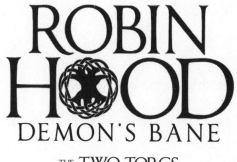

DEMON'S BANE

THE TWO TORCS

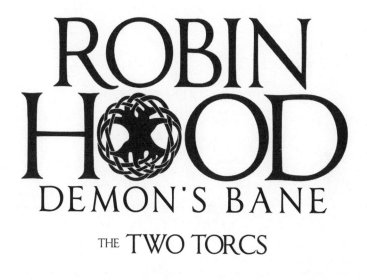

ROBIN HOOD
DEMON'S BANE
THE TWO TORCS

DEBBIE VIGUIÉ + JAMES R. TUCK

TITAN BOOKS

ROBIN HOOD: DEMON'S BANE
THE TWO TORCS
Print edition ISBN: 9781783294381
Electronic edition ISBN: 9781783294398

Published by Titan Books
A division of Titan Publishing Group Ltd
144 Southwark Street, London SE1 0UP

First edition: August 2016
2 4 6 8 10 9 7 5 3 1

Did you enjoy this book? We love to hear from our readers.
Please email us at readerfeedback@titanemail.com or write to us at
Reader Feedback at the above address.

To receive advance information, news, competitions, and exclusive
offers online, please sign up for the Titan newsletter on our website:
www.titanbooks.com

To Ann Liotta, my oldest friend, I would battle demons
with you any day.
–DV

Always to the Missus.
–JRT

PROLOGUE

The world had gone white.

Everything lay under a rime of hard frost, sheeted over with ice, slick and deadly, waiting to take down man and beast alike.

Even the heart of vast Sherwood lay locked in the grip of winter, only the mighty oaks stood unbent beneath a frozen burden. Limbs were bare against the dull sky, bushes and undergrowth pressed down by the weight of snow. The deer had stopped moving, stopped digging for food long gone. They retreated to hidden hollow and sad shelter, hunger-staved sides and jutting ribs shaking as they huddled together for what meager warmth they could make.

He stalked carefully, moving with barely a ripple through the low groaning of the trees. Stopping on a ridge he stood, looking down over a deep hollow in the earth. Even in the numb of the cold he could feel the life that shivered around him. His spirit felt larger than his body, as attuned to the mighty forest as the sun is attuned to the sky. He had come to hunt, to take a life to sustain others. His goal for the day was to see red spilled on white, to breathe the steam as his prey cooled. He had prepared to offer the life to God, a sacrifice of necessity.

But something was different.

He was transfixed, his body thrumming inside to the vibrations of the earth beneath the ancient wood.

Movement caught his eye, pulling him from the white.

A badger, skin loose from winter's privation, shuffled up the hill toward him, low to the ground on stubby, curved legs.

Another movement broke the white. A covey of three foxes trotted from the other side of the valley, angling toward him, their lush fur brushing small icicles off shrubs with a soft tinkling sound. Foxes were hunters like him—they could move silently, creeping like shadows without a sign that they passed by, but these bounded like domesticated puppies.

A flurry of snow fell beside him. He looked to the source and found the limbs of the oak and ash above him crowded with small creatures. There were squirrels, rabbits, and dozens of birds from small sparrows to raptors the size of his chest. Over the ridge trundled a bear, shaggy and stumble-footed from hibernation cut short, but massive and mighty with claws the length of his palm.

His hand flew to the quiver on his back, fingers closing on the shaft of an arrow.

The black arrow.

His skin tingled and grew tight. Small muscles along his body began to twitch, and his mouth tasted like the morning smelled after a hard rain.

Once, when he was younger, first running through Sherwood, he'd been too inexperienced to read the signs of an oncoming storm through the canopy of the forest giants. Unaware until the forest turned black and water began to shower him, he was caught in a thunderstorm. At first he stayed in the wood, enjoying the warm summer rain that fell in runs and splashes through the branches and leaves of the trees, the power of the storm muted far above. Then he continued on to the edge of a field, one of the interior pockets of open sky and low grass.

From under the canopy of a massive oak he looked out at a sky as gray and solid as the blacksmith's anvil. The expanse split with blasts of lightning so fierce they tore the clouds apart with white light. The rain in the opening pummeled the grass, flattening it and covering it with inches of water that fell too fast to be absorbed by the thirsty earth. Hail pounded down into the miniature lake, sent water flying back up, and he was reminded of the story of God's almighty wrath against the Egyptians.

He didn't know who the Egyptians were, but watching the storm, he could understand the concept of God's wrath, terrible and beautiful at the same time.

The thunder that followed each lightning strike rolled against the full front of his body and he felt it in the marrow of his bones. Suddenly his teeth hurt in the back of his mouth and every hair on his pre-teen body stood on end. He began to move backwards, back into the forest, feeling as if the eye of the wrathful God had turned upon him.

Lightning struck the oak beside which he'd been standing.

The blast of it knocked him flat, his eyes scrubbed of the ability to see, and his ears closed with the concussion of the strike. He didn't remember losing consciousness, but in what felt like an instant he opened his eyes. His muscles wouldn't stop twitching under his skin, and the back of his mouth had that peculiar taste in it.

It felt like lightning had struck *him*.

It felt the same way now.

But different.

Similar.

Familiar.

He could sense the animals around him, one and all—not just see, but *sense* with all of his body. Each heart, from the ones the size of acorns to the mighty boulder of blood-pumping muscle inside the bear. Every one of them beat in time with his.

One by one, the creatures stopped in a ring on the hill below him, all of them looking up at him. Predator stood beside prey, the white steam of their breaths collecting and combining to make a ring of fog.

His hand fell away from the arrow, not pulling it from the quiver, but the connection remained.

He turned to his left and found the King of the Forest there.

The stag towered over him, looking into the distance, crown of antler threatening to tangle in the branches. The mantle of fur over the stag's back glistened with hoarfrost, glittering in even the low winter sun, as if he were not just the King of Sherwood but also the Lord of Winter itself. As if he were an elemental, a primordial guardian of the wood.

He was close enough to lay his hand on its flank.

The animal turned its head, staring at him with an implacable eye the color of midnight. He fell into that eye, his spirit—the one that had felt so large just moments ago—tumbling like a child taking its first steps. He was overwhelmed. His nostrils filled with the musk of the forest, the pungency of life that made his head swim. The stag's heartbeat thundered through him, bouncing the bottoms of his boots on the hard snow beneath them.

Then the thunder calmed and settled, less the roar of the waterfall and more the rush of the river. Beyond the circle of lives below him on the hill, he could feel all the life in Sherwood. It pressed his skin, insistent as it penetrated him with the unknowable mystery of Creation itself.

Unable to withstand even another minute he turned and walked back down the ridge, the feeling fading with each step, yet etched in his memory.

WITCHSTONES AND CHILDREN'S TEARS

CHAPTER ONE

"I hate this cursed place."

Will turned in his saddle to face the speaker. Doing so meant he had to adjust the rapier strapped to his hip, tugging the hilt back to clear the sheathed blade from the quilted cloak he had wrapped around him, but he hated talking to someone without looking at them.

Even if he despised that someone.

"Do you hate it because you think it cursed," Will asked, "or do you think it cursed because of your hatred for it?"

The merchant on his own horse didn't look over. Between scarf and cap, his eyes zigged and zagged in their sockets, trying to take in every limb on every tree that arched overhead. He was a soft man, not fat, but cushioned by a life of comfort and ease without work. The type of man who eagerly exercised someone else's power. Always an underling, an overseer, a lapdog but not a lackey.

He snarled, and it made the soft flesh of his face jiggle.

"You watch that sharp tongue of yours, Will Scarlet, else it gets cut out of your head. You know as well as I do that Sherwood is haunted." He closed one eye and spat on the ground, an old ward against evil, then crossed himself. "And worse," he added.

Will looked at the canopy above them. Interwoven branches

of oak, hawthorn, and ash screened against the weak winter sunlight, diffusing it into a verdant haze that darkened the closer to the ground it fell. Off the road the forest became near night, twilighting away to pockets of pure dark.

At night, he wouldn't be able to see his hand in front of his face.

"I'm riding with you to protect Locksley's goods and keep you safe from ghosts, goblins, and fey." Will's hand was still on the hilt of his rapier. He flicked open his cloak as his voice dropped, low and dangerous. "But it won't be my tongue you find sharp, if you threaten me again."

The soft man jerked around in his saddle, so violently it made the horse under him stumble a step or two sideways. His moon eyes were full.

"I... I... I meant no disrespect!" A pudgy arm in a thick wool sleeve wiped across his mouth. "It's the forest. It makes me nervous, and I speak without thinking."

Will Scarlet's voice took on a cruel tone. "Frightened by children's ghost stories and old wives' tales of will o' the wisps? I'm surprised Locksley trusts you to deliver his goods for him."

The merchant's voice dropped to a harsh whisper. "It's not the ghosts that get to me. It's the Hood."

Will sighed, breath pluming into the air. "Oh yes, the Hood—the scourge of Sherwood, swooping through the trees and robbing any merchant who dares take the only road to market." He made a show of yawning. "I'm sure you'll find him just as real as the will o' the wisps."

"He *is* real," the man insisted. "He stole my brother's merchandise just a month ago. Robbed him, stripped him naked, and sent him back tied across his horse with an arrow in his arse."

"Well, the good Lord Locksley has also paid me to keep arrows out of your arse. That is, unless you like that sort of thing."

The merchant looked sharply at the man who rode beside him. Slim and small, Will Scarlet was like a snake in fine clothing. His movements either nonexistent or too quick for the eye to follow. He rode on a silver-trimmed saddle of imported leather. A red velvet jerkin, with family crest embroidered on the breast, fit tight to a slender chest. Linen ruffles spilled from the throat and cuffs of his shirt and the wide brim of a felt hat was pulled low over a boyish face with dark eyes and a sly grin. Many ladies of the court had succumbed to that smile.

Rumor was a few men had, also.

In particular John, the acting king.

Will didn't say anything for a long moment, dark eyes cold as black ice. Then he chuckled—a soft rasp, a scuff on leather.

The merchant tittered, a hateful, nervous giggle brought on by the unsure feeling that he had just avoided some terrible consequence he couldn't even imagine. His eyes jumped away, returning to the forest canopy above.

"Locksley neglected to tell me what we're transporting on this fine winter's day." Will looked at the large wagon trundling along behind them. A sturdy carriage the size of most huts from the village, it rolled on wide axles and stout wheels built to carry heavy loads. They squeaked through ice-crusted puddles left in the muddy earth by an earlier storm, a mix of wet sleet and fat droplets of rain.

The sides were thick wood planks banded and roofed with iron, the only windows thin slits cut high near the roof. The iron door on the side was fastened with a lock the size of his head. The behemoth was pulled by a pair of steady, dull horses guided by the sallow-faced boy who was the merchant's apprentice.

"It must be worth a great deal," he added, "to warrant a rolling fortress such as that one."

"I only know that we are to deliver goods, wagon, and all to the Kraeger Estate on the other side of Sherwood."

"We're not going to market?"

"No. Whatever is in that wagon gets delivered directly to Lord Kraeger."

Will's eyes narrowed. "Curious." Pulling back on the reins of his horse, he brought it to a stop. To his left, in the shadows of the forest, flared a small light.

Suddenly a flaming arrow streaked the air by his face, stinging him along his cheek, then thudded to a stop, quivering in the wood of the wagon inches from the head of the merchant's assistant. The boy sat for a long second, mouth hung low in shock, before tumbling sideways and falling in the mud. Scrambling to his feet he ran, a flurry of elbows and heels that disappeared down the road back to town.

The wagon shuddered to a halt, though the cart horses were unaffected by the commotion.

The merchant cursed, twisting in his saddle and sawing the reins. His horse lurched and stomped with a sharp whinny that shushed as soon as it hit the trees. Jowls shaking, he whipped his head around, looking for the source of the arrow. Will instead pointed down the path in front of them.

A man in a hood stood in the center of the road, an arrow notched in a stout longbow and pulled tight against his cheek.

"The Hood!" The merchant's voice hissed between his teeth. "I told you he was real."

"Yes, you did," Will growled. "Color me surprised."

A voice, gruff and deep, rolled down the road toward them.

"Dismount with your hands away from any weapons."

The merchant leaned in. "What should we do?" he whispered loudly.

Will rolled his eyes. "I suppose we should dismount and keep our hands away from our weapons." He swung his leg over his horse's back, dropping gracefully to the ground. He scowled at the squish of mud under his boot heel.

I shouldn't have worn the calfskin.

The merchant's descent from his horse was far less graceful. At least the man managed not to fall on his face, though. By the time Will looked again the Hood was only a few feet away. The bow was still pulled back, the wicked iron point of the arrow aimed at the merchant. Razor-sharp edges gleamed in the low light, the fangs of a snake poised to strike. At such a short distance not even bone would stop it, if the man in the hood let it loose. Will put his hands in the air.

The merchant stood, dumbfounded. Will whistled, low and quick. The merchant looked over, mouth hanging open. Will moved his hands and jutted his chin. The merchant raised his arms, dark moon stains showing in his armpits even through the thick winter tunic.

A cowl of leather hung low over their attacker's face, obscuring it in shadow. All that could be seen was a ruthless glint deep where an eye would be.

"Open the wagon."

"I... I c-ca-can't." The merchant's bottom lip slapped against his chin in a quiver.

"Then you are of no use to me..." The Hood stepped closer, voice grinding from under the cowl. "...and I'll kill you where you stand."

The merchant's mouth jabbered, no sound coming out. Will saw the Hood's fingertips slip slightly on the bowstring, preparing to let loose the shaft.

"He has a key to the wagon," he said quickly. "On a chain around his neck."

The merchant's eyes cut over at him. "Why would you tell him?"

"Don't be a fool, man. Locksley isn't paying you enough to lose your life."

The Hood lowered the bow. He kept his fingers on the notch of the arrow, but let the pressure off.

"Listen to your foppish friend here," he said. "He's trying to save your life."

Inside Will's head he snarled.

Foppish?

The Hood's foot lashed out, kicking the merchant in the belly, leaving a big smear of mud and pushing him back in a stumble toward the wagon. The man staggered and turned, pulling a key on a chain from under his tunic, all the while gasping to get his breath back. Jerking his head, the Hood indicated that Will should follow.

He did so, still burning over the insult.

Pudgy hands lifted the heavy lock. The key *click-tapped* around the keyhole, dancing in a shaky hand. Finally slipping it in, the merchant turned the key and pulled the lock. The ring of it opened, the weight of the lock itself causing the whole thing to swing and slip and fall to the mud below.

"Open it, fool, and let me see what I've won from that black-hearted bastard Locksley today."

The merchant grabbed the handle. Wrenching the door wide, he screamed, "You win your death, outlaw!"

Out of the darkness of the wagon rushed soldiers, armed to the teeth and with murder flashing in their eyes.

The first soldier out was a giant, arms bulging under a mail shirt, quilted tabard emblazoned with the Locksley coat of arms. Behind him came three of his sword brothers, all wearing the same royal-blue tunic sewn with the same rampant lion.

The sword in the giant's skull-crusher hand was long steel with a vicious point left from the days when savages from the North came to rape, pillage, and plunder. It was thick and heavy and made for killing. He swung it with a roar that would have made the blade's original barbarian owner proud, the cold, cruel blade aimed to cleave the Hood in two before he could raise his bow.

Quicker than a blink the Hood drew and shot, his wicked arrow *thunking* deep into the dirt of the road, sinking halfway up the arm-length shaft.

Right through the foot of the soldier.

The giant's roar broke, becoming a scream of pain. Pinned to the earth by the arrow, he faltered. His body twisted, drawing up in agony.

The Hood swung the longbow, stout yew cracking across the giant's temple, driving him to the ground with a splash of mud.

The arrow shaft broke and pulled free in a boot-darkening spurt of blood.

The other three soldiers stopped, watching their sword brother fall right in front of them. They looked at him as he lay sprawled at their feet, then up at the man in the Hood who stood almost casually in front of them.

Will lowered his hands, watching.

"Surrender." The Hood's voice came from under his cowl.

One by one, their eyes narrowed as anger sparked between them. Will could almost see the thoughts forming in their skulls as hands tightened on weapons.

Who does he think he is?

There are still three of us and one of him.

He shook his head.

Fools.

A soldier, young but already battle-scarred with a livid line that ran from his brow, around his eye, and across his cheek, pointed at the man in the hood. He stepped over his fallen companion.

"Who do you think you are?" he demanded. "There are three of us and—" A fist crashed hard and savage across the soldier's jaw.

The man dropped to the ground, a puppet on cut strings.

So predictable.

Before the other two could move the Hood spun, driving his boot deep in the stomach of the man on the right. The soldier bent sharply in half as he lost his breakfast on the road. The bow whipped down, clubbing him across the back of his skull. He dropped to his knees, slowly falling to his side.

The man in the hood flipped the bow in his hand as he turned. The last soldier was just raising his sword when the bow fell, hooking over his head. The Hood leaned back, jerking the bowstring tight across the soldier's throat and yanking him off his feet. Planting a foot across the soldier's shoulders, the attacker pulled up, bow bending sharply in his hands.

Will began counting in his head.

He didn't get past twenty before the soldier stopped struggling, and was out cold.

The man in the hood held the bow tight for another three-count before releasing the pressure. He unhooked the string from under the soldier's head. Straightening slowly, he kept his head down in his hood, shoulders rising and falling as he breathed deeply.

He's tired.

Will pulled his rapier from the scabbard without a sound.

Behind the man in the hood the merchant snuck, jagged knife in hand. Piggy eyes glittered in their flesh pockets, jowls split wide with dark, murderous lust. The knife swung back, ready to strike, to bury itself hilt-deep in the kidney of his target.

The butt of Will's sword bashed across the back of the merchant's head, splitting the skin wide below the edge of his cap.

The soft man dropped like a felled ox, mud splashing as he struck the road face first.

The Hood whirled, hand drawing an arrow from the quiver across his back. Then he stopped, staring at Will and the deadly point of the rapier, hovering between them.

The silence of the forest closed around them, circling them in an eerie, unnatural hush.

"You're welcome," Will said as he sheathed his rapier with a quick movement, and then shrugged his cloak back around him.

The man in the hood relaxed, letting go the arrow and slouching back.

"I was wondering if you were going to help, or just watch me do all the work." He reached up. Calloused fingertips flipped the leather cowl back, revealing a face nearly as dark as Will's. The features were harsher, cut from heavier, swarthier stock than his own, but the similarity was there.

"Oh, please, the day Robin Longstride can't handle four Locksley thugs by himself is the day you should come out of these woods and take up cross-stitch with the nuns at the convent." He shook out the ruffles at his cuffs, letting them fall down to cover his hands. His fingers were nearly frozen. "Besides, I would be of no help seeing that I am… what was the word? Oh, yes, 'foppish'."

Robin smiled, a small pulling at the cheeks, unrecognizable if Will hadn't known what it was.

"Did that hurt your feelings?" the bowman asked. "Do you stand there offended, in your mighty fine hat and your fancy padded cloak?"

"I can't help being handsomer than you, outlaw." Will sniffed. "And it *is* a very fine, very *warm* hat."

"I find myself very jealous of it."

Will waved away the statement with the flutter of a ruffled cuff.

"Don't be. It would look all wrong on you. Your ears stick out too far. Best continue with the hooded reaver look you're perfecting."

Robin knelt next to the giant soldier, who still lay unconscious. His hand closed on the handle of the Viking sword, retrieving it from the mud. Wiping it clean on the end of the giant's tunic he hefted it, looking down the blade. Hammered into the steel, along the blood-groove, were letters cut from darker iron.

Will leaned in. "What does it read?"

"*Ulfberht.*"

"Who is Ulfberht?"

"No one knows." Robin twirled the sword, swinging it easily through the air. "Whoever Ulfberht was, however, he made the finest swords ever seen. They are rare and near unbreakable. This blade alone is worth a hundred English swords." His voice dropped as he lifted the blade again, eyes glittering as they ran along the sword's clean lines and razor-sharp edges. "It's amazing that a raw, pagan barbarian could create something so wonderful."

"I know it's lonely here in Sherwood, but do I need to leave you and that sword alone for a turn?"

"Very funny." Robin thrust the blade out toward Will. "Take

it and sell it. It will feed many families."

"I think you should keep it."

Robin's eyes darkened. "Take it. You know I want nothing from Locksley—not for myself."

"Keep it." Will picked up the other three swords and slid them under a lashing strap on his saddle. "Locksley has just proven that he's willing to trap and kill you. The other merchants will soon follow his lead." He threw his hand up to stop a protest. "If there had been even one more soldier, you would have been in real trouble, Robin. Don't be reckless. You need a sword, and it might as well be the best one."

Robin pinned him with a glare.

He stared back, knowing he couldn't blink or he would lose the argument. Then the outlaw's brow furrowed, settling in for the contest.

Will's right eye began clawing under its lid, scrabbling in its socket, wanting desperately to twitch, to blink, to wink. It felt wet, the strain of not blinking, of not looking away, wringing tears from it. He was about to break when Robin let out a sigh, and looked down at the sword in his hand.

"You're right, my friend. I'll keep it."

Will smiled at his victory. Such things didn't happen often, so he savored them when they did.

Robin slipped the sword into his belt and clapped Will on the shoulder.

"That cart is too big for only four soldiers," he said, turning to look. "Let's see what else Locksley has provided for the poor."

Together they walked to the open door. Will stood back, letting Robin go first. He was startled when his friend jumped back with a sharp, harsh curse.

"What is it?"

Robin didn't answer, continuing to curse Locksley's name, his parents, and his ancestors.

Will stepped up and looked inside.

Eight men, bound, gagged, and blindfolded turned their faces toward him from inside the wagon.

"Locksley, you son of a bitch," he said.

The huge stone was warm under Glynna Longstride's palms, the surface smoothly rippled as she caressed it. Her fingers sought out the marks carved into it, slipping along edges worn soft by untold years of weather.

Rain and wind, snow and ice, heat and dust had beaten this stone for a thousand lifetimes, yet it stood resolute, defiant of all the efforts of the elements to wear it to nothing. It loomed above her head, leaning slightly to the east, pointed accusingly at the sun.

She moved closer, pressing her cheek to the surface. Her stomach brushed against it, and some energy passed through her, rambling and knocking low down to tickle the nether of her womanhood before spiraling up her spine to the base of her skull. She shivered as if touched by a familiar lover, one who knew her body as a musician knew his instrument.

Witchstone.

"Peel yourself away from there."

The voice pushed through her pleasure, separating her from it. She turned, lifting her face but keeping her stomach and hands firmly on the stone. The field around her lay white. Striding across the stark plain came a man cut from the night. His armor stood out sharply. Each plate, every link of mail, even the long-bristled fur of the collar was a light-drinking darkness, a black as pure and uncut as expensive ink.

The only color showing on him was a gleaming sigil upon his chest, a symbol cut in lines and swirls of heart's-blood red. She did not know what the symbol stood for, but when she touched it her fingers burned for hours.

His pale skin and white hair became lost in the haze of light reflected off the snow, and as he drew closer it appeared as if he were only a pair of wide ebon eyes and a sinister mouth of ruddy lips floating above a cruel carapace.

He dragged something with him as he walked, so that his footprints were wiped clean in a swath of smeared snow. He stopped a few feet from her.

The smile twitched her mouth.

"You didn't bring the little prince?"

The man snorted. "It's cold."

"I noticed."

"However, I brought you a present."

He turned, dragging his burden around from behind him.

It was a man.

A monk.

Bound hand and foot, he had a knotted piece of rope cinched around his head for a gag.

The man was young, not much older than Robin.

Her heart twisted at the thought of him, and she felt it in her face. She stepped away from the witchstone, toward the captive. The moment she broke contact the winter cold howled against her exposed skin, drawing it taut across her face and hands. She pulled her cloak tighter around her.

The monk looked up at her, eyes wide. They were set a bit deep in his skull but pretty, curving down at their corners. They were the eyes of a poet, a man who could talk a summer girl out of her dress, though only if he had been born first. Second sons went to the monastery, became monks. Only God wanted the castoffs, taking them in from the poor, putting them to purpose. Denying them even the chance to talk to girls, much less talk them into bed.

She squatted, holding her stomach as she did. Immediately the pressure on her lower back eased. She wouldn't be able to stay down very long, but it would feel good while she did.

She touched the monk's face. It was cold, feeling like wax except where his short stubble scratched her palm. Spittle had frozen in the corners of his mouth, cracking on the surface of lips gone dark blue.

"He's adorable."

"He's not that kind of present."

"No?" She pouted for the man in black's benefit. "But I'm not hungry."

"Not that kind either. He has information. I want it."

She smiled and a light flickered deep in her eyes.

"Oh, good," she said. "A *plaything*."

CHAPTER TWO

A pale lace of frost covered the window glass, catching the buttery glow of the fire that crackled and popped in the hearth behind her. It was low, but still cast enough heat to penetrate the linen gown and the scant garments underneath.

Marian's back was dry and warm as a loaf of fresh-baked bread, but the front of her was so cold it felt damp, clammy. The two sensations kept her concentration sharp and she embraced them, considering first one and then the other in turn.

Anything to keep her mind occupied.

Over the edge of the frost crystals she could see the top of mighty Sherwood. The barren trees alternately held patches of snow in nets of woven branches, or gaped open, letting it fall to be swallowed in the depths. The wood looked like a vast checkered blanket laid across the western part of the kingdom.

It was so bitter cold out there in the wilderness.

She turned from the window with a jolt and a flap of cloth. The warmth of the room brushed across her face, feeling hotter than it was because of the cold on her skin. She crossed the room in three swift strides, reaching her bed. Stepping high, she went over the bed instead of around it and dropped on the other side, falling into a hard wooden chair.

Leaning forward she pushed the mattress away from her,

sliding its soft mass across the slats until a space opened as wide across as her forearm. A sheet of leather had been tacked to the slats, allowed to droop between them to form long pockets in the apron.

Between each slat lay a weapon.

A sword taken from a locker at the stables. She didn't know who its owner had been. There was no mark on the plain wood grip or the simple leather scabbard, but the blade itself had been well cared for, honed to razor sharpness by hours of passing a whetstone over the edge.

Next to it lay the Duke of Raleigh's family saber. The handle gleamed with inlaid pearl and gemstones held by gold and silver wire. The scabbard matched, a line of rubies tracing out the sigil of Raleigh's family. This sword had become hers when her friend and servant Chastity liberated it from the Duke's drunk and sleeping form at the bottom of a stairwell, after one of King John's debauches.

The ancestral blade had been near impossible to pull free from its sheath, gummed in by years of neglect and disuse. It had taken creative thinking and a thorough application of oils to break it free. She'd been afraid that when it finally gave way, that the blade would be worthless—a ceremonial plaything, a decoration and nothing more—but it was made of good Spanish steel, stout on the spine and sharp on the edge, a heavy weapon made for cleaving bone.

A half-dozen knives were scattered between the slats, as well, from a wide-bladed kitchen knife to a thin poniard with no edge but a wicked point for punching through armor, to a small chirurgeon's blade not half as long as her littlest finger.

To one end lay a fire-hardened cudgel, the wood black and varnished to a dull sheen, the knot on the end of it bloody red like mahogany. A leather thong wrapped the handle and the knuckle was dimpled from the dozens of skulls to which it had been applied.

To the other end lay the war hammer.

King Richard's war hammer.

Her fingers stroked the handle, sliding over the worn oak stave and the slick strap of steel nailed to halfway down its length, there to reinforce the mounting of the head. She touched it, rubbing her finger pad over the point of the deadly spike that jutted from the back, opposite the wide, flat face. Tiny grooves squiggled on the surface of the steel, like worms after the rain, cut there by the torn edges of all the armor plate it had punched through.

This hammer had been in Richard the Lionheart's hand when he ended the war between Geoffrey the Dark and Sir Lidamont, over the hand of a woman from Iberia. Geoffrey the Dark still walked with a limp because of this hammer, and the woman from Iberia still rubbed ointment into the puncture in Sir Lidamont's side.

She'd found it in a cache, hidden away in one of Richard's secret gardens, and had taken it before it could be discovered by John or one of his men.

A knock came at the door.

It was a familiar one, but nevertheless she tugged the mattress back in place, standing and smoothing her dress as she did.

"Enter," she called. A key clattered in the lock for a moment before the door swung inward, pushed by a short figure swathed in a dull-green wool cloak. Snow that clung to the shoulders hadn't yet begun to melt. Turning and locking the door behind them, the figure pushed the cloak up and over. It came loose in a wad that was tossed aside, revealing a young woman in rough clothes too small for her generous curves. A mop of blonde curls waved in the air, crackling as she shook herself.

"Och, it's cold out there, Princess!"

"I went last time."

"I know." Chastity rubbed her hands together, moving toward the fire.

Marian moved close. "Any word?"

"About what?"

Marian hesitated. "My uncle."

"Not a peep. No news either way."

"Damn." Marian's voice came out a growl.

Chastity laid a hand on her shoulder. "No news isn't bad news."

"Crusading armies send word back when they land. That's what kings do."

"Doesn't mean he didn't land."

"Then what *does* it mean?" she snapped angrily.

Chastity stepped back and Marian felt the small distance like a dash of ice water.

A blossom of shame opened inside her. She sighed, clearing the tightness in her chest with the deep breath.

"I'm sorry."

Chastity shrugged. "I know it's tough for you, Princess. Even without John and the Sheriff and their mischief, I know it's hard."

Marian had no words. None. She turned away so that Chastity wouldn't see the despair in her eyes. She missed her uncle more than she ever thought she could miss anyone, and in these moments—the quiet moments—her missing him turned from melancholy to anger and back again.

It was exhausting.

"Be strong and of good faith," he had said. *"I will return."*

The rightful king's last words directly to her.

Uncle Richard, you had no idea what you were leaving me to face.

She knew deep in her gut that none of the messengers she'd sent had made it through. Yet there *had* to be a way to reach Richard.

If he's even still alive.

The thought came unbidden to her, filling her with an instant sense of terror. She prayed every night for his safety, sometimes weeping into the wee hours of the morning with the fervency of her prayers.

He wasn't the only one she prayed for. She also prayed for her cohorts, those who had donned the mantle of the Hood to try to spoil King John's plans. Particularly for Robin. Then she prayed for the children of the nobles, the young ones who had been stolen to keep their parents in line. The children nobody could find.

"Still no word on where they might have taken the little ones?" Marian asked, knowing already what the answer would be. If Chastity had such news, it would have been the first thing from her lips.

"No," the young woman admitted. "No one seems to have any idea. They can't be in the castle, though. There's not been food leaving the kitchens unaccounted for."

Marian took a deep breath. "You don't think he's killed them, do you?"

She waited for an outburst from Chastity, a reassurance that even John wasn't that stupid or heartless. It never came, and Marian turned to look at her friend.

Chastity had gone pale.

"I don't know, milady." The formality in her tone told Marian everything she needed to know.

"You think he has."

"I *pray* he hasn't."

"As do I. Let us think, though. If he has kept them alive, and they are not here, where would they have been moved to?"

"Somewhere secure, where they couldn't escape and no one could find them. There'd have to be soldiers with them, and at least a few servants to handle the cooking and the like."

Marian nodded. "Have any servants gone missing since the children were taken?"

Chastity frowned. "I cannot say for certain. I know there are a few I haven't seen in a while, but no one moves about the castle as freely these days, so that may mean nothing. I will find out, though."

"It would be a start, at least. If we could find the children and rescue them, put them somewhere safe, then maybe we could convince the nobles to unite against John."

"It's a lovely plan, Princess. It might even work if…"

She trailed off and Marian nodded.

"Yes, if…"

If the children are still alive.

She folded her arms across herself, seeking to keep out the cold that had nothing to do with the weather raging outside. She thought of those little ones, hungry, frightened, possibly even freezing to death somewhere if they were still wearing only the clothes they had on when they were seized. Even if John hadn't killed them, it was possible the pox had, or that this cursed winter would soon enough.

Snow melted under the three-dozen men who knelt in the courtyard of the monastery. They curled into themselves, arms pulled close to their bodies, legs folded tightly under them. Numb fingers moved stiffly, painfully over worn knots in prayer ropes. The cold numbed their legs, their hands, their faces, and the slickly razored patch of scalp in the center of their tonsures.

The cardinal stood in front of them, watching the wisps of their breath as they prayed. The cold wiped away the distraction of the world, giving an overwhelming physical discomfort that corralled the mind into a place where prayer could be truly transcendental. God could be found there, in the icy wind and the bitter temperature. The cold could also kill a man, without him realizing it.

He watched their breath—especially Brother Kincannon, the thinnest of the monks there. As his body grew colder inside his breath would show less and less. If it disappeared, then the man might not live through the night.

Kincannon's breath was a near transparent curl, like that of wood shaved from a joist or joint by a carpenter.

Moving his eyes along the rows of brown-robed monks, the cardinal counted one more time and, satisfied with his tally, he clapped his hands together, breaking the hum of murmured prayers with a sharp *crack*.

His palms tingled painfully afterward.

One by one the monks all looked up, some jumping as if they'd been struck, others moving slowly, as if rousing from a deep sleep.

"Rise and return inside," he said briskly. "Food has been laid out, and warm mead to revive your insides. You have dined with Christ Almighty, now sup with each other in good fellowship, cleansed and braced by this exercise."

They rose, the younger and sturdier helping their elders, as was the way of the order. In small groups they filed past him, some rushing forward into the halls of the monastery. One monk in particular waited toward the end of the line. He seemed not to feel the cold as sharply, given the breadth of his middle and his stoutness of limb.

The cardinal tilted his chin up, indicating to the fat friar that he should wait. As the door shut behind the last of the line, the monk spoke.

"Yes?"

The cardinal smiled, even though the cold air made his teeth hurt.

"Surely the mighty Tuck isn't cold."

Friar Tuck sniffed. "Not at all, but you said there was warm mead."

"There will be enough" the cardinal reassured him. "I won't make you tarry long."

"Is there trouble? Something from the castle?"

The cardinal shook his head. "Nothing from there… but we are missing a brother."

Friar Tuck nodded. "Stephen. He's been gone since mid-morn."

"Which one is Stephen?"

Chubby fingers waved in front of Tuck's face. "The one with the eyes."

"Ahhhh… where is he?"

"Not in the cold praying. Maybe he is inside, with the mead."

The cardinal said nothing.

Friar Tuck touched his arm. "Is there a reason for worry, Francis?"

The cardinal shook his head. "No, not yet. Check his cell and the infirmary. He may be sick from this weather."

"He's good stock, but it's possible."

"I pray he is," the cardinal said, then he paused. "I have a bad feeling. A sense of dread in my stomach."

"Something you ate?" Tuck offered.

"I've been fasting for God's wisdom for the last three days."

A frown twisted the friar's face. "I hate fasting."

"I'm surprised you remember what it's like."

Tuck grimaced. "Maybe the boy left because of your sharp wit."

Stephen rolled his large green eyes from side to side as he knelt, trying to watch the man in the pitch-black armor and still look at the woman in front of him. Behind her loomed the witchstone. The ancient marker was haunted, cursed even. If his hands and legs hadn't been tied tight, he would have scrambled to his feet and run away.

The man was still at his back, just on the edge of his vision if he wrenched his neck all the way around, but the pain that shot up into his temple from the strain made him impossible to see clearly. Instead he was simply a sinister black streak—a shadow, a haint that hovered just past where he could see.

Something warm and moist touched his face.

His head jerked, causing the woman's fingertips to skim along his cheek and across his mouth. He recoiled as far as his bonds would let him, sucking sharply inward at the pool of spittle that sloshed out around the knotted rope between his teeth. The edge of her nail just nicked the juncture of his lips, right above the hemp, stretched taut and so very thin that the skin split in a sharp burning pain—so much more than it should have. It made his left eye twitch and stutter.

The taste of raw iron bloomed across his tongue. The woman kneeling before him looked over his head.

"Let's take that silly rope out of his mouth."

A blow to the back of his head drove it forward, his chin crashing into his own breastbone, his teeth grinding down on the knot. They were going to break, crack, and splinter into shards that would be driven deep into his gums, leaving them bloody ruins. His would be the mouth of a gargoyle.

Something hard dug under the rope where it went around his skull, tearing hair out as it pushed and shoved. The gag was yanked deeper into his mouth, his lip tearing further at the cut and his jaw cracking as the joint of it slipped in its mooring, not quite dislocating but pulling apart, straining the tendons in a punch of hot pain that rolled from his chin to his temple and back again.

Tears streamed down his face and he couldn't see anything, his eyes shut so tightly they pulsed red behind their lids with each hammering heartbeat.

He felt his mind begin to drift in the fog of intense, unrelenting pain. Another jerk, and the pressure disappeared.

The ends of the rope fell around his face. They were smooth, cut by something sharp. The woman reached up and tugged gently, pulling the rope from his mouth. The relief that washed over him made his head spin.

She lifted his chin with a soft finger. "Better?"

He moved his jaw, trying to get it to slip back, to feel right. It *was* better. The blinding pain faded to a persistent, throbbing ache.

He nodded as he swallowed bloody spit.

"Good." A scrap of cloth embroidered with a star pattern covered her hand. She moved it to the corner of his mouth, dabbing at it. "There, there, you should be right as rain by morning."

He stared at her, watching as she pulled away the cloth. She studied it for a moment, as if considering the wide splotch of his blood that stained it. Carefully, she tucked the stained cloth into the bodice of her gown. The sight of her fingers slipping under the hem and between pale mounds of her breasts moved him, and he hardened under his robes.

The pain in his mouth slipped his mind.

"What's your name?"

He swallowed. Her face looked so kind, so full of concern.

"It's Stephen, Lady Longstride."

Her eyebrow arched up. "You know me?"

He nodded. "My family helps with your orchard harvest every autumn. I have seen you every year of my life... until the last one."

Her shoulders moved back, lifting her chest. "You looked at me every year? Watching me as I toured the groves while you worked?"

He turned his face away, cheeks burning as he flushed.

"I did. It's why I was sent to service."

Sharp fingernails scratched the front of his robe, tracing down his stomach and swirling around the hardness in his lap. "So you are new to the church?"

He nodded.

Glynna Longstride looked over his head at the man who still stood behind him.

"He's a baby monk. He will know nothing."

"The long night is coming. We will not get another chance and I won't risk it." The voice growled behind him. "He knows *something*. It may be piss in a bucket, but it can be a start."

Glynna sighed and adjusted herself, one hand on her thigh, one on the swollen stomach that stretched from her otherwise lithe frame. Settled, her eyes focused on him again.

"Our dear Sheriff of Nottingham believes you own knowledge we need," she said to the monk. "Is that true?"

He scooted forward. The movement pulled on his bound hands, making the pain in them flare, and then ease as he shifted.

"I know nothing, milady, nothing at all. I barely know my way from one end of the monastery to the other."

"Ask him about the *Relic Grimoire*," the Sheriff prodded.

Glynna snarled. With seeming effort she pushed it aside and smiled.

"We are looking for a book, Stephen," she said. "A specific book."

"We have books."

"This would be a book someone is trying to keep out of sight. We think it has been hidden in the monastery—so think, has anyone acted differently?"

"No ma'am, not since Bishop Montoya..."

The growl from behind cut him short. "Forget that idiot."

Glynna Longstride snapped her fingers.

"You're a bright young man," she said to Stephen. Her hands slid over her stomach to her breasts. She cupped them, lifting them slightly. The collar of her blouse pulled lower, and even more of her cleavage rose to his sight. "You pay attention to things around you."

He licked his lips, and tasted blood.

"Tell me who at the monastery shares in the conspiracy?"

"I swear on my own life," he pleaded, "I know nothing."

"Nothing?"

"No, ma'am."

A sly smile pulled her mouth sideways and her eyes went dark and hooded. "Good." Reaching into her blouse, she pulled out the handkerchief and shook it out. The blood had spread, turning almost the entire cloth a dull brownish red. It was far more blood than had been dabbed away from his mouth. Lady Longstride lifted the cloth to her face slowly.

Every inch it rose, dread stacked in his stomach like stones growing in size, until he couldn't breathe, feeling as if the stack had invaded his throat from inside him.

The bloody cloth hovered, only a breath away from her mouth. Her tongue, bright pink and longer than it should have been, lashed out, brushing against the cloth, lapping at the blood.

Lapping at *his* blood.

Lady Longstride swallowed, her throat working as if she'd

taken a long draught of liquid—more than a mouthful, far more than a lick. She looked at him with intensity and her lips parted, her voice coming in a husky whisper. "Bind to me, lash to me, cleave to me. *Mine to take.* Mine to own. Mine to *possess.*" Shoving a wad of the bloody cloth into her mouth she began to suckle it, drawing against it with a heave of chest and a fluttering of eyes.

Obscene sounds came from her—vulgar noise as she shifted and suckled harder. Stephen's bowels went to water with terror. She heaved and sighed around the mouthful of cloth with muffled squeals and moans, and he could feel it hot and moist against his face, the tiny droplets of her breath freezing on his cheek.

She lurched at him, flinging herself forward, her thick blonde hair whipped across his face and she lay against him for a long moment, breathing hard.

He could smell her. She was sour, acrid, like a poison.

"Are you quite done?" The Sheriff spoke from above them.

Slowly, Lady Longstride pushed back, kneeling in the snow. She shook her hair back and looked up. Stephen couldn't take his eyes off her. A tiny corner of the cloth stuck out from lips that looked swollen, engorged. She reached up and pulled it, the soaking cloth slipping from tightly pressed lips.

It came out completely clean.

Her eyes locked with his.

Her mouth opened.

"Mine to destroy."

For a long moment nothing happened, save for his heart trying to beat its way from his chest.

Then the burning started.

It grew in his calves, warming, heating, then boiling. It rose, scorching as it did the blood in his veins. Panic made his head go fuzzy.

Hands clamped on his shoulder. Glynna shook him.

"Tell me who conspires to hide the book!" she hissed in his face, her voice rising, her breath like hot copper.

The heat climbed inside him and he could feel the things that made him—the organs and the viscera—cooking, turning hard and rubbery or soft and chewy. It hurt, oh God, it hurt so much.

God.

Christ.

Mary.

"Tell me!" She shook him again and the heat climbed another notch.

He was abandoned. Left to die at the hands of his obsession. God had turned His face. Christ had closed his eyes. Mary had walked away from him.

Only Lady Glynna Longstride was near.

If he told her, maybe she would spare him, save him, stop this pain.

His heart lay like cinder in the furnace of his chest.

The church had left him to Hell.

The fire lapped at his throat as he spoke, crying out through his panic.

"The cardinal," he said. "The cardinal and Brother Tuck. They talk in low voices and keep to themselves."

Lady Longstride smiled and laid her hands on each side of his face. The fire inside him lessened, falling away, giving him respite.

"Thank you, Stephen. You are a good boy."

As he began to open his mouth to say that he loved her, she spat in his eyes and dropped her hands away.

Instantly he went blind, screaming as the fire in his blood howled its way to his brain.

CHAPTER THREE

Darkness and thirst and pain.

These were the things John Little had known all morning.

Lids held shut by a length of hemp spun tight with a stick and secured by a knot in his hair. The edges of his eye sockets were chafed, the bridge of his nose sanded raw by the rough fibers of the rope. The pain was constant but small compared to the sharp fissure of pain that ran down his parched throat.

The rag shoved between his teeth tasted foul and slimy. It wicked away all the water in his mouth leaving him near mad with thirst. His jaw throbbed with grinding agony having been forced wide, tendons straining until they creaked with every breath he forced past the damned gag that kept trying to crawl down his gullet.

His shoulders, back, and legs were knots of fire as the muscles spasmed from being forced into one position for hours. Since morning he'd been shoved to the floor of the wagon, hands bound behind him. He'd listened as the conveyance shuddered to a stop, and the men who guarded him prepared their weapons. They jumped out, making it rock on its axles, tossing some of the other men against him. One landed across his leg, his weight driving nails of pain deep into the strained muscle. A short commotion was punctuated by loud and creative cursing.

"Locksley, you son of a bitch," someone said. Hands grabbed him roughly. The relief of being lifted was short-lived as he was dragged forward and pushed down. He knelt in what felt like mud that seeped, frigid and wet through the knees of his pants.

Fingers pulled his hair as they shoved under the blindfold. The rope pulled tight, squeezing across his temples and pushing into his eyes, making flares of false light inside his lids.

"Hold still," a voice said above him. He tensed as something scraped the skin of his scalp—it was narrow and pointed and definitely sharp. A harsh tug sideways, and true light flooded his eyes. He blinked away the pain, and the world stuttered back into focus, going from black to blurry to only slightly fuzzy on the edges.

In front of him stood a slim man holding a slim dagger. John squinted, straining to focus, to see who this was.

Will Scarlet, John thought with confusion. *He's the only one who would wear a hat like that in the forest.*

Turning his head to the side he found his seven neighbors kneeling next to him. They all slumped, shoulders curved, heads hung low in their blindfolds and gags. All but one. The Old Soldier wasn't bowed, much less broken. Seeing the old man, ramrod straight with his head high, made John force his own spine upright.

Along the road lay the soldiers who had put them in the wagon that morning. They sprawled in the mud, beaten to unconsciousness but still breathing, although the biggest of them lay in a puddle of blood. His heart thrilled at the sight, glad to see them in such a condition. They were the ones who had dragged him from his bed.

Dragged him from his wife.

He hadn't gone easy.

Will Scarlet grabbed the gag and slid the knife between cloth and skin. Another sharp yank cut the filthy rag. John spit it to the ground.

The slim man smiled. "Let me get you some water." John

tried to speak, but his voice stuck to the sides of his throat. Lips feeling like they had been peeled and dried, he swallowed, trying to find enough moisture to release his words. Barely a whisper came out.

"Free... my... hands."

"Not until we know why you're tied in Locksley's wagon." A different voice. There was someone else there. John leaned, eyes sliding past Scarlet and finding the second man who stood on the other side of the road.

"I'm John Little," he growled, and anger pushed his voice past the rawness in his throat. "Longstride knows me. Hell, he knows *all* of us." Scarlet turned, looking at Robin. The bowman nodded once. Eyebrows drawn but not questioning, Will moved beside John, leaning against his shoulder as he reached behind him with the dagger. The feather of Will's hat brushed along his cheek, tickling, making his eye twitch. He ignored it, staring at Robin.

A small tug and the ropes parted like water. Immediately the burning cramps between his shoulder blades loosened in a rush of relief. Both arms were dead, useless from being constricted, void of all feeling from shoulder to fingertip.

Will moved away to begin cutting another man free. John struggled to his feet. His mind felt disconnected from his hands, so that he had to push the thought at them to clench and unclench, trying to force feeling back into them.

He stared at Robin, marking the difference since the last time he had laid eyes on him. Young Longstride had become leaner in his time as an outlaw, the soft fat of luxurious living carved away by surviving off the land and fighting John's men. He looked... darker.

His swarthy skin had always been different from his family, from his little sisters, God rest their souls, but now it was even more pronounced. It might have been the dim light of Sherwood, or the fact that Robin was dirtier than John had ever seen him— certainly since he had moved from boy to man.

No, not a man, John thought angrily. *A man lives up to his responsibilities, instead of running away.*

Needles of pain filled the space between skin and muscle in his hands as blood began to flow through his veins again.

"What are you staring at, Little John?" the hooded outlaw asked quietly.

"Don't use that name," John snarled. "That name is for friends and family. Your father could use it, but not you, Robin." His voice was harsh, and not just because of the aftereffects from the gag.

"I used to call you that."

"I used to call you Lord."

Silence fell between them.

Done cutting the last man free, Will moved to stand beside Robin. The others moved to stand behind John, except for the old man. Old Soldier stood equal to John, not behind nor in front of, but beside. Except for him they all moved slowly, still recovering from being bound in one position for hours. A water skin passed between them.

One by one they took it, drinking long and hard. It came to John and he handed it immediately to the old man. Old Soldier took a quick swallow, just enough to wet his mouth before handing it back. The water was ice cold and tasted of river moss and waxed leather.

It was more delicious than wedding wine.

"Do you really trust them?" Will asked Robin.

Robin said nothing.

John spat a mouthful of water onto the road between them. His throat eased with the liquid, the thirst slaked and the pain dulled.

"He should trust us. He's known some of us his entire life. Not that it made a damn bit of difference to him."

The old man put a hand on John's shoulder. He looked down at it. The back of the hand was liver-spotted. Veins gorged with thick blood mapped the surface under parchment-thin skin, the knuckles swollen and scarred from the bite of sword through shield. Yet they did not shake. They were as steady and as strong as the man's voice.

"Be fair, Little John."

John bit back a growl.

"Fair? You tell me, Old Soldier, was it fair for little Lord Longstride to abandon our lands? Was it fair that we fell under the reign of Locksley, just because Robin decided to piss off in this wood and play outlaw with sticks and string?" The men who had been cut free began to murmur behind them, their voices swelling in appreciation of John's words.

Old Soldier squared off against him, not threatening, but showing fearlessness in the face of the big man's wrath.

"You know the circumstance…"

"Yes, I know! We all do." His eyes narrowed and he leaned in. "Do you not remember burying little Becca and Ruth? *We* dug their graves, side by side, shoulder to shoulder. *We* buried the wee ones." John's heavy hand traced the sign of the cross. "God bless and keep them."

"What are you talking about?" Will's hand was on his sword hilt, an unconscious reaction to John's shaking rage.

"I don't have to answer to you, Scarlet. I'm a free man."

"Because we just freed you!"

John said nothing. The pain had passed, and now his hands simply remained clenched. He could feel the weight of his blood in them, the heaviness of his rage. He glared at Robin over the fop's hat. Robin stared back at him, eyes flat and dark.

He looks guilty, John noticed. *Good. He knows what he has done.*

"If you are a free man, why did Locksley have you locked in a wagon bound for Kraeger's land?" Will Scarlet asked.

Old Soldier stepped forward. "Locksley took over Longstride Manor when Lord Robin—"

"*Don't* call him Lord." John spat.

"Don't give me orders, Little John." Old Soldier's voice was even, patient. He waited a moment to see if John would reply.

When the big man didn't, he continued. "When Lord Robin left us. Locksley has occupied our land with soldiers, and taxed us heavily. This morning he gathered the eight of us, had his soldiers bind us, then informed us we'd been sold into the service of Lord Kraeger."

Robin spoke. "I didn't leave you in slavery."

John lunged forward. "No, you *abandoned* us into it. Without a rightful Longstride to hold the land, Locksley came in under the Sheriff of Nottingham's hand."

"He had no right," Robin said, his voice low and menacing. "I'm still alive. Your homes should have been left alone."

"The Sheriff doesn't give a damn what's right," John countered, "and he's not the only one these days." The men behind him grew louder, muttering their agreement.

Old Soldier and Will Scarlet both moved toward him. Tension grew. John's chest swelled as they did so, drawing in air, preparing to fight.

"*Stop.*"

The word cut through the air.

Robin pushed past them. Both men moved aside, allowing him to step within arm's length of John Little. The two men stared at each other, Robin looking up, John looking down.

Robin spoke first.

"I had to leave."

"You were a coward." John's face twisted in a snarl.

"I did not mean for hardship to fall on you."

"I don't care what you meant," John replied. "I'm still here in this cursed wood, separated from my wife, and all because of *your* actions."

Robin took a deep breath. "When the pox took my sisters…"

"Your sisters would be ashamed of you." John's voice was a knife. "I'm glad they're in Heaven, and cannot see you now."

The words fell like thunder, leaving a brittle, hollow silence in their wake. No one moved. No one breathed.

Robin's fist lashed out.

Viciously it smashed John across the face in a blinding burst of pain. Too quick for him to react, too fast to see it coming. One second the two men were glaring, the next he couldn't see past a red wall of pain.

His nose was broken. That much he could tell. He stumbled into the men behind him, the only thing that kept him from falling to the ground. They shoved him away and he went to one knee, his world a throb of red and black hurt.

Weight struck him in the chest, riding him to the ground. Blow after blow clanged against his face, his neck, his head. His ears closed, the only sound he could hear was the smack of fist on flesh.

After what felt like hours the hitting stopped.

He couldn't breathe, couldn't lift the weight on his chest, couldn't draw air past the blood in his nose. He blinked away panic, the world coming back into focus as he gasped air through his mouth.

Robin was above him, one knee pinning him to the ground.

The outlaw's teeth were clenched, a bloody fist raised over his head. His face moved close to John's. Teeth bared and a feral, fever glint in his dark eyes, Robin spoke, his voice low and dangerous.

"*Never* speak of my family again," he said. "I am *not* the boy you once knew."

Little John turned his head. His tongue worked and he spat a clot of blood into the dirt. He tried to speak, couldn't. His eye pulsed, slowly swelling closed with every heartbeat. Swallowing the iron tang of his own blood, he found his voice.

"You're not the man, either," he replied. "Try that again when I haven't been beaten by soldiers, and the story will end differently."

Robin let go and stood. He looked at his hands, studying knuckles painted with John's blood. He took a deep breath, let it out. With red fingers he pulled his hood back over his head, turned, and stepped away.

Scarlet reached out to grab his arm, then clearly thought

better of it, his hand hanging in the air.

Robin paused. "Sell the swords, the wagon, and the horses. Give the money to the families of these men."

"I'll see it done." Will said.

Robin nodded, walking toward the dim forest.

"Gold won't take away your guilt." John dragged himself up from the mud, pushing through the pain, coming to his feet. "Walk away, Little Longstride, and leave us to fend for ourselves once again."

Robin kept walking.

"What am I supposed to do now?" John bellowed. Tears streamed down his face. "I can't go back to my wife. I'm an outlaw now, just like you. We *all* are."

Robin reached the tree line on the side of the road.

"This is your fault, Longstride! All of this is your fault."

Robin didn't turn.

"Sherwood is not my forest." His voice carried past the edge of the hood, over his shoulder. "Live here or leave, I don't care. Just stay the hell away from me." With that he melted into the trees, leaving John to his rage.

He turned on the man with the feathered hat. "What of you, Scarlet? What call do you have to be helping an outlaw, when the nobles think you're one of their own?"

Scarlet went pale, but whether from fear or rage John couldn't tell. Nor did he much care at that moment. His life was already over.

Old Soldier reached out a hand and touched him on the arm. John wanted to snap at him, but his respect for the man held him in check. Old Soldier had been a King's man in his youth, but more than that no one knew of him—not even his name. John had seen him once or twice as a boy, when the king would pass through the land visiting landholders and their people. The man he knew now as Old Soldier had been never more than a step away from the king's side.

Years ago, not long after John had become a man himself,

Old Soldier had come to Longstride Manor and taken up a plot of land, working side by side with the rest of them. His actions always spoke louder than any words. He was a friend to the people, and wiser even than he was old. John had never seen him without his mail shirt on—not even in the field.

Finally Scarlet replied. "He is my cousin," he spat out, "and he's right, this is a free forest. When was the last time any of you could ever truly say you lived as free men, who did as they pleased?"

There was muttering among the other men.

"Never," John snarled. "And no matter what you or that outlaw think, we're still not. Free men could go home to their families."

Scarlet narrowed his eyes. "If you can't go to your families, maybe you should consider bringing your families to you."

"We can't live in the forest," John protested.

"We wouldn't be the first who had," Old Soldier rubbed his grizzled chin thoughtfully.

He was right.

John knew it—he just didn't like it.

They had no other choice. They couldn't risk endangering their families by returning home. Yet maybe, somehow, someday they *could* bring their wives and their children to be with them. For now, though, they had to stay away.

"But everyone knows Sherwood Forest is haunted," one of the other men said, fear making his voice quiver on the edges.

"It is haunted." John put his head in his hands. "Haunted by us."

CHAPTER FOUR

The fire popped and spat tiny embers toward his legs. They didn't reach him, burning out before they could. The flame had died to little more than coals, leaving the room dark. He leaned on the mantle, chin on his arms as the remaining heat radiated against the front of his body.

The edge of the mantle had been worn over time, the cedar under his forearms rounded instead of an angled block, the wood fibers smoothed to a slick, hard surface with no splinters. His father had stood in this very place almost every evening, his big arms crossed, mighty head bowed so that his shaggy beard, uncut for decades, could hang and sway from the up current of heat.

His father had taken up so much more room at the mantle. His own arm didn't fill the worn-in place, just as the man didn't take up as much room in the kingdom as his father had.

A noise, a shoe on flagstone floor.

"What do you want?" He didn't turn. He'd had one too many whiskeys, and felt no need. Not in his house.

"Lord Locksley," a voice said. "Forgive the intrusion…"

"Finish intruding before you ask forgiveness."

The voice behind him faltered. "Lord?"

He turned then, shoulders rolling on the front of the mantle as he brought his face around to see who had interrupted his reverie. A man he did not recognize stood by the door to the study. A heavy wool cloak wrapped him, covering floor to throat. The cloak's blood-red color, dark in the shadows, marked him John's, the sitting king.

Locksley waved his hand. "Get on with it."

The king's man nodded. "You are required at the castle."

"Why?"

The man blinked. "Why?"

"Why?"

More blinking. "Why?"

Instantly Locksley was across the room, hand wadded in the man's cloak before he could react. He pulled the man close.

"Say 'why' one more damned time." Locksley shook him, and the man shoved back with all his strength, breaking free. He stumbled away, fumbling under the edge of his cloak to grab the hilt of his sword.

Locksley held up a finger.

"Don't make that mistake, laddie," he said. "I'll gut you here, and feed you to a pack of wild dogs."

The king's man stopped, hand flexing and unflexing on the hilt of his sword.

"Let it go, son."

The man dropped the edge of his cloak.

"Why am I being summoned at this late hour?" Locksley said, and he waited.

"I was ordered to fetch," the man said angrily, "not told why."

"Then feck off with you." Locksley turned away in dismissal. "I'll be along shortly." Again the sound of shoes on stone, and the door closed behind him.

The room grew silent, save the crackle of the coals.

Locksley sighed.

"You may as well come out, and get it over with. I know you are skulking in the shadows."

Robin stepped to the edge of the dull orange glow.

It had been months since Locksley had set eyes on the younger man, the last time when he'd laid his claim to his land. Robin set fire to Longstride Manor as he disappeared into the depths of Sherwood. He'd been more than a boy then, but not much more.

Before him stood a man pared down by survival. Robin had grown shaggier, his dark hair hanging down along his shoulders, the edges raw cut by knife instead of shears. Hollow cheeks had been shaved to hard edges by living as an outlaw. Dark clothing made him a shadow in a shadow.

He had the look of a winter-starved wolf.

"Clever using the other man's entrance to cover your own." Locksley picked up his cup and took a sip.

"Why did you sell my men into slavery?"

"You waste no time on pleasantries."

Robin stepped closer, the light casting up over his features.

He has her eyes. The color is wrong, but the shape is right.

"There is no room for polite conversation between us." Robin scowled. "Answer the question."

"They aren't *your* men," Locksley said. "You abandoned them. I bought the property."

"They aren't property. They are free men."

Locksley slammed his cup down. "They are *responsibilities*! Mouths to feed. You didn't plant enough, and the fire took part of what you did. Between the lack of harvest on your piddly land and the taxes levied by the throne, there is not enough. Kraeger needs strong backs, and he had good gold to buy them. I now have fewer people to feed, and more money to care for the wives and children."

Robin snarled, a low animal sound that rolled out of the left side of his mouth.

"Don't pretend to be noble," he said. "You act only out of spite for my family."

"I bought the land out of spite," Locksley acknowledged, and he lifted his chin, "but I made the hard choices out of nobility, and because they were the right choices to be made."

Robin stood there, quivering in the half-light, fists tight by his side.

"You run at the call of your master, John the Usurper," he said. "You support his abuse of the land and the people. How *dare* you claim nobility?"

"You'll learn one day that noble is not just how you are born, but how you act," Locksley said. "Abandoning your responsibilities isn't noble."

"Kissing arse to a tyrant isn't either."

"Staying alive is the first rule."

"I'll take my freedom."

Locksley barked out a laugh. "Surely your freedom has been terribly cold and hungry this winter."

Robin's eyes glittered in the firelight. "I'm going to kill you."

Locksley's guts turned to iced water. He saw the sword hilt jutting off of Robin's hip, and his mind measured the distance between them. As he did, he cast back to the day he'd gone to collect taxes at Longstride Manor.

The planks shook under his feet. He threw himself sideways, shoulder hitting the boards as a hurley crossed the space where his skull had just been. He rolled, stopping in a crouch, sword halfway drawn from its scabbard.

Robin stood in front of the door, hurley in hand and swinging back for another try. The planks still vibrated where the boy had dropped from the roof of Longstride Manor. He was bare-chested, filthy from the waist up, his dark hair matted with dirt. He looked like an ancient Pict—dark, savage, and full of murder.

Locksley felt the whiskey in his own blood, dulling him.

No, he thought, *I'll never close on him before he cuts me down.*

Locksley stood straighter. "You will be hunted down."

Robin chuckled. "I'm already hunted."

"Then do your dirty deed, low-minded savage."

Robin shook his head. "You buy your life with the bread you feed the families of Longstride land. Care for them while the traitor holds the throne. They are your ransom from my wrath." He stepped back into the shadows. "But sell anyone else into slavery, and you won't see the arrow until it is jutting from your chest."

He made no sound as he disappeared into the shadows.

It took several moments for Locksley to be certain he was alone in the room. He lifted his cup with a trembling hand, and drank the rest of the whiskey it held.

Will felt pity for Old Soldier and the others—even John Little. Being cut off from their families was not what they would have chosen for themselves, but they were out of options. Men without options were desperate men, and often given to doing things that were ill-advised and rash. He knew as much from his own situation.

"Come with me," he said. "I know a place in the forest where you can build camp. You'll be safe there."

Little John spat on the ground, and looked as if he might be ready to say something more, but Old Soldier stepped forward.

"Take us there," he said in a calm voice.

Will had learned early on in life that the quiet ones were the ones who always bore the most watching. Old Soldier was a man with whom he would never want to cross swords, and he was grateful for his cooperation now.

He indicated the two horses that had been pulling the cart.

"Take them with us," he said. "You can take turns riding, and a good horse is a useful thing. Take the merchant's horse, as well."

Two of the men quickly set about freeing the beasts. Once they had done so, the men looked around at one another.

"What's wrong?" Will asked, eyeing the guards and wondering how long before they started to wake up.

"We don't know how to ride," one of the men finally confessed.

Old Soldier turned and mounted the larger of the two beasts with ease.

"I'll teach them," he said.

One of the men took firm hold on the bridle of the merchant's horse. Little John took the lead rope of the other cart horse.

"Until then, we'll walk," he grunted.

Will tried not to stare. The horse was a big one, built for heavy labor, and yet Little John was so large that he made the horse look more like a child's pony.

"Suit yourself," Will muttered, turning his own animal's head deeper into the forest.

Old Soldier walked his mount a couple of paces behind, allowing Will to lead. He couldn't help but notice that the grizzled old man, though he likely had not been on a horse for years, still had a more relaxed seat in the saddle than Will himself did. It was enviable.

The place he had in mind was a few hours' hike into the thick forest, far enough that they would not be found. Only Robin and his allies ventured so far in. With each step they traveled, though, he could feel the unease growing, like a steady itching on the back of his neck.

When he could stand it no longer he turned in his saddle and glanced back at them.

"What's wrong?" he demanded.

"The forest is haunted," one of the men said, his voice low, his eyes darting.

Will shrugged. "Leave the haints and the fey alone, and they'll leave you alone, as well," he said. "They want even less to do with you than you do with them."

"How can you be sure of that?" Another man spoke up, somewhat fearfully.

"Have you seen what an ugly lot you are?" Will asked.

They stared at him for a moment, blinking, then to his surprise Little John was the first to guffaw at this quip.

The others followed suit until all were laughing. With a small sigh of relief, Will turned forward again.

"You got lucky," Old Soldier commented, softly enough that only he could hear.

"I was counting on my luck to hold," Will replied. "Besides, a man who has lost his sense of humor has truly lost everything."

He paused, then added, "They're going to be alright." He knew perfectly well, however, that he was trying to reassure himself.

"I'll help train them," Old Soldier said, his voice still soft.

"Train them for what?" Will asked.

"For war," the old man answered. "That's where all this is headed, after all."

Will shook his head. "I hope it doesn't come to that."

"But it will, and hoping one way or another won't change anything."

"What will you need?" Will asked. He wasn't ready to admit that Old Soldier was right, but at the very least it would give these men something on which to focus. That was a very good idea.

"We could make some weapons—bows and arrows, staffs—if we had the tools to cut the wood. Beyond that, swords. As many swords and knives as can be laid hands upon."

"I'll see what I can arrange," Will said. "I'll try to get some food to you as well."

"Unnecessary, we can eat off the land."

"Alright, then. I should be able to get some blankets," Will said, thinking of how bitterly cold the winter was, even so early in the season.

Old Soldier shook his head fiercely. "We don't want them making a home. Home makes you soft. It's what you fight for. The more comforts and luxuries they have, the faster they'll forget that we are at war."

Will nodded slowly. "Tools and weapons then."

"Weapons, then tools."

Will indicated the bundle behind his saddle. "You can have the ones we took from Locksley's men."

Old Soldier nodded. "It's a start."

When they finally reached the clearing, Old Soldier nodded as though satisfied with Will's choice for an encampment. A creek bordered one side, and would provide fresh water. This deep in the forest, there would be an abundance of game. Tall grass, brown and brittle with the winter, bordered another section. It was close to where Robin most often spent his nights, since retreating into the forest. These men would need his cousin's help and guidance, even if he wasn't ready to take on that responsibility. And if Old Soldier was right, Robin would soon need their help as well.

The men began to spread around the open space, exhibiting an assortment of emotions, until Will was getting that itching sensation on the back of his neck again. This time, though, he didn't think it was because of the men themselves. He needed to go back, before his absence was noted.

"I will not be able to return for several days at least," he said, "but I will see to it that you get what you asked for, and as swiftly as possible. We are not entirely without allies. So, if you see a fat friar or a lanky bard, try not to hurt them. They are on our side."

Old Soldier nodded and clasped Will's hand, a sign of respect. When they let go Will turned and rode quickly from the clearing, hating that he could not do more for these men who had been wronged by Locksley.

CHAPTER FIVE

Some days Friar Tuck felt as if he didn't have enough prayers to go around. There were so many in need. The poor were being devastated by the harsh, early winter, so soon after the pox, and having been squeezed nearly to death by King John's tax collectors. He could no longer pray for them each individually—there were too many. That hurt him deeply. Even worse, the majority of his prayers dealt with greater issues—the defeat of John, the return of Richard, the safety of those who fought for the realm. His knees hated the cold stone floor, yet he spent more and more time on it, praying with his heart and soul.

"Friar, are you alright?" It was a quiet little voice, interrupting his latest devotions.

He opened his eyes and found a child staring at him wide-eyed. It looked to be a boy, judging from the clothes and the haircut, but it was really Lenore, a girl orphaned by the tax collectors. Her father had been a well-respected merchant, and her mother a kind soul. Friar Tuck had taken Lenore in, disguising her for her own safety. There was too much darkness in the world these days, and he couldn't risk others taking advantage of her simply for who she was.

"Yes, I'm fine," he assured her. "Is there something that is troubling you?" he asked, heaving himself up off the ground and staggering for just a moment as he realized that his left foot had fallen asleep. He gripped the back of one of the pews, and stomped to awaken it.

"A man is asking to see you," she replied timidly. "He wears the fanciest clothes I've ever seen."

Will Scarlet. Tuck would wager just about anything on that.

"Fetch him in here," he said, then he moved to the back of the chapel, where there was a small alcove. Lenore left and quickly returned with Will, who looked to be in as sour a mood as Tuck had ever seen.

"Thank you, boy," Will said absently. Lenore nodded, and then departed. Will glanced around and moved close to Tuck, his movements furtive.

"I'm surprised to see you here," the friar admitted.

"Is there someplace safer?"

Tuck shook his head. "I'm not certain there is one," he said. "One of our brothers is missing, and it bodes ill. The cardinal is concerned... but, that is not what has brought you here."

Will glanced around and then dropped his voice. "We... liberated a group of men who had been sold into slavery on Locksley's orders. I have relocated them to the glen where we have met on many occasions prior to our... adventures. They are in need of supplies, but all they wish for are tools and weapons." He paused a moment, then corrected, "Weapons, and tools."

Friar Tuck frowned. "No clothes, blankets, or food?"

"No. There is one among them, Robin only ever called him Old Soldier. The man insists that we only send weapons and tools. He sees a war coming, and he wants to help, train the men to fight when the time comes."

A chill touched Tuck's spine. He marveled for a moment at the fact that he had been moved by what King Richard had said, so long ago, and had been ready to follow him off to war, had the cardinal not forbidden him from doing so. It turned out that he'd had no need to go off to war, since war seemed insistent on coming to him.

He took a deep breath. "I will do what I can. The tools will be easier than the weapons."

"I told them to expect you."

"I'll take as much as I can gather right away. They will be in need of comfort, as well, and spiritual counsel. Regardless of what the man said, I'll take some blankets, and our woolen robes. There's no reason they should have to pass the first of many cold, lonely nights in the forest without someone to ease their minds, and help share their burdens." Then he added, "A little ale might help to warm their bodies and lift their spirits as well."

"So long as it is not all drunk before you arrive," Will commented with a small smile.

"You mind I don't box your ears," Tuck said gruffly, but the smile just broadened.

"I must be off," Will said. "John will be wanting to see me. I'll have to tell him that there is indeed an outlaw haunting Sherwood, and that Locksley isn't just making that up."

"Be careful, Will," Tuck said, placing a hand on the other man's shoulder. "I worry for you and Marian, every day, in that nest of vipers."

"So do I," Will said with a sudden, intense seriousness that was unusual for him. "Sometimes I have nightmares…" He drifted off, and then shook his head, clearly not wanting to discuss them. "Suffice it to say, the sooner King John is off the throne, the better."

Tuck nodded, his concern deepening. He knew what it was like to have disturbing dreams. He knew how much worse it could be when they sometimes came true.

It was with a great deal of reluctance that Will rode away from the monastery.

Every time he left the castle, he returned with an even greater feeling of dread, and his stomach was already in knots even before he drew anywhere near the keep. He was playing a dangerous game with John, and every day he prayed to God it wouldn't be the day that he lost.

The fear and anxiety caused by his role as spy, combined with the ever-increasing sense of evil that permeated the place, were taking their toll. He did his best to keep up appearances. Robin, Marian, even the good friar needed him to be strong, indeed merry. It did no good to let them see the dread in his heart, as it would only add to their own.

It used to be that Alan-a-Dale could be counted on to raise people's spirits. Of late, though, the bard had taken it upon himself to fill the role of truth-teller, or soothsayer. That was all well and good, but sometimes what people needed was hope. Even if it was a lie. Though he kept his horse at a walk, Will arrived at the castle far sooner than he would have liked. He felt his chest tighten as it came into view. By the time he arrived in the forecourt, though, a fake smile was firmly in place. He tossed the reins to a stable boy, and then sauntered into the castle with as much arrogance as he could muster.

He encountered the steward almost immediately, and the man quickly led him into John's presence. The prince was at his desk, poring over some documents. He looked up as Will approached, and smiled in the way that made Will's blood run cold. It was like watching a serpent trying to smile, and knowing all the while that it intended to kill you.

"Leave us," John told the steward.

The man bowed and then left the room—perhaps too readily. Will wondered for a brief moment if he was lurking just outside, listening to their conversation. Then he dismissed the thought as irrelevant.

"Well?" John said, leaning forward eagerly.

"There is indeed an outlaw," Will reported, "one of impressive physical prowess. Locksley is not making that up, and he stole the entire shipment. Once I had ascertained that the Hood did exist, I didn't waste time beating a hasty retreat.

I wasn't about to risk my neck, not without first being able to tell you what I saw."

"You were right to leave quickly," John agreed. "After all, you were really there to be my eyes and ears. Other… allies of mine cannot enter the forest with the same ease that you can."

Will bowed slightly, even as his mind quickened with the information. He had suspected as much. The Sheriff couldn't enter Sherwood proper. Some magic must be keeping him at bay, for which they all could be immensely grateful.

If only there was a way to spread that magic over the entire country, Will thought wistfully. Still, the more they knew about their enemies, the better chance they had at defeating them.

"I am happy to be of service, my liege," Will said.

"Now I have another task for you," John said, nodding. "One that will be infinitely more agreeable."

Will very much doubted that, but he smiled broadly.

"And what is that?"

"I'm calling all the nobles here, to arrive in six weeks' time. Then we shall hold a week's worth of festivities, culminating on the feast of the winter solstice. I would very much like your help in planning everything—there is no one better suited. You are so clever with matters of court."

"Your Majesty flatters me," Will said with mock delight. "I would be honored to take on such an exciting task." His mind was already racing.

John had made no bones about his contempt for the nobles, so he had to harbor an ulterior motive. Hosting the lot of them for an entire week, with festivities and a feast? Whatever the prince was planning, it had to be big, and something terrible. The door opened and the steward entered.

He was accompanied by the Lady Marian.

"You wanted to see me," she said perfunctorily when she had stopped beside Will. She did not look at him.

"Yes, my dear," John replied. "In six weeks' time we will be entertaining the nobility. As the ranking lady of the castle, you will be responsible for the duties of the hostess. Together, you and Will Scarlet must make sure that everything is perfect for our guests." His tone turned mocking. "I trust that working closely together won't pose too much of a problem?"

Marian flushed, but kept her voice steady.

"I'm certain everything will work out perfectly," she said.

"Good," John responded. "Steward, see that messengers are sent with these letters." He picked up the pile from his desk.

The man moved forward to take them.

"Will, Marian," John said, turning away from them, "I will summon you again to discuss the specifics." With that he gave a wave of his hand, effectively dismissing them. Marian turned on her heel and stalked toward the door. Will bowed, then followed at a much slower pace.

Behind him, John spoke again to the steward.

"I want you to make certain that tomorrow night's shipment, bound for Scotland, leaves precisely on schedule," he said. "It is vitally important that the *valuables* on board that ship arrive safely at their destination. We can't risk sending an envoy that large through Sherwood."

Will's heart skipped a beat as he wondered what John could be sending to Scotland. King Richard's cousin, Henry, currently resided there. Might John be sending him a bribe of some sort? Perhaps to back John's claim to the throne. His stomach lurched slightly at the thought.

Ahead of him Marian paused, and almost started to turn around, then seemed to think better of it and kept going. Will exited the room a couple of feet behind her, and he closed the door carefully. He listened for a moment and then shook his head. Either John and the steward had ceased talking, or they were speaking too softly to be heard.

He moved away from the door, signaling Marian to walk with him. They made their way down one of the hallways until they found an alcove where they were unlikely to be disturbed.

When they stopped walking Will looked at her.

"We need to stop that shipment," they said in unison.

Marian frowned. "Alan is off and away. It will take more than the four of us to deal with a group of soldiers."

Will smiled.

CHAPTER SIX

The cold ride sharpened Locksley, clearing his head. One thought kept rolling through his mind, turning and turning, taking on the rhythm of the hoofbeats beneath him.

Robin Longstride is the Hood.

He'd known about his men being sold off, used as bait in a trap for the Hood. As a child Robin had long shown an affinity for the bow, winning contest after contest, even against trained soldiers.

Robin was the Hood.

The bane of his existence as chief tax collector.

Son of his sworn enemy.

Son of the only woman I ever loved.

He arrived at the doors that led to the throne room. The king's man—the one who'd come to summon him—stood to the left, frowning. As Locksley stepped closer the man reached for the door. Locksley held up his hand.

The man stopped, and his frown turned to curiosity. Locksley kept his hand up, standing in place as he turned the revelation over in his mind.

King John would reward him generously for this information, yet what could be done with it?

Robin remained in Sherwood, unreachable, secure in the labyrinth of the mighty forest. His father was gone with King

Richard, his siblings dead, and his only other relative, well... working directly for John. There was no leverage that might draw him out.

That wasn't entirely true. There were the people in Locksley's charge at Longstride Manor, but Robin had given his warning. If harm came to them, Robin would kill him, even if it meant his own death in the process. Victory meant nothing if he wasn't around to savor it.

No, knowledge was power. He knew Robin's secret. He would hold that weapon until it could best be wielded.

He dropped his hand and nodded to the king's man, striding forward as the door was pulled open. The throne room was gloomy, the walls covered in long sections of dark cloth. The last time he'd been there the walls had been blank, expanses of bare stone marked by light areas where once had hung ancient tapestries that depicted scenes of history and religion, tapestries put in place by King Richard, by his father before him, and his father's father before that.

King John had removed them in his first month as acting king.

The room's only light came from a ring of guttering lamps, mounted on iron poles around the dais of the throne. The dull blue flames in them jerked and spat sparks against the insides of their globes.

People were gathered around the throne. They were far enough away to be indistinct, although he recognized John by the ridiculous scepter he always clutched while holding court, as if it conferred weight to his station. Near him was the dark spot that was the Sheriff of Nottingham. The man looked like an obsidian blade with his black armor and his streak of lightning-white hair.

As he approached the people they turned toward him. With each step the lateness weighed heavier on him. He had many complaints about King Richard, but the man had never called him to attention at such an ungodly hour.

King John tilted his head, wide crown sliding on his dark brow.

"Glad you could come," he said, sarcasm edging his voice, and he indicated two men who knelt beside the throne. Their hands were bound, their heads bowed. One of them wore a blue tabard. He couldn't see the insignia, but he knew in his heart of hearts it was a rampant lion. "Some of your friends have returned."

The heavyset man raised his head. Locksley's stomach tightened at the sight of the familiar face.

Mendly Mercroft, seller of goods and items of curiosity.

The man he'd tasked with trying to kill the Hood in ambush.

Locksley cursed in his own mind.

The last to turn toward him was the Sheriff, pivoting on his heel and stepping aside.

Seated behind him, obscured from view, was Lady Glynna Longstride.

Locksley cursed out loud.

Lady Glynna giggled.

He was stunned that she was alive. The summer plague had claimed her daughters, and he'd thought it had taken her, as well—but here she was, bright-eyed, fair-skinned, her hair luxurious against her bosom...

...and immensely pregnant.

Her belly jutted out from her tall, athletic frame, swollen to enormous proportions, the size of it pulling her skin taut and thin so that light blue veins marbled the entirety of it. Her blouse had been pulled up over it, leaving it exposed like a pale moon rising over the horizon.

Thin, squiggling symbols had been painted on its surface in curving lines. They pulled at his eyes, one row of flame-script pulling his eye left and another pulling it right. His eyes began to water and he had to blink and look up at her face.

Alive, he thought, *and with child. It cannot be.* He'd seen her just a few months back, when he'd sought to collect taxes on her household. She'd shown no sign of it then. Could this be Longstride's child, conceived before he sailed to the Holy Land?

He pictured her before, long and lithe, no sign of having borne four children, and his mind tumbled further back.

To warm summer days of his youth, and the difference in her after just one child. The subtle widening of her hips, the light crackle of stretch marks on her stomach, hidden in the crease of her hipbone, the fullness of her...

"Why do your men always fail?"

The question jerked him back to his present situation. His eyes focused on John as he leaned forward on the throne, staring. The Sheriff stood beside Glynna, his hand slid under her hair, black gauntlet-covered fingers just coming around the other side to splay against her throat, lying against her fair skin like the legs of some tremendous spider covering the artery there.

Her eyes were closed and she leaned back against his touch. Her lips turned up in a sly, wicked smile.

No...

He blinked, wanting to shake himself, but refusing to show that much weakness.

"Excuse me?" he said.

King John stood. "I asked, why do your men always fail?" Raising the heavy scepter in his right hand, he gestured at the two bound men. The staff was a rod of hardwood, coated in gold. The top of it bore a fist-sized lump of gold that had been worked into the snarling head of a ravening wolf.

A wolf with curling horns.

"More to the point," John continued, "are you in league with the Hood?"

Locksley's eyes went wide, and he took a step back.

"You accuse me of treason?"

"Treason, or incompetence," John growled. "Which is it?"

His skin grew hot under his clothes. "Neither."

"Then why is the Hood *always* taking the taxes that have been collected?"

"He doesn't," Locksley protested. "We deliver most of..."

The Sheriff's voice cut him off.

"Any delivery he attacks, he takes."

Locksley looked at the Sheriff. The man unnerved him.

"Do you hire cowards for the job?" the Sheriff continued. "Men who lay down at the sight of a rogue and a bandit?" The man stared at him now, dark eyes glittering in the shadow of his brow.

"My men always fight." He stepped closer to the dais, closer to the two men bound there. He snapped his fingers. "You two, look up, let me see your faces."

Mercroft and the guardsman did as they were told. It took him a second to place the name of the guardsman. He was a young man, new to Locksley's service. In fact, he was one of the men who lived on Longstride land. *Barkley? Benton?*

Bentley. The man's name was Bentley. An ugly bruise cut across his throat, a wide line of mottled flesh. A dark line of dried blood bisected it, curving over his Adam's apple and under his jawline, the mark left by a rough sinew bowstring.

"See their injuries?" He gestured toward Bentley's throat. "They fought."

The Sheriff snorted through his nose.

"The fat one bears no injury." Glynna's voice was a purr as she stroked her face along the armored fingers at her jaw and cheek.

Mercroft's eyes went wide and he began to stammer, lips smacking and jowls shaking. "H-he struck me from b-behind! You can't see it for my hair!"

"So you were running away?" the Sheriff asked.

"No, no, no, no... I was trying to stab him! I was!"

"Then how was he behind you?" Sinister humor sparkled in the Sheriff's eyes.

Mercroft's mouth moved, but no sound came out.

Bentley's head dropped to his chest. The soft sounds of his sobs came to Locksley's ears.

The Sheriff met eyes with King John, who still stood in front of the throne, scepter in hand. The Sheriff nodded once, a quick up and down of his head.

Dread filled Locksley's stomach.

He leaned forward, a protest in the back of his teeth.

King John took one step, drew back his scepter, and smashed it into Mercroft's face.

The heavy gold ram's wolf sank into the space where Mercroft's left eye met his nose, the bones of the man's face folding like they were made of cloth, and in an instant the merchant Locksley had known for three decades didn't even look like a man anymore. Blood and bone splinters sprayed, drenching the side of Bentley's head. As the gore struck him like a wet slap he screamed a long, pitiful wail, high pitched and mewling, like an animal being slaughtered.

John's face pulled into a wide, gleeful smile. He tugged on the scepter and Mercroft's body shuddered. The thing had lodged in the collapsed skull. John put his foot on the dead man's chest, grasped the scepter with both hands, and yanked. It came free with a long, lingering squelch that hung in the air, not quite echoing in the room.

Mercroft's body slumped sideways, falling against Bentley. The young man was screaming, his wail now undulating as his body convulsed, trying desperately to get away from the bloodied corpse but still bound hand and foot.

John twirled, his long robe slinging out from his lean body, showing a hairless, blood-spattered chest. His spin brought him closer to Bentley and he swung the gore painted scepter up in an arc, to bash it against the young man's jaw.

The scream ended.

The impact bounced Bentley on his knees, his head twisted sharply by John's blow. Locksley could see he was already dead. The lifeless body of the young man leaned out, pushed by the weight of dead Mercroft against him, and tumbled off the dais. It fell onto the tiled floor, landing on his neck which creased like a letter to be sent.

John tossed the scepter into the air. It spun in a lazy arc from his right hand, across his body, and into his left hand.

The Sheriff spoke.

"From this moment forward, any time your men fail to stop the Hood from taking a delivery, one of them will die."

Locksley turned to look at him. He'd gone numb, left hollow at the casual destruction of two men. *His men*. One he almost counted as friend, the other he'd taken as a responsibility.

His words to Robin burned deep inside him, below the dullness of shock.

"And make no mistake," John continued for the Sheriff. "Fail us many more times, and *you* will be that man."

Locksley realized his hand was shaking by his side. He clenched it to make it stop.

"You are dismissed," Glynna chirped. "Fare thee well."

He turned and stalked out of the room, cursing the name Longstride with each step.

Friar Tuck carefully maneuvered the heavily laden wagon through the forest, heading for the clearing where Will had told him the men would be. He had brought with him tools, such weapons as he could get his hands on, and two casks of ale.

He had been fortunate, as well, in that Alan-a-Dale had stopped by just in time to accompany him on the short journey. The young man would help in cheering the men.

"It's starting," Alan said softly, interrupting Tuck's thoughts.

"What is?" he asked.

"Everything. These men must be convinced to rally around Robin, to help the cause. If they stand with him, others will, then others, until we actually have a chance at something other than being slaughtered."

"You're in a good mood," Tuck said drily.

"I am, actually. Just because I'm being pragmatic doesn't mean I'm in a bad mood."

"Still, I'd appreciate a little less pragmatism and a little more optimism when we get where we're going," Tuck grunted.

"I'll endeavor to give what is needed."

That was what worried him. Alan had been a little too blunt lately, and honest, and it was upsetting to say the least. Maybe bringing him along had been a bad idea. It was too late to turn back now, though. They were almost there.

And at the end of every day, even blunt, too honest, and in a foul mood, he would rather be in Alan's company than anyone else's.

As they rolled into the clearing, the man known as Old Soldier stood, alone and alert, a sword in his hand. He slowly lowered it as he nodded to Friar Tuck.

The old man let out a whistle and the tall brown grass rustled and shifted as two men rose up out of it. Tuck started as one man clambered to his feet not a dozen paces away from him. He hadn't even seen him hiding there.

"They're already making a good start of things," Alan said for his ears alone. Tuck pulled the horses to a halt and climbed down from the wagon. He strode forward and clasped Old Soldier by the arms.

"Bless you," he told him.

"Friar, we were expecting you."

Friar Tuck glanced around. "I'd hate to see what would have happened if you *hadn't* been expecting me."

"Have you brought us tools, and more weapons?"

"I brought all that I could," the friar replied. "Plus I brought some ale to help ease the transition, and chase away the cold."

Old Soldier smiled. "I'm sure the men will welcome it. We've already killed dinner for the night, so it will be quite the feast."

"Caught some rabbits?"

"Better than that, my friend."

Better turned out to be a deer. Tuck had no idea how they had managed to sneak up close enough on the beast to fell it with a sword. At the camp proper, the wagon was quickly unloaded by the other men and a fire was built. Chunks of deer meat were soon roasting and Tuck found his mouth beginning to water. At last the ten of them gathered around the fire and one of the men began carving off slices of meat while another passed around cups of ale. A quieter group Tuck had never experienced, and that included those of his brothers who had taken vows of silence.

"Come, don't be so glum," Tuck urged at last.

"Were you expecting to find a bunch of merry men?" Little John asked, before spitting on the ground. "Well, excuse me if we'd rather be somewhere else than this."

"Would you rather be in chains, imprisoned or as slaves, or in your graves, perhaps?" Alan asked, his voice soft. "When you think of those options, this doesn't look so bad."

"There are plenty of places worse," Old Soldier averred before taking a bite of meat. "Fresh air, plenty of food, good comrades, and a purpose to life. That's more than any man can ask."

"Yes." Alan agreed. "I have spent many nights in nature's embrace and have enjoyed them all, even in a winter such as this."

The men grumbled in their cups, but they grumbled in sullen agreement.

Yet somehow, even Tuck's modest life at the monastery seemed like a luxury in comparison.

CHAPTER SEVEN

The Sheriff had summoned his best spell casters. His impatience with the Hood was growing, and he had a new task for those who worked dark magic.

He waited in the small hut where they would gather, letting the last arrive before making his own presence known. It always gave him pleasure to see their shocked faces. It also drove home to him how incredibly stupid humans were, since they seemed to be surprised every time.

All except Glynna. The woman was a lot of things, but stupid wasn't one of them. She had never been a part of his plan, but because of her, some things were working out even better than he could have hoped. She peered at him adoringly, the only one who didn't shrink even a little bit at his darkness. In fact, she loved him for it, and he had been surprised to discover that love could make someone more loyal than even fear. She stayed apart from the others, seated by the fireplace on a bench originally designed for small work with hand tools that was of a height to make her comfortable in her condition.

He admired the fall of her hair from his shadows as he listened to the conversation in the room.

"Why have we been summoned?" Agrona the necromancer leaned over the arm of her chair, thrusting her chest toward the sorcerer beside her. The man had slid down in his own chair, allowing his long body to spill off the edge, legs wrapped in the tatters of a monk's robe, the cloth age-eaten and grey. His hands rested on his chest like crossed spades, the knuckles swollen and raw red. Along his cheeks were patches of crumbling skin the color of ash that flaked and dusted the long gnarl of beard that hung from his jaw.

"Why ask me?" The Mad Monk's voice rolled through the air between them, years of reciting incantations not meant for human throats giving his words odd inflections on and between their syllables. "I am no more privy to a reason when summoned than you."

The moment he began speaking, all the others in the room grew quiet, eyes on the two of them.

"Ah, but you are infinitely more curious than I."

The monk scoffed. "That is simply a lie."

"From these lips?" Her fingers slid across her chin, nails scraping the edge of her bottom lip just enough to make it swell and become plump. "Never." Dark eyes glittered. "Surely you have something in that mad, swirling head of yours."

He stared at her. Slowly his hands slid down his body until they clutched at his own jutting hipbones like milk and blood spiders. He sniffed deeply through a hawkish nose. "It may have something to do with the upcoming solstice."

"A solstice is special," another witch muttered, barely loud enough to be heard.

"Ah, but not like this one. This solstice only comes every one hundred generations. The druids had a name for it, I believe."

Enough! the Sheriff thought from his place of concealment.

Dropping his magick with a shrug, he appeared in the center of their gathering. Most of the people reacted sharply, jerking away from the sudden intrusion, reeling from the backwash of eldritch energy. Only the Mad Monk and the necromancer remained as they were; only Agrona did so with a smile on her face.

"What progress have you made in countering the magic of

the forest?" he demanded as he moved from the center of the room, pinning each person with his eyes.

"We… we still haven't found a way to break the geas that keeps you from entering," the insane monk replied. "It is ancient, primordial. It's like nothing I've worked against before."

The Sheriff was not surprised, however. Frankly he would have been surprised if this motley assortment had managed to make *any* progress in that regard. Normally he would show his disappointment, choosing one of them to be an example, but not this day.

"Keep at it," he commanded, "but I have a more immediate need, something that must be addressed at once."

"Is it the long night?" the necromancer asked, slithering her way across the floor toward him.

Instantly he could feel Glynna's hatred of the woman, like a physical force. The woman was not long for this world, he feared. A shame, since she had her uses. Best to get something out of her while he could.

"I need a potion," he said. "One that, when it makes contact with the skin, drives the victim into a state of pure paranoia, so that they are gripped by fear, suspicion."

There were people protecting the Hood. Of that he was certain. If he could undermine their trust in him, at the very least he could remove the outlaw's safe havens. At the most he might bring him down without sinking either sword or arrow into him. The best way to do that was to turn the Hood against his own allies. Thus he needed to turn the man into a pariah.

Murmurs went up around the room. Finally a voice from the back replied to his instructions.

"It would be easier to make something that, if drunk or eaten, would produce the same effect." The murmurs turned to agreement.

"Easier, yes, but not what I require," the Sheriff said, putting just a hint more menace in his tone. The murmurs ceased.

"It will be done as you wish," the necromancer said. As she

did, he could feel Glynna's hate deepening, and he couldn't help but smile.

He wondered how the woman would die.

Tuck tugged at the buckle on the harness. Despite the cold, it was slippery with horse sweat. He looked over the back of the docile animal.

"You could help."

Alan-a-Dale smiled. "I could, in theory."

The friar pulled the harness, clearing it from the back of the animal and hanging it on the stable wall. Before he could turn back, the horse wandered into its stall and began eating from a bucket of oats.

"What theory?" he grunted. "The theory that you are too lazy to help?"

Alan made his face very somber. "The theory that my fingers strum the song of Avalon. They must be preserved at all cost."

Laughter brayed out of Friar Tuck's mouth, making the horse snort in its stall.

Then the two men walked toward the stable door, shoulders brushing together.

A shadow crossed their path.

"Francis!" Friar Tuck exclaimed as the cardinal stepped into view. The friar moved slightly to the left, making a small distance between him and the bard.

Alan tilted his head, fingers touching his brow lightly in deference. The cardinal returned the bow with a smile.

"What brings you to the stable?" Tuck asked.

"I came to find our esteemed druid," the cardinal replied, nodding toward Alan. "I have need of his knowledge."

"It is yours," Alan said.

"Follow me inside to my study, then, where we can talk privately."

"Of course."

Friar Tuck spoke as the cardinal turned to go. "Do you wish me to attend the door?"

"No, we shall be fine with Alan's sharp hearing." The cardinal put his hand on Tuck's shoulder. "You may continue to look for brother Stephen. He still hasn't turned up."

"I will find him."

The cardinal smiled. "I have faith in you."

"But what is in this shipment, and why should we care?" John poked at the fire with a stick as thick as a man's wrist. Sparks danced around the blackened tip, rising up in the swirl of hot air. The men of the camp huddled around the freshly dug fire pit as they listened.

Marian put her hands on her hips.

"It's the noble children," she said. "John is shipping them to Scotland for ransom."

"Well, to be perfectly honest—" Will held his hands out. "—we don't know for sure that it is children being shipped."

"What else could it be?" Marian snarled.

Will shrugged, deflecting her anger. "Gold, supplies, oil for the Sheriff's armor? It might even be books. He has a real addiction to books, according to the tax collectors."

Marian bared her teeth, her anger unabated. "He collects all these things, but the children are the tools with which he holds his power over the nobles of the land." She clenched a fist and held it in front of her, shaking with rage. "We should have moved to save them before now. I cannot believe we are so selfish."

Little John laughed, spitting out the bitter humor. "Selfish is having the balls to come ask us to help a bunch of noble children. We were dumped in this cursed forest by not one, but *two* nobles!"

The men around them murmured in agreement.

Old Soldier stepped forward to stand beside the fire. All chatter ceased.

John threw his stick into the coals, upper lip curled in anger. "Go ahead and say it, old man," he growled. "Get it over with."

For a moment Old Soldier just stared at him.

"We weren't put here by children," he said.

"So?"

Old Soldier's face twisted, the creases by his mouth becoming deeper as his lips pulled back over teeth still strong enough to pull meat from bone. His breath pulsed between those teeth, spilling white into the cold air.

The men around Little John eased back.

"Children are not responsible for the sins of their fathers," he continued, the intensity of his words building. "They suffer the worst for them, more often than not." Old Soldier pointed a thick-jointed finger. "You know that more intimately than most."

The words struck John like a hammer blow to the chest. His shoulders bowed, pulling together to drop his chin. He gave a shudder, and tears shimmered on the end of his lashes before shaking free and dropping to soak into the beard that covered his jaw.

Old Soldier stepped forward and put his hand on John's chest, directly over the giant's heart. He murmured, so low that no one but John could hear it over the crackle of the fire.

"I'm sorry."

John nodded, still looking down at the ground, shaking more tears free.

Old Soldier spoke over his shoulder to Will and Marian.

"He won't kick a fuss anymore."

Before either of them could respond a voice cut across the gathering like a butcher's knife through a piece of meat.

"It doesn't matter. This is not your fight."

The lock on the door rattled, making them stop talking and draw closer to one another.

They already huddled for warmth, gathered in the center of

the room away from the cold stone of the walls. Once winter set in, Rory, son of Lord Montjoy, had them all pull their pallets together. A few of the children had resisted, but once the true chill set in, they joined the rest.

Rory also forced them to get up often and move about, to stay active with games and exercise. When they huddled he made them all tell stories and answer questions and tell jokes, anything to keep the seriousness of their situation from settling into their spirits.

He was the only child of Montjoy, twelve years old and the pride of his family. He spent every moment trying to act just as his father would, and Lord Montjoy would not have let them suffer any more than they had to.

He held faith in his heart that his father was going to rescue him. He didn't know when or how, but his father loved him and would not leave him behind. Yet as more time passed, the faith turned hard and stony, transforming from true belief into a stubbornness. He didn't know how long it had been, trapped in the one room, but it seemed like months. Certainly the seasons had changed. There was no privacy aside from the half a blanket sacrificed to cover the entrance to the chamber-well. That allowed them a bit of dignity when attending to their personal business, and it cut the draft that came from the long well that ran down the inside of the tower wall.

The only interaction they had with the outside world came twice a day when guards brought food and water and the occasional change of clothing.

Some of his fellow prisoners were as young as four and five. The nights were the hardest for them.

The door lock rattled again, and Rory clambered to his feet, instantly missing the warmth of the circle.

It wasn't time for a meal.

Something new was happening.

For a moment—a hard shining moment—he expected the door to open to reveal his father, coated in the blood of their captors coming to rescue him, and a tear formed in the corner of his eye.

The door swung open.

A paunchy man in a fine robe of wool and fleece walked in, flanked by two hulking guards clad head-to-toe in black armor. The man wore a heavy gold crown on his head and his left hand held a scepter with an animal head on it. The crown sat low above his ears, pushing dark blonde locks to lay flat on his brow.

He walked in and stopped. His face drew in on itself, and he waved his hand in front of it.

"Well, you little whelps have been closed up in this room for a very long time." He breathed in and out through his mouth. "Noble birth doesn't keep you smelling fresh as a rose, does it?"

Rory watched the man. There was something about his movements that made him seem... unpredictable. Dangerous.

"Well, what have we here?" The man sauntered over, drawing so close that Rory had to look up. "Who are you, standing so tall and proud like a little lord?"

"Rory Montjoy," he replied, "son of Samuel Montjoy."

The man tapped his lower lip, eyes turned up to the ceiling. "Montjoy, Montjoy, Montjoy... hmmmmmmm." He frowned and dropped his eyes back down to Rory. "Don't know him at all."

A pang shot through Rory's chest. "Are you the king?"

"I am," the man replied gleefully. "Call me John."

"Are you here to rescue us?"

The laughter brayed from John's mouth. It blasted into the room, loud as a trumpet. Somewhere behind Rory, children began crying.

"No, Rory the mighty." John bent, leaning until his face was even with Rory's. His breath was sour when he spoke. "I'm the one who put your little arse here."

Rory's whole body tightened. Suddenly it was hard to breathe.

King John's eyes widened, and he grinned. "Oooooh, you want to hit me, don't you, son?"

Rory didn't answer, but his heart pounded in his throat, and the edges of his vision tunneled red in rage.

John straightened.

Rory glared at him.

John pulled a dagger from his belt.

Rory didn't step back.

John turned the dagger handle first and touched Rory's chest with the pommel.

"Take it."

Confusion swirled through Rory's anger.

"Take the knife, *boy*." John pushed the dagger, jabbing him in the breastbone.

Rory took the dagger. He held it in his hand, unsure of what to do.

"You have a choice." John's face smoothed into seriousness, brows drawn together under the edge of the heavy crown. He pointed behind Rory at the other children. "You can take the most annoying brat here, the one that won't shut up, the one that won't stop crying, the one that you all hate, and you can stab out their eyes. Do that, and I'll let you all go free."

Rory stared at him.

"You have to take *both* eyes though."

Rory's hand flexed on the handle.

"What's one blind brat, compared to getting out of this room?"

The crying spread, bubbling up from the huddled children. Either more had started, or the ones already crying grew louder.

Rory could hear, inside the sobbing noises, the wet sniffle cough that was Miriam. Miriam who made that same sound every night when the light faded from the room.

All.

Night.

Long.

It wasn't loud, but it was incessant, crawling into Rory's brain through his ears and curling, curling, curling inside his skull like an animal that just could not get comfortable.

"You've chosen." John waggled his eyebrows, eyes glittering.
Rory stabbed him with all his might.

Shove the damned thing deep like you mean it and get that blade up in his guts with a twist.

He swung the blade up, pulling with his shoulder, pushing with his thighs, aiming for deep under the ribcage just like his father had taught him.

John's hand clamped on his arm faster than Rory could see him move. Fingers wrapped completely around Rory's wrist, jerking him to a stop.

The dagger halted inches from John's side.

All the anger inside him drained like water from a broken cistern, spilling down his thighs and into the floor beneath him.

John wrenched him close, hand squeezing. The pressure on his wrist blossomed to pain, sharp and hot all the way to his armpit. Something snapped and it shot into his intestines, making him hot and greasy in his guts.

The dagger clattered to the floor.

"You could have saved the whole world with that," the king hissed. "If you weren't a failure." John's breath forced its way down his throat as the man put his nose right on Rory's face. "No wonder your father abandoned you."

Rory didn't see the slap that drove him to the floor.

As the world faded to black he heard John say, "Leave this one, he's worthless."

The words chased him all the way to the black.

Marian turned.

Robin stood on the ridge just above them. The cold wind rolled from behind him, causing dark locks grown longer to lick out from around the hood of his wool tunic. In the gloom of the woods he looked darker, almost sinister. She could imagine how merchants felt when suddenly set upon. It would be as terrifying as a wolf attack.

If the wolf appeared out of nowhere.

And shot arrows at you.

A long sword hung from his hip, something new. It added to his air of menace. Arrows could be used to harry and confuse, but a sword—especially a broadsword like that—was used only to cut or to kill.

They don't call them bastard swords for nothing.

Her hand found the pommel of the long dagger that lay along the crease of her hip, under her robes. She touched it, giving it a little tug, not quite enough to release it from its sheath. It was nearly as long as her forearm, almost a short sword, the blade curved slightly with a thick spine ridge for strength and an edge honed to shaving sharpness. She'd ground off the cross guard, leaving just blade and grip so there would be no snag if she ever needed to draw it.

Robin's eyes cut down to her hand, and then back up to her face. His mouth twitched, but his eyes stayed dark.

He's as haunted as the woods themselves.

She shook the thought away.

"Robin…" Beside her, Will began to speak.

Robin put his hand up.

Will stopped talking.

Robin pointed at Marian and Will.

"I'll have a word with you two." He turned his back and walked away.

Will looked at her. "I guess we follow him?"

"Oh, I'll *follow* him, to be sure." Anger at the presumption that she would simply obey jumped into her throat. "But if he thinks he's the only one who will be talking, he's got much to learn."

CHAPTER EIGHT

The bolt squeaked as it was pushed into place, iron rubbing on iron and in need of oiling.

Alan held the sound in his mind and rolled it around, turning it one way and then the other, examining it to see if he could replicate it with the ancient harp that was strapped to his shoulder. The deeper end of the sounds it could produce were made with iron strings. He could ask the blacksmith to fashion him a simple iron band to round the middle joint of his first finger. With this in place he could simply tap upward to the thickest part of the thickest iron string, unworn by playing.

"Thank you for joining me."

The sound of it should be the same squeak of a thrown bolt but amplified by the yew-wood frame, Alan realized.

It would work excellently in the saga of Dagda, The Goodly Wise, a harper himself who kept Uaithne, Stroker-of-Strings, as his personal harp. The Fomorians captured Uaithne and carried him off. The Goodly Wise gave chase with his son, Aengus Og.

At the Fomorian camp they crept to the tent...

The tale continued to unwind in his mind, twisting away to one of the many nooks and crannies that formed the maze of a bard's memory.

* * *

"I said, thank you for joining me."

Alan blinked at the cardinal.

"No thanks needed," he said.

The cardinal studied him, head cocked slightly to the side. Alan studied him back, noting the thinness of the other man's skin, worn by age into wrinkled parchment. Cardinal Francis was still a fit man, but well into the winter of his life. His hands only trembled slightly, and his eyes were more than clear—they were piercing, able to divide a man body from soul.

The cardinal smiled. "What were you cataloging in that wonderful head of yours?"

"The sound of mishap."

"Esoteric, as always."

"Not always, but at times."

The holy man placed his hands on the table. "I need that talent exactly, so I do not mind." He reached into his robe and withdrew a small bundle of waxed leather. Unfolding it revealed a book not much larger than a man's palm.

Alan recognized it.

He'd accepted it from a wiry monk in Ireland, then carried it across the sea and into the dark depths of Sherwood to a tiny, ancient chapel. He'd given it to Friar Tuck, as requested.

A secret book carried in secret.

King John's tax collectors have sought a book, he mused, *from the beginning of their reign of terror.*

The connection was so sharp, it made Alan sit straighter in his chair. Cardinal Francis put his hand over the small book, not quite touching it, letting his fingers hover.

"Do you know what this is?"

"No."

Francis flipped it over, revealing a sigil carved into the bone plate that formed the cover. The symbol blasted itself into Alan's mind, a roar of chaos in the highly ordered system of his brain. It squirmed through the tiered knowledge granted to him by his druidic training, layer upon layer of information carefully placed in the whorls of his thoughts. The bard's stomach flipped, and everything he'd eaten that day threatened to spew out of him.

He closed his eyes and took a breath, drawing air deep inside. Holding it, he used the weight of his full lungs to center himself, taking the symbol and shoving it to the side, locking it into a box he could use to observe it, but keeping it quarantined from the rest of his knowledge.

He opened his eyes to find Francis staring at him.

"I wondered how this would affect you."

Alan shrugged. "It was... uncomfortable."

"Not any longer?"

Alan could still feel the symbol prickling at its box. "Not too much." He sat forward. "Is this the book John seeks?"

"I believe it is."

"Why?"

"This is the *Relic Grimoire*."

"That makes... sense."

The name sparked knowledge inside Alan. A volume made from the bones and skins of saints killed in the Roman Coliseum by the dark magician Kursoa, with the intent of making the most blasphemous spell book in existence. St. Jonathan the Mystic had rescued it from the magician's hands before it could be completed.

He had used the book to record his own visions before returning it to the church, where it presented a dilemma. Should it be destroyed as a vessel of dark magic, or revered as an item composed of the last remains of some of the very first martyrs for Christ?

"You are aware of the history?"

Alan nodded. "But not its content."

Francis sighed. "St. Jonathan had... interesting ideas."

"I assume you've read it, and there is some reason you want to discuss it with me."

"The vision inscribed within tells of the splitting of the oak, the dark splinter, the absent king and his shadow, and the gathering dark."

"All in one record?"

Francis nodded.

"Then it confirms Merlin, Taliesin, Melchior, and your own St. Jonesius."

"Fully and completely," the cardinal agreed. "It ties all their disparate parts into one unified prophecy. It also confirms other details from dozens of other sources."

"So Jonathan was a scholar of prophecy, and he compiled them?"

"No," the cardinal said. "He had no way of knowing of any of these. He was a first-century father of the church. He predates everyone save Merlin and Taliesin, and he had no way of knowing they existed, much less their predictions."

"Then he is the clear key."

"Yes."

Alan's eyes narrowed. "What else is in that book?"

"*The lion roars across the sea, as his shadow thickens at home.*"

"Sounds like Richard… and John."

"It does."

"Yet prophecy can be shaped by the times of the interpreter."

The cardinal's face hardened. "I'm not seeking the worst, and I am no fool."

"I didn't think you were."

"Still, you implied…"

Alan's long fingers waved it away. "A word of caution is all," he said calmly. "It is part of my calling."

"So you agree with my interpretation."

"I have no reason to doubt it."

Francis nodded. "Good." Looking down at the book, he nodded again, "It also talks of the oak as the King of the Forest."

Alan kept his face unreadable.

"Now is not the time for secrets, son," the cardinal said.

Alan considered Cardinal Francis. He'd thrown himself into the rebellion formed by the older man, because it felt right. The people—*his* people—suffered terribly, and anything to ease that had to be done. He knew Francis to be a good man, a godly man, but the knowledge in him was sacred, kept secret for the protection of the ancient ways.

Did he *trust* Cardinal Francis?

Francis didn't press as Alan came to his own decision.

"The tree you speak of is the Oak of Thynghowe. It is the Heart of England herself, an ancient guardian in the center of Sherwood," he said.

"Do you know where it is?"

Was I wrong in my trust?

"No one knows where it is. The tree stands between this world and the otherworld. Its roots tap into the spirit while its branches spread into the physical. Legend states that as long as the Thynghowe stands in Sherwood, then the land and people will be safe. Only a true child of the forest can find it."

Francis nodded, his eyes off in the distance. "And its connection to the kingship?"

"It is the guardhouse of sovereignty itself."

"How so?"

Alan shook his head. "That is not clear. It may be metaphorical or actual. One way or another, the mighty Thynghowe protects the sovereignty of Avalon."

Francis closed his eyes and sat back, hands across his stomach. The quiet grew between them. It pressed against even Alan's hard-learned druidic patience, but he did not break it. There was something coming, and he would wait for it rather than press and spoil it.

Cardinal Francis did not open his eyes when he spoke.

"What do you know of a woman of ancient blood, who can hold sovereignty in her hands?"

"Because I damn well *said* so."

Marian threw her hands up. "That is no reason at all."

Will leaned on a tree watching Robin and Marian argue. They

were on the other side of the ridge, away from the camp. He was sure they could all hear the argument, even though Robin and Marian thought they were keeping their voices low. The crisp, cold air carried sound much further, especially through bare branches and shrubs shrunken under frost.

"Is it not?" Robin countered.

Marian moved closer. "Robin Longstride, we have let those children suffer too long."

"This isn't about the children."

"Then why did we traipse all the way out here in this God-forsaken wood?"

Robin's voice went soft and low.

"The forest hasn't been forsaken by God."

Will pushed off the tree and moved slowly forward. He recognized the quiet edge in his cousin's voice. The last time he'd heard it, men had bled.

Marian took a deep breath. "It was a long ride and cold besides. Forgive me."

Robin looked at her. He took a half step forward then stopped. He nodded.

"Always."

Will stopped moving.

"Well and good." Marian's mouth twitched a small smile before pulling into a hard line. "Now stop being stubborn, and let us use these men."

Will shook his head and stepped back to the tree. He shifted against the rough bark, trying to get comfortable.

"They always like this?"

Will jumped as if bit by a snake. He jerked his head and found Old Soldier standing there, hands cupped around his mouth for the warmth of his own breath. A twinkle of amusement flickered in his rheumy eye.

Will pulled himself together. "Not so far."

"There's a fire there betwixt 'em. Maid Marian's had backbone her whole life, like both her parents before her. A woman like that won't let you rest 'less you're doing your very best." Old Soldier nodded knowingly. "She's a good fit for him."

Will looked back at Robin and Marian. She moved her arms in circles, shifting from foot to foot. Robin stood resolute, and the only change in his position was to cross his arms.

Old Soldier leaned close and whispered "Didn't mean to startle you, Will Scarlet."

"You didn't, Old Soldier."

The old man chuckled as they both watched the dance before them.

"Those men are angry." Marian shook her head. "They *want* to fight."

"Their anger doesn't make it their responsibility."

"We're talking about *children*."

"The men are commoners, so it's not their children."

Fire burned in her guts, roiling up inside her. He didn't understand. He didn't *care*. How could he stand by? She would convince him, compel him, make him come around. She snarled, the words spilling out of her.

"Children, innocent children locked away and at John's mercy since…"

"Marian."

It was one word, spoken softer than before, and it cut her short.

Robin opened his mouth to speak and faltered. He pushed back the hood of his jerkin, using his fingers to scrub his scalp in frustration. Marian watched the dark locks of it shake around. She'd seen Robin full of laughter, full of anger, somber and brooding, and wistfully near melancholy. She'd never seen him frustrated, and unable to express himself.

It made her want to go to him, to pull him into her arms and press his head down to her shoulder.

To her bosom.

The thought of it brought a body memory of something

that had never occurred. It hit her full force, and for a brief moment—a split second—she could *feel* him pressed against her. His lithe body, firm in its strength, touching against her from thigh, to hip, to stomach, to chest.

Her breath caught, and deep in the most intimate part of herself she felt a longing she'd never experienced before.

Oh, Robin.

"Yes?"

His voice startled her and she realized she had spoken his name out loud without meaning to.

"Uh, oh, carry on, I'm listening."

His head tilted sideways, cocking at an angle as he studied her.

"These men gathered here are from my family's land," he said. "Some I've known my whole life. When my father left, *I* was responsible for their well-being, but I hated it. Every minute spent working that damned farmland was torture. It's why I joined our rebellion."

"The rebellion is needed…"

He put up his hand. "I'm not saying otherwise, but that's just not why I joined it. I wanted away from Longstride Manor, and fighting against John with you was a way I could justify it to myself. So I ran with you and the others, fighting his corruption but not because it was corrupt. If I had wanted that, I could have gone to court, joined the other nobles and made a stand. Instead I ran through these woods and fought fat merchants with good friends." He paused for the briefest moment, not looking at her, then added, "And a beautiful woman."

She caught the words.

Robin continued. "My hatred of my father, the idea that I was better than digging a field, and the thrill of fighting in our rebellion is why I allowed Locksley to take my family's holding. It was selfish, completely selfish." He looked up at her. "Because of me, those men lost their homes and families. None of them will lose their life as well. We fight this fight alone."

Her resistance broke. "Then we will rescue the children ourselves."

He nodded. "As it should be."

BITTER ASHES
SWIRLING TO
EARTH

CHAPTER NINE

The ship rocked gently under their feet, bobbing slightly. The ice rimming the hull had been broken, smashed by the crew so that the ship could sail freely from the southern harbor.

It crunched and chafed, covering any noise they might make.

Wind blasted over the water, ripping across the deck and cutting them to the bone. For stealth and fighting they had worn as little as possible, leaving behind layers of clothing in favor of simple wool pants and tunics, dyed black, and wool cloaks only big enough to cover them.

The moonlight poured down from the clear winter sky, bathing everything in a weird silver glow. It had allowed them to watch from the edge of Sherwood as a regiment of soldiers had escorted three wagons to the harbor. In its light they watched the soldiers open the wagons and drag out huddled figures covered in blankets. In the crisp air the sound of weeping was clear.

The southern harbor was old, small, and rarely used. It was more treacherous to sail from there than the one King Richard and his men had used. Perfect for things that needed to be done away from prying eyes.

They had watched as the huddled figures were walked up the gangplank, taken aboard, and put into the hold of the ship. Once they were secured, a portion of soldiers with them, the crew had begun their preparations as the rest of the regiment turned the wagons and headed back toward the castle.

The sailors went to quarters, and the rebellion made its move.

Robin's hand held the hatch's rope handle. He nodded at Will and Marian.

"Once I drop down, you follow," he whispered. "We can deal with the guards if we move quickly." He looked past at Friar Tuck and Alan-a-Dale. "You two watch for sailors."

One by one they returned his nod, each of them gripping a weapon. Will had his rapier and Marian held Raleigh's saber. The fat friar carried an axe handle with no blade, just a stout stick of wood, its business end blackened from being fire hardened. Alan brandished two Scottish dirks each the length of his forearm. Their blades were nicked and notched from use, proof that they were of sturdy construction. "Wait." Marian held out her hand.

Robin turned to her.

"Something doesn't feel right." The moment his hand closed on the hatch handle, her skin had begun itching. Not the dry-winter-skin-against-wool itch, to which she had become accustomed, but the feeling that something with too many legs crawled across the bends and folds of her body.

"We don't have time for this," Will hissed.

Robin glanced at his cousin, then back at Marian. He raised an eyebrow in a silent question. *What feels so wrong?* Her mind turned. Perhaps it was just the winter and the wool, after all, that made her itch under her clothes. Maybe her sense of unease was worry about the mission. They were about to attack soldiers. They had surprise on their side. Their chances were good.

She looked at her compatriots, capable fighters all. In Robin, one more than capable.

A small sound came through the wood of the hatch. A cry from a young throat, cut short before it could really start.

Gripping her sword tighter, she nodded to Robin. He took a

deep breath, and pulled the hatch up.

Light blasted out, scouring the vision from Marian's eyes.

The world went black-red, her vision only saved by the fact that Robin took the brunt of it. Raw force slapped the front of her body, making her step back. Immediately her mouth filled with the acrid taste of spoiled milk, and all she could smell was sulfur. Tears streamed down, freezing to her face as she blinked to clear her eyes.

Behind her Will, Tuck, and Alan all cried out. Only Robin in front of her stayed silent. Black fog replaced the glare, and swelled around them from the open hatch making Robin hard to see, even though he was only a foot in front of her, and moonlight still poured from the open sky above.

A sword punched out of the swirling dark, and Robin barely had time to knock it aside with his own blade, the cut so close it sliced the hem of his cloak.

He fell back, pushing Will and Marian with him. Everything was darker than it should be. He would be blind if he hadn't jerked back just in time for the edge of his hood to shield his eyes from most of the blast.

Someone yelled behind him, a male voice but he couldn't tell who. His attention was focused on the people spilling out of the hold.

There were soldiers, armed to the teeth with long swords, and among them were men and women, some older, some younger, dressed in strange clothing that looked nothing like uniforms.

He blinked away the black on the rim of his vision and leaped forward, bringing the fight to the steel of the attackers.

Will watched Robin sweep his sword to parry two soldiers who struck in unison. His cousin, first to battle.

Then he reached out his hand, brushing Marian's hip. She

lurched toward him, eyes streaming tears down her cheeks, soaking into the black scarf she had covering her mouth. His own eyes hurt from the magic blast, but she had gotten worse than he.

"Get behind me," he hissed. "I can still see, mostly."

Soldiers not fighting Robin circled around toward her, and he did not like the look of the people in the robes. He pulled at Marian and stepped around her, rapier out and ready to strike blood.

Alan-a-Dale elbowed Friar Tuck. "Can you fight?"

"Always." The big monk hefted his bludgeon.

"Then stop being lazy." With that, the bard launched himself at the people in the robes.

Robin's sword sang off the steel of the soldiers, slashing tabards into shreds and cleaving deep into the rough iron mail beneath. The rings held, too tough and too flexible for him to shear through, but he creased them, plowing them deep into muscles like a saw.

Two fell to his blows, then two more. He struck hard enough to feel each impact in his own chest, the thud of steel against bodies.

He cursed himself for leaving his bow and quiver with the horses, over the ridge and inside the forest. If he had his bow he could have made short shrift of these soldiers, even in such tight quarters. Instead he bashed and hacked until, one by one, each of them lay still on the ship's deck.

Sucking air into burning lungs, he looked to find Marian and the others. They fought the cadre of robed people, swinging their weapons, which appeared to *clang* off empty air before striking. He took a step toward them when the sound of cracking wood made him turn back toward the hold.

Wooden planks that formed the deck, timber that had been

cut and planed and slotted together, all of it now buckled, pulling apart and slapping back together into a haphazard pile. On the other side of the disruption stood a tall man in a monk's robe with dark eyes full of insanity. He gestured with the over-knuckled hands of an arthritic, and shouted words in a language Robin didn't recognize. Even so, they made his ears burn deep inside.

Witchcraft.

Agrona moved nearer the Mad Monk. The clash of battle around her was lovely—chaotic and exciting. She felt it between her thighs, warming her from the cold.

The clang of swordplay drew her attention and she turned. A slim, hooded figure parried with a soldier twice their size, yet their skill and determination set the soldier retreating. The hooded figure attacked with the ferocity of a starving wolf, swinging his heavy saber in sharp, chopping arcs.

Agrona murmured a spell, rolling it off her tongue and into her hand before slinging it toward the brave fighter. It was a minor magic, barely anything at all. Agrona was a priestess of the dead, though barely an acolyte when casting against the living, yet the spell struck true and the hooded figure faltered, just for a second.

Just long enough for a soldier to dart in and swipe the edge of his blade across the shoulder, black wool parting to flesh, pale in the moonlight for a split second before blossoming red.

The figure growled in pain, a hard animal sound, and lunged, his attack spinning the two off into the chaos and out of Agrona's sight.

She turned back toward the Mad Monk.

His magic rolled against her as he gestured wildly and yelled in Northern Enochian, a language dead for centuries. The decking had ruptured, making a pyramid of splintered wood.

She moved closer as he changed his gestures and his voice dropped into an octave too low for a human throat.

Her skin flushed hot even in the cold winter air, and her mind processed the spell he now cast. It rolled through the gray folds of her mind like lamp oil, and lit hot and bright behind her eyeballs.

The gods-damned fool is going to set the whole ship on fire.

Robin took a step forward, dropping his shoulders, preparing to leap over the hole in the deck, to drive his sword into the sorcerer on the other side. Smoke began to curl from under the kindled wood and flame licked from the edges of it, catching as if the wood had been soaked in pitch.

The smoke burned his eyes, blurring his sight as he moved.

He tensed, body low and ready to spring, when a dark shape knocked the sorcerer aside and out of his sight.

With the smoke, he couldn't tell who it was that took the man down. Another movement made him turn, and he found Marian fiercely fighting a soldier. She and Will were of similar size, and the cloaks they all wore were fashioned to make them indistinguishable for most people. Still, he would recognize Marian no matter what. Pluck out his eyes, and he'd still be able to see her.

Her shoulder was bleeding.

He pushed off, closing the gap, and slammed the pommel of his sword hilt against the soldier's skull. The man's knees buckled and he dropped to the deck, and then slumped forward.

He stepped over the man and moved to her.

"You are hurt."

She shook her head. "It's not bad."

"Looks bad."

"It's fine." She pointed with her saber. "The ship is on fire."

He looked. The flames had grown, and were crackling in harsh snaps over the noise of fighting.

"There are no children here," he said. "We have to get off this ship."

"Get Will and Alan," she responded. "I'll get our Friar."

* * *

"You bitch! What were you thinking?"

The Mad Monk climbed to his feet, brow creased and his dark eyes crackling with anger.

Agrona leaped up and shoved him.

"You fool," she said, "you can't call down banefire while we are still on board this damned ship. I love the dead, but I do not wish to join them—not yet."

He looked at her as the smoke around them grew. His mouth had parted slightly, lips soft in the bristle of his beard.

"You love me." There was awe in his voice.

She snorted. "You aren't that good in bed."

He smiled a wicked smile. "Oh, I will be now."

"You'll never get the chance, if we cannot get off this vessel. Your fire lies between us and the gangplank."

His arm wrapped around her, scooping her up against his chest like a father with a child.

"I'll have my chance," he said, and in four long strides he reached the rail of the ship.

He began chanting.

Then he stepped up, and stepped off.

Back on the shore, Tuck spun one way, then another, wishing he still had hold of his weapon. As it was, all he could do was shout out warnings to the others. His terror was practically choking him, and he struggled to keep his voice strong and not let the fear close up his throat, as it was threatening to do.

Turn around.

He listened to the voice in his head and twisted just in time to see a humpbacked man rushing toward Robin. There was a flask in his outstretched hand, which he cocked back as if making ready to throw the contents.

"No!" Tuck bellowed and threw himself between the two men

just as the liquid in the flask was released. It hit him squarely in the face and he screamed as he expected to feel hot oil or burning acid removing his skin.

It took him a moment to realize that he felt nothing but wet. He blinked open his eyes and stared at the man who was, in turn, staring at him, eyes wide in a kind of fascinated wonder. Suddenly blood bubbled out from the man's lips. Tuck looked down and saw a sword protruding from his chest. He tumbled to the ground and Marian pulled her sword free.

"Are you safe?" she shouted.

He could barely hear her over the din, but managed to nod.

"What was that?"

Poison.

The thought came, horrific and sudden. He tried to swallow down his panic. There was no reason to frighten her. Not yet.

"Nothing, I suppose," he managed to shout back.

It *had* to be poison. Why would the man have thrown something harmless? It made no sense.

He could feel his heart pounding in his chest. If only the man wasn't dead, maybe they could have forced him to reveal the truth. As it was, the flask was smashed on the ground, and there was no way to tell what it once had held.

"Get out of here!"

He turned. Robin was shouting to him—to all of them. He wanted them to leave. Were they losing? Were the others dead? He looked around, trying to pick out other cloaked figures among the smoke and flame, but he couldn't.

Dead, all dead, he thought.

Then he saw someone mounting a horse. He got a good look at the boots. Fancy. They had to belong to Will. What was Will doing mounting a horse? Maybe he should, too, if he could get one to stand still long enough for him to try and haul his girth onto it.

Alan was there, pulling a horse forward, his cloak over its eyes to keep it from shying away from the flames that were engulfing the ship.

Something in Tuck's chest broke and relief flooded him at the sight of the slender bard. He hadn't realized how much he'd been worried for him.

"Get on," Alan said.

"No, you take the horse. I'll…"

Alan pushed him. "I can run faster and farther than you, and I know the forest. Get your fat arse up on this horse and give the horse its head. It will get you to safety."

Tuck quit arguing, grabbed the saddle, and began pulling himself up.

CHAPTER TEN

Marian's mind raced frantically as she kicked her horse faster and faster away from the scene of the ambush. Images of burning men filled her mind, and she prayed that none of them was Robin.

The others would be regrouping at the monastery no doubt—except for Will who might make his way straight to the castle in an effort to avoid suspicion. He would look for her there, and worry when he didn't find her.

She couldn't think about that right now, though. They needed Richard to return. Only he could help set things right, and it was time to stop sending emissaries, most of whom couldn't even grasp the full extent of the danger that they were in. It was becoming more and more of a struggle to leave the castle unseen, and this might well be her last chance, her one hope to get word to the king.

Even if it meant going herself and leaving behind those she cared for. She tried not to think about what might happen to Chastity in her absence. The truth was, if they didn't stop John and the Sheriff, they were all as good as dead anyway. She had to have faith in her friends, too. Chastity was clever. She was a survivor, and Marian had to believe she could outwit the others, and either find a way to hide in the castle or to escape, if it came to that.

She rode through Sherwood. The forest had ceased to hold any terrors for her. It was far safer than the open road. The messengers she'd sent had been too afraid of the forest to use it for passage to the northern harbor. She was not. Whatever had befallen them on the road—whatever the creature was that had attacked her—she hoped it would not be watching.

Her shoulder burned like fire, but she could not stop and inspect her wound. There would be time enough for that once she was aboard the *Kestrel*. Beneath her she could feel her horse trembling in fear. Whether it was from the fight or from the forest she did not know. She put her hand on the animal's neck and tried to whisper soothing words to it. At the same time she was wary, knowing that the horse could easily be sensing a danger that she couldn't.

After a minute the animal seemed to relax, but Marian remained alert. The closer she got to the harbor, the more she worried that someone or something would try to stop her. She could not afford to be caught, not now. There would be no explanation for her appearance, or the fact that she was there.

She considered abandoning the cloak in the forest, but couldn't bring herself to do it. She might still have need of it. Besides, if more than one of them was found, then their enemies would have proof that more than one person was masquerading as the Hood.

That is, if the rest weren't already dead.

She swallowed around the lump in her throat, urging herself to focus. She couldn't help any of them at that moment, but she could save whoever was left… if she could just make it to the king.

When she was within minutes of the harbor her heart began to pound even harder, and she wanted to kick her horse into a full run. Inside her mind, though, a small voice whispered vigilence. This might be the most dangerous part of her journey and she couldn't afford for it to end in failure simply because she abandoned caution.

She slowed her horse to a walk and forced herself to listen as hard as she could. The edge of the forest came close to the harbor, but she would still have a lot of open ground to cover once she exited the safety of the trees.

Something brushed her hair and she jerked, startling her mount. She twisted in her saddle and forced a sigh when she realized it was just a branch. A couple more steps and she saw a flash of movement out of the corner of her eye. She turned just as another limb seemed to suddenly stretch out beside her, and catch at her cloak.

Marian blinked rapidly. She was seeing things. That had to be it. She was overly agitated by everything that was happening.

Yet she could have sworn the branch actually had moved.

Another one caught her hair, and then another. A root seemed to thrust suddenly upward from the ground and her horse tripped, nearly falling. The beast whinnied in fear and Marian lacked the words to calm him. Around her the forest began whispering, and she felt chilled to the bottom of her soul.

It doesn't want me to leave, she realized at last. *But why?* Why were the trees suddenly acting alive, and trying to keep her from her destination?

All the old stories came flooding back to her, about the forest and its fey. Was it trying to do her mischief? If so, why wait until now? Or was it something else?

A warning, perhaps.

Her heart pounded painfully hard in her chest, and her horse began to lift its feet higher, eyeing the ground with clear suspicion.

"Please," Marian heard herself whispering. "Please, I have to make it to the harbor. The lives of so many depend on it."

No.

She blinked, stunned. She had heard the word whispered on the wind, as clear as any word ever spoken by man.

"I must."

Can't.

"I *will*."

No answer this time. All around her the trees started shuddering, as if shaken by a fierce wind, although there was none upon her skin. Then it was as if they shrunk back from her slightly. She could see light, the edge of the forest. Ten more strides and her horse stepped free of the trees, coming onto a small rise that overlooked the end of the harbor.

Marian looked down.

The entire dock was on fire.

They were all of them dead men. Will kicked his horse harder, streaking through the forest. At a signal from Robin they had scattered. He could hear guards chasing behind him, practically feel the breath of their horses upon his neck. Scatter and regroup, that was the plan.

This had been a trap, and Will knew he needed to get back to the castle as soon as he could, before someone realized he hadn't been there when this debacle took place. Marian had taken off seconds before him, though in a different direction. He didn't have time to go chasing after her, though. She was smart, and a better rider than most men. She could make her way back to the castle. Hopefully at least one of them would make it. If they were together the odds increased that they would be caught.

He heard a whistling sound and ducked just as a sword cut through the air where his head had been a moment before. He cursed and kicked his beast harder. He didn't know how many men had followed him. Outrunning them, then, was his best chance at survival.

In his right hand he gripped his horse's reins and in his left he held a sword. The hood of the cloak kept falling farther down, blinding him, and he kept shoving it back up, trying not to jerk his horse's head as he did so, and wishing he dared remove the hood completely.

He heard a sudden sound to his left, swung with his sword, and connected with something that let out a shrill scream.

Something hit the ground and his horse leaped sideways to avoid it. With his stomach twisting in agony he prayed that he had killed one of John's soldiers, and not one of his own comrades.

There was a sudden shrieking sound on his right and he barely managed to switch hands as he ducked beneath an arcing sword that seemed to burn the air where he had been. He thrust with his blade, felt it connect, and kicked his horse faster. He had to find a way to lose them quickly, so he could get back to the castle unobserved.

Marian felt as if she was going to be sick as she forced her horse down the hill to the harbor. The *Kestrel*, Richard's fastest ship— the one she had meant to board to go and bring him back—was in flames. Her crew were dead, lying on the docks. One man, the captain by the look of him, lay with his stomach split open and guts piled on the ground beside him. His eyes were frozen in a look of horror.

Two other ships, trade ships by the looks of them, were each sinking slowly below the water, scuttled.

Whoever had done this could still be close by. She felt a prickling along the base of her skull and she turned, then kicked her horse back toward the safety of the woods.

The forest had tried to warn her.

Somehow it had known.

Marian's stomach twisted into knots as the full impact of what she'd seen hit home. These were the only ships left behind when Richard set sail on the crusade. With the ships destroyed, there was no escape. There was no way to get word to Richard.

They were trapped, and no help would be coming.

CHAPTER ELEVEN

Will managed to leave his horse at the stables without being seen. No one knew he had taken the beast out that morning, so he should be safe in that regard.

He made his way quickly to the kitchen, heart still in his throat. He had no idea if he'd lost the last of his pursuers, but he'd managed a few seconds to bury his cloak at the edge of the woods just in case.

Once inside the kitchen he was relieved to see the woman in charge, Jansa, who according to Marian was friendly to their cause. Fortunately, given the time of day, she was alone in the kitchen when he put in his appearance. He was out of breath and disheveled, and when she saw him she looked clearly taken aback.

"Can I help you?" she asked.

"I hope so," he said, grabbing a bottle of wine and taking a seat. "Have you seen the Lady Marian today?"

"No, I haven't."

"Damn," Will muttered under his breath. He quickly uncorked the bottle and took a long swig, then splashed a little on his clothes.

"You are a friend to my lady, yes?"

The woman's lips tightened. "Yes," she said. "Why do you ask?"

"We are both dearly in need of friends at the moment. Friends who understand discretion," he said, taking another long swallow.

"That's potent stuff you're drinking," she warned.

"I'm counting on it. Why don't you have a seat and join me, and we can pretend we've been swapping stories for hours."

"Why I never…" she said, and she bristled.

"My life might well depend on it," he said, lowering his voice. "Milady and I would be ever so grateful."

He was taking a huge risk, trusting in the woman and her ability to keep her mouth shut. He had no other choice, though. Either he was going to be under suspicion, or he wasn't. If he wasn't, then nothing would ever come of this. If he was, then he needed an alibi, and if Marian wasn't back at the castle yet, it certainly couldn't be her. After a moment standing there, frowning, Jansa pulled up a stool and picked up a glass, which Will filled. She brought it to her lips, but he noticed that she barely sipped it.

"Now, did I tell you about the time that I won a bet with old Lord Raleigh about who could hold his liquor better?" Will said, louder than would be considered normal. He slurred his words slightly.

"No, you didn't," Jansa said.

"I bet him fifteen gold coins that I could stand upright longer than he could when drinking."

"That's a large sum to wager," she observed.

"It was an incredibly large sum to wager, given that at that particular moment I didn't even have *one* gold coin on me," Will said, letting his voice swell with pride.

"How cheeky of you! What would you have done if you had lost the wager?" Jansa asked, taking another sip of the wine. She pursed her lips at the taste of it.

"It wouldn't have been good, I'll tell you that." Will took another gulp from the bottle. "But I had a secret weapon."

"Really? What sort of weapon?"

"Thanks to years of being bored at mass, I've learned how to stay on my feet even when I fall asleep or pass out."

"Impossible!" she scoffed enthusiastically.

"No, not impossible," he said, holding up a finger. "The trick is to lock your knees, and to balance yourself perfectly straight above them. Then you have nowhere to go."

"Oh, I think you're full of it, Will Scarlet," she said.

"I'll tell you what I'm not full of. Wine—at least, not yet. I think we need another bottle," he said, turning the now empty one upside down on the table.

"Another one?" she exclaimed.

"Yes, and then I'll finish telling you about Raleigh. You should have seen the look on his face after we'd each gone through an entire bottle of my uncle's best stuff."

A voice cut the air behind him.

"I've been looking everywhere for you."

Will turned around and saw the steward, flanked by two guards, standing in the doorway of the kitchen.

"Steward! You're just in time to hear the story about when I out-drank Lord Locksley. Or wait, which story was I telling?" he asked, turning to Jansa.

"You were telling me about out-drinking Lord Raleigh. The fifteen-gold-coin wager."

"That's right," Will said, pounding the table. "Did I tell you about out-drinking Locksley yet?"

"Not yet."

"Okay, first Raleigh, then Locksley. So, I had bet him those fifteen gold pieces I could stay standing longer."

Will was slurring his words even more, and waving his hands about in the air. His head nodded in cadence with his words.

The steward cleared his throat, and Will turned to look at him, letting his head roll a bit loosely on his neck. Although he was trying to give the impression of a relaxed, inebriated man, nothing could be farther from the truth. His heart was pounding, and he just hoped that if he started sweating in fear it would be taken as sweating from the drink.

"Oh, you want me to start from the beginning?" he asked.

"No," the steward said, looking skeptical. "So you have been here the entire time, telling your sordid stories to the cook?"

"Why not," Will said with a grin. "She knows where all the best wine is. Besides, I came in here looking for one of those new kitchen girls, you know the one with the curly black hair? She's a fetching one, isn't she? She's out doing something or other with vegetables, so I figured I'd wait."

"The king wants to see you," the steward responded. "Now."

"Oh." Will rubbed a hand over his face. "Does he want me to bring some wine with me? Does he already have some?" he asked, standing and heading over to the counter for another bottle.

"No," the steward said coldly.

"Loss his... I mean, his loss," Will said with a sloppy grin. He weaved slightly on his feet. "Lead on!"

He didn't risk glancing at Jansa as he left the kitchen. He followed behind the steward, and the guards flanked him on either side. His heart felt like it was in his throat, and he wanted to be sick. This could be it. His charade might be over, and he could be dead in the next few minutes. At least he could try to bluff his way to the very end.

Maybe if they killed him, it would deflect suspicion away from the others. It was small comfort, but he found a tiny measure of hope in the thought. He didn't want to die, but if he had to do so, theirs was the cause worth dying for.

They made it into the throne room where John sat on the throne, the imposter in all his obnoxious, pompous pride. Will forced himself to give his most charming smile while still staggering slightly.

"My king," he said, "I was just regaling some others with hilarious tales. Would you like to hear one?" He swept into a courtly bow that was slightly unsteady.

"There are times when I'm quite convinced all you think about are the appetites of the flesh," John said, his voice cold.

Will winked. "In my experience those are the most entertaining pursuits, my liege."

"There are serious matters at hand," John growled, and Will endeavored to stand a little straighter.

"What troubles you?" he asked, attempting to show genuine concern.

"We have a traitor here in the castle," John said coldly.

"Surely not!" Will burst out, acting appropriately appalled, and hopefully not overplaying his hand.

"Yes, someone quite close has been conspiring against me."

Will swallowed hard, struggling for the right words to say. It was as if he could already feel a noose tightening. He took a deep breath even as he realized he might instead feel the cold steel of a sword as it severed his head from his neck.

"I have a hard time believing that someone would be so foolhardy," he said, licking his lips and shaking his head slightly. He wished at the moment that he *was* good and drunk. Maybe then he wouldn't feel this crushing fear that threatened to choke him.

"And yet someone has been," John replied. "I'm certain of it. A convoy was attacked today and, there is only one in the castle who could have known of it in time to warn the Hood."

"Who is it you suspect, my king?" Will asked.

John raised his hand sharply and Will fought not to cringe backward as he expected one of the guards to descend on him. Instead he heard the door open and he turned in time to see four guards escorting Marian into the room.

Instead of diminishing Will's fear, the sight only galvanized it.

"What is milady doing here?" he managed to ask.

"Haven't you guessed?" John purred. "She is the traitor."

Will turned and forced a smile onto his face.

"Ah ha *ha*, an excellent jest indeed, my king," he said, struggling to keep his tone light. "You almost had me fooled."

"It is no laughing matter. There is a traitor amongst us and I am convinced it is her."

"Even if there is a traitor, how could it possibly be her?" Will said, hiccupping. "When has any woman that pretty had half a brain in her head?"

Will was deeply relieved to see that Marian wasn't wearing the cloak, or anything else that would resemble that of the Hood's costume. She was wearing a rather plain dress, likely one she usually used for riding. He did detect a few drops of blood showing through on the one shoulder, though. She must have been struck in the battle.

He just prayed John hadn't noticed.

"She was caught riding back to the stables just minutes ago." John leaned forward and stared accusingly. "It was she who passed information about the convoy to the outlaw. Of that I have no doubt."

Will shook his head in mock disbelief.

"I don't even know how a woman so sheltered as she would even go about finding an outlaw," he said.

"I don't think you give women enough credit for deviousness," John replied. "Especially *this* woman…"

"She's actually quite the simple girl, Highness," Will pressed, and he raised an eyebrow. "If you recall, she even allowed me… well, past her gates." At that he burped.

Marian's face flamed red.

"You bastard," she growled.

Will waved his hand, dismissing her outburst. "Even if it is true, your Highness, she's your niece. So what can be done? You'd need proof before you could make the accusation in public, especially since she is *your* responsibility." He was walking a fine line, he knew—one that might get him hanged right along with Marian. Still, he had committed himself.

Might as well see it through to the end, he thought, and he grimaced inwardly at the choice of words.

"Besides," he added, "if she is a traitor, we might yet find a use for her." At that he fell silent. All he knew was that if John made a move to harm Marian then he'd have to act—even if it got him killed.

John smiled and Will's stomach twisted harder at the sight. It was an evil smile.

"I can think of a *few* uses she might still serve," the usurper said, and he turned to face his prisoner. "For now, Marian, you shall be banished to the tower. You are not to leave it unless I send for you."

"You can't do this," Marian hissed.

John laughed, long and low, and it made Will's skin crawl.

"My dear niece. It is already done."

Friar Tuck was unused to riding horses. Driving carts or traveling afoot was far more comfortable for him.

After a short period of galloping, which had seen him nearly thrown from the animal's back half a dozen times, he pulled the beast to a walk, which then seemed ponderous and slow.

"I could walk faster than you," he muttered.

The horse flicked back an ear as if half paying attention, but it didn't move any faster.

The truth was, he *would* have preferred to get down and walk, but he was still shaking from the encounter, and didn't trust his legs to support him. He wasn't even sure where in the forest they were, exactly. He should have paid closer attention—though he'd been too busy hanging on for dear life.

Tuck looked around, hoping to see something that looked familiar. There was nothing. Not a tree, not a bush. The only thing even remotely familiar was the music.

I'm going to die, lost and alone in the cursed forest, he realized. He could feel bile rising in the back of his throat, and his heart began to pound as hard as it had done during the midst of the fighting. He was lost. He was done for.

Music?

Tuck blinked, suddenly aware of the sound that was drifting through the trees. It was faint, but he recognized the instrument that made it. He offered up a prayer of thanksgiving as he urged his horse in the direction of the music.

A couple of minutes later he came within sight of a rock upon which sat the bard, Alan-a-Dale, his long fingers strumming the harp. The bard nodded at him, and then ceased his playing.

"I thought you might need some assistance finding your way," he said, voice and face both much more serious than they normally were. There was a streak of blood on his cheek, and the rest of his skin was pale around it.

"How?"

"I told you I could run fast and far, and that I knew the forest."

"I'm grateful to see you in one piece," Tuck said, abandoning the playful banter he usually shared with his old friend. "And your assistance is much appreciated."

"We should all be grateful to be in one piece," Alan said as he stood and returned his harp to its normal resting place on his shoulder. He stepped closer, and as he did, Tuck looked around.

"Do you know the way to the monastery from here?"

"I do, but that's not where we are going," the bard responded. "The cardinal thought it prudent to meet elsewhere, in light of everything that's happened."

Tuck felt a chill pass through him. Since the death of Bishop Montoya, he had once again found the monastery a place of peace and sanctuary. Then Stephen had gone missing. He wondered if the cardinal's reticence had something to do with the missing monk. The world was upside down and he, for one, was growing tired of it.

"How have you made it there and back so swiftly?" Tuck asked. He knew Alan didn't enjoy riding horses either, and he didn't have one near him now.

"I spoke with Cardinal Francis before we left," Alan said.

A terrible suspicion entered Tuck's mind then. What if Alan had betrayed them? What if he was leading the friar into a trap now? He took a deep breath, trying to force the thoughts from his mind. Alan could be trusted. He was one of *them*, and he'd proven his loyalty time and again.

Yet the doubt would not be denied.

"Why did Francis speak with you, and not with me?" Tuck

asked. It made no sense. He was the cardinal's closest confidant. Perhaps Francis didn't trust him anymore. Tuck bristled at the thought. *After all we've been through, he had no right to exclude me.*

Instead of answering his question Alan frowned.

"Are you sure you are well?" he asked.

"Why wouldn't I be?" Tuck demanded.

"You're acting... unlike yourself."

"Well, if I wasn't being kept out of your, your... secret deliberations, then I wouldn't be acting strange," he growled.

"I assure you, my friend, there were no secret deliberations. The cardinal simply asked me to make certain everyone made it to the new rendezvous point, since both he and I knew the location."

No. Alan was lying. Tuck was sure of it.

He took a deep breath, trying to ease the squeezing sensation in his chest. His head was buzzing and he was tired—more tired than he could ever remember being. Still, he saw nothing for it but to play along with the minstrel's schemes, at least for the time being.

"So, lead the way," he growled.

Anger had been Robin's near constant companion for so long now he had lost track of the days. For the moment, though, anger had been replaced by fear. He slipped silently as a ghost through the forest, hoping and praying that the others had made it out safe.

Back at the scene of the ambush, it had been his intention to leave none of their enemies alive. One man had escaped, though. He was wounded and wouldn't last out the night, but still Robin had followed after him as soon as he could. He'd worried what the man might say before he died.

He had found the man's body on the road just outside the forest. He was dead, but not from the wound that Robin had inflicted. The corpse was half-eaten, and just seeing the remains left a bad taste in his mouth. He wondered if one of the Sheriff's pets had been responsible. He just hoped the man had died before being able to tell anyone what he had seen.

He was heading toward the monastery when he encountered the cardinal heading away from it. The man was walking briskly, clearly with a purpose and a destination in mind.

"What's happening?" Robin asked sharply.

Cardinal Francis looked up at him in genuine surprise. "Apparently more than I expected, if you're not with Alan. He was supposed to lead everyone to a new meeting place," he said.

Robin shook his head. "Things went... badly."

He leaned down and offered the cardinal a hand. The man swung up easily behind him, surprisingly spry for his age.

"Let's just hope the bard was able to tell the others," Robin muttered, fear wrapping itself around his heart.

CHAPTER TWELVE

Even though things had gone horribly wrong, Alan knew that it could have all turned out much, much worse.

They had been lucky, really, to escape with their lives. As he looked around at the worn faces, he could see the toll the stress was taking on each of them. Robin's anger was slowly fading and being replaced by a sense of helpless frustration. Cardinal Francis wore the look of a man resigned to his fate. Friar Tuck was jumpy, constantly looking over his shoulder as they all sat on the giant felled log that was their meeting place.

"If they were smart, Will and Marian have made for the castle," Alan said softly, "hopefully arriving before they were missed."

"What if they're at the monastery looking for us instead?" Tuck growled.

"I left instructions with Lenore, in case she saw them," Cardinal Francis said.

"You put her in danger?" Tuck snapped, his skin growing even paler than it already was.

"No one looks twice at a child when they're seeking information," Francis said. "She knows enough to hide from strangers, but she's met both Will and Marian. She will be fine."

"They knew we'd be coming," Robin said, his voice angry.

"It was more than that," Alan responded. "They lured us out.

There were no children, no cargo was being sent to Scotland."

"No, it wasn't," Robin agreed. "Once I was free of pursuit, I circled back and checked the roads," he said. "They were empty—no carts, no wagons. They only held soldiers."

"What do we do now?" Friar Tuck asked. "What happened to the men who attacked us?" He peered over his shoulder, as if one of the soldiers might materialize at any moment.

"All the soldiers are dead," Robin said. "The wounded one who escaped was…" He paused, and frowned. "He was attacked, and eaten by something. The man was dead when I found him."

Alan couldn't stop the shudder that worked its way down his spine.

"So as long as Will and Marian aren't caught sneaking into the castle, we are safe from discovery for now," Francis said. "We should heed the warning of what just happened, though. We have to view every activity as a trap, whether it is or not, and take appropriate precautions. John's men will be better armed, and their numbers will increase."

"We need help," Alan said quietly.

"And where exactly do you expect it to come from?" Friar Tuck asked.

"There are others with cause to hate John and his allies, just as much as we do," he answered.

"No," Robin said.

"No what?" Tuck asked.

"He's talking about Little John and the other men we freed. But I won't put them in harm's way." Robin shook his head. "I won't let them down again," he muttered.

"You never let them down in the first place," the cardinal said gently, but Alan could tell that Robin would never believe it. He needed to be convinced.

"It's their lives, their country as much as it is ours," he said. "They deserve a chance to decide for themselves if they will stand and fight." He let that sink in, then added, "The more we can rally to our cause, the greater our hope of success."

"And the more we'll have to bury," Robin said bitterly.

"We can't trust anyone else," Tuck said. "Not even Will and Marian—why aren't they here? How can we be certain they didn't lead us into that trap?"

Alan blinked at the friar in surprise.

"What has happened to you?" he asked. "You've been acting strangely, ever since the fight."

"I just don't like being stuck like a rat," Tuck growled. There was more to it, though. Alan wasn't sure what, but the friar's demeanor, his attitude, they were just… *off*. This wasn't the man he'd known for so many years. Something more was at play than fear and shock, he was sure of it. Whatever it was, however, it would have to wait. They had more pressing business to discuss.

"There are others who have been rendered homeless by the usurper and his lackeys," Alan said quietly. "Left penniless by the tax collectors. We can no longer keep them safe where they are, and the forest seems to be the only place that the Sheriff and his men cannot go." Robin and Tuck both glowered at him. He shrugged his narrow shoulders. "The forest protects those within it. It will protect them, as well."

"Consider the extra burden this would place on Little John and the others," Robin argued. "I will not ask them to bear it."

"They are already training for war," Alan replied. "This will remind them what they are fighting for, and it will add new warriors to their number."

"You're a bloody savage," Tuck growled. "You always have been. How can you understand what good Christian people need to live?"

Everyone froze at the words.

"Something *did* happen to you in the battle," Alan said. "Were you struck by anything?"

"Do I *look* wounded?" Tuck replied angrily. "You're imagining things."

"No, Alan's right," the cardinal said, "there is something amiss."

"Maybe it's because I've had enough," Tuck said, clambering to his feet. He was shouting now. "You lot have been conspiring together and excluding me. It's only a matter of time before you betray me, give me up as the Hood to save your own skins!"

Robin stood, his face twisting in concern, and he placed a hand on the friar's shoulder.

"There was a moment, during the battle," he said. "A thin man attempted to throw something at me. You jumped in front of him, and it struck you, instead." He peered closely at the holy man. "What was it?" he asked.

"Water, for all the damage it did," Tuck answered. "I shouldn't have bothered trying to save your worthless hide." He turned and stormed off suddenly into the woods.

They all stared after him and after a moment, Alan broke the silence.

"Whatever was thrown, it clearly wasn't water."

Marian paced, tracing the confines of her new room in the tower. Her prison. Furious one moment and filled with despair the next. She had to find a way to stop her uncle, even if it meant strangling him with her own two hands. Unfortunately, it wouldn't be that easy. All too well she remembered Robin's description of what had happened the night he had crept into John's bedchamber and attempted to kill him. John had demons on his side.

She supposed she should be grateful that he hadn't had her killed outright. Shut up here, though, she might as well be dead. He had rendered her useless. She couldn't spy, she couldn't fight—all she could do was pray. Even that felt ineffective, as though the evil swirling around and through the castle was somehow blocking her supplications. Yet the chaos in her mind served a more important purpose—to help her avoid the truth.

She had killed a man tonight.

Sword through the chest.

She had taken a life. Marian had only been in the tower for

a handful of hours, and already she felt like she was going mad. Abruptly the bolt on the door of her cell shot back. The door opened and Chastity entered, hastily bolting it again behind her.

"I brought you some things," the younger woman said, balancing a platter of food in her left hand and holding a squirming baby fox in her right.

"Champion," Marian said, moving quickly to take the fox into her arms. She buried her head against his fur.

"Didn't think you could leave either of us behind, did you?" Chastity asked as she put the food down on a table by the narrow window.

Marian lifted her face. "I need you to get word to Will," she said.

Chastity cocked her head to the side. "Best wait a day or two, until everyone's not so jumpy, Princess."

"It can't wait," Marian insisted. "He needs to know that I went down to the other docks—the ones in the north harbor. The ship waiting to take a messenger to Richard had been burned, the crew killed, butchered like animals. All the other vessels had been scuttled, as well."

Chastity gasped and covered her mouth with her hands.

"So we can't get word to Richard," Marian said, hating the tremor in her voice. "Will needs to know that. We mustn't risk delay, for he might try to send a messenger of his own, and they'll be killed. He might even try to go himself, as did I.

"We can't afford to lose a single ally."

The middle of the night and Will was still up, pacing in his room. It was a miracle that he and Marian weren't both dead. He should be grateful for that, but anxiety was eating him alive.

It was only a matter of time before John grew tired of dealing with the princess and had her executed. And he would follow. When she was gone, suspicion for any leaks coming from the castle would fall directly on him.

There had to be a way to implicate someone else, one of John's allies. That would relieve the pressure on them, and rid them of one of their enemies all in one blow.

The steward.

He was the logical choice—unless, of course, he had known about the trap for the Hood. Then trying to put the blame on him would be worse than useless. It would be a noose around his own neck. One that he could almost feel tightening now.

Will had a vision of himself, asleep in his room, when suddenly there was a pounding on his door. Before he could rouse himself soldiers would flood in, led by the cursed Nottingham.

He closed his eyes and shook his head, trying to tell himself he was being paranoid. John didn't suspect him.

A sudden knock caused him to jump, and he nearly yelped. His heart raced out of control. The knock had been soft, not the pounding of a soldier's fist. Still he stood, as if frozen to the spot. Finally he forced himself to take a deep breath, and make his legs move.

When he cracked open the door, he sagged in relief. Chastity was standing there, a shawl pulled tight about her shoulders. He opened the door wide and she slipped inside before he closed it again.

She turned. Her normally rosy cheeks were pale, and the air of mischievousness that usually clung to her was notably absent.

"Has something happened to Marian?" he asked sharply. "Is she alright?"

"For now, though the Lord only knows for how long," Chastity replied. "She wanted me to warn you not to send an emissary to King Richard. She rode herself today to the harbor, and found the king's men dead. His ship on fire."

"What are you saying?" Will asked, feeling his chest tighten even more.

"We are cut off," she replied. "There is no way we can get word to King Richard." Her eyes bulged with fear. "We are on our own."

Will sucked in his breath, his mind racing. Until now he had believed they were playing a waiting game, trying to keep John in check until Richard could return and set things right. A sudden, bleak thought struck him like a physical blow. What if Richard was already dead? There were a thousand dangers in the king's path. John's betrayal was but one of them.

His legs refused to hold him anymore. He staggered over to a chair by his writing table, and slumped down in it. He fought the urge to bury his head in his hands. Instead he forced himself to look up at Chastity. Her shoulders were shaking, and he realized with a start that she was crying.

It seemed so unnatural for her, the opposite of her normal, quick-witted, saucy self. It drove him back up to his feet even though he himself felt on the verge of collapse. He crossed the floor between them and took her in his arms. She stiffened for just a moment, and then buried her head against his chest.

"I'm so scared for her," she sobbed. "She takes the most awful chances."

"Marian is strong, and she's the king's niece. John wouldn't dare hurt her," Will said, lying for the girl's benefit. John would kill any of them if he suspected betrayal.

"Yet I had the most terrible feeling as I walked the halls tonight," Chastity said. "I heard something, in my mind. I heard the bells tolling, as though for a wedding, but all around there was the sound of people weeping. Then in my mind, I saw an old woman, and I asked her what had happened. She said, 'The Hood is dead and woe has come upon his lady.'"

"It was just a phantasm," Will said. "A trick of the imagination."

Chastity shook her head violently and straightened so that she could look him in the eye.

"It wasn't," she protested. "As a child, a week before my father died, I heard my mother weeping for him in my dreams. A few years later, I saw a vision of my mother's grave, even before she passed." She pushed away from him. "Mark my words, the Hood is going to die.

"I'm afraid Marian will die with him."

CHAPTER THIRTEEN

Glynna Longstride awoke, the remnants of a particularly dark dream singing through her blood. She stretched, the fur coverings of the bed rubbing luxuriously against her skin.

Her eyes sought out the dark corners of the room, looking for her love. Others could not see him when he chose to hide in the shadows, but she could. They didn't understand that he was the very shadows themselves.

He wasn't there, however, and she felt a tickle of disappointment until the substance of the dream came back to her. Then she sat up, excitement crackling through her. She had devised the perfect way in which to kill the hated necromancer woman.

Glynna glanced over at the clothes she had dropped on the floor earlier that evening. She had grown to despise the cursed things which bound her, kept her imprisoned. She took a deep breath to clear her thoughts, then she reached deep down, touching the darkness that was growing inside her.

Turning her mind outward, she focused, raised her arms, and swirled them together.

Shadows suddenly spun around her, settling for a moment upon her skin, only to take flight again. She wanted to cloak herself in them, and knew she would be able to do so soon.

However, as the shadows flew back to the corners from

whence she had summoned them, she realized that day had not yet come. It would soon, though. With a small snort of disgust she stood, and set about finding something suitable to wear.

The Sheriff had been keeping his dark allies close to him, so they would be available quickly when summoned. Thus, the woman she hated had taken to sleeping in the hovel where they all met. No doubt she hoped to curry favor, or dreamt that he would notice her devotion. As if he gave a damn about the likes of her. He used her—as he used all of them. They were tools, and ones that could be replaced.

Glynna paused. He would not be pleased when she broke one of his tools, but surely he would understand, and forgive her for it. He would probably even love her more. She smiled at the thought.

Lifting a quilted cloak from the wardrobe, she pulled it out and flung it around her. Made of a tightly woven linen the color of a canary, it was stuffed with goose down and wrapped her like a blanket. The seamstress had affixed ram's-horn buttons that went from throat to mid-thigh. The inside had been lined with a thin silk, too thin to contain all the pinfeathers, so here and there a few small quills poked through to scratch and slip across her bare skin.

Covered enough to leave the room, she went in search of the necromancer.

He was the strongest man in England. Everyone knew that. Why, then, were his arms so exhausted that the muscles were shaking, while Old Soldier stoically notched another arrow into his bow.

"I can't do another one," John protested as he stared at the arrow the old man had driven into the ground in front of him.

"You can and you will," Old Soldier said, as calmly as if he'd been discussing the weather.

"I can't, I tell you," John said. "My arms are on fire. We've been shooting arrows for over an hour now, and I can't take anymore."

Old Soldier let his arrow fly. The slender piece of wood raced through the air with a soft whooshing sound before embedding itself next to its brothers in the target tree. Then the old man looked up at him, eyes glinting with a hard light.

"Is that what you'll say in the heat of battle?" he asked. "'Stop, I can't take anymore.' And what will your enemy say to you?"

John felt himself flushing. He hated it when he was chastised. Sometimes he deserved it, other times he wasn't so sure, but it always made him feel squeamish in his belly.

"In the heat of battle, there'll be no time to think," John argued. "The passion, and the fear it has stirred up, will see me through."

Old Soldier stared at him, and made him feel stupid.

"On the battlefield, passion, fear, those only last so long before your body can't keep them up," he said. "You know what comes after those? Exhaustion and then resignation. I've seen many a great fighter bested by a lesser man because he resigned himself to his fate. He stopped fighting in *here*," Old Soldier continued, tapping John's chest over his heart. "And in here," he added, tapping John's forehead.

"You give up in either of those places, you let yourself feel the pain and the exhaustion, and you're dead. All I've taught you means nothing, and I'm left helping your widow bury you. Is that what you want?"

"No," John said, licking his lips.

"Then I don't give a damn how tired you are. You don't stop until I tell you that you can. Is that understood?"

John nodded.

Part of him hated Old Soldier in that moment—wanted to pick the man up and snap him in half like a twig. Old Soldier had seen things that John couldn't even imagine, though, and he had survived. If John wished to survive, he had to do as the old man said. Even though all he wanted in the world right then was a cool drink, a morsel of bread, and a tree to sit under.

Another part of him realized that he should be honored. The old man didn't drive everyone else half as hard as he drove John. That meant he respected him, expected him to be capable of great things. It was good to have someone believe that much. It helped take a bit of the burn off, as he forced himself to pick up the arrow and notch it.

He pulled back and let the arrow fly. It went straight and true, and buried itself in the tree next to Old Soldier's last one.

"Good," Old Soldier said. "Ten more arrows, and then we'll switch to sword training for the rest of the morning."

John gritted his teeth and nodded. He refused to let the old man see him hurting anymore. He made a vow to himself and God, then and there, that he would not yield a weapon until the old man had. He was, after all, John Little.

Strongest man in England.

Put me away. Hide me.

Agrona blinked herself out of the trance she'd been in, the image of her mother dissolving like early morning mist. They had been prodding the spirit of her sister, trying to draw her out of the relic that lay slimy across her knees. The shinbone left a streak of goo on her robe as she lifted it up and placed it into the black oak box beside the dry bones of their mother. Closing the lid, she slid it under the edge of her pallet and stood, all in one sinuous motion.

The door rattled.

"Come in—" she said.

It opened before she had finished speaking, and Glynna Longstride strode into the room.

"I do not need you to *allow* me entrance."

The words whipped across Agrona, and she fought to keep her temper in check.

"This is where I have made my home," she said. "I was welcoming you."

Glynna kept moving until she stood close enough to touch the necromancer. Her icy blue eyes narrowed.

"Quite the accommodating little bit, aren't you?"

"Only to some," Agrona replied.

"Only to those with power."

Agrona tilted her head at the accusation, considering it, and considering the woman who threw it. She took in Glynna's long, lithe form. Even with the pregnancy, it was laden with sensuality. Lust dripped off her like droplets after a shower. It perfumed the air, a heady scent of sex and power. Agrona stepped closer.

"It is intoxicating to find someone worthy of attention."

"Worthy as the Sheriff?"

"Worthy as he." Agrona licked her lips. "Worthy as thee."

Glynna reached out, grasping Agrona's wrists, drawing her sticky hands to the buttons on the robe. As Agrona's fingers began to work, Glynna inhaled deeply. Agrona knew the other woman could smell the must of bone, the tinge of rot, the warmth of womanhood—and there, down in the layers of it all, the blackberry smoke and grave-dirt scent of her lover.

The ram's-horn buttons fell away. The robe parted around her stomach. She hitched her shoulders and it slipped down her arms to puddle at her feet.

Agrona drew in a sharp breath.

When she could, she whispered. "Sweet Goddess, thou art *glorious*."

"You desire me as you desire the Sheriff?"

"I do, milady."

Glynna brought her hands up to her collarbones, sliding her palms down to cup her breasts, swollen to the point of ridiculousness. She squeezed them and the flesh went translucent. White and the blue veins stood out like woad painted on a corpse.

Then Glynna reached down, and Agrona rocked on her heels.

Long, slender fingers slipped below, caressing around the swollen stomach and then under, disappearing from the necromancer's sight. Yet she could *feel* them against her own skin, as if she were the one being touched.

She bit her lip to hold in a moan.

The other woman raised her hands, cupping Agrona's face and pulling her close. The necromancer tilted her chin up, lips parting as she stopped against the taller woman's distended, pregnant stomach.

Glynna leaned down, their lips close enough to brush.

"Whose are you, little corpse-talker?"

"Yours, milady," Agrona gasped, her breath closed tight in her chest. "Yours and our lord's."

Glynna's tongue flicked out, swiping across Agrona's bottom lip. The necromancer's knees buckled at the crackle of power that stabbed through her.

Glynna chuckled then, holding the other woman up.

Agrona's hands found Glynna's belly, the skin under her palms tight as a drum. There was a sharp kick under her right palm. It cleared her mind just enough to speak.

"My sister was a midwife."

"Was?"

"Our lord sacrificed her."

"Good for her."

"We talk more now," Agrona said. "I can force her to share her knowledge with me, when your time comes."

Glynna brushed her bottom lip against Agrona's.

"She is dead?"

Agrona nodded.

"Tell her I said hello."

Then Glynna's mouth fell, latching onto hers. Her lips were soft and hot, so very hot. Agrona's head swam as the other woman's tongue invaded her mouth, insistent, pushing past her teeth. There was a split second of ecstasy as raw lust poured over her like fire-warmed honey.

The tongue in her mouth kept pushing.

It shoved, swelling as it went into her throat. She choked around it, the urge to gag jerking her forward. She pushed, trying to get free, to get breath, to get away, but Glynna's hands were iron around her head. The tongue, the thing, in her throat began to squirm, to crawl its way deeper inside her.

Panic stampeded through her as red spots clouded her vision

from the edges. She couldn't breathe, couldn't speak, couldn't *think*. She could only feel the invasion of what was once a human tongue, burrowing inside her.

The darkness took her as it unleashed spikes that tore the soft tissue inside her. The last thing she saw was Glynna Longstride's eyes, glittering with hate and insanity, just inches from her own.

"Was that necessary?"

Glynna dropped the dead weight and turned, wiping her mouth with the back of her hand.

The Sheriff of Nottingham leaned against the doorway.

His pale hands and face seemed to float in the dark that gathered around him, his ever-present armor drinking the light from the room.

Heat jumped inside her, leaping from point to point in her body like embers in a raging forest fire. She was ecstatic to see him, and could not tell from the tone of his question if he was angry with her, though angry would be fine.

His punishments could be so exquisite.

She smiled a wicked smile. "Necessary enough."

In an instant the Sheriff was beside her. He hadn't walked across the room, he just suddenly was there. He looked down at the dead woman on the floor. The body had collapsed in on itself like a drained wineskin. He looked back at Glynna and raised a pale eyebrow.

"How did she taste?"

Glynna parted her lips and leaned toward him. "See for yourself."

It was three days before Will felt it was safe to leave the castle. Even so, he found himself glancing frequently over his shoulder to make sure he wasn't being followed as he headed toward the monastery.

He was wrapped in a fur-lined cloak that did little to fend off the creeping cold that seemed to seep into his bones. In his room at the castle he kept the fireplace burning night and day. He told himself it was just imagination that made it seem as if his room—and indeed, the whole world—grew darker and icier by the day.

There were many preparations to be made for the upcoming solstice. He secretly wondered if Marian still lived because of the festival, or something associated with it. At the last such gathering John had orchestrated a horrific series of hangings. Will still saw them in his mind's eye, women and children, killed without remorse.

He would not watch Marian be executed, and he prayed it didn't come to that. Will rounded a bend in the road and saw a lone figure trudging toward him, baskets swinging from the stick he held across his broad shoulders, head down against the cold winter wind. Will relaxed as he recognized Much. The miller's boy had done a lot of growing in the last couple of months. His shoulders seemed broader, and his face thinner.

Then again, a lot of faces seemed thinner these days. With winter settling in prematurely, he couldn't help but wonder how the people were going to survive it. He thought of the fine meal he'd enjoyed just that morning, and felt a surge of embarrassment that he had a full belly, while so many did not. It was a monstrosity what John was doing to the people. Even the men living in the forest ate better and more often than their families did in their homes.

They should all seek refuge in Sherwood.

"Hail, good fellow," Will said as he drew close to Much. "Where have you been so far this morning?"

"As far away as the stonecutter's home."

"Wasn't the father taken by the pox?" Will asked, straining to remember. So many had died from King John's curse, it was hard to remember them all.

"And the oldest son," Much agreed. "His wife and two young

sons are left. My father sent me to check on them, make sure they had enough." His brow puckered in concern.

"And do they have enough?"

Much shook his head. "My father instructed me to leave some food with them, and they cried and thanked me. I felt bad, though, because I knew it would not last them long."

Will's fists clenched where they held his horse's reins. It should be up to the nobles to care for the people. With King John squeezing them so hard, though, the nobles scarcely had the food needed to feed their own families. All others were going to have to fend for themselves during the harsh months ahead.

Most would be reduced to begging, and he feared that a great many would end up dead. There was an obvious course of action. Robin wasn't going to like it, but he had to hear it nevertheless.

Cardinal Francis knew deep in his soul that Will's arrival was a dark omen. The tide was turning against them. He'd felt it for days, but had not wanted to admit it to himself, let alone the others. The more time he spent in prayer and fasting, the more he knew his own days were numbered.

"We are cut off from Richard," Will said, as he finished relaying what the Lady Marian had seen when she rode to the harbor.

No ships to send word for help. No ships on which to escape.

For Francis, there was something far worse than being cut off from King Richard. He was cut off from Rome herself. At the very thought, he shuddered deep inside. Unlike some of his brethren he had never wanted to be Pope, never wanted the responsibility for so many souls. His entire time in the Church had been spent as a scholar, an adviser.

He closed his eyes.

Francis was still those things, and he would continue to be those things for whatever time was left to him.

He opened his eyes and looked at Will.

"There's something more," he said. "What is it?"

"The people," Will said, and the cardinal shot him a curious look. "So many of them are starving, or will be before this winter is even half over. Between the pox, the taxes, and this unnatural early cold, they are hard pressed even to find scraps of food."

"And you have a suggestion of what might be done," Francis guessed.

"I think they should be sent to Sherwood," Will said.

Francis leaned back in his chair. Robin wouldn't like that, but it wasn't his choice to make. Besides, if the portents were true, young Longstride was going to have to forgo his lone wolf ways, and learn to lead. The people needed a leader.

They'll need him even more after I'm gone.

"I agree," he said quietly.

It was the logical choice—and if it prepared Robin to step up to his destiny, then all the better.

Will nodded, but there was hesitation in his eyes.

"Don't worry," Francis said, guessing the source of his trepidation. "I'll tell Robin."

"Thank you."

"You should return to the castle before you're missed," the cardinal cautioned. "We can't afford to lose you."

Will nodded and rose. A minute later he was gone, leaving Francis alone with his thoughts.

Yes, his time was definitely nearing an end. There were things that had to be done, however, before it arrived. Most importantly, he had to find a way to see Lady Marian. He had something he needed to give her.

CHAPTER FOURTEEN

"What do you mean the boats have been scuttled?" Cardinal Francis looked hard at Friar Tuck. "Do you need me to define the word?" he asked sternly.

"I know what 'scuttled' means," Tuck growled. "How did it happen?"

"John's men did it."

"They feared someone might send word to King Richard."

"It appears so."

Friar Tuck began to pace, the wool of his robe crackling with static electricity as he swung his meaty arms around. The chamber they were in was small—five steps across and nine steps long. The stout monk seemed to fill the space, his anger radiating off him in waves.

"Calm yourself, my friend." Francis raised his hands, palms out. "It is bad news, but we shall persevere."

"Do you not know what this means?" Tuck exploded. His round face had gone red, darker on the edges of his jowl line.

"I do." Francis kept his words measured.

"We are without hope!" the friar cried.

"We are never without hope, my friend."

Tuck locked eyes with him. "Tottering old fool."

Francis drew himself to his fullest height.

The moment has arrived, he thought. *You leave me no alternative.* Reaching into his robe he removed a small bottle with a cork and uncapped it. Friar Tuck turned to cross the small room again, hands balled into fists and his head down like a bull preparing to charge. Francis slung the contents of the bottle on his friend.

"In the name of Christ I bind you," he cried.

The anointing oil slung from the bottle in an arc, slapping across the fat friar's chest. It sparked purple and sizzled.

Friar Tuck froze, mid-stride.

Francis slung the oil at him again, this time up and down. The oil struck him again, from brow to belly. The oil sizzled and sparked once more, before soaking into the coarse wool robe. The stain of it formed a rough cross.

Jaw clenched, Tuck growled.

"What are you doing?"

"I anoint you, Tuck, in the name of the Father and by the authority of the church. The works of evil are denied, the chains of iniquity are broken."

"Leave me the hell alone!" Friar Tuck bellowed.

"There is no power over you but the power of Christ Almighty!" Cardinal Francis struck Friar Tuck in the face with an open hand. The monk, who was thirty years younger and a hundred pounds heavier, dropped to his knees as if felled by an axe.

Francis could feel the magic spell that laid over his friend. It made his skin crawl and feel dirty. The air smelled sour in the small room.

"It burns, Francis!" Tears streamed down Tuck's cheeks. "Why are you doing this to me?" he cried. "I trusted you!"

The words punched Francis in the gut, but he had to hold strong. This wasn't an exorcism—Friar Tuck hadn't been possessed, but he was under the influence of dark magic. It could not remain unchecked. To leave it thus would endanger them all.

Then Tuck began to howl in pain.

Francis had to be strong. To see this through.

"In the name of Christ, I command the demonic forces to depart," he cried. "You are banished to the pit."

Tuck screamed then, a shrill sound that broke at the end.

"Be bound, devils, be broken, spell," Francis continued. "Be free in Christ, Brother Tuck." He turned the oil up over Friar Tuck's head, letting the last of it drip onto the monk's face.

It ran into his mouth as he screamed.

Bards, by the necessity of their vocation, were always moving, always traveling. They never stayed in one place too long. It was more than their position that dictated it, though. Every bard was born with a wayfaring spirit, a driving force that scratched at the back of his mind and chewed away at his guts if he stood still for too long.

Alan had stood still for far too long, and it was starting to affect him in a very real, very intense way. Over the past fortnight he had begun sleepwalking, his unconscious mind attempting to address the problem that his waking mind refused to sort out. News that the boats had been destroyed caused him a rush of sheer panic. Not that he'd ever crossed the sea to France. Knowing that he couldn't, though, made him feel as if he was being closed in, caught like an animal in a trap. He fought the urge to flee up north, to Scotland, to see if there were boats there that could take him off the island.

Unfortunately, Alan had a duty he couldn't ignore. He'd known that responsibility might trap him here, once events were set in motion. He just wished there had been another way.

The sense of community, of bonded brotherhood, was unusual for a person of his profession, yet there was merit to it. Being tied to the plans of others was uncomfortable, though, even when he was exercising his gifts.

Alan stood at the door of the stonecutter's home. Much had described the family as having the poorest chance of surviving the winter on their own. When the stonecutter's widow opened the door, and Alan observed her hollow cheeks and fearful, bloodshot eyes, he knew the young man had been right.

One of the gifts that came with being a bard, a student of the old ways, was the ability to read people, to know the contents of their hearts. The woman before him did not believe she would survive the week, let alone the winter. For her, hope was in shorter supply than food.

In Sherwood Forest there would be food and shelter, but it would not be an easy life. It would require each person to want to survive, to be willing to fight for it. There was no fight left in the woman he faced.

There was movement behind her, and then her two sons stepped forward, curiosity drawing them like moths to a flame. Both were younger than ten, and both still had fire in their eyes.

Alan swallowed.

"My lady, I am here to help your sons," he said. Most likely the woman had never been called a lady in her life, but she deserved the kindness, the show of respect, given what he was about to ask of her.

"How?" she asked curiously.

"The coming winter will be long and harsh," he said. "I can take them someplace where they will be warm and fed, and will live to see it through." He paused, to allow his words to sink in. Then he asked, "Will you send them with me?"

Curiosity turned to understanding, and tears sprang to her eyes, but she nodded her head swiftly, evidence that she knew how dire their situation was.

"Will you take them with you now?" The way she asked it said that she hoped he would.

"Yes," he replied. "Gather whatever warm clothes they have, and we will leave as soon as you are ready," he said.

She nodded and disappeared inside the house. The two boys turned to stare after her, then looked back at Alan, eyes wide.

To her credit, the woman was swift, returning almost immediately with two small bundles. She handed one to each boy.

"Audric and Haylan, you're going to go with this man," she said, bending down to look into their eyes. "He'll take care of you," she said, giving each of them a hug.

"You aren't going with us?" Haylan, the younger one, asked, a tremor in his voice.

"No, I need to stay here, but I expect you to be good boys," she answered, struggling to keep her voice firm. "Be strong for each other."

The older one said nothing, but Alan could tell by looking at his face that he knew he'd never see his mother again.

The woman rose, dashing away a tear.

"God go with you then," she said to him, "and thank you."

"You are welcome," Alan said softly, then he turned to the boys. "Alright then, follow me. We are going on an adventure."

Audric, the older boy, took the younger one's hand and nodded. There were tears on his cheeks, but he was doing his best to be strong for his little brother.

Alan turned and began to walk back down the path to the road. The boys trailed a step behind him.

As much as he wished he could have taken the mother with them, the woman had given up all hope of living, and she would have been a burden they could not afford to carry—one that might have got them all killed. It was a hard choice, but it had to be made.

That was why Alan had been chosen for this task. It would have been impossible for Cardinal Francis to leave anyone behind. The decision would have broken him. He wouldn't have been able to do it. As it was, the bard breathed out deeply, exhaling his regrets.

He couldn't afford to have them.

He wouldn't let himself have them.

This job was one he alone could do.

"Where are we going?" Haylan finally asked.

"Somewhere safe," Alan said.

"That would be nice," the boy replied.

"I don't want to go somewhere safe," Audric said. "I want to kill the Sheriff." With that he lapsed into a sullen silence.

I hope you never get the chance, Alan thought, though he did not speak. *If you do, it will mean that we have failed.* He forced himself to turn and smile down at the boy.

"Don't worry," he said. "There are plenty of dragons in this world to slay. I'm sure you will have your chance."

The quarterstaff had always been Little John's weapon of choice. Because of his size and strength, he could spin it with great speed and force. He could break another man's bones and feel it in his hands when he did.

It turned out that sword fighting, though also requiring speed and strength, was an entirely different skill and one that was much harder for John to master. The sword he held was short, almost like a child's plaything in his hand, and yet its deadliness was driven home to him again and again by Old Soldier.

A dozen shallow cuts leaked blood onto his skin. If it had been a warm spring day, instead of the cold of winter, his arms would have been red from shoulder to wrist.

He lunged, shoving the sword forward at the old man, who casually flicked his wrist and parried, knocking Little John a half step sideways. Before he could pull back and slash at Old Soldier's head, he had another burning cut on his forearm.

"Dammit!"

Old Soldier grinned.

"Stop smirking, you old bastard."

"Why?" Old Soldier asked. "I'm enjoying this."

"When's the last time you faced a worthy opponent?"

"Not any time recently."

"If I got my hands on you..."

"How likely is it that anyone will let you do that?" Old Soldier gave an amused cough. "Even the missus could keep you at arm's length."

At that, John's mind went immediately to his home. He missed his wife desperately, and the longing of it sounded like a church bell inside his chest.

Old Soldier read the look on his face.

"Soon, my friend."

"Not soon enough," Little John spat bitterly.

Alan gave Audric and Haylan a nudge toward the campfire and the men who stood around it. A man with a crooked shoulder stood with him.

They watched as both boys squatted by the fire. One of the other men there handed them each a turtle-shell bowl filled with stew.

"They'll have to earn their keep," the man said. "That's as we all agreed."

"They will."

"Shelter's limited."

"They won't take up much room."

"Food's even more limited."

"It will be provided."

The man grunted.

"What is your name?" Alan asked.

"Aiden," the man replied. "Aiden Peter's Son." He looked sideways at the bard. "Why do you ask?"

"I want to report to Lord Longstride *exactly* who will be responsible for the safekeeping of those two boys."

"Well, now—"

"He will be glad," Alan continued, "to know you care so much that they will eat before you yourself will."

"I never said..."

"No, you didn't. I did." Alan turned to walk away. "And a true bard never lies."

* * *

Both men sat against the wall, soaked in sweat.

Friar Tuck leaned against Cardinal Francis, his giant head against the stone.

"Thank you," he said.

"Thank Christ."

"Amen."

Silence between them grew.

"It must have been the liquid I was struck with on that ship."

"That is what I assumed," Francis said.

"Will I be susceptible from now on?"

"You will have to maintain spiritual diligence."

"That is a yes."

"It is."

"Fasting?"

"Mayhap."

They fell to silence again.

After a long moment, Friar Tuck pushed himself over a bit to make space.

"Why did it happen to me?"

"It was a spell. An attack by the enemy. As you may recall, it was aimed at Robin, not you."

"Yes, but why did it work?"

Cardinal Francis said nothing.

"Is it because of sin in my life?"

Cardinal Francis said nothing.

"Is it?"

Francis sighed. "Sin can be a doorway to this kind of thing," he admitted.

"Is it—"

Francis cut him off.

"You indulge your appetite."

"It isn't anything else?"

"I would say not."

"Not even...?" He let the words trail off this time.

"No." Francis's voice was firm as the stone beneath them.

Silence came again, this time it held for a long time before it was broken.

"So, that's it," Tuck said. "We have no way to contact Richard." He heard and hated the defeat that was so clear in his voice. "Nor Rome either, to warn her of what's happening."

"Take heart, my friend," Francis said. "All is not yet lost. It just seems that way."

"The true king of the land is needed here, in order to heal it."

"There may yet be another way to accomplish that very thing."

"What do you mean?"

"It might be time to use the book."

Friar Tuck regarded his friend and mentor for a long moment, trying to find words with which to express his concern. As if reading his mind, Francis put a hand on his shoulder.

"Do not be afraid," he said softly. "It is for this very crisis that we sought out the book, and had the bard bring it here, instead of leaving it in Ireland."

"You knew?" Tuck asked. "Even then?"

"I feared," the cardinal answered. "And I knew that if my fears were correct, we couldn't risk being cut off from so powerful an object."

"Taking it to Marian is a risk, and she's already lost so much."

"Before the end," Francis said, "sacrifices will have to be made. Each of us will need to prepare our souls for that."

CHAPTER FIFTEEN

Marian put down her cross-stitch and uttered a frustrated sigh. The thread had tangled and knotted, becoming unusable. She'd have to cut it out to continue the pattern. Even that was too much to ask of her distracted mind.

Standing, she stretched and then moved across the room to the window. Scraping away the frost with her finger, she looked out over the top of Sherwood Forest, normally a verdant blanket stretching as far as she could see. It now lay black.

She had been trapped here for three weeks, and longed desperately for freedom. The masons who built the castle long ago had cemented bars across the opening to keep the tower's occupant from tumbling out. Installed for safety, they simply reminded her that she was a prisoner.

The scrape of an iron bolt made her turn toward the door. Chastity bustled in carrying a tray with Marian's supper on it. She was early, and she had an air of furtiveness about her. Leaving the window, Marian met her in the middle of the room.

Voice hushed, she asked, "What's wrong?"

"There is a visitor here to see you."

"No one is allowed to visit me here," Marian replied, and her eyes closed to slits. "Who is it?"

"I don't know," Chastity said. "He wears a monk's robes."

The young woman turned her eyes to the floor, and added, "but he keeps his face hidden inside a hood."

"A monk?" She wondered if it was Friar Tuck, with news from the outside. As unlikely as it seemed, it was as good an explanation as any. Marian looked down at the dressing gown she wore. "I'll need to change."

Chastity nodded, mouth pulled into a tight line.

"Give me a few minutes to prepare, then bring him in," Marian instructed. Chastity turned to go, and Marian caught her arm. "Is there any word from Robin?"

The younger woman shook her head, strawberry-blonde curls bouncing. "That gives me a bad feeling," Marian admitted as she shivered, struggling to dismiss the thought. She shook her head, putting it away. "For now, however, there is a monk awaiting me in the hallway."

"Get dressed, milady. I'll bring him in shortly." Chastity turned and slipped out the door, leaving it unbolted.

They were both taking a huge risk. Marian wasn't allowed to have visitors, but if the monk had come to her, it must be important. From the wardrobe she pulled a demure dress, one she always reserved for mass. Before the tower, when she was permitted to go. She slipped it over her head, and it hung where it used to fit. Adjusting it as best she could, she stepped into well-worn boots.

She picked up the shawl her mother made when she was a wee child, and draped it over her unbrushed hair. By the time the door swung open, she was at least presentable.

The monk entered, walking with a stooped, geriatric shuffle, folds of simple brown cloth draping him from head to foot. He trundled in, head bowed, face hidden in the shadow of his hood, a shadow made darker by the flickering candlelight.

Chastity stayed at the door. "I'll keep watch, milady."

Marian nodded and the serving girl stepped out, pulling the door closed for privacy.

Marian held her arms out in welcome. "Well met and God

bless, Father. I am glad to see a servant of God," she said. "What brings you to the castle?"

The monk did not move. He did not speak. He simply stood, bent nearly in half, for a long moment. He appeared to be... listening.

"Father?"

Marian was about to speak again when the monk straightened and pushed back his cowl.

Silver hair shone in a tonsure, a halo around his head. Their eyes met, and her heart locked inside her chest. This "monk" was the cardinal himself. There had to be a pressing reason for him to take such a risk. Her thoughts flew to Robin, filling her with fear that maybe something had happened to him.

Her breath caught in her throat.

The cardinal closed the distance between them and his hands gripped her shoulders. He looked down at her with eyes as green as Sherwood and still clear, despite his age.

"It is good to see you looking well," he said, and he smiled. "We knew that you had been imprisoned, but beyond that..." He let go of her, and stepped back.

"You're risking everything by being here," she said, suddenly realizing that she was shaking. She stopped herself—just barely—before giving in to the temptation to lecture him.

"Just listen," the cardinal said. Marian tilted her head and he continued. "A very important time is upon us. I bring a mission from God to lay at your feet, a task that will require much of you, but it must be done."

"I've proven before that I will do all that I can, give all that I have," she answered, "but as you see for yourself, I'm useless now, trapped here in this tower."

"You might be trapped at the moment, but you shall not be much longer here. It is dark days in Avalon, and you have been chosen for a time such as this. Your role is to be much changed... and will become much greater than what it has been."

Her heart began to beat faster.

"What do you mean?"

"Our rebellion is not working," he said, sadness appearing in his voice. "The darkness is flooding in faster, and our efforts to staunch the tide are quickly becoming futile. There is more that can be done, though, that *must* be done. The Lord Almighty chose you before you were born."

He paused, but she didn't know what to say.

The cardinal stepped close.

"Do you know the story of your parents?"

Marian nodded.

After all the years that had passed, the thought of them still made her chest tighten.

"In your veins runs the blood of the original people of this isle, and the blood of their conquerors. You are the perfect embodiment of England—a true Celt with the bloodline of conquest. You are the truest heir to the kingship of Avalon."

"Me?" She was taken aback.

His hand touched his chest. "I have been destined for the church since I was a child. My father was a priest before me, and his father before him, but grandfather *converted* to the truth of the church, from a life as a druid, the holy people of our ancestors. They foretold this day, and the crisis in which we find ourselves now.

"I had my suspicions about you, always, and recent events have made things clear. My family has been looking for you throughout the ages. The darkness is falling and you are our only hope."

"Cardinal Francis, I've been trapped in this tower for three weeks," she said. "How much worse have things become?"

"The season is fully upon us, and the poor are starving to death," he said. "We are doing everything we can, but they are too many, and we who would help are too few. The winter is bitter, the worst any of us—even the oldest—has ever known.

"John and the Sheriff are growing bolder even as evil gathers around them. The people are oppressed, treated as chattel and slaves. Abused and robbed, they turn on one another. Desperation drives them to avarice, for the arms of sin always open widest to the hurting and the betrayed.

"Across the land sorcery begins to rear its ugly head as witches and wizards and devil worshipers grow bold." He took a deep breath and shook his head sadly. "Children have started to disappear in the night, and the signs show that if things continue unchecked, the Devil himself will walk the earth. It's as if that day at the southern harbor was some kind of unleashing of all manner of evil."

Marian gasped in horror. She had heard him speak of the prophecies, the darkness they were facing, but it made her dizzy to hear how bad it had grown in such little time.

"What can be done?"

Reaching deep inside his robes he pulled out a dark square small enough to fit in his palm. It was a book covered with holy symbols and bound shut by a braided leather cord.

"This is the only thing that can stop John's reign of terror and *you* are the only one who can use it."

He pressed the book into her hands.

The effect was electric.

Energy jolted from her fingertips as they encountered the hard, bone plates that made the book's cover. It sang up her arms, tracing crackling power in a rush of blood set afire in her veins. Her heart beat inside her chest like a bird trying to escape a cage. Numbness swept across her lips, and the strength poured out of her knees like water.

The cardinal's hands locked around her elbows, keeping her from falling to the floor. He studied her with a narrow eye.

"You feel the power of the relic in your hands," he said, as if to confirm his own observations. "God truly *has* marked you for this task."

She nodded, but was unable to speak.

"Then you must take this book to the Heart of England before the next full moon," he continued. "The portents indicate that soon John will reach the height of his power, and he will make his gambit for the throne. What occurs next will determine the destiny of this land."

"The next full moon?" she said, her wits returning. "But that's—"

"Yes, it's the solstice, but not just *any* solstice. The druids named it the Gateway Solstice. It occurs once every hundred generations."

"And where is the Heart of England?" she pressed. "How can it be found? Is it here, in Richard's castle?"

"No child," he said, taking her arm. He led her to the window and pointed. "*There* is the Heart of England, protected round about by the mighty Sherwood Forest." He turned to her, "You must take the book to the center of the forest and find the ancient Oak of Thynghowe. There your course will be revealed."

"I don't understand."

"When logic fails you must go on faith."

"But how will I get there?"

"There is another whom, I believe, has been prepared for such a time as this. Robin must take you. Only together can you do this. Your task is fraught with peril. There are guardians that must be passed, tests to be endured." He sighed deeply, shaking his head at the thought. "Robin alone has the strength, cunning, and integrity to keep you safe and deliver both you and the relic to your appointed destination. He has already faced and defeated some of the forest guardians, so only he can understand what you will be up against."

"I will gladly do this, but how am I to escape?"

As if to punctuate her words, footsteps echoed from the hallway, followed by the sound of voices.

Panic lashed the cardinal's voice.

"Hide the relic, child!" he hissed. "Do not allow the book to leave your possession until you are in Robin's hands—and remember, you must go to the Heart of England *before* the next full moon. If you miss the appointed time, then all will be lost, and England will fall." He pulled the hood over his head again, and resumed the stooped appearance of an older man.

Clutching the tiny book in her fist, fighting her own panic, Marian looked left and right for a place to hide it. She turned from the cardinal and pulled up her skirts. Fingers working swiftly she tucked the book into the garter tight around her thigh, then dropped the skirts with a silent prayer it would go undiscovered.

The door banged open and she turned.

"Well, what do we have here?"

King John shoved Chastity before him. She stumbled and fell to the ground, scrambling instantly to her feet, moving out of the way of John and the two soldiers who were following him.

The two were masked, harsh iron helms covering their features, only black slits through which they could look out. They loomed behind him, impossibly broad. They were far taller than any men she had ever seen, the tops of their covered heads nearly brushing the ceiling. Yet their backs were stooped slightly, and humped. Deadly curved blades that looked to be stained with blood swung from thick leather belts. A stench emanated from them that made her involuntarily press her hand to her face.

There was something wrong here—something terribly, dreadfully wrong—and she struggled to comprehend what it could be. All she knew for certain was that fear was creeping through her, threatening to paralyze her.

Looking away from them, her eyes fell on the usurper.

He had changed.

John wore a mantle of midnight, inky shadows that seemed to move and slide over one another, like a slithering ball of snakes. On his head sat a crown built from the skulls of small creatures. Their empty, fragile eye sockets stared at her.

She stepped forward, moving between John and the cardinal. She pushed her fear aside, reaching in her mind for a response.

"I called for this monk because I haven't been to mass in too long, and needed reconciliation," she said. "I did not mean to be a trouble."

From the depths of his hooded cloak, the cardinal spoke weakly. "I'll take my leave."

At a motion from John, the two soldiers shuffled forward, blocking him with their bulk, mail-gloved hands clamping on his arms.

"You'll go nowhere." He looked at Marian, eyes slit as he studied her. "How did you send for him, Princess?"

Marian hesitated, unsure of what to say.

"I fetched him, sire." Chastity stepped forward, head down.

John turned his attention to the serving girl, eyeing her narrowly.

"You chose well, wench. This is no simple monk you've brought to us today." John's voice sounded almost pleasant, lilting over the words as he stepped close to the hooded man. In the next breath he turned, words curdling into a harsh snarl. "Where is it?"

"The monastery?" the cardinal replied. "It's on a hill just above—"

The wet smack of a fist striking flesh cut his words short.

Marian winced.

"I know about the book, fool!" John spat. "You will tell me where it is."

Marian blinked, intensely aware of the weight pressed against her leg. The symbols etched on the cover blazed in her mind's eye. A small portion, the tiniest bit of the feeling she'd had when touching it, trilled through her. She thought of the urgency he'd expressed when he had entrusted it to her, as if he knew the book itself was in danger.

"The only book I know is the Holy Writ of God." Francis's voice was strong. Unwavering.

A second blow knocked the priest's legs out from under him. He hung in the hands of the soldiers. She knew he was willing to die to protect the book and its secrets, but she would be damned if she watched it happen.

"Do not lie to me!" John's fist raised again.

Marian darted forward, throwing her body between the coming blow and the cardinal.

"Stop, just stop!" Her hands shoved hard against John's chest, pushing him back. "Haven't you done enough?"

His mouth curled, revealing sharply pointed teeth.

"Insolent whore!" He pulled a knife from his belt, the blade notched from hard use, but still sharp. "I'll teach you a lesson you'll never forget."

Anger boiled in her chest. She stepped closer, fists clenched.

"You wouldn't dare," she gritted. "The king will flay you alive if you harm me."

"My brother is not here."

"He will return."

"Do not be so sure, little Princess. Death has no respect for royalty."

"You've never spoken truer words, *Prince John*."

The cardinal spoke behind her. "It is alright, Maid Marian. Let him do his worst. God is in control."

His words brought back his warning and commission to her from just moments before. He trusted her with a task, and that task was more important than the both of them. She turned to face him. The skin over his left eye had swollen shut, and a split on his cheekbone bled freely, blood running down parchment-thin skin. He looked at her intently, and she could read in his eyes what he was thinking.

The book is what John wants. Our lives are forfeit if he finds it. All of our lives...

Maybe there was hope for the cardinal's survival. As long as John thought he knew where the book was, then the monk should live. Maybe she could orchestrate a way for him to escape, if not today, then tomorrow. Chastity would help her, call in all her favors with the other castle girls.

Hope flared briefly inside her.

She stepped aside.

"I will have that book," John hissed.

"There is no book," the cardinal said. "It's a rumor, a lie spread to bring fear to all who defy the Lord God. A story to check the vipers that would destroy this land, usurp the king, and blaspheme the Most High."

"I don't believe you," John said. "I know the book exists, as it has for centuries, watched over by your predecessors—and now by you."

"You're mad." The cardinal's voice was quiet, but even.

Silence fell like thunder. It stretched into the room, the warning of a coming storm.

"Take him to the dungeon," John said. "Strip and search him."

The soldiers nodded. As one they dragged the cardinal to the door. He looked at her over his shoulder, his eyes telling her one last time to be strong. Then as they left the room, John stepped close to her.

"That will be the last visitor you ever see."

She wanted to demand the cardinal's release, to insist upon his safety, but she held her tongue. The holy man's exhortation, to safeguard the book and deliver it to its rightful place, repeated inside her head. She also feared that if she pushed, he would cut off her access to the few servants loyal to her—particularly to Chastity, whom she needed now more than ever.

King John turned on his heel, stalking out without a backward glance. The door slammed shut and Marian blinked after him, not sure if she had seen him actually touch the door or not. It was almost as if he had waved his hand in its direction, and it had closed on its own.

Chastity rushed to her side. "Are you alright?"

Marian nodded. "I will be."

Striding to the window, she pushed open the glass and pressed her face between the bars, drinking deeply of the crisp air. The clean scent of the forest rolled across in a light wind, scouring away the raw anger and fear that burned inside her.

Head clear, she turned and walked to the bed.

She took a deep breath.

"I need to find a way to escape."

"We can figure something out," Chastity said.

Marian glanced at her.

"I don't want harm coming to you," she said firmly. "Even if I manage to escape, all is for naught if I can't quickly find the man I'm looking for."

Chastity raised one eyebrow. "Any particular man?" she asked, her voice uncertain.

"The Hood."

"Oh." Chastity stepped back. Her hands fidgeted with the fabric of her skirt. "There is a price on his head. Even if word could be sent to him, he wouldn't dare come anywhere near here. He's too smart for that. They say John *hates* him. He'll skin him alive if he ever catches him. No one knows his true identity. Some even claim more than one man is the Hood."

Marian had never trusted Chastity with the secret of the Hood, although she wouldn't have been surprised if the smart young woman had guessed at it. Certainly she might have guessed at Robin's involvement.

"You know who he is," Marian said.

Chastity licked her lips.

"I reckon I do. Doesn't make him easier to find."

"If you go into the forest, he'll find you," Marian said, unwilling to send her to Will or Friar Tuck. If Chastity was followed then their lives, too, were put in danger. Robin could protect himself—and Chastity, if it came to that.

"I'll go myself," the girl said. "Tonight."

"Not tonight." As much as it pained her, Marian shook her head. "They'll be looking for us to make some sort of move, forced by panic to make a mistake."

"Then tomorrow night," Chastity said.

"Yes," she agreed. "Hopefully that will be soon enough."

Chastity nodded. "Tomorrow night I will find him."

Marian's hand touched her friend's arm. "Thank you. You have no idea how important it is."

"You say it's important, that's enough for me, Princess."

Chastity turned and went out the door. The scrape of the bolt being thrown rang like church bells at a hanging.

CHAPTER SIXTEEN

His bare feet stuck to the flagstones, just slightly, as he moved back to the brazier and dropped the iron pliers on the hot coals. The wet jaws of the tool sizzled against the embers as blood boiled away and the tiny scraps of flesh stuck to the rough teeth began to cook.

The blood underfoot was turning tacky.

"Was that fun for you?"

John turned to the doorway where the Sheriff stood.

"I find myself enjoying things like this more and more as we go forward."

"I was talking to him, Princeling." The Sheriff tilted his head, indicating the man hanging from his wrists in the center of the room.

"Oh," John said, "he's not talking."

The Sheriff walked over, standing close to the man, studying him. He was naked, in good shape for a man of his advanced age. His skin hung loose on a slender frame with very little paunch.

"He told you nothing?"

"No."

The Sheriff grunted.

John felt the disapproval across the cell.

"He's stronger than he looks."

"A compulsion spell didn't work?"

"Not on him."

The Sheriff grunted again, and leaned close to Cardinal Francis's face. The older monk's eyes were swollen, turning black, and the side of his lower lip hung loose, torn free at the edge. The Sheriff sniffed deeply.

"Is it true? Are you that strong?"

The cardinal swallowed hard, throat working past the raw burning that had stolen his voice, struggling to speak.

"Come with it, monk," the Sheriff said. "Speak freely."

The man's voice was tiny, barely a whisper, and broken as if poured over salt.

"I am... nothing." He swallowed. "Christ... in me is strong."

The Sheriff stepped back, lip curled in disgust.

"I told you," John said.

"Your cursed Nazarene won't keep you from dying," the Sheriff told Cardinal Francis.

The holy man's mouth moved, but no words came out.

"Leave him," the Sheriff said, moving toward the door.

"Where are we going?"

"I'm going to put an end to that damned monastery."

"Do you want me to come with you?"

The Sheriff turned and looked him up then down. "No, Princeling, but I do want you to put your clothes back on."

As he left the room, John called behind him.

"I didn't want to get blood on them."

Much the miller's son was used to being ignored.

It was right and proper that he was ignored. Who was he after all? The only son of a poor miller and his wife, born late in their lives when both had forgotten how to interact with a child. He didn't feel it as a lack of love—despite the hard work his father laid on him—just a distance. He'd grown up alone in a house with two other people, quiet and isolated. He didn't talk much, didn't draw notice, and so people ignored him.

He paid attention to them, however. *Close* attention. People had a funny way of saying the truth when they thought no one was around to hear them.

He'd stumbled upon one of those moments on the road.

Walking back toward his father's mill, after fetching needle and thread for his mother from the village market, he'd been pushed off the road by a regiment of soldiers. At their head was the Sheriff of Nottingham astride a cobalt-black charger. It was the biggest horse Much had ever seen, its chest and shoulders knotted with muscle upon muscle as it strode down the lane. Passing by, its long head swung toward him. Dark marble eyes fell on him and he swore they blazed red in the sunlight.

The Sheriff did not look down. He sat spine straight and staring ahead. White-blonde hair hung from his scalp in a thick braid. The Sheriff's face was clean-shaven, the skin smooth over sharply angled cheekbones and jawline. A straight and patrician nose jutted over a mouth with thin, villainous lips.

His hand rested on the hilt of a long bastard sword that rode his hip. Hatchmark lines cut the pommel, forming a ruby red star. It was the same red star that blazed from his breastplate, the symbol somehow sinister in the eye of the beholder. Much couldn't see where the Sheriff ended and the mighty warhorse began, the man's black leather armor blending perfectly with the beast beneath him.

Behind him marched a column of dog soldiers, King John's personal guard and the right hand of the Sheriff. The ground rumbled beneath their boots, making the grass shake and sway. These were the soldiers who'd arrived with the Sheriff just days after Prince John had been installed in the castle. These were the soldiers who took everything when the Sheriff came to collect the taxes that seemed to be needed every few days.

These were the men who destroyed property, and took prisoner any who couldn't pay.

They marched in perfect rhythm, hobnail boots rising and

falling in lock-stepped unison. Each carried a weapon, some a fierce sword, some a powerful war hammer, some their own deadly instruments twisted with blades and spikes and chains that looked like they'd been forged in the furnaces of Hell itself. The same fiery red pentagram glowed on their black steel breastplates, like lava under cracked basalt.

Much fought to keep his mouth closed as they marched by.

Behind them came what was left of King Richard's men. Too old, too out-of-shape, or too cowardly to join the king in the crusade. They were a motley assortment of men, eyes downcast, unshaven, unkempt. Their armor was shabby, their weapons spotted with rust and pitted by corrosion. They dribbled along behind the Sheriff's men in straggled groups of two or three.

After a moment's thought, he crouched low in the grass, watching and listening for all he was worth. The last two soldiers dragged their feet as they walked past with their horses. They acted as if they really didn't want to reach their destination. With each step they took, the gap between them and the rest of the regiment grew.

Much crawled closer to the edge of the road as they drew near to his hiding place. Their voices came to his ears.

"...used to be something," the taller man said to his companion. "I was a sergeant of the guard."

"I remember," the shorter one said. He was older than the tall man, armor pushed out across a stomach it wasn't forged to fit. "You were an arsehole about it, too. I'm glad you're the same rank as me now."

"I'm still higher rank. *I'm* a private first rank."

"You made that up," the short one replied glumly. "We're all just privates since the Sheriff took over the garrison."

The taller man grunted. They took a few more dawdling steps before he spoke again.

"I don't like them."

The shorter guard shrugged.

"They don't care."

"Damn Hessians."

"Those ain't Hessians."

"How would you know?"

"My wife's half Hessian."

Tall man looked at him. "I didn't know that."

"Why would you?" the short guard said. "Regardless, those soldiers ain't Hessian, but they *are* King John's men."

"He'll go too far one of these days."

"Maybe, but so what? Who'll stop him? Every witch and devil in the land is enslaved by him," the short one said.

"And what does that make us, that we consort with the man who deals with dark forces?"

"Smart," the short one replied. "Survivors. Alive and well-fed." They stopped walking as the short one pulled off his boot and shook out a small stone. "Unlike everyone else."

"But God—"

"God has abandoned this land. At least He will after today. He's off in Jerusalem with the king, and cares nothing for the likes of us. We have to take care of ourselves." He slipped his foot back into the boot, shivering from the cold.

"It doesn't feel right."

"What doesn't?"

"The monastery."

"What has the monastery ever done for you? All they've done for me is take my tithe so the monks don't have to work." The short one spat on the ground and started walking again. "I say good riddance."

The lanky soldier began to walk, shaking his head. "Burning the place still seems wrong."

Much recoiled in horror. He stumbled back, sliding down the side of the ditch. His pants scraped against loose stones, tumbling them free to beat the dry winter rushes. He froze at the noise, praying they'd not heard him.

If they did, they gave no notice.

"If we drag arse enough," the tall man said, "it will be ashes by the time we arrive. We might work for the devil, but we don't have to participate in all his handiwork."

The two kept walking, voices fading from his ears as Much backed away from the road. When he thought it safe, he fled toward home, cutting through the edge of Sherwood.

I have to tell Father.

His father would know what to do.

CHAPTER SEVENTEEN

Young Much spilled out of the trees where the forest crept close to the river. He and his family lived in a small house behind the mill.

He was surprised to find the mill empty. Even here in the midst of winter, midday was the time of hustle and bustle, the village wives coming in to have their corn or grains turned to meal and flour, but the building was shuttered and the door barred. Things had been different this winter, harder, and people brought in less, but still the door should have been open. His scalp went tight with worry.

Moving quickly, he entered the house, pausing for a second to let his eyes adjust from the sun outside to the gloom inside. His mother only allowed candles or lamps at sundown, making them last longer to save money. His vision was just beginning to adjust when the smell hit him.

Blood.

The air in the house was rich with the iron tang of blood.

His mouth went dry, heart clenching into a fist that squeezed his throat shut. He pushed through the front room, moving toward the back of the house. He didn't call out—he couldn't—but his mind raced.

What has happened to my parents? he wondered frantically. *Bandits? The Sheriff's men?*

Noise came then from the back room, the room where they ate their meals. Light spilled under the closed door.

He crept to it.

Put his hand on the rough wood.

Pushed.

The door swung open.

The warm glow of candles washed over him, carrying the sweet scent of honeyed beeswax. The table was covered by the body of a stag. It was a massive, majestic creature, a true prince of the forest. A slender arrow shaft jutted from its breast where its heart had been pierced.

Robin of the Hood smiled at him from behind it.

Relief flooded him as his mother and father came in from the kitchen. They were alive and well. Understanding followed the relief. They'd closed the mill because of Robin, to keep his visit a secret and to keep his gift of game a secret, as well. Meat was a rare thing for the family, a visit by the great man even rarer.

Robin stood straight and tall, face shining with a light that made him look like one of the angels that Friar Tuck would tell stories about. St. Michael the Archangel made flesh. He wasn't the biggest man Much had ever seen, but he filled the room with his presence. He was a king and an outlaw, the dark justice of Sherwood. Not everyone knew that, but Much knew, because Much listened and watched, and those at the monastery had trusted him when they were battling the pox. Just being in his presence made Much feel like he could be better, *wanted* to be better, nobler, more heroic.

He smiled back, he couldn't help it.

"There's the lad with the ears of a fox and the eyes of a hawk," Robin said. "I can tell even now that you have brought news of great importance. It burns in your eyes."

Much swelled with pride and snuck a quick look at his father to see if he'd noticed the praise Robin had given him. His father nodded at him, and Much thrilled for the second time.

The moment passed, though, as Much remembered the

urgency of his information. The smile left his face as quickly as it had come.

"I have news, but it isn't good."

"Go ahead and say it, son," his father urged.

Much swallowed. "I overheard two soldiers on the road. There were a whole lot of them. They said the Sheriff plans to burn the monastery."

The news fell into the midst of them, and lay as still as the corpse cooling on the table.

"He wouldn't dare," his mother breathed after a moment of silence. Her hand flew into the sign of the cross.

"Wouldn't he?" his father asked. "He dares much since his arrival. He's taxed us to poverty, and hurt our friends and neighbors. He's evil personified."

"But the church!" His mother tore at her apron, cheeks red and wet with tears. "How could he?"

"I assume with torches and fuel, Capricia." His father's voice was as harsh as his words. "Now get a grip on yourself!"

Robin stepped around the table. All cheer was gone from his features. His face shone with a dark light, features carved into hard lines. Much imagined the Angel of Death's countenance would look exactly like that. Robin picked up his bow and headed for the door.

Much scrambled out of the way.

Robin stopped and laid a hand on his shoulder.

"Thank you, lad."

"Where are you going?" Much's father asked.

"To put an end to this tyranny once and for all." Robin's eyes glinted darkly. "Even if it kills me."

Three times.

Three times that morning, imps of the devil had interrupted Friar Tuck's supplications to the Lord, showing him dark and frightening visions so disturbing he'd barely been able to speak.

He'd always had such visions, though sporadically. Since Cardinal Francis had broken the devil's hold on him they had intensified, coming almost every night and with a clarity that shook him. They boded ill, not just for the day, but for the future of everyone in Nottingham.

Tuck was sure of it.

The village on the edge of Sherwood Forest was one of his personal favorites to visit. The walk from the monastery was a bit long for his short stride, but the road was even and it gave him time to think. He passed villagers in the snow-covered fields, looking for stragglers of wheat or corn, tending shivering sheep and cattle who ate frozen chaff, and combing roadside plots of weeds for any wild vegetables that might be hardy enough to grow beneath the hard, cold ground.

They hadn't waved to him, hadn't looked up, simply continued to work. They were good people, simple and made pure by hard work, good harvest, and the word of God. It was the way life had worked for generations. It was what the people deserved.

They deserved protection.

They deserved their king.

God's plan had been usurped.

The village chapel was where he met those who should protect the people in the absence of the nation's true defender, King Richard. God had called the Lionheart away to other tasks, across the ocean to defend the true faith.

More than once, however, Friar Tuck had thought that the king might have been heeding a different voice.

Then he would do penance for harboring such thoughts and suspicions.

But really, it was hard for him to dodge those fiery darts when tyrants were left in charge, tormenting the people and taking from them the precious little they had.

Soldiers came at the backs of tax collectors like a plague of armed locusts, to strip the people of the fruits of their hard work. They forced the villagers to load wagons full of their harvest to be taken away, leaving behind only scraps and starvation. The desire to express his wrath in a physical way rode him hard.

His burden on behalf of the people weighed around his neck like a stone.

He believed—no, he *knew*—that God would not long suffer his children to remain in such a state. Had not God himself called up heroes to fight for the people in the world? To lead them into battle?

One in particular.

Even if he was reluctant to accept his destiny.

Tuck left the chapel, making his rounds. The visions he'd experienced that morning remained vivid in his memory.

During the morning's visions, he'd heard the incessant chattering and whispering of imps and demons, plotting even now to make the plight of the people harder. They schemed to plunge England into a state of darkness, to cut it off from the Creator, and make it a loathsome place where the Devil himself would walk freely. A desolation from which he could launch attacks against all of Christendom.

The first vision had been of a dark place, deep in the heart of some forgotten, God-forsaken wilderness. Everything was dead. Everything. Trees once majestic and laden with life had been reduced to twisted husks. Nothing grew in that place— no animals, no birds, not even the lowest crawling thing. The stench of death and evil lay heavy upon it. Something terrible had happened there, something so foul and blasphemous that the place itself had been cursed for the remainder of time, and even Almighty God had turned his back upon it.

Then the demons revealed the end of the first vision. It was of Tuck himself standing in the middle of that wretched place, screaming desperately for God to hear him.

But the Lord was silent.

The second vision blasted his soul as the first one faded.

He saw a spoiled bog. Dead creatures floated on its surface, bloated and rotting, half-submerged by the weight of their slowly dissolving flesh. The air was so rank, so choked with poison, that he could not breathe. A man—no, a creature—rose out of the bog as though ascending from Hell itself. When at last it stood free of the scum-crusted pond it was more than a foot taller than the average man.

Strange designs were tattooed onto its arms and chest, spilling under raw skin across slabs of muscle. Antlers grew from its head, tangled and gnarled like a bramble of wicked bone, and its feet were not feet at all but black cloven hooves. Its eyes glowed the crimson of spilled blood. A horsehide cloak and loincloth were its only coverings.

It threw back its head and laughed, and out of its mouth spilled perversions and filth to which the friar had been forced to listen. While he watched this abomination, the imps whispered in his ear that the doom of Robin Longstride was at hand, for here was his slayer.

Friar Tuck tried desperately to shake off these dark thoughts as he headed across the square. There were things to which he needed to attend, and besides, one could never trust demons to tell the truth. Their currency was lies and perversion.

These thoughts kept him from noticing the figure who watched him with amusement from a few feet away.

"You look to be in better spirits," a voice said. "Have you been at a secret cache of good monkish whiskey?"

Friar Tuck stopped mid-stride. Alan-a-Dale sat on the edge of the village well. He'd donned a salmon-colored tunic, which was tucked into blue-checkered pants. A lemon-and-grass cloak pinned over both made him a bright splash painted on the dull backdrop of the village.

A simple wooden flute hung from the silver scale belt at his waist. With it he could form a tune or charm a sparrow. His ancient yew harp rested in slender hands and he wore a heavy gold torc around his slender neck, both of them older than even the monastery.

He was a minstrel, a skald, the very image of a Celtic bard

stepped from the pages of a book. Alan strummed the harp, lifting his smooth voice along the scale.

Oh, I once knew a friar who loved him some ale
Had it for breakfast and supper without fail
He drank and he drank until he was ever so fat
I wonder what the good Lord would think about that

The bard ended with a flourish and a laugh.

"A full belly and a warm hearth are all the thanks I get," Tuck growled, "for looking after the wretched, depraved souls, lost and wandering in the devil's own wilderness." He gave Alan a serious look, and added, "Souls such as your own."

As he wondered why Alan was approaching him in public, instead of contacting him at the monastery or in the forest, Tuck tried to rid himself of the third vision the demons had shown him that morning. Yet as he stared at his friend's smiling face, he couldn't help remember what he had seen.

The demons had shown him Alan-a-Dale, draped in chains of black iron, trapped in a dark and terrible dungeon.

Beaten.

Tortured.

Swollen, his face was nearly unrecognizable, cheekbones broken and his skin painted with his own blood.

Bards were sacrosanct, untouchable, accorded great leniency in return for speaking the truth. Their satire could be so harsh that it could cut skin, yet they were depended upon for news and gossip, sought by king and peasant alike.

In the vision, Tuck had watched as a figure cloaked in darkness pulled a wicked knife from a bucket of hot coals. It glowed red, and as the vision had dissolved into darkness, all that was left were screams and the smell of cooking meat in his nose.

He shook his head to clear the image from his mind.

"Let's go into the chapel," Tuck suggested for the benefit of prying ears, "that I might better pray for your wayward soul."

Alan nodded, and followed him inside.

As soon as the door was shut, Tuck turned to him.

"What has brought you here," he hissed, "dressed as such?"

"I've decided it was high time I took my position as a true bard."

Friar Tuck frowned, but remained silent.

"What is it, my friend?" Alan asked, and he smiled. "Do I not look fine?"

"It makes you a target," the friar replied.

"I am already a target," he said. "We all are. Mayhap this way I can draw the fire from the rest of our merry band of fellows."

"That's not the point."

Suddenly the church door flew open, crashing against the wall and causing the statues of saints to jitter and jig inside their cubbyholes. Tuck spun as quickly as his girth would allow.

"This is the house of God," he bellowed. "Show some respect."

Alan-a-Dale touched him on the shoulder.

"Don't be so harsh," he said. "It's just a lad." Tuck could see how Alan would make such a mistake. Slender and wiry, in the androgynous, pre-bloom stage of youth, and dressed in the rough clothes of the village boys, Lenore was very tall for a girl—taller than the friar himself already. She was short of breath, as if she had run a long distance. Her cheeks were full of color, eyes wide with panic.

"What is it?" he asked her. "What's wrong, child?"

"The Sheriff," she said between gulps of air. "He's coming."

Friar Tuck blinked. The Sheriff rarely put in an appearance himself, usually relying on his lackeys to do his dirty work. Whatever was happening, it couldn't be good.

"Go out the back door and return to the monastery," he said, shooing her away. "Go! Quick like a bunny."

She nodded, gathered herself, and scampered through the church.

As soon as she was gone they heard the clop of horse's hooves approaching on the road at a rapid pace.

"What does the devil's bastard want today?" Friar Tuck hissed.

"Perhaps to confess his sins," Alan offered sarcastically. "I'm sure they are many."

Moments later, a tall, angled form darkened the doorway, blocking the afternoon sun from outside. Black eyes glittered from the shadow cast by a shock of white-blonde hair. White teeth flashed, and the friar couldn't tell if it was a smile or a grimace.

The man stepped in, swinging booted feet, the hobnailed soles chiming out small sparks against the flagstone floor. A wide-bladed sword hung from his hip, and one gloved hand was on the hilt as he entered the church. Friar Tuck bristled, fighting to keep his lip from turning up in disdain.

"Sheriff, good morning to you," he said, forcing his voice to stay even, but the Sheriff of Nottingham ignored him. His eyes slid over to the bard.

"What are you doing here?"

Alan bowed with a flourish. "Even a humble bard must take the time to confess his sins."

"Get out."

"Do not think you have power over me."

The Sheriff bared his teeth. "I am the law."

"No, I am the law." Alan drew himself upright. "I am the law and the lore and the lyric."

The Sheriff looked at him, his face gone from scowling to interested, as if he had never seen Alan before.

It made Tuck nervous.

He touched his friend's arm.

"Thank you. I can handle this."

Alan bowed again, picked up his harp, and walked away without a backward glance, leaving the Sheriff and Friar Tuck alone. Outside the door Friar Tuck counted at least a dozen soldiers, armed to the teeth. A heaviness was in the air and he dreaded to find out exactly what the Sheriff's latest atrocity was going to be.

"I've been collecting taxes for John today, instead of Locksley," the man announced.

"I see."

"So many can't seem to pay." The Sheriff's hand stroked his sword hilt, making the rings of his mail shirt whisper against one another like conspiring snakes. "Some will have to go to prison for this, of course."

He held his tongue.

"Others I know once held certain items of value, trinkets and heirlooms that might be applied to their debt, but it seems many of them have been seized by a sudden fit of piousness, and have given these things to the church."

It was true. Many of the people gave their most valued possessions to the church, rather than see them go to Prince John. It was the same in villages across the countryside. Tuck personally had helped dozens of families save their treasures in that manner.

"People give what they can to the service of the Lord." He shrugged, palms raised.

"They give the church what they should be giving to me," the Sheriff snarled, his mouth twisting. He looked feral, like a rabid animal. "I mean to get it back."

At that he lifted his hand. Soldiers poured into the church, their boots shaking the floor, bodies shoving aside the wooden pews.

"What's the meaning of this?" Tuck demanded.

The Sheriff spoke over his head, addressing the soldiers.

"Search the place," he commanded. "Take anything of value."

"This is the house of God!" Tuck protested. "You can't do that!" He lunged forward to block one soldier's path.

The soldier just drove his sword hilt into the priest's stomach. Friar Tuck fell to his knees, gasping for air, fighting to keep his breakfast from spilling onto the floor.

"God lives in Heaven. He has no need of earthly things," the

Sheriff spat. "John, on the other hand, lives here on Earth, and his need is great. Move out of our way or—"

"Or what?" Friar Tuck demanded, struggling to his feet.

The Sheriff smiled. "Ask your friends at the monastery."

Suddenly Friar Tuck realized there was a commotion outside the chapel. Shrill cries and shouts of alarm sang through the doorway. Terror flooding his chest, Friar Tuck shoved past the soldiers and stumbled outside.

The air was gray.

Confusion flared inside him.

Fog on a winter day? The cold, brisk air should be clear. Lord, how can this be?

His eyes searched, past the huts and the homes, past the road that cut through the countryside and up over the ridge. There, in the distance, he saw a crimson glow and a column of black smoke coiling like an angry serpent into the blue, blue sky. Then he knew.

The monastery is on fire.

CHAPTER EIGHTEEN

A fist smacked the side of Lenore's head. It wasn't intentional, just a clenched hand in the confusion of a panicked crowd, but it still watered her eyes and rang her ears.

She fell against a woman, bouncing off an ample hip. Taking a deep breath, and ducking her head, she pushed on.

The air grew thick with smoke, making it hard to see. Hard to breathe. She pulled her tunic collar up over her face. It helped, but a cough settled deep in her lungs, a tickle midway down her throat that she swallowed to hold at bay.

Someone dropped a bucket of water in front of her. It landed flat, sloshing water onto the dirt but staying upright. The hand that let it slip didn't reach for it and without thinking, Lenore snatched it up.

Water to the fire… water to the fire… Have to help!

Her thoughts jumbled, confused and falling all over one another. Above people's heads she could see the top of the monastery walls and the sooty black smoke that billowed into the sky. This was her home, the place where she'd lived for the last year. She had to do something to help.

The bucket was heavy, dragging her arms down, icy water splashing over her waist as the bottom of the pail bounced off her legs. Her feet slipped as she got closer, the heat of the flames melting the snow into a muddy slick around the walls. She shoved people aside with her shoulders as she pushed forward. The crowd parted and she tripped into the heat of the inferno, spilling the water over the slowly browning grass.

A black-armored soldier ran his sword through Friar Hanson, just three feet away from her.

She screamed as the blade folded the monk in half. Friar Hanson turned his face toward her as he lay over the soldier's gauntleted arm. His mouth moved, but no sound came out, only blood spilled from his lips and onto his chest. Brown eyes, eyes that had been so kind as he taught her the basics of mathematics, fluttered then drooped half-lidded as their light went out.

Something broke in Lenore's chest. It split wide, spilling a boiling torrent of rage into her. Screaming through clenched teeth she charged the soldier. He looked up in surprise as she swung the heavy wooden pail at his head. The hardwood rim crashed against his helmet with a *clang* that jolted all the way down her arm.

Shoving the dead monk off his blade he growled, the noise tearing through the roar of the flames behind him. He turned and backhanded her, the slap knocking her off her feet and driving the air from her lungs. The rough links of the mail glove tore the skin along her jaw.

Stepping over, he straddled her, one booted foot on each side as she lay in the puddle created by Father Hanson's blood. Lit from behind by the inferno, he looked monstrous. Rage had flown from her with his blow, and now cold fear—colder than the muddy ground upon which she lay—settled into the marrow of her bones. He *seethed* above her, all glittering eyes, sharp teeth, and an evil blade that dripped the life of someone she knew.

Oh, God, please save me.

Alan-a-Dale's eyes burned from the acrid smoke that stacked the air in layers. A woman stumbled in front of him and he snatched her arm, holding her up. If she went to the ground she would be trampled. She turned wild eyes up at him and jerked free. He watched as she ran. Trained by years at his vocation, his mind instantly began turning the incident into verse.

> *With trembling step and halting gait*
> *The frightened deer made her escape*
> *Running far and running free*
> *From the fiery flames she did flee*

It would go into his song, fulfilling his duty to record the inferno at the monastery, giving it a proper place in history… but later, much later. He filed it away, pushing the snippet to the back of his mind, then turned to look for Friar Tuck. He had to find his friend.

He'd seen the girl-child, Lenore, as she'd gone toward the garden around the back of the monastery, just outside the brick walls. He pushed and shoved in that direction, hands raised to protect the ancient harp strapped to his shoulder.

There, he thought, spotting her just ahead.

He'd seen the concern in Tuck's eyes. The monk would be hunting for her, making certain she was safe, so he trailed after her, bumping and shoving against the villagers who crowded around, some trying to help, most stumbling in shock and awe at the level of destruction.

The monastery provided an anchor to these people, offering stability and hope for something beyond the toil of life. It was the house of God, but also the hospital for the village, where the monks applied healing arts to body, heart, and soul.

Now it had been laid low by consuming fire.

He broke through the crowd. A wall of heat nearly knocked him flat, intense and merciless. Black-armored soldiers stood close to the structure, unaffected by the waves that threatened to dry the eyeballs from his skull. They used their blades to drive monks back into the inferno, hitting them with the flat steel like balls in a child's game.

Faces split in wolf grin
Blood dript upon their chin
They lay flame to the house of God and all trapped within

Alan swallowed the acid that lurched into his throat. There was nothing he could do for them. He turned away, sick in his heart, moving along the front of the crowd, looking for the young girl.

He found her on her back next to a dead monk. A soldier crouched over her with murder in his eyes.

The Sheriff's man raised his bloody sword, mouth twisted in a snarl. Alan took a step then stopped.

The girl was good as dead. There was nothing he could do. He was too far away. He had no weapon.

No weapon.

Slender fingers scrabbled at the well-worn straps that bound the yew-wood harp to his shoulder. They parted in seconds, releasing the instrument from its position of protection and honor. The grooves in the spine of the harp called to his fingers, the arch of the harp notched to lovingly cup his cheek. Thick calluses brushed across the taut strings made of brass, iron, silver, and gold. They hummed to life, the vibration buzzing through the bones of his face—not music, not yet, but the promise of it.

He *did* have a weapon.

The most powerful weapon of all.

He was a bard of the old tradition.

Woe be to the man who trifled with him.

Swimming through the heat, he moved toward the soldier. As he drew near his hand struck the strings, calling forth a razor-sharp chord. It rang out, and Alan felt the Awen spark inside him.

The music flew straight and true, striking the soldier. He jerked his head, black iron coif jingling ring upon ring, to look at the bard. Alan kept walking, fingers plucking out note after note. It was fuel to the fire of the Awen, stoking the furnace of the

Celtic spirit inside him until it burned as hot as the monastery.

He was the Singer of the Song, the Keeper of the Truth and Law, the Voice of the People.

He was an awenydd, a bard.

His voice rose, spilling from his throat and carried across the distance by the music of the ancient harp. The soldier staggered. The world fell away as he sang of truth and light.

> *Melt away o' wax of evil*
> *Blow away o' smoke of iniquity*
> *Fall before the strength of*
> *The Goodly-Wise and the Many-Gifted*
> *Righteousness shall prevail over thee*
> *And cut you off at the knee.*

The soldier staggered with each line, hips folding and knees buckling. Lenore scrambled, scurrying away. Alan kept singing, power pouring off him with each note, with each chord he struck.

Finally the soldier crumpled to the ground, greenish ichor spilling from under his black iron helmet as he howled in agony.

Caught in the song, Alan didn't see the blow that felled him.

Lungs burning and legs trembling, Friar Tuck reached the monastery.

It was a column of red flame and black smoke. Back at the chapel, when he had turned back from the doorway to accuse the Sheriff, he found himself alone.

The man had vanished. So he did the only thing he could.

He ran.

Soldiers were milling about, blades and firebrands in their hands. The flames trailed from the ends, as if not wanting to separate from the inferno inside the walls. Despair washed over him. This was his home—had been since his family had delivered him to the service of the Lord, the fourth son and one too many mouths to feed. He bore no malice for them. At this point in life he didn't know them any longer. Any pain that came from their abandonment had been lost in his love for priesthood. *This* was his family.

The brothers here his kin and kith.

To see it destroyed left him gutted.

Knees weak, he began to fall to the ground before a sharp thought drew him upright.

"Lenore!" he shouted as he ran around the burning structure. The heat was nearly unbearable, beating at him through his coarse robes. Every doorway was blocked by flames. He could see no way in. Hanging out of one of the windows was the body of a monk on fire. He ran to help, but backed away when he realized the man, his brother in the Lord, was already dead.

The villagers milled about and he could hear the horror in their words. Their cries echoed in his heart.

Something had changed. As recently as a week ago, the Sheriff would *never* have done something this bold. Could it be true? Had he really made a deal with the Dark One? Or was there something he knew that the rest of them didn't?

Fear clenched his guts.

Has King Richard been killed? Is John now our ruler, and the Sheriff free to do as he wills? As he passed the well house a low, bitter sobbing caught his attention. All around him people wept openly, but this was quiet, muffled, as though someone didn't want to be heard. Listening closely, he followed the sound. A few feet away, behind the woodpile, he found Lenore—huddled in terror, bitter tears streaking down her face.

"Thank God," he whispered, sinking to his knees next to her. "Praise be to Jesus, you weren't in there, child."

"It was the Sheriff's men," she croaked, her voice raw. "They taunted the monks, wouldn't let them escape, and told them that all men of God had the same fate coming to them, or worse." Her words struck him like a fist.

Or worse? What could be worse than this?

He shuddered at the very thought.

As he looked again at the flaming structure, at the body of his dead brother monk smoldering in the window, he couldn't imagine what worse would look like. Lenore's trembling hand caught his sleeve and he looked down.

Eyes wide and unblinking in shock the girl spoke, voice thin and thready.

"One of the soldiers tried to…" she began, and her words trailed off.

Fear caught in his throat. "What is it child? Are you hurt?"

"He saved me. The man with the harp. But…" She turned her head. "I'm sorry I ran away."

"Alan-a-Dale?" Snatches of his vision flashed in his mind. He lifted her to her feet. "Where, child? Show me!" Lenore shook herself and took a deep breath. In her face he saw the determination he had seen before. The girl had a fierce spirit and it was coming to the surface now. She nodded once sharply and turned away, moving around the flame-torn monastery. Friar Tuck started after her, offering a prayer that they would not be too late.

The fire was glorious.

The Sheriff of Nottingham reveled in its destructive beauty.

Flames spit high in the air, smoke rolled across the ground seasoned with the roasted meat of holy men, and the air was spiced with fear, confusion, and agony.

It felt like home.

Soon it *would* be.

He swung down from his mount, sliding one hand on the sleek skin of the nightmare. The hell-horse nickered and stepped aside. Black-armored soldiers gathered behind it, forming rank. The inhabitants of the monastery were done for. Dumb villagers stood in a herd of mooing humanity, joined by a sorry lot of soldiers left from the Lionheart's retinue.

He glared at them. Slaves to be subjugated, all of them. Terrorized into obedience. Fodder and food for the engine of King John's reign under Hell's authority.

Under *his* authority.

Soon and very soon.

On the ground the bard pulled himself to his knees.

This one could be a problem.

He stepped toward the fallen minstrel. The bard looked up at him, eyes still glassy from the kick that had knocked him flat. Even dazed, the man's hands clutched the harp to his chest, holding it above his own heart. The sight filled the Sheriff with hot rage.

Teeth clenched, he reached for the handle of the sword that hung off his narrow hip.

The bard's eyes sharpened and grew wide as wicked steel slid from its scabbard with the sinister chime of metal on metal.

The Sheriff smiled. He was going to enjoy gutting this one, using his sword to carve the lungs from the bard's chest. There would be no more song then. He would use the dark arts to keep the man alive, leaving only a mewling piece of meat when he was done.

He raised his sword.

"Stop! In the name of Christ Almighty, stop!"

Pain slammed into him from the left, crackling along the nerves under his skin. He whirled, looking for the one who would dare order him in *that* name. A friar ran toward him, wobbling on thick, stumpy legs. It was the one they called Tuck. The scrawny girl dressed as a boy was running beside him.

He swung his sword around, a wolf-grin appearing on his face.

"Fat friar, how do you like the hearth I stoked for you?" he said. "I made sure to laden it with the finest meat in the land."

Friar Tuck stumbled to a stop, legs kicking along the scorched grass.

"You dare mock the deaths of holy men?"

"I dared to kill them," he said, and he shrugged. "Mocking the act seems well within my rights."

"Blasphemer!" the priest screamed, anger running down red cheeks in the form of tears.

"By my very nature," he agreed, and he stalked toward Friar Tuck. "How does it feel to be the last priest in all of Avalon, fat man?"

The soldiers began to form a circle around them, eyes glittering red under black iron helmets.

The last priest. He blinked. *Francis.* Francis had been going to try to see Marian. What had they done to him?

"You won't destroy the word of God," Tuck managed to say around the lump in his throat.

"Mayhap not, little friar." The Sheriff stepped close enough to touch the priest. "But I will destroy every mother's son who speaks it."

"I'm not afraid of you, devil-spawn." Friar Tuck's hands clenched into fists. "*Get thee behind me.*"

Pain flared across the Sheriff's skin, a cold ache of righteousness. He snarled at it, shaking his head to clear it away. Then he leaned forward.

"Fool! My men are already behind you."

Friar Tuck's eyes widened as Lenore screamed. He turned to see a soldier clamp hands on her arms and lift her from the ground. She thrashed and kicked, trying to fight free, but his grip was steel and she only dangled, helpless. While he was turned, more hands closed on him. The Sheriff's men had him and he could do nothing.

The Sheriff lifted his sword.

"I will cut off the body of Christ at the head, priest."

The sword swung back over his head.

"And I shall enjoy every pulse of blood from the stump of your fat neck!"

The blade flashed like unholy lightning.

Two arm-length arrows punched through his chest, sinking to the feathers and bursting out the back of him in a spray of gore.

The Sheriff looked down.

"Well, I'll be damned."

Much couldn't believe his eyes. The Sheriff didn't fall!

Instead he jerked around, the sword in his gauntleted fist thrown wide from the impact of Robin's arrows, but he stood on his own feet.

Friar Tuck pulled away and ran over to scoop up a boy and carry him to the bard, who had staggered to his feet. The soldiers that once held them turned and drew weapons.

Much ran after Robin, trailing behind as they crossed the field. His eyes drank it in as Robin pulled arrows from his quiver and shot in smooth motion. The shafts flew faster than he could follow, streaking through the air to magically reappear, embedded in the bodies of the dog soldiers. By the time Much had run ten steps, Robin had dropped as many of the Sheriff's men.

People ran past, finally having seen too much. They fled to their villages to huddle and hide and see how things happened. One man knocked into Much and fell down. He tried to help him but the man scrambled away with a curse. Much looked up and saw that Robin had left him far behind.

The hooded archer fired three arrows into the faces of three dog soldiers. Much could hear the hollow melon *thunks* as arrowheads sank to the back of iron helmets. Another black-clad soldier, this one too close for Robin to shoot, swung a mace. Rusted iron blades swirled off the hardwood bat, jutting like the poison teeth of a basilisk.

Robin fell to the ground and slid under the swing, death-blades cutting the air where he had been. He slid to a stop, pulled an arrow, notched it, and sank it under the soldier's armpit. It jutted ont forget。

out the other side of his torso in a jolt of black gore, hitching up the arm that held the club and making it drop the thing. The soldier took two steps and tumbled to the ground.

Robin stood, his features still obscured.

Then the Sheriff faced him, fingers touching the feathers that sprouted from his breastplate. He looked the same as before, cold, icy, imperious—more frightening with his face pulled into a sneer.

His voice was smooth and fluid when he spoke.

"So you are the infamous Hood who has been interfering with my tax collecting."

Robin said nothing.

The Sheriff began to pull on the end of an arrow. It drew out of him slowly, pulsing blood around the shaft as it slid.

"This hurts you know."

"If you remove it, I will replace it."

"I think you can see that it won't matter. All you do is make me angry." The shaft came out with a squelch. The Sheriff dropped it to the ground and moved his hand to the next. "Besides, you are out of arrows, archer."

Robin slung the bow across his shoulders. "I have more. They worked fine enough on your men."

"They will be lazy until sunset." The Sheriff knelt, dropping the second arrow beside the first. He wiped his own blood off on the grass. Much could swear he saw it smoke and sizzle. His mailed hand closed on the hilt of the dropped sword and he stood. "If I let you live until then, they can join in your torture for the pain you put them through." He shrugged. "Most likely I'll carve your liver here, and have it for my reward."

Robin drew the sword hanging from the baldric at his side. Much had seen it earlier, made note of it because Robin never carried a sword. It was a yard of shining steel, heavy and thick with a hilt the size of a man's fist. Dark markings ran up the blade, but he couldn't read them from where he was.

The Sheriff stalked forward, swinging his sword back and

forth. It crackled in the air.

Robin spoke, jaw set in a clench.

"Help the others, lad," he said to Much. "Get to the forest and run. I'll catch up." He glanced to the side. "Be brave!" He turned back to the Sheriff in time to raise his sword and block a thunderous blow that would have clove his head to the teeth. It drove Robin to the ground. He scrambled, swinging wildly with his own sword, seeking to get space.

"Go!" he bellowed at Much.

Much went.

He reached Friar Tuck, the bard, and the boy. His hands closed on the rough wool robes of the priest.

"Come on! We have to make it to the Forest. Robin said!"

Friar Tuck planted his feet, jerking Much to a stop. Shoving the boy and the bard toward him, the priest spoke.

"Take them," he said. "I cannot leave Robin to face that devil alone."

Much pulled hard on Friar Tuck, using the muscles he had earned hauling full sacks of meal. He felt guilty and breathed the hope this wasn't a sin.

"Robin said we *all* should go." Friar Tuck looked at him sharply. There was a black splatter of the Sheriff's blood across his face. Much tugged again. "He *said*. He can beat the Sheriff, we have to run."

The bard laid a hand on Friar Tuck's arm. "We should go."

The priest nodded and shouldered himself under the weakened minstrel.

"Help with the other side of him, lad."

Much took the other arm across his shoulders. The bard clutched the harp in a white-knuckled fist. It banged against Much's chest, making little humming chimes with each step as they began to cross the field to the forest.

The other boy picked up a short sword that lay on the ground. Behind them Much could hear clanging steel and shouted curses. He couldn't look back with the Bard's arm over his neck, couldn't bear witness to the fate of the man he looked up to so desperately. He could only obey and run.

With each step, he prayed for Robin's safety.

CHAPTER NINETEEN

Robin was losing. The Sheriff was better with a sword than he was. He was faster, and possessed a strength unknown to mortal man.

He cursed himself for not having the black arrow with him. He had not expected his visit to the miller's family to be anything other than pleasant. Thus the arrow was safely hidden, deep within the forest. He would never make the same mistake again. The weapon that could bring both life and death would never leave him—not if he survived this.

Still he swung his sword, blocking every blow as he kept losing ground, inch-by-inch. He was going to have to flee. That truth was a bitter taste in his mouth, a clawing in his stomach, but if he did not run, he would not live. The Sheriff wasn't human, else the arrows would have killed him. If what the creature said was true, his men weren't human either.

Too long have we been fighting a human war against inhuman opponents, he thought fiercely. *That must stop.* He breathed a prayer, asking for strength, that God would let him live to protect those who could not protect themselves.

Surely Friar Tuck and the others would have gained the safety of Sherwood. The mighty forest seemed to be the only thing that could stand in the Sheriff's way. They needed to figure out why that was, how to extend its protection, and how to prevent it from being breached.

His opponent's sword whistled past his head, nicking the hood and nearly taking off his ear.

His arms were burning with the strain of parrying the man's blows. Even as Robin retreated, step by step, he did so with purpose. Behind him lay the trees. He needed to draw the Sheriff closer to them.

Friar Tuck was exhausted and almost numb from shock when he, Much, Alan, and Lenore arrived at the camp. Their arrival was heralded by a lookout, and soon he was face to face with Old Soldier and Little John.

"What has happened?" Old Soldier demanded, his voice like burnished steel, strong, resolute.

"The Sheriff and his men burned the monastery," Tuck said. "They killed... all my brothers." The grief was there, raw and terrible just below the surface, but held in check by the dreamlike state he felt he was walking in.

It wasn't real. It couldn't be. How was Nottingham so emboldened that he could destroy the representatives of God? Was it because he knew they were cut off from Rome, and that the Pope remained unaware of how dire things had grown?

Next to him Lenore wept quietly. Alan and Much were both silent.

Little John had recoiled in horror, crossing himself. Even Old Soldier looked rattled.

"The Sheriff, he's a monster," Much said quietly. "Robin shot him twice, arrows through the chest, and he did not even fall."

"Where is Lord Robin?" Old Soldier asked.

"He sent us to safety," Tuck answered. "He was battling Nottingham. The man truly is a demon, walking abroad by some dark magic, as Much said." Guilt gnawed at his insides like a starving dog worrying a bone.

"If that's true, then Longstride will be dead," Little John said, voice strained.

Silence fell among them.

"I'm not that easy to kill," a voice spoke up suddenly.

They all turned to see Robin staggering into the clearing, bloody and so battered as to be almost unrecognizable. Relief surged through the friar.

"The Sheriff?" he asked, daring to hope.

"He can't enter the forest, just as we've heard," Robin responded grimly. "Unfortunately, he's also unkillable, just as the rumors have said... just like that bastard John."

Tuck thought of the black arrow. Before he could ask, however, Robin locked eyes with him and gave his head a short, sharp shake.

Then Robin's eyes drifted past Friar Tuck to fall upon Much. "If the Sheriff is to be believed, the soldiers we killed will rise again at nightfall."

Tuck's blood ran cold at the thought, and he involuntarily crossed himself.

"Did any of them see you?" Robin asked, addressing Much.

"I don't know." The boy hesitated a moment and then nodded. "Some of the villagers did."

Robin nodded grimly. "Then we shouldn't take chances. If one of the soldiers revives, and remembers you, they might look for you at home and focus their revenge upon your family." He spoke the truth, and every man there knew it.

"I'll run straight home to warn them," Much said, his face pale.

"Take care that you are not seen," Robin instructed, "and when you reach them..."

"Bring them here," Old Soldier said. "We can settle them in the forest with some of the others."

"What of you?" Little John spoke up, pointing a shaking finger at Robin. "Did the Sheriff or his men recognize you?"

Robin shook his head. "I managed to keep my face disguised. The identity of the Hood should still be a secret."

* * *

Much's heart was in his throat as he ran for home. There was still plenty of daylight left. If the soldiers would wake at nightfall, then he should be able to reach home and get his parents to safety before any of them could remember seeing him.

He was grateful to Robin for thinking of that. He never would have. He hadn't even done any fighting, just followed Robin and watched in awe. That wouldn't stop the Sheriff or his men, though. They were cruel. Less than men. *Demons*, as Friar Tuck had said.

He held to the forest as long as he could before bursting out of it close to home. His feet flew down familiar paths that he had walked so many times, laden with goods to trade. His heart pounded harder and harder and his legs burned but he dared not slow down. They'd have just enough time to pack a few things before leaving. They wouldn't want to leave their home, but they'd understand. He'd tell them Robin had sent him, and then they'd listen.

At last the mill was in sight and his heart swelled with relief to see it standing. A moment later, though, something cold touched him. There was something wrong. The door was open wide. There was no smoke rising from the chimney, though it was growing even colder as the day drew to an end. A fire should be burning on the hearth for his mother to use to cook dinner.

There was a stillness to the place that terrified him.

He wanted to stop, turn, and flee back to the safety of the forest, but he couldn't. He had to know. His feet drove on, running even faster up the path as his mind screamed that it was dangerous. It was as if he had no control over himself, like he was compelled to move forward.

Then he smelled something burning... something terrible.

He grabbed the edges of the doorway and jerked himself to a sudden halt. A moment later he crashed to his knees with a cry. His father lay, blank eyes staring at the ceiling, his shirt coated in blood. A few feet away his mother lay in the fireplace, her body half its normal color and half charred like a bit of meat fallen into the fire.

He didn't look away as he retched.

Even as he did, though, his mind tried to work. The Sheriff's men would come alive at night. They couldn't have told the Sheriff that he had been there, and he was sure the Sheriff hadn't seen him, his attention focused on Robin. Some of the villagers had seen him, a couple in particular. One of them must have told the Sheriff about him. It was terrible, unthinkable. They knew him, his family. They were friends. Yet the truth was there to see, no matter how terrible it was.

Someone he knew had got them killed.

He had to leave, before someone could come back, looking for him. His parents should be buried, and properly, but he knew deep down he couldn't be the one to do it. He hadn't the time. He needed to make his way back to Sherwood, and pledge himself to fight beside Robin and his men. Old Soldier would train him and he would avenge his parents.

Much forced himself to his feet, tried to think through the haze that clung to his mind. He made it to his room, grabbed some clothes and his warmest boots. He wrapped them in a blanket from his bed. He moved back into the living room and he took his father's axe from the wall. It was the only weapon his family possessed, though it had only ever seen use as a tool.

He was about to go out the front when he remembered something else. He turned and stared at the small door that led to his father's private room. It was like invading a sacred place as he opened the door now, stooping to get inside.

With reverent fingers he took the boxes that held his father's tobacco and the jug with the sweet, fermented currant drink that his father had shared with him but once. These were his now. He felt the weight of them in his hands, and another weight on his shoulders, like the remembered weight of his father's hands.

He closed his eyes, allowing the weight to work upon him. He could smell his father in this room, almost hear his rare laugh, and he couldn't help but feel that he'd been given a blessing by the man who had given him life.

Without a word Much turned and slipped from the room. Out of habit he closed the front door of the house as he left. Then he set his steps toward Sherwood. His pace quickened as he noticed the sun sinking toward the horizon. Night was coming. The demons would be waking up.

The tears froze on his face as he walked back to the camp.

THE MANTLE OF WINTER MOURNING

CHAPTER TWENTY

Will spent the day working on the plans for the feast King John would be hosting in just over a week's time. Even as he ordered food and materials, and spoke to various household staff, there was an itching in the back of his mind.

He convinced himself he was being paranoid, that Chastity's fear had rubbed off on him. He didn't know why he was putting such stock in the girl's vision anyway—such things weren't to be believed.

Of course, as he was learning, he didn't have to believe in dark things for them to be true. The girl had been so afraid, too. He had seen her express many emotions, but never abject terror. He had held her in his arms for many long minutes while she cried. Then it had taken everything in him to let her go when she was finished.

Since then his thoughts had been on her more often than not. She was beautiful, her charms beyond dispute. There was a strength about her that fascinated him. Maybe it was because she was one of the few women who had never shown any interest in him. There was no denying that the chase could be an intoxicating thing.

He sighed. Chastity was Marian's maid and friend. Pursuing her was unwise. It might also prove impossible. If the rumors were true, then she was well-named. Will shook himself.

He had pursued many an alluring female but none had so occupied his thoughts. Maybe when all this unpleasantness was behind them, he would consider it. Until then he had plans to make, plans to foil, and he still needed to figure out a way to frame the steward.

It was dark and there was only a sliver of a moon out when Chastity made her way from the castle. Fear washed over her in waves. Fear not for herself, but for the Lady Marian, whom she was leaving alone in a nest of vipers.

Chastity was not accustomed to being afraid. All her life she'd been quick, clever, strong as a boy and twice as smart. Many a time she'd defended her name and her virtue with her fists and a good swift kick. More often than that she'd bested her opponents with her wits.

Of late, though, the fear had been creeping in. It had started with the vision of the Hood dead, and his lady brought to woe. Even then she'd suspected that Robin was the Hood and Marian his lady. Having acknowledgement just made it all worse. She didn't want harm to befall either of them. England *needed* the Hood. Even more it needed Marian, particularly if anything happened to King Richard, God save him.

She didn't know what she could do to stop the vision from coming true. She just knew that she had to. Chastity couldn't stand it if something happened to Marian, who had not only been her lady, but had also been her friend since they were both very young. Marian was everything that was good and right in the world. She was someone to believe in.

She took a deep breath, waiting for the guards to clear the corners of the wall, then she ran, fleet as a deer across the small stretch of open ground where she was most likely to be caught.

She made it to a patch of shrubs that concealed her and gave herself a moment to catch her breath. She was dressed in dark clothes from head to toe to match her need for stealth, and kept her eyes moving, making sure that no one was following her.

No one, and no *thing*.

Chastity had caught just the barest glimpse of one of the Sheriff's pets a few nights ago as it wrapped itself around his collar, pretending to be naught but a fur stole. She knew better, though, and kept a careful eye out for it or any other minions that might do the Sheriff's bidding.

She'd planned to charm a groom into letting her borrow a horse, but had decided it was safer if no one knew she was leaving the castle. It would be a long walk, but at least none would be the wiser, except for Marian.

Slipping further into the bushes, she moved quiet as a mouse. Her wary eyes darted ahead and behind. At last she began to move at a faster pace—she'd need speed to make it to Sherwood on foot and accomplish her mission.

There was an elusive scent on the wind that seemed to disappear and reappear periodically. The farther she made it from the castle, the stronger it became. It was smoke. Not the warm, smoky smell of a hearth fire, but a deep, acrid stench. Something sickly sweet floated on the air with it, and the stronger the scent became, the more her insides twisted.

She didn't want to know where the smell was coming from.

When she finally made it to the forest she began to breathe a bit easier. The stench wasn't as strong, and she was off the roads and safe. Most folks were afraid of Sherwood, of the haints and fey that were said to roam it. She didn't discount the existence of such creatures, but after seeing what the Sheriff and Prince John were capable of, she didn't fear them, either. There was no darkness in the forest that could equal the one outside it.

Once among the trees she was confronted with a new problem. Marian had said she wouldn't need to find the Hood—that the Hood would find her. Chastity didn't know why, but it sent a little chill up her spine to think about it like that. How could Robin know if she stepped foot in Sherwood unless he, himself, was one of the fey?

She didn't know, and she shrugged aside the thought. Marian had sent her with a job to do, and she planned to do it. It might just not happen exactly as her lady had said.

It was dark in the forest but there was just a little light, enough that she could see a few feet in front of her.

She began to walk slowly. A blast of wind startled her, lifting stray hairs from her neck with a touch that seemed almost human. She pressed a hand over her heart and kept going.

She walked another couple of minutes, trying to accustom herself to the sounds of the forest around her. Her feet crunched in the snow. The wind whistled in the leaves. Nearby a small animal rustled in a bush.

Leave.

She started, spinning around.

There was no one there.

Chastity couldn't hear anything over the sound of the blood pounding in her head. She stood a moment, fists clenched, defying whatever had spoken, daring it to show itself. She couldn't deny the fear that was blossoming inside her. She couldn't leave, though.

Turning slowly, she resumed her course. She walked a couple more minutes and had just begun to relax when something brushed against her arm.

Run away.

Spinning, she took off at a sprint, then pulled herself to a stop. It was as though her body had been compelled against her will. It had cost her valuable ground, running back toward the tree line.

Heart in her throat, she forced herself to turn back around.

"I will not leave," she said, her voice low. "I need to find the Hood."

Only silence answered her.

Even the wind and the animals had grown quiet, and the absence of sound was more frightening than the disembodied voices. She began to walk, purposefully putting one step in front of another. When she came back to the spot where she had been, she tensed, waiting to see if the voice would come again.

It didn't, but she did see a thin twig that crossed her path. It was the hand that had reached out and touched her. She took a deep breath and reminded herself that there was worse outside the forest than there was inside.

It was well after nightfall when Much made it back to the outlaw camp. The men there welcomed him and shared his sorrow, and before long he realized that he was one of them. A man without a home. He did have a cause, though—one for which he would fight.

He found a place to put his stuff, a little plot of dry dead grass just for him. It wasn't like home, but it would be home until things were set right again.

The men offered him some food, but he wasn't hungry. Old Soldier told him that eating was wise, even if he didn't feel like it. Much relented and put some of the meat and bread in his stomach. He felt a sense of accomplishment when he didn't immediately vomit them up.

Soon the others began to bed down for the night. Much lay down as well, but he wasn't tired. His mind was busy reliving everything that had happened that day. It seemed like impossibly much for a single day. He wanted to cry there in the dark, but the tears wouldn't come, as if too stubborn or too proud to reveal themselves.

He heard a bird call, and it struck him as strange. He turned and saw a shadow standing in the tree line.

It took him a moment to realize that it was Robin. He didn't know how he knew—the face was obscured—but he just did. The line of his shoulders, the bearing Robin couldn't shake no matter how primitively he chose to live.

As he watched, the bird that had called—a raven, he believed—swooped down and perched on the man's shoulder. It leaned its head toward the man's ear and twittered, as if it was telling him a secret. Much stared in fascination as the man nodded, and then turned and melted into the forest.

Without hesitation Much rose. He wanted to know very badly what the bird had told Robin. He didn't know why, but it felt important. He walked into the forest, trying to tread lightly but knowing that he made a terrible amount of noise compared to the person in front of him, who seemed to make no more sound than a shadow as he moved beneath the trees.

He finally came to a stop, unsure of which direction Robin had gone.

"There's an intruder in the forest."

Much turned, somehow not surprised that Robin had managed to walk up behind him undetected.

"What will you do?"

"I will go and see what she wants. Stay here with the others. I might have need of you later."

Much dipped his head in acknowledgment.

Robin laid a hand on his shoulder. "I was sorry to hear about your family," he said, his voice kind.

"Thank you," Much said. He couldn't help but wonder if the raven had told Robin about that, too.

She was going in circles. All the trees looked the same, and the path had dwindled to nothing but a wider expanse of snow that masked a jumble of low growth gone brittle in the cold. She hadn't found her own footprints, but for all she knew the forest was covering them. Chastity finally paused to rest herself a moment and try to get her bearings. She'd done her best to walk in a straight line, but the forest could be deceiving and the canopy overhead kept her from getting her bearing. She was a little surprised that she hadn't heard anymore whispers. They had faded as she made her way deeper into the woods.

At least she *hoped* she was deeper in the woods.

A sudden low growl caused the hair all over her body to stand on end. She turned her head slightly to the left and saw a pair of glowing eyes, staring fixedly at her. Her first thought was of the Sheriff's nightmare pets, and she clamped a hand over her mouth to keep from screaming.

A second growl came from her other side, and she turned quickly. Another pair of glowing eyes were upon her. This pair was bobbing up and down slightly, moving toward her. Seconds later she saw a giant wolf, fangs bared, its sides lean with hunger.

Behind her more growling. She didn't know how many of them there were, and forced herself to stand still, wishing that she had more of a weapon than the dagger tucked into her bodice. For the first time since Marian had commanded her to carry it with her, she felt as if she might need it.

She also realized, however, that it would be useless against an entire pack of starving wolves.

She shouldn't run. Someone had said that once when she was little, and she struggled to remember who. If she ran, they would chase her and tear her to pieces. She turned slowly, trying to determine how many there were. They circled around behind her and then stepped slowly forward, five of them. She moved away and they kept walking toward her, adjusting their course a couple of times until she had the distinct impression that they were herding her somewhere.

Yet they never attacked.

The pace picked up, and when she tried to slow down, one growled and moved closer. She resumed her normal walking speed and he dropped back with his brothers. At last they stopped walking, and so did she, wary of what might lie ahead in the shadows.

The wolves stood for a moment, heads cocked to the side as though listening to something, and then they melted back into the forest.

She stared, trying to catch a glimpse of them, but they were gone. She turned around, wondering where it was they had brought her. She listened, but heard only the sound of wind and woodland creatures. Was there something she should do, say, to draw the attention of the Hood?

A raven landed on a branch nearby, letting out a piercing cry that caused a chill to snake down her spine. The bird regarded her, staring at her as intently as the wolves had.

"I need to speak with you," she said out loud.

Only silence greeted her. She had been foolish to think that it would be otherwise. She started to take a step forward, but then stopped as she felt cold steel touch her throat.

"There are far worse things in this forest than wolves," a voice rasped.

CHAPTER TWENTY-ONE

"I do not fear what is in the forest," Chastity said, half of the mantra that she'd been repeating to herself for the last hour.

"What are you doing here?" The voice whispered in her ear, so close that she could feel his breath.

Normally she would have driven her elbow into the stomach of the man standing beside her, taking her chances with him and the knife he held. Instead, something urged her to stand completely still and answer his question.

"I am come with a message from my lady, for the Hood," she said. "It is urgent."

At least her voice was steady, which was surprising given the panic she felt.

For a long moment he didn't reply.

"It's dangerous to walk alone in the forest."

"More dangerous still to walk alone outside the forest," she countered.

The cold steel lifted from her throat and she did her best not to show her relief. A moment later Robin walked in front of her, eyes narrowed.

"Is something wrong with Marian?" he asked.

"So many things are wrong," Chastity said. "John has locked her in the tower, and she needs to escape. The cardinal came to see her yesterday, and John and his men took him prisoner. I fear for his life."

"Why does Marian need to escape?" Robin asked sharply.

Chastity shook her head. "She did not tell me why, just that it had to be done and done quickly."

"So quickly that she bid you to come tonight?" Robin questioned.

"Yes—I would have come last night, but we feared they might expect it," she replied. "As I said, there is no time to waste."

Robin frowned. "Has word reached her of what happened today at the monastery?" Robin asked.

"No, we have heard nothing," Chastity said. Then she asked, "Why?"

Robin hesitated, and suddenly she knew. "When I was making my way to the forest, I smelled smoke... and something more."

"The Sheriff burned the monastery, and killed every man of it, save Friar Tuck and the cardinal."

Chastity had thought herself hardened to the horrors committed by John and his monsters, but this shook her to her core. Burning tapestries was one thing. Burning holy men was quite another.

"Then we have even more cause to fear for Cardinal Francis's safety," she said, voice quavering.

Robin nodded. "It would not surprise me if he was already dead."

"Something has to be done."

"It will be," Robin said, his voice carrying a dark promise.

"What shall I tell my lady?" Chastity asked.

"Tell her I am coming for her," Robin said.

"John is planning a great gathering of the nobles on the solstice, with games and a feast," Chastity said. "They are scheduled to arrive in two days' time to begin a week of festivities leading up to it."

"Then I will arrive with them," he answered. "Tell her to be ready."

Chastity nodded.

"And now it is time for you to return."

"I have lost my way," she admitted.

Robin whistled softly, and a gray shadow appeared at his side. It was one of the wolves that had been herding her earlier. Robin put his hand on the wolf's head and the animal looked up at him. Something seemed to pass between them and Chastity blinked, wondering at the connection the two were sharing. She knew from the things that Marian had said, and the gossip she heard from others, that he had always been more at home in the forest than in a house. This was different, though. The change in him was profound. It was as if he had become part of the forest, an element of nature unto himself.

"He will show you the way home," he said, removing his hand from the beast's head.

Chastity nodded.

For the first time she was afraid of Robin.

Marian had been up all night, studying the book, reading it nearly non-stop since the cardinal had pressed it into her hands.

She couldn't risk going to sleep, though. Fear drove her onward—fear that someone might discover it, and take it away. She couldn't allow herself to be separated from the book before she'd gleaned the information she needed. The combination of diligence and study left her beyond exhausted.

Cardinal Francis had revealed that she and Robin needed to take it to the heart of Sherwood, before the winter solstice. Something would happen there that would help them in their battle against John. Every second seemed to be slipping, the solstice marching steadily closer while she was no nearer to her objective.

Panic welled up as it had more times than she could count. She forced herself to breathe. They had acted as quickly as they dared. It would have been madness had Chastity tried to leave the castle the night before.

Recklessness would doom them to failure.

She turned her attention back to the tiny pages. From what she could gather there were challenges, guardians to be met and defeated before they might reach the heart of the forest. This matched what they already knew. Robin had been forced to do battle in order to acquire the elixir that saved them all from the pox. When they asked what had happened to him, he had been reluctant to give any details. Whatever it was, she hoped the experience would serve them in good stead.

Will found himself tormented by restless dreams. Chastity's sense of foreboding was contagious, and the sense of dread stronger within him.

He picked up a black nightshirt and made ready to depart, leaving his rapier behind, even though in the dark of the castle he wanted it strapped to his hip. Instead he settled for a wicked-sharp poinard he could slip into the top of his boot. Moving down the stairs, he went from the upper sleeping quarters into the main halls of the castle. Pausing at the stairway that led to the tower, he was tempted to go up and check on Marian. He resisted. To do so would simply arouse suspicion when he was stopped by the guard outside her door.

His thoughts turned to Chastity.

He was nobility, while she was a common wench, at least in the eyes of John and his retinue. Will could go and find her chambers without causing any suspicion at all. So he went around the back of the stairwell, and proceeded down into the bowels of the castle, where the servants quartered.

It grew darker and darker as he moved deeper into the castle. Torches hung unlit. Arrow slits were covered in oilskin as protection against the cold winter air. Every thirty steps there was a landing. His breath fogged the air for most of the journey. Perhaps he'd chosen the wrong stairwell.

He'd never been to the servants' section.

Thoughts of Chastity's blonde hair and bright eyes kept him moving.

After dozens of steps he noticed that his breath no longer showed in the air, and he was noticeably warmer. Was it just a little brighter down below?

He slowed, and heard someone talking.

So he stopped, considering whether he should carry on, or turn back. As he did so the voices became louder, and shadows danced up from below. His decision was made for him.

He turned and dashed up to the next landing, grateful for the soft leather boots he wore. Once there he found a niche and pressed himself back into the deepest shadow, pulling the collar of his nightshirt high over his pale face.

The sound from below became clearer as it drew closer.

Voices.

No, a single voice.

One person.

Prince John.

But two sets of footfalls, one much heavier than the other, and the metallic chime of metal rubbing metal.

The sound of armor.

"We need to find a way to put water down there," John said. "By the time I am at the top of these stairs, my hands have crusted over."

Silence, save for the footsteps.

"I could have you haul it down," John said.

The steps were closer, and the light much brighter.

"Why do I even talk to you?" John said harshly. "You are a giant lummox—no voice, no opinion. I might as well be talking to myself."

They were just around the corner now. Will pulled his collar up further to his face, shrank deeper into his pocket of shadow, and went as still as possible.

The light flared, and John stepped into view on the landing, carrying an oil lamp in dark hands.

Will held his breath.

Behind John came a gigantic figure, hunched to avoid the ceiling. It stopped walking and turned its head toward the usurper, studying John. A sound came from it that sounded like a dog choking on a bone lodged in its throat.

John stopped and swung the lamp toward the figure, revealing a suit of armor that covered its wearer from crown to heel, and looked very similar to what the Sheriff wore.

John regarded the leviathan.

"I know your purpose better than you do."

The figure made noise again.

John shook his head. "You do not. I am not bound by the demands of my creation. I am a human, not a creature called."

The figure stood silent, but its head tilted.

"Damn you, livestock."

The figure still didn't respond.

John turned and continued up the stairs, muttering to himself. The giant followed, clanking with each step.

Will held his breath until he couldn't hear them anymore.

He couldn't breathe.

The muscles along his ribs had given out long ago. He couldn't push up, couldn't lift his weight off his outstretched arms. Couldn't take a full breath, only sip the air.

He couldn't think. His mind was in a fog of pain that chased his thoughts.

He hung, hands long numb, and drifted in and out of consciousness.

Someone touched him and he jerked, trying to pull away from the agony that was certain to follow.

"Easy, easy," a voice murmured.

He tried to open his eyes, to look and see, but one was sealed shut, the skin around it swollen to the point of splitting open.

The other had been plucked out on the first day of his torture.

He couldn't make his voice work to ask, his throat scraped raw from hours of his screaming.

There was a noise, a *click*, and then a soft metallic *ching*. The pressure on his hands and arms lessened. His feet touched flatly on the ground, but his knees and thighs had no strength to hold him up so still he hung, waiting.

The voice was close again when it spoke.

"Oh my God, Cardinal Francis. How did this happen?"

He tried, but could not speak.

Something cold touched his mouth. He opened it and a trickle of cold water ran past his tongue and down his throat.

It was taken away before he'd slaked his thirst, and he moaned when the cup left his mouth.

He could hear the person in front of him, softly weeping.

He pushed his voice, trying to be clear.

"Who is this?"

"Will Scarlet."

"You can't be here." Panic made his voice seize up. His throat closed and he coughed.

It felt like his guts were being twisted from inside him.

"Let me get you down."

Hands pulled at the knotted rope around his wrists, still on the hook.

"Stop." He flailed, throwing all his strength, despite the agony.

Will's voice cracked, turning plaintive. "I can free you."

"You can't." His lungs clenched like a fist. "John will know."

"I won't leave you."

"You... will."

Silence fell as he gathered his strength. In the black of his blindness white spots swirled around.

Finally he was able to speak again.

"Leave me, Will," he croaked, "but you have... to do something first."

"What?" Will's voice sounded like a child's.

"I cannot bear... another visit... from John." He swallowed.

He had more to say. "Don't let me… betray you."

"W-what?"

"Please." If tears could have fallen from his damaged eyes he would have wept with desperation. "Be faith… faithful, Will."

There was silence, broken only by his own labored breathing and the soft, caressing sound of weeping that quietly filled the room.

It continued, undisturbed, then after a moment of nothing, Will seemed to be fumbling with something. Hands on leather.

He said a small prayer for Will Scarlet's soul, then he felt the knife in his ribs. The pain was as nothing, the warm embrace of a long-lost friend before sending him home.

CHAPTER TWENTY-TWO

Marian sat by the window, waiting as night fell. Champion was curled up on the bed, already fast asleep.

Chastity had made it back safe that morning and told her that Robin would be coming for her. Together they had worked all day with tools that Chastity had been able to smuggle in to remove a couple of the bars from Marian's window. But the climb down was sheer, and would prove nigh impossible.

The nobles would begin arriving the next day for the week-long festivities John had commanded. She shuddered as her mind conjured up nightmare images of the things John might be planning. Plague, hangings, torture—the prince had proved himself a maestro of evil. Whatever horrors he had arranged, he would save the worst of them for the culmination of the festival.

For the solstice. One week. That was all she had. One week to save her country, her people. Every second that passed was an agony, an opportunity lost, as they moved steadily toward destruction.

The key rattled in the door and she jumped, then turned to see Chastity enter, looking pale and tired.

"What's wrong?" Marian asked, rising to her feet.

"Will has left the castle to make final preparations for the festival," the girl said, her brow puckered in worry.

"I'm sure he'll be fine," Marian said.

Chastity nodded, but the worry remained.

With a start Marian realized something.

"You like him, don't you?"

Chastity flushed and dropped her eyes slightly. "Him? I wouldn't give him the time of day," she said with a sniff.

"There's no need to lie about it," Marian said, crossing to her friend and touching her cheek.

Chastity looked up at her.

"I don't want to," she said sincerely, "but I find he's on my mind more often than not of late."

"There are worse matches that could be made," Marian said softly.

Chastity waved her hand, dismissing the thought. "He's a noble and I'm a servant, and there's only one kind of match happens that way. That's not for me. I want something that lasts more than a night."

"Extraordinary times," Marian said. "We don't know what is and what is not possible," she added, her heart aching for her friend. "Does Will feel the same way?"

"Will Scarlet feels the same for anything that wears a skirt," Chastity muttered, dropping her eyes again.

Marian paused. What Chastity said was true, but she wanted to believe in the possibility of a happy ending. Hope was in such short supply these days.

"It does not mean that the right woman can't turn his head and capture his heart," she said softly.

Chastity looked up sharply. "Do you think that's true?"

Marian took a deep breath, then nodded. "Richard once told me that my father was quite the ladies' man until my mother caught his eye. It took only her looking at him to calm his wild ways. So, yes, I think it can happen, and I think that you're just the right woman to tame Will Scarlet."

"Your father *was* a very handsome man."

"So I have been told."

Chastity smiled. "We both have men that need taming, just in different ways."

Marian smiled back. "Now, go and try to get some sleep. I know you're tired, and we'll need all our wits about us tomorrow."

"Yes, milady," Chastity said with a quick curtsey, in one of her rare shows of decorum. She turned and left, locking the door behind her.

Marian sighed and said a prayer for her, and for Will. She'd noticed Chastity's growing interest in the rogue before, but now that interest seemed to have blossomed into full-fledged infatuation.

She stood for a moment, trying to convince herself to go to bed. What she had told Chastity was true; they both needed rest so they'd be ready for whatever tomorrow brought.

A sudden cold draft caused her to turn. She barely suppressed a cry of alarm when she saw a man climbing through the window. It took only a split second, though, for her to recognize Robin.

He dropped to the floor in her room and straightened.

"You sent for me?" he asked softly.

"Yes, though Chastity led me to believe I should look for you tomorrow," she said, forcing herself to speak. She was still startled by his sudden appearance. "How... how did you manage to climb up?" she asked.

He gave a crooked smile. "It wasn't easy."

She stared at him, feeling the need to memorize every line of his face. He was like a dark apparition that had come to her, more dream than man. She shook herself, seeking to break the spell which gripped her.

"We need to go to the heart of Sherwood," she said. "Cardinal Francis told me, and the book confirms it." At his curious look, she quickly told him of the nature of the *Relic Grimoire*. "Once we reach our destination," she continued, "we have a task that has been appointed for us, one which will help us save England."

Robin frowned, taking it all in.

"Even I've never been to the heart of Sherwood," he said. "If what you say is true, it will be a perilous journey."

"Yet it is one which we must make together," she said, "and quickly. John is planning something for the winter solstice, heaven knows what, and we must complete our task by then if we are to hope to stand against him."

"I will go." He looked resolute.

"We both must go," Marian insisted. "Apparently I am part of the key, for a reason that stems from my heritage. You need to get me there safely. Cardinal Francis was most clear on that point."

"Do you know what has happened to him?" he asked.

Marian shook her head, her heart squeezing painfully in her chest at the thought of their friend and mentor.

"I do not," she replied. "However, Chastity told me about the monastery, the monks... I'm afraid I haven't much hope for the cardinal, not in John's hands. He knew the danger in coming here, though. He wouldn't have risked it if this wasn't our best chance at stopping the usurper, and whatever he has planned."

He frowned, but then nodded slowly. "We will go together."

"I'm ready."

Robin shook his head. "Not now, not tonight. I barely made it here without being seen. Two of us could not make it out. Tomorrow night when the nobles are here for the revelries, then it will be much easier to act amid all the distraction."

Marian moved to her bed and retrieved the book from its hiding place. She turned to Robin, clutching it with white knuckles.

"Then take this," she said. "If it were to fall into John's hands... I can't even imagine."

"They have already decided you don't have it, or they would have taken it before now. It's safer here with you for the night."

She hesitated then folded the object against her chest.

"How will you leave, then?" she asked. "There's no way out but to fight, is there?"

"Most likely," Robin said with a nod.

"Then why risk coming here tonight, if we can't act until tomorrow?" she asked.

He didn't answer right away.

"Because you asked me to come," he said finally, "and I did not want you to wait any longer than was necessary." He looked sheepish. "It wasn't the best of plans, I fear."

There was so much she wanted to say to him, but words escaped her. They stood there for a moment, regarding each other. At last Robin spoke.

"I should go while I'm still able."

Marian nodded, not trusting herself to respond.

He could not remember when Marian had looked more beautiful. She wore a simple dress of forest green, no decorations or finery. Her hair was pulled back and hung in waves down her shoulders. She looked elemental, like a force of nature. He had an overpowering urge to take her into his arms and kiss her.

He knew if he did, though, that she would intoxicate him more deeply than any wine, and he would never make it away from the castle alive. As much as it pained him, he knew he needed to go, or risk everything for which they'd been struggling so hard. There were too many others whose lives depended on them. He had to think of those others, and not himself. Whatever existed between him and the Lady Marian, it would need to wait until England was free, and their lives were not bound to fighting John and the evil he had brought upon them all.

He swept low in a bow, unable to say goodbye, then turned and climbed quickly through the window. The wall outside seemed sheer, but was marked with a great many chinks in the stones and mortar. Climbing down would be the easy part.

Making it away from the castle would be more difficult.

The forest seemed darker, more unforgiving to Will as he rode through it. It was as though there were eyes upon him with every step, and they were not the eyes of friends.

The further he rode, the more vivid the sinking sensation in the pit of his stomach. He would not find Robin. Maybe that was why the forest felt so hostile to him, without his cousin there.

I'm just imagining things, he thought, chastising himself. It was the only explanation. Of course, in order to believe it, he'd need to convince himself that he hadn't seen glowing eyes staring unblinkingly at him out of the darkness. He knew not whether they belonged to woodland creatures or fey, and was in no hurry to discover the truth.

When at last he reached the camp he discovered that he was right about Robin. He was angry, though, to discover that his cousin had gone to see Marian. Not only was it a foolish move that put both of them in danger, but it also meant Will had risked leaving the castle for naught.

He did finally find Friar Tuck, and the heaviness in his chest returned tenfold. More than anything he wished he had different news to bring to the friar. He pulled Tuck and Alan aside, so they might speak without being overheard by the others. Old Soldier and the others might be on their side, but his news was not for their ears.

"Will," Tuck said, putting a hand on his shoulder, "it is good to see you, and to know that you are alive and well. However, I think you've traveled far tonight for a reason, and it's time you told us what it was."

Alan nodded his agreement. There was nothing to do but get to the point.

"Cardinal Francis is dead," Will said. "John tortured him."

"John killed him?"

Will hesitated, tears on his cheeks, before nodding and looking away.

There was absolute silence for a moment as the terrible truth sank in.

"He's gone?" Tuck asked, swaying slightly on his feet.

"Yes."

"He was taking a book to the Lady Marian," Alan said. "Was he able to give it to her?"

"I believe so," Will replied. "I only hope whatever is in that book is worth the terrible price he paid." In his heart, he had a hard time believing that it would be. Francis hadn't gone with them on their raiding missions as the Hood, but he had been a part of them, nonetheless—a leader if any of them were.

"I am alone," Tuck said, his voice heavy with grief and weighed down with the burden of responsibility.

"We don't know that," Alan said softly. "This is just one portion of England. We don't know that he's destroyed the other monasteries."

"We don't know that he hasn't, either," Tuck countered, his voice breaking. "And unless we can get word to them, we're as good as alone."

He wasn't wrong about that, but Will didn't think it would be helpful to agree.

"Nobles will be coming from all over to attend John's celebrations," he offered instead. "Perhaps we can ask them, and get an idea of how things are in other areas."

Alan nodded. "I'll be attending. Hopefully I can hear the whispers, convince a few people to talk."

"It's too dangerous," Will said quickly. "They know you were at the monastery, trying to stop them from burning it."

"It will be a public event, and they wouldn't dare touch me there. Bards are sacrosanct," Alan replied defensively. "Our position has protected us all for centuries, and it will continue to protect me," he added more quietly.

"Very well," Will said, though he didn't share the bard's confidence. "But we shouldn't arrive at the castle together. We don't need anyone making the connection."

"Agreed," Tuck said heavily. "You should go back now. Alan can travel in the morning, to arrive with some of the nobles."

They talked for a few more minutes, then Will bade them farewell and set out back toward the castle. He was nearly free of the forest when his horse pricked its ears forward, suddenly alert. He drew the animal to a stop, wondering what it was sensing.

"This is a surprise," a voice to his left said a moment later.

Will relaxed slightly. "I was looking for you," he responded. "I bring terrible news. Cardinal Francis is dead."

Robin nodded, lips in a grim line. "I was afraid that might be so."

Will frowned inwardly. He hadn't expected Robin to break out the sackcloth and ashes, but he had expected a little more of a display of grief. Before he could say anything, however, his cousin spoke again.

"We have to help Marian escape tomorrow night," he said, "while the festivities are taking place."

Will blinked. "That's going to be easier said than done."

"Nevertheless, it needs to happen," Robin insisted. "I will see you tomorrow night."

Before Will could reply, he had slipped into the darkness and vanished.

"I just hope it doesn't get us all killed," Will said to no one in particular.

CHAPTER TWENTY-THREE

Locksley had grown to dread the King's gatherings. People always died. John was dangerous and, worse, unpredictable. He recalled the hanging of Lady Minter and her daughters. That had taken place under the guise of a public concert.

This particular gathering was supposed to last a week, which meant more opportunities to be killed.

He hoped the opportunities would be just as plentiful to organize the other nobles into some sort of resistance. Not that he thought it would actually work. The families still had children who were being held by John, and as long as that was the case, no one would dare oppose him.

In that regard Locksley was one of the lucky ones. He had no children to threaten. Yet he still had people who depended upon him. People who could be hurt. Thus, whenever he left home, he instructed that if he didn't return, each man, woman, and child under his care was to be given food, a weapon, some gold, and sent away.

His steward had remained behind to execute this last wish, should it be necessary, before fleeing himself. At least this way his people couldn't be used as an example, just to frighten others into submission.

There were dozens of people milling about the great hall.

Locksley didn't move among them, nor did he seek to make his influence felt. This evening he simply watched, looking for anything that might provide a clue as to why they were all really there.

Despite a roaring fire, the air was chilly. After half an hour, the only unusual thing he had observed was the number of soldiers who had filed into the room, lingering near the exits. It boded ill, and he was glad he'd worn his sword. It wasn't the ornamental one used for ceremonies, but rather the one that had been carried into battle by five generations of his family. Its steel had been stained with the blood of many enemies, and it would stand him in good stead should the worst occur.

He turned this way and that, taking in more of the room, and his eyes lit on John's toady, Will Scarlet. The man was making his way through the crowd toward him. Locksley felt his eyes narrow. He had no argument with Scarlet, but there was no love lost between them. Will was a cousin to Robin. Worse than that, he was a silver-tongued serpent who could smile and lie to your face while stabbing you in the back.

"Pleasant evening to you, Lord Locksley," Scarlet said as he came to stand before him, a fake smile plastered firmly in place.

"I seriously doubt it, Scarlet," Locksley growled. "You're John's constant companion. Why don't you tell me what he has planned, and spare me the surprise."

Will raised an eyebrow. "You mean he hasn't told you?"

"No, and I'll wager that the only ones he might have told are you and the Sheriff."

Scarlet chuckled. "You flatter me, but in this instance, I am not in his confidence."

"Then maybe you should be as worried as the rest of us," Locksley suggested. He had to admit that he wouldn't be entirely sad to see the man's perennial smugness wiped away by a hangman's noose. Scarlet frowned suddenly. Locksley turned to look behind, wondering what he had seen. More soldiers were quietly entering the hall, moving along the walls. They were all heavily armed.

"I don't like this," Locksley said.

"You're not the only one," Scarlet said so quietly that Locksley wasn't sure for a moment the man had actually spoken.

Before he could say anything in response, however, a trumpet sounded, heralding the arrival of the king. They both turned to look.

John swept into the room, arrogance rippling off him. One step behind him was the cursed Sheriff. The man frightened him, far more even than John. They were both evil, but there was an unnaturalness to the Sheriff that was unnerving. Next to the Sheriff walked Glynna. Locksley felt his chest constrict at the sight of her, so clearly consorting with the monster.

John ascended to the throne in the center of the room. Two chairs were close by, and Glynna took one. The Sheriff elected to remain standing for the moment.

Behind them walked two servants carrying an ornate table, which they put down close to the foot of the throne. Everyone took a couple steps forward to get a better look as the servants stepped away. On the table lay several scrolls and some pens that gleamed strangely in the light.

Locksley could hear the muttering around him. He disliked what he saw even more than the rest. Some of the nobility present were from the far reaches of the kingdom. A couple, at least, were being exposed to King John for the first time. He couldn't help but wonder what they were thinking. He hoped some of the others would have warned them already about what to expect.

Somehow this table wasn't what he had expected.

John looked suddenly at Locksley, as though the weight of his thoughts alone had drawn the twisted prince's attention.

"You are wondering what these are for," John said. It wasn't a question, but was stated as fact.

"Yes," Locksley said, feeling compelled to answer.

"You see, tonight is a very special night," John continued, scanning the room. When he spoke again, his words were louder.

"Tonight you will do something that will bind us all together. You will swear a blood oath of fealty to me."

There was a moment of stunned silence.

All around him the nobles exploded, voices raised in anger and frustration.

"Give us back our children first!" one shouted.

"After what you did to the monastery?" someone else bellowed. "You're insane!"

Rebellion was in the air. Finally John had pushed them too far. Now was the time to take action, to strike while their blood was up. Perhaps it was a chance to put a stop to the madness.

"Enough!" Locksley roared, striding forward with a hand on the hilt of his sword. Scarlet tried to grab his shoulder, but he shrugged him off.

The crowd parted before him like water, and within moments he was standing before King John, who stared at him through narrowed eyes. The man looked more like a serpent than he usually did.

"You have something to say, Locksley?"

Locksley considered his words. Considered the cost. The decision weighed on him as he felt the pressure of everyone's eyes on him. He could sway the room with whatever he decided to do next.

He took a deep breath.

"What you are asking is treason," he said so that all could hear. "No man here can swear any kind of fealty to you, while King Richard yet lives."

"A situation that will be shortly remedied, I assure you," John said, his eyes opening wider with confidence.

A chill ran through Locksley. He and Richard had encountered their differences, but the king was a thousand times better than his brother.

The thought occurred to him now that John might have an ally in Richard's camp, someone intent on making sure that the king never came back to claim his throne, or save his people.

If that was true, then it was up to him and the rest of the nobility to save England. Someone shouted something behind him, but he had eyes only for the usurper.

"Long live King *Rich*—"

Will winced as the Sheriff cut off Locksley's head with one clean blow. The body slumped straight to the ground and the head bounced twice, then rolled to land at John's feet.

So intent had the noble been on John that he had never seen the Sheriff move around behind him. Will had tried to shout a warning, but Locksley must not have heard him.

All around him the other nobles flew into a panic. The soldiers that had been lining the room now moved forward, pressing inward, slowly driving them toward the table with the cursed scrolls and pens.

One man stepped forward and laid his hand on a pen, hissing in pain as it cut into his flesh. Blood ran down his fingers to the tip, and he signed his name to the scroll. As he did so the blood lit with a tiny flame, burning itself dry with a stench filling the air.

Will just stared in horror. He wanted to shout, to scream, to run forward and drag the man back and tell him not to be a fool. He did none of those things. Instead he just watched as his own father was the first to swear fealty, sealing it with his blood.

Shame washed over him. Was his father that much a coward? Surely he could see that John and Nottingham were the very essence of evil. Will's uncle would never have signed. Nor would Robin.

Nor can I, he thought, realizing that John would likely require it even of him. He started moving, backing slowly toward one of the side doors, trying not to catch the attention of the soldiers. He glanced around, looking for Alan or Marian. He saw neither. He kept casting his eyes back and forth, desperate to find his allies. They needed to get out of there, and *now*.

His father stepped aside, and the nobles began to line up. Will could see him staring at a black mark that swirled up from his fingertips, wrapped itself around his wrist, and then disappeared beneath the sleeve of his shirt. Foul magic. He had signed the devil's scroll in his own blood and now he was bound.

There was no help for his father, or the next noble who was already signing the scroll. Will didn't know if they would be freed even if John was killed. Maybe the mark would kill them, and drag them to Hell along with him.

The room had been cold a short time earlier, but he was sweating profusely, almost as if he could feel the fires of Hell lapping at the edges. He tore his eyes from the line of men who were busy sealing their fates, and looked around again.

There, just inside the one door, he saw Chastity. Her skin was pale against the crimson color of her dress, and even through his fear and horror he couldn't help but notice that she looked beautiful. Between them, though, stood four soldiers. One of them glanced at Will and took a step in his direction.

He cursed under his breath.

"Good men of the kingdom, listen to me!"

Will twisted his head to see Alan standing on top of a table, harp in hand. His blood ran cold at the sight.

Alan-a-Dale drew himself to his full height. His hand struck the harp on his shoulder, drawing out a clash of notes, discordant and brash enough to lock everyone's eyes on him.

"Men of Avalon!" he shouted. "Heed the word of the True Bard of the Everlasting Isle!"

John raised his arm to point, and Alan struck his harp again. The noise made the prince wince and draw back.

Alan lifted his hands, arms out to show the splendor of his clothing. He knew the sight of it would spark the spirit of the men gathered before him. They were Celts from the blood of

Celts, and their hearts would sing with the bard.

"The time has come to end this charade," his voice cut through the chaos. "There is an usurper in our midst, a sickness to be cut out. The throne, the very sovereignty of this mighty island, rests not with weak-blooded men, not with those who would turn to dark ways. This is the Summer Kingdom, a kingdom of light. Your rightful king has not forsaken you, so do not forsake yourselves. Feel the Awen spark in your soul. You are bondsmen of the king, guardians of this kingdom."

He pounded the harp and it roared out thunder from its strings.

"Rise up! Gather ye steel to ye fists and paint your face with woad! Hear the song of sovereignty! Hear the song of righteousness! Hear the song of England!"

All eyes were on the bard, who Will knew was beyond his help. He could not waste the distraction that the man had provided, though. He walked right past the soldiers who were staring from Alan to John and back again.

As he reached the door he heard John roar an order. He forced himself to keep moving. He made it out of the room and into a corridor. He had only taken half a dozen more steps when a hand clamped down on his shoulder.

"Where are you going?" a soldier growled at him.

Will spun out from underneath the man, leaving his half cloak in the brute's fist. He sprinted down the hall.

Time had run out.

Ahead of him he saw a flash of crimson disappear around a corner. Chastity, it had to be. He skidded around the corner just in time to see her yank a dagger from her bodice. He stopped, reached out, but she didn't see his hand.

A moment later the soldier ran around the corner and Chastity plunged her dagger into the man's throat. Blood sprayed everywhere as he fell. She shoved the bloody knife back into her bodice, and then grabbed Will's hand and pulled him down the corridor.

She wasn't leading them to the front of the castle. It finally dawned on Will that they were headed for the kitchen. They burst into the room and found a dozen servants hastily preparing the menu that Will had actually chosen for the night's dinner. Once the nobles had finished signing, the devil was going to throw them a party.

Only the head cook looked up as they made their way through.

"You haven't seen us," Chastity whispered to the woman as they raced past her.

Seconds later they were outside. There were no soldiers to be seen, and Will guessed it was because the majority of them were inside.

"Marian?" Will asked.

"I'll get her," Chastity said. "Meet us at the edge of the forest."

Will shook his head. "No, I can't leave without her."

"Go," the girl insisted. "I promise we will join you shortly."

He was about to object when she suddenly stood up on her toes, grabbed his face in her hands, and kissed him.

She pulled away a moment later, skin flushed.

"That's a promise, too," she said, her voice husky. She turned and ran back into the kitchen.

Marian's imprisonment wasn't common knowledge, and she wasn't sure how John planned to explain her absence, but at least it gave her an opportunity to escape unobserved.

She had packed a small bundle of warm clothes, including the trousers she usually used for riding. She had her secret dagger strapped to her leg, and the book carefully tucked into her bodice. Champion was asleep in the crook of her arm. She was ready to go, and the excitement and fear had worked together to make her sick to her stomach.

When Chastity unlocked the door Marian pounced.

"We have to go, now," Chastity said, face strained.

"Lead the way," Marian said, and she didn't waste time asking what was wrong.

She had expected Chastity to be stealthy, and for the two of them to spend a long time making their way out of the castle. Instead the girl took off at a run. Marian was surprised, but she sprinted after her.

Chastity took a few turns that led them away from the main entrance, and soon they were racing toward the kitchen.

They were running past one of the walls that bordered the throne room when Marian gasped and nearly doubled over in pain. She could feel evil emanating from the chamber, thick and malignant, and her entire body seized, her muscles cramping, her throat constricting. Everything about her reacted to what was happening.

"Come *on*, Princess," Chastity hissed, grabbing her arm and trying to pull her forward.

Marian wanted to go, wanted to run, but her legs gave out, depositing her on the floor. Her body started to convulse. Terror filled her. Nothing like this had ever happened to her before.

She looked up, and it was as though she could see black tendrils snaking their way out of the throne room, through the very walls. Everything they touched turned black, and they snuffed out torches as they passed through them.

She wanted to cross herself, but she could barely lift her arm. Chastity leaned down and tried to pick her up, but it was as though Marian's limbs were all leaden, and she couldn't help her.

Chastity sobbed in frustration.

Marian forced her arm upward. She was able to grab the book and push it into the girl's hands.

"Take Champion and go," she said, her throat tight and her tongue thick. The words sounded like gibberish to her as they came out of her mouth.

Chastity must have understood, though. She took the book, scooped up the fox, and ran for the kitchen.

The girl was out of sight when Marian heard the sound of running footsteps, coming toward her from the opposite direction. It took every ounce of will and all of her strength to turn her head.

The Sheriff's soldiers were racing up to her. They seized her, lifting her in their arms, and carried her into the throne room.

Inside the walls appeared to be a shimmering, moving black as though the shadows themselves had come alive. The only lights in the room were dim, failing a little more with each passing second, their flames dwindling.

There was a line of nobles in front of the throne, faces pale, eyes glazed. Black marks swirled up their hands from their fingertips, and on the throne John sat, simpering, enjoying his victory. He looked at Marian, and a cruel smile twisted his features.

"So nice of you to join us, my dear."

CHAPTER TWENTY-FOUR

Lenore's insides were twisting with hate. She was hidden in the bushes that lined the road leading from the castle. Lights blazed throughout the structure and people had been arriving for hours. Her hands were slick with sweat. In the left one she clutched a small dagger.

Something important was happening tonight. She knew that from what she'd heard Friar Tuck say to other people when no one noticed that she was listening. There were men inside that castle who had killed her parents. Men inside who had killed all the brothers at the monastery. If something was happening tonight, if there was a chance to kill them before they killed anyone else, then she wanted to be a part of it.

A sudden rustling in the brush behind her startled her, and she turned just as Much stepped through.

"What are you doing here?" she demanded.

"Wondering what *you* are doing here," Much said. "Friar Tuck wouldn't approve."

"I can take care of myself," she said, showing him the dagger.

"Do you know how to use that?" he asked.

She thrust the dagger at one of the plants and then sliced off the leaves of another.

Much hunkered down beside her, nodding in approval.

"You're going to use it on someone," he said.

"Yes."

He nodded again, but didn't say anything about trying to stop her, which was good.

"So, why are *you* here?" she asked.

"Something's happening. I'm here to help if I'm needed," Much said.

"You do that a lot," she said. "Help."

Much shrugged. She had known him as long as she could remember and she'd never thought much about him. The last few days, though, he seemed older to her, wiser somehow. Lord Longstride trusted him. That had to mean something.

"Neither of you should be here," a voice said from the darkness. Lenore spun around and came face to face with Lord Longstride himself. The man was dressed in dark clothes. A hood was pushed back off his head. He held a longbow in one hand, and there was a quiver of arrows on his back.

He reminded her of the stories her father used to tell her about the avenger of Sherwood. Sometimes she watched him and wondered if Lord Longstride was that same man, immortal as the forest itself.

"Look!" Much said suddenly, excitement in his voice. Lenore turned back around and saw a lady running out of the castle. She was dressed in the finest dress Lenore had ever seen.

"Is that the Maid Marian?" she asked.

"No, that's her servant, Chastity," Lord Longstride said, his voice taking on a hard edge.

Moments later soldiers sprinted out the door, chasing the lady.

An arrow sang past Lenore, the wind of it ruffling her hair.

Lord Longstride was shooting at the soldiers.

A figure emerged from the other side of the road and ran forward, sword drawn. The woman ran into his arms, and together they turned and headed for the bushes.

A soldier swerved and put on a burst of speed. He swung a wicked-looking sword and slashed the man across the back. A moment later the soldier fell as one of Lord Longstride's arrows buried itself in his chest.

The man and the woman made it into the bushes on their side of the road, and Lenore moved toward them with Much beside her.

"Are you alright?" Much asked the man.

"I'll live," he hissed through clenched teeth. Lenore stared in surprise at the woman, who was clutching a tiny book in her right hand and a squirmy fox in her left.

"Where's Marian?" Lord Longstride demanded as he ran up behind them.

"Captured by John's men," the woman said with a sob.

"Likely so was Alan," Will added.

Lord Longstride cursed. He turned back toward the castle, and then cursed again. Lenore turned to look. The Sheriff's men were filing out of the doors. They set up a perimeter of swordsmen around the castle. On the top of the wall she could see a dozen archers taking position.

Lord Longstride turned and put his hand on Much's shoulder.

"Much, get them all back to the camp. You'll find two horses tied up a hundred yards down the road. Fetch the men from the camp, and bring them here. We need to rescue the Lady Marian and the bard before John kills them both."

Much nodded. Then he put an arm around Will, helping to support some of the man's weight. Lenore put away her knife and ran around to help support the man on the other side.

"Hurry," she heard the lady say, but she wasn't sure if she was talking to them or Lord Longstride.

Together the four of them moved down the road, leaving the lord behind. There was going to be a battle tonight. Then maybe she would have the chance to get her revenge.

Old Soldier paused, whetstone against the steel across his knee. Carefully he put the small stone back in its pouch and stood, keeping his sword in hand. He faded back into the thicket, and waited for whoever was coming down the trail toward the camp.

It didn't take long for the snow-covered undergrowth to part and reveal Will Scarlet, being helped along by a voluptuous maiden and the miller's boy. Just a few steps behind them, knife in hand, came the orphan Friar Tuck had dropped off. He let them pass, then slipped in behind them, following them to the camp. Climbing to the top of the small ridge on the westernmost side, he watched the quartet enter.

"Ho, men of the forest, awaken yourselves!" Will cried out.

The men at the fire had already turned, Will's shout brought out the ones huddled in tents and lean-tos.

Little John strode up, thick arms swinging.

"What is the meaning of this?"

Will eased himself down onto a stump. "Everyone needs to gather their weapons and come with us back to the castle."

"Why would we do that?"

Will shifted, wincing. The woman moved behind him, examining the wound through his cloak and tunic.

"Robin has called for you."

"That isn't a reason."

Much leaped forward, closing on the far larger man. His hands had knotted into fists.

"Damn you, John Little! Heed the call!"

John looked down at Much. "Check your passion, lad. It could land you in a world of hurt."

Much spat. "Oh, *now* you find courage? Against me?" He spat again, this time on John's boot. "The much-vaunted man of strength, mighty John Little, with only the bravery to fight someone a quarter his size."

"You scrawny..." John drew back. Much didn't flinch, narrow eyes staring at the giant of a man.

John swung.

* * *

Something struck him from behind, knocking into his shoulder and pushing him forward a half step. Pressure circled his arm, gripping it tightly. He turned his head and felt something sharp under his beard against the big vein in his throat. Lenore's face was inches from his, teeth bared in a hard white line as she clung to his arm like she had climbed a tree. Her breath smelled like a man's as she spoke.

"Touch him, and you'll be smiling under your whiskers."

He froze, unsure of what to do. The knife was at his throat, but he could feel her body on his arm beginning to tremble from the strain of hanging on. In just a few moments she would fall, he was sure of it.

But would she slit his throat as she did?

Anger roared up in him at the helplessness of the situation.

He felt the knife pull away, just slightly, as she slipped down his arm.

His other hand curled into a claw, moving to snatch her off him and dash her little bird skull against the ground.

"Enough."

The voice cracked across the camp like lightning striking a tree.

Every head turned, John's included, to look up at Old Soldier on the ridge. He stared down at them, steel in his hand and steel in his spine. For a long moment, time hung in the balance.

Then he spoke.

"Lord Longstride has need of us," he said. "Pick up a weapon, each of you, grab your sorry excuses for balls, and be quick about it." He pointed around the camp with his sword. "Anyone who chooses not to come—" He stopped with his sword pointed directly at Little John. "—begone from here before I return, or I will gut you and leave you to fend off the crows and the ravens.

"Do not test me on this."

It only took moments for everyone to scramble to readiness. Old Soldier turned to the forest and set off at a pace hard for a man half his age. In twos and threes all the men followed him.

"Where do you think you're going, serving girl?" Little John asked Chastity, who was sorting through the cooking utensils until she found a wide-bladed knife meant for cutting meat. It had a stiff spine and a sharp edge, and it would do.

She turned on him, eyes blazing. "My friend is captured by John. I'm going to help free her. She is my responsibility." She looked him up and then down. "I will not wait here like a coward."

John dropped his eyes. He couldn't argue with that. She had a sense of duty, a master she was willing to die for. He had once been willing to die for Robin, but that was before…

Chastity gathered her skirts and sliced through them with the knife. A few more slashes made quick work of the bottom hem, turning it into strips that she used to tie the material into pantaloons that she tucked into her boots. She grabbed a small blanket, sliced through the center of it, and stuck her head through. It hung over her shoulders as she turned, and ran to the back of the line of men and children who were following Old Soldier.

As she disappeared he looked around and found himself alone in an empty camp.

"Damned fools," he muttered.

The fire crackled beside him.

"Damn stupid fools, every one of them."

A log popped in the fire pit.

"An old man, a bunch of refugees, and some children."

A cold wind blew smoke in his eyes.

"Damn them all to *hell* for being idjits."

Little John picked up his quarter-staff and set off toward the trail they had all taken.

CHAPTER TWENTY-FIVE

In the span of just a few moments everything had gone wrong. Alan looked around him. The blackness—a physical manifestation of evil that filled the throne room—was making him sick, twisting his innards round and round. He had seen many dark things in his time, abominations and desecrations, but never anything like this.

The nobles stood around the room, listless, as though their very souls had been sucked from their bodies. Looking at the stack of bloody scrolls John had next to him, Alan thought it likely that they had been.

Dark magic was clearly present in those scrolls, and the act of signing with their own blood had done something to each of the men who had pledged their loyalty. Better far that they had resisted him.

Each man who refused, died in the act.

Alan shuddered, wondering just how much further John was going to go, and what his intentions were. Whatever they might be, they could not be allowed to come to pass. He was stripping the people... and the land.

The last time Alan had walked alone in the woods, he had heard a weeping sound as though the earth itself was in torment. Nothing was going to survive John's madness and ambition.

Alan glanced over at Marian, who had been tied to a chair to keep her from trying to escape again. Her skin was unnaturally pale, nearly translucent. He could see veins throbbing in her hands, neck, and face. The poison in the room was having an effect on her as well—a profound one.

The cardinal had been right about her. She was the one to save them. If only he could save her first. Yet he didn't have his instrument. It was across the room. His hands, too, were bound, so even if he did have it, he couldn't play. That left only his voice.

The greatest weapon a bard possessed.

"Prince John, heed my words." he said, letting his voice echo around the room. "There is no victory here for you. You oppress the people of this land, a land carved by the very hand of the Creator and set as a beacon on a hill. The Goodly-Wise and the Many-Gifted will not see this people laid to waste.

"We are ancient. We have stood against evil before, and we will continue to be steadfast. Turn aside and honor your vow to the rightful king, Richard the Lionheart. Forgo this mad quest to usurp the sovereignty of England. Turn toward the light of wisdom and knowledge.

"Choose to follow darkness at your own peril."

Silence rang at Alan's last words.

John began to clap… slowly, each one a mocking reverberation.

He descended from his throne, snake-like eyes locked on Alan's. The bard stood, chest out, unwilling to give an inch of ground. His was the right. His was the truth.

"I have met a couple of your kind before, bard," John said as he came to stand before him. "So arrogant, so smug, feeling like you know everything and the world should listen to you. I can respect that on some level. You know what your problem really is?"

Alan stood, unblinking, refusing to answer.

"None of you know when to hold your tongue." John flashed him a wicked smile and suddenly there was a curved knife in the man's hand. "So I shall do it for you." He nodded to the soldiers. "Hold him," he barked.

The guards on either side of Alan grabbed his body and head, even as he realized what John intended.

He clamped his lips shut.

John just stabbed him in the face, knife prying his jaws apart. Then pain unlike any he had ever known coursed through him as blood filled his mouth. Everything went black.

Marian screamed in horror as John cut out Alan-a-Dale's tongue. It was the ultimate desecration, the worst thing that he could have done to the bard. Alan slumped unconscious, and as John held his tongue aloft the guards let the bard fall to the floor.

John was laughing, blood dripping down his arm as he paraded around the room with the tongue held high for all to see. At last he stopped and turned to look at Marian.

"Oh, don't feel too sorry for the bard, little Princess. Your turn is coming," he said with a cruel smile. "And we have something much more special in store for you."

"You will pay for this, all of you," Marian warned. Her eyes flitted between John, the Sheriff, and Robin's mother. Clearly the woman had bound herself to the Sheriff. Marian didn't know if Robin was aware.

"Actually, it's you who will pay," John said. "And them," he added, carelessly waving a hand at the nobles who were standing around the room like statues.

"You are not king, and you never will be. The earth will spit you out. Richard will return and the rightful king will sit on the throne," she said. "You have surrounded yourself with darkness, but the light always wins."

John chortled as though she had said something funny.

"Not always, dear niece, and not this time. No, I *am* king, and soon I will be the greatest king. The King of all the West."

"A sorcerer is what you are," Marian spat.

"Yes, but Sorcerer King of all the West is a little too long a title, don't you think?"

"So, you admit it," Marian said, raising her voice and looking around, hoping against hope that at least one or two of the nobles still had their wits about them. None seemed to react at all.

"Don't look to them for help," John said, following her gaze. "They are all now bound to me, their wills are mine."

"You sold your soul," Marian accused.

John shook his head. "No need to sell anything if you have the right spell. Say, a spell that will raise an arch-demon and bind him to you," he said, eyes glancing toward the Sheriff.

Marian's blood ran cold. An arch-demon. The Sheriff just continued to stare with his unnatural eyes. She looked past him, and tried to make eye contact with Glynna.

"Lady Longstride, help me," Marian said, her voice pleading.

Glynna turned and looked at her as though seeing her for the first time.

"Why, whatever is the matter, my dear?" she asked.

"The Sheriff is a demon, and John means to destroy everything."

Glynna smiled at her. "Not everything, dear," she simpered. "But then again, you won't be around to know, will you?"

"What does she mean?" Marian asked, turning back to John.

"Oh, I forgot to tell you. To seal my kingship, only one little thing is left—and, you, my dear niece, are going to make the perfect sacrifice."

Robin had been watching the castle for hours, his fear for Marian gnawing away at him and driving him toward insanity. Too many times he'd had to control himself. Rushing in, getting killed, would leave her defenseless.

Not helpless, though. Not Marian.

He prayed that her strength remained enough.

At last he heard the sounds of movement from behind him, still coming from a way off.

It was another ten minutes before Old Soldier crouched down next to him. The others arrived in groups, and remained back a few steps. Fifteen souls ranging in age from a young boy to an old man. He prayed it would be enough.

"We are here, Lord Longstride," the man said.

Robin didn't correct him. The title chafed him, but he knew it was important to Old Soldier.

"There are almost no soldiers around the right side," he said, pointing. "They've focused mainly on the front and the side where the kitchen is, since those are the easiest points of entry."

"Begging your pardon, Lord Robin, but I spent years as the king's right hand and shield. I know this castle."

"You know a better way in?"

"That I do."

Robin nodded. "So, let's hear it."

"There's a secret way into the dungeons—there to get the king to safety if need be—which they likely don't know about. It can be accessed through the king's garden. They won't have but a guard or two in the dungeon. We arrive on the inside, and then fight our way outside."

Robin clapped his hand on the man's shoulder.

"Lead the way."

CHAPTER TWENTY-SIX

Prince John looked like a fool, prancing around the room, crowing over Marian and the bard. Glynna could tell that her love felt the same way. There was no change of his countenance as he stared at the little prince, but she could feel his contempt. The little fool had been going on for what had to be hours. She wished he would just get on with it already.

She leaned back against Nottingham, who stood behind her.

"All the boys lusted after that one," she said, pointing to Marian.

"She's no match for your beauty," he said absently, stroking her hair with a gloved fist.

Glynna thrilled at the compliment.

"Maybe not, but a match with her would put a man one step away from the throne." Before he had left, Philemon had urged Robin to try to claim the Lady Marian for himself. The thought of Robin as royalty was laughable to her. The boy had never cared anything for power or responsibility. He was content to play in his woods like a child.

Robert would have made a good king. He was away playing soldier with his father, though. Like as not they would both be killed. It didn't matter, though. Even if they did come back, they would find things much changed. A new power would be on the throne, and she very much doubted it would be the little prince.

She rubbed her stomach absently with one hand while she continued to watch John lording it over his prisoners. Such a waste of time. Torturing them, she could see, but all this talking was so… boring.

"Soon, my pet," the Sheriff rumbled in her ear, as though sensing her impatience. It was nice to have someone who understood her—all of her—so completely.

"It's just so tedious," she whispered.

"Let him gloat while he can."

He pressed icy lips to her temple and she felt it low and deep inside her body.

Idly she wondered if any of the nobles had any fight left in them to protest the sacrifice of Maid Marian, and if they even knew it was happening. Somehow she doubted it. The black marks they had earned from signing the scrolls bound them to the darkness, and the darkness was far more jealous than the light, fighting to the death for what was its own.

Of course, it didn't matter, since most of the nobles were all snugly tucked up in guest rooms all over the castle. They had been escorted there by the guards a little earlier. Most of them would be asleep by now.

Sleeping the sleep of the wicked, she mused.

The Sheriff tensed. She could feel it where her body was leaning against his. She twisted her head to look up at him. His dark eyes were fixed on the far wall, where there was a door. He shifted her weight forward so that she was standing on her own feet. Then he began to move.

Shouts came from right outside the door.

"It is time for you to retire for the evening," her love told her. "Quickly, before these idiots gain entrance and make everything even more complicated."

She pouted. She'd much rather have stayed and watched him kill every last man who dared to intrude. No, she'd just have to wait to lick their blood off him when he came to bed. Moving toward the door that would lead to the staircase nearest their room, she paused and turned. The main doors flew open. Four men ran in, blades dripping the blood of the guards outside.

She frowned. It wasn't much of an assault. Were it not for the surprise, they'd be dead already. Somehow she thought there would have been more.

They crept up the stairs from the dungeon. Old Soldier had been right about the secret passageway. At the top it was a simple matter for Robin to put an arrow through the throat of the lone guard. Then they flooded out of the dark, dank basement and made for the throne room, where the sounds of battle had just begun.

A moment later they burst through a back door, one usually reserved for the king alone. Robin stepped in and quickly moved to the side as he let arrow after arrow fly. Men streamed past him, fanning out around the room.

Much headed straight for Marian, as Robin had told him to. He covered the boy's progress with his bow, felling any who stepped in front of him. All the while Robin was trying to keep an eye out for the Sheriff. He could hear the black arrow in his quiver as though it were singing to him, begging him to take it out and use it.

Much reached Marian and frantically began untying her. His feet slid in blood that was pooled on the floor. Robin tried not to think of whose blood it might be.

His fingers kept flying, each arrow was barely notched before it was buried in another enemy. Those who had come at his call streamed into the room, attacking the Sheriff's men with a host of different weapons. As grateful as he was for the help, it became harder to find clean targets. He didn't want to risk shooting one of his own people. He had full faith in his aim, but in the heat of battle people moved quickly, and a friend might suddenly be where a foe had been only a heartbeat earlier.

Old Soldier was in the thick of things, bodies piling up around him. He was a magnificent sight with blood dripping from his sword as he yanked it free from another of the Sheriff's demons who crumpled to the ground.

Ten feet away from him, though, Aiden was not doing nearly so well. The man had not always been the bravest, but he had charged into that room with the rest of them.

One soldier lay dead at his feet.

Robin quickly put arrows through two others that were converging on him, but watched helpless as a third seemed to rise up as though from the floor itself and ram a sword through Aiden's gut. He heaved the poor man into the air and then tossed him aside like a rag doll.

Rage filled Robin as the lifeless body hit the floor.

Chastity made it to Marian's side just as the miller's son finished untying her. Together they got her to her feet, but Chastity was dismayed to discover that Marian couldn't stand.

The sickness that had taken her seemed worse now. Her mistress's face was pale, her skin nearly translucent. Her eyes were glassy and bloodshot and there was no tension in her body. She could barely even hold her head up straight let alone move her arms or legs.

"We'll have to carry her," she told the boy.

He nodded, and before she could do anything he had hoisted Marian up into his arms as though she weighed nothing.

"Take her back the way we came," Chastity ordered.

Much nodded and started to run for the back of the room. She began to follow but then stopped, turning to look for Will. He'd been wounded earlier, and she'd never had a chance to find out how badly. Fear prickled along her skin.

At last her eyes fell on a hooded figure some distance away from Lord Longstride, struggling against a soldier. Though she could not see his face, the quickening of her pulse was all she needed to know that the hooded fighter was Will. With her very next breath, though, her fear increased as she realized that there was blood dripping down both his arms.

She ran toward him, yanking the dagger free of her bodice and ramming it into the neck of the soldier Will was fighting. The man hit the floor and she reached out to Will.

"We have Marian," she said. "Much is taking her back out the way we came. Go, protect them, I'll alert the others."

Will nodded and turned to go. She sucked in her breath as she noticed that a patch of blood on his back was quickly spreading. He was wounded worse than she had feared.

She forced herself to turn and scan the room, looking for the rest of their compatriots.

The Lady Marian weighed almost nothing, and Much was nearly to the door that would lead back out the way they'd come. He could see it just up ahead. Then, suddenly, a dark figure seemed to slither into the space between him and it.

Much slid to a halt and stared in awe and fear at the Sheriff who transfixed him with eyes that seemed to burn like flames.

"Give her to me, boy, and I won't hurt you."

It was a lie. Even if it wasn't, there was no way he was giving the lady to him. He took a step back, looking around for Robin—who was no longer where Much had last seen him. He turned back as the Sheriff began to stride toward him, a sneer twisting his lips.

"You can't run from me, boy," the man growled. "Don't even try." Then, from out of nowhere, Lenore raced into sight. She threw herself onto the Sheriff's back and began stabbing at him with a dagger. He roared in surprise and fury and twisted, trying to reach her.

Much darted around them and made it through the doorway. He ran and didn't look back until the sounds of fighting had faded into the distance.

* * *

Tears were streaming openly down Friar Tuck's cheeks as he untied the bard that had been his friend through so many years and so many trials. They had taken Alan's tongue. It was unthinkable, but true.

Alan had revived at some point and struggled to stand on his own. Chastity ran past.

"We have Marian," she shouted before she disappeared from view.

He heard a clamor of noise and he turned just in time to see a host of nobles enter the room, moving stiffly and carrying swords. Each of them had a glazed look on their face as though they were sleepwalking.

Or under a dark curse.

Friar Tuck crossed himself.

It was time to go. Crouching down, he put his shoulder into Alan's stomach and then stood, the bard draped over his shoulder, and made his way to the exit.

Will was hurt bad. Every step was getting harder to take as he chased after Much and Marian. At last he came upon them, just short of exiting the castle, clearly waiting for someone to give them orders. The rest should be coming soon. He prayed they would.

Suddenly he could hear screams, carrying far more clearly than the sounds of battle. It chilled him to the bone. Had he not already been shaking from his injuries it would have been enough to cause his knees to quiver.

He looked at Marian and all he could think about was Robin, and how much his cousin loved her. Robin was still back there, fighting. He just hoped Chastity got to him soon.

* * *

Little John swung his sword, cleaving in half the demon that had been on the verge of killing Audric. Rage roared through him. The boy was too young to be here. The others shouldn't have let him or his brother come. It just showed how selfish they could be, putting children in harm's way.

"We're leaving!" the castle girl who served Marian shouted as she raced past toward the far side of the room. He scooped up the boy under his left arm and turned to go.

As he did he saw Timothy, one of his friends since youth who had worked the fields with him. He was disarmed, standing before a soldier. John hefted the sword in his right hand, and then threw it for all it was worth. Propelled by his massive strength, it impaled the soldier.

"We're leaving!" he shouted, and Timothy needed no second warning.

"Nice move," Old Soldier grunted as he fell into step.

"What's wrong with them?" John asked, coming to a sudden halt as he saw nobles moving around the room, some fighting, others just waving their swords in the air, all of them moving stiffly as if they were made of wood.

"I don't know and I'm not going to stick around to find out," Old Soldier said grimly.

Sound strategy.

As their men began pouring back down the tunnel, Will looked for Robin. He felt relief when he saw him helping another who was limping. There were many wounded and others who had not yet shown. He saw Jansa, the woman from the kitchen who had saved his life, running down the corridor, clutching the hand of a child. He was glad she was getting out. She and some of the others passed them, Old Soldier shepherded some more.

At any moment the soldiers would be coming, in numbers too great to fight. They were never going to make it, not without some sort of distraction. And Robin would be fool enough to stay until the last straggler left, getting himself killed in the process.

Much stood, moving from foot to foot, looking to him for an order. Marian was in the boy's arms, pale, but looking resolute. Will coughed, and blood bubbled up on his lips. He reached out and put a hand on Marian's arm.

"What would you do to save Robin?" he asked.

She paused. "You asked me that question before."

"I'm asking it again."

"My answer is the same," she said. "I'd do anything."

"Unfortunately, my answer is the same, too," Will said. He touched her cheek. "Take care of him."

"Will, what are you—"

He turned and ran back toward the throne room, passing the others, and pulling the hood of his jerkin up. He had an arrow in one hand and a sword in the other and he stabbed and thrust with them both until he had made it back inside.

Prince John turned.

"You!" he thundered.

"Yes," Will said. His heart was pounding in his chest as he reached up and revealed his face. He could do this for Robin, for Marian, to give them a fighting chance. He took a deep breath.

"I am the Hood."

"*No!*" Chastity tried to shout, her heart stopping within her. Her words came out only as the faintest of whispers. She had been just about to enter the corridor when Will had come running back into the hall. She understood now what it was he was doing.

"Stop!" John thundered.

The soldiers had been about to rush from the room after the others. At his command, they stopped. The nobles who had been milling aimlessly about stopped as well. All eyes turned to John as he strode toward Will, his face contorting.

"You!" he said again.

Will smiled, that rakish, charming smile she had found so endearing and childlike. Only now there was blood on his lips, and it made the expression seem sinister instead.

"Of course, you fool. Who else could it have been?" Will said, his voice mocking. "I nearly laughed myself to tears when you thought Marian might be the spy in your castle. It was me all along, and the steward worked with me."

Chastity blinked.

"Bring the steward!" John roared.

Two soldiers left hastily. Moments later they returned with the man who looked like he was about to crawl out of his own skin.

"Do you know who this man is?" John demanded of the steward, a shaking finger pointed at Will.

"My liege, that is Will Scarlet," the steward said, voice trembling, eyes bugging from his head. He probably thought that John had lost his mind. He might as well have.

"It's alright, my friend, you don't have to cover for me anymore," Will said to the man, his voice gentle. "John knows I'm the Hood."

"The Hood?" the steward gasped. "Surely not, I mean no, I don't know any such—"

"It's alright," Will repeated. "I've always loved you for your courage, your loyalty to Richard. Don't let it fail you now."

The steward stood, open-mouthed.

He was still standing there, staring, an instant later when the Sheriff ran him through.

"Goodbye, old friend," Will said as the steward's body hit the floor.

Will coughed, and more blood appeared on his lips. That was when Chastity realized what he was doing. He was dying, and he was using his final moments to save the others. Tears burned her eyes and streaked down her cheeks.

"So you want us to believe that Marian knew nothing of your masquerade as the Hood?" the Sheriff asked coldly.

Will rolled his eyes.

"That girl child doesn't understand anything about the way the world works. The night I failed to kill John, I tried to hide in her room. She woke and I had to attempt to seduce her so that she wouldn't discover the true reason for my being there."

"So, she's not even the object of your affection," the Sheriff said.

Will laughed. "No, Marian's not my lady."

Chastity blinked. Her vision came roaring back to her. People weeping because the Hood was dead, and crying "woe to his lady." The bells would toll, the people would spread the word that the Hood was dead and that woe had befallen his lady. Her. She didn't know what would become of her, but she knew that she could not let him die alone.

She dropped her weapon and rushed forward. She threw her arms around him. He was cold, so very cold, as she pressed shaking lips to his, blood coated her mouth. She pressed her face against his chest and began to sob. The vision hadn't been about Marian and Robin. It had been about her and Will.

He collapsed into her arms and they fell together to the floor. She cradled him in her arms, his blood seeping into her clothes.

"I should have kissed you sooner," he said.

"I kissed *you*, remember?" she responded, suppressing a sob, trying to be strong for him and knowing that she was failing. A light appeared in his eyes and he smiled at her so gently it broke her heart.

"I love you," he whispered, for her ears alone.

THE HEART OF
SHERWOOD

CHAPTER TWENTY-SEVEN

When they made it to the clearing in the woods, Marian tried to dismount. All her muscles seized, though, and she started to fall. Robin caught her and set her on her feet. She grabbed hold of her horse's saddle, leaning against the beast for support as she tried to get her limbs to stop shaking.

Around her she saw tired, defeated faces. Most of them were covered in blood. Worst of all was Alan. His face had pulled into a rictus, the muscles twisted around his mouth. Blood darkened his jaw like a beard, dried into a thick crust from the line of his lips to his collar. To take a bard's tongue was inhuman.

It would have been far kinder to kill him.

"Lenore, has anyone seen Lenore?" Friar Tuck called. He must have guessed the truth, because he began to weep.

They had lost too many today. Not the least of which was Will. There was a good chance Chastity was dead as well.

Marian made it to a seat on a tree stump and tried to gather her wits back together. All around her she could hear the sounds of weeping. Not loud, but heartfelt. She watched as Robin added a couple of drops from a small vial into a cup of water. She suspected that it might be the last of the elixir that had saved so many from the pox.

A minute later her suspicions were confirmed when Robin

bade Friar Tuck distribute it to all who were injured. Tuck took the cup and poured a few drops into Alan's mouth. The friar then turned and began ministering to the others.

Robin stood for a moment, hands clenched into fists at his side. Marian recognized the look on his face. Hopelessness. She knew that had to be what it was, because it was what she was feeling deep in her own heart. He stood another few seconds, then turned and melted into the forest.

He probably wanted to be alone. She could understand that. The urge was great to slink off quietly by herself. However, if there was one thing she knew at that moment, it was that none of them should be alone.

She glanced around at the others. Everyone had someone they were speaking with or attending to. They kept one another warm, and did their best to cope. She couldn't tell if any of them had even noticed that Robin had gone. She lingered a few seconds, then rose and followed him into the woods.

The darkness of the forest wrapped around her as soon as she stepped from the clearing. The trees loomed above her, sentinels keeping guard over the goings on beneath their branches. Sherwood had fascinated her as a little girl. There was something about it that had always felt comforting, reassuring to her.

Yet there was a little part of her that was afraid when she was within its borders. She always had the sensation that there were a thousand eyes on her—birds, beasts, even trees. Then there were the others.

Fey. That's what people called them. The creatures that lived in the wood that were neither man nor beast. Most were said to be imbued with some sort of magic. Even as a young child she hadn't been able to dismiss the stories as easily as others. She had always felt deep down that there was truth to them. She'd also wished she was brave enough to run off to find them, and have adventures.

She'd nearly done it once, not long after her parents had died. She'd been on her horse and she'd outrun her keepers. She had stopped at the edge of Sherwood and stared into it, unblinking, for what had seemed like an eternity. She could swear she heard voices whispering, calling to her...

Marian.

"Robin?"

She turned, thinking she'd heard someone say her name. There was only the dark of the forest, though. She realized that she had been walking for a couple of minutes, so lost in thought that she didn't know where she was or even how to get back to the camp.

Her heart began to beat a little quicker. Lost in the forest, just as she'd dreamed about as a young girl. She spun slowly in a circle, breathing in the rich, heady aroma of earth and trees, growing things and dying things. As she completed her turn she accepted that she was entirely lost.

She could shout. Hopefully someone at the camp would hear her and come to bring her back. She remained silent, though. Even though it was night and she was tired and dark things lurked in the shadows, she felt no fear. Robin called this forest home, and she refused to be afraid of Robin's home.

"Robin," she called again, her voice barely a whisper that floated on the air for a moment, and then vanished.

Something moved behind her. She didn't hear anything, but she just *knew* there was something there. Something brushed against the back of her hair, and she turned to stare into Robin's eyes.

He was looking down at her, his lips parted slightly as though he were on the verge of saying something.

She expected him to drop his hand, but instead he stroked her hair lightly as he continued to stare at her.

Around them the forest was alive. She could feel it like a singing in her blood. She took a step closer to him and pressed a hand against his chest. He bent down and kissed her, his lips feather soft against hers.

She gave herself over to the kiss and, for a moment, all the pain and the fear seemed to vanish. She let herself lean into him, relishing the feel of his warmth and strength as his arms went around her. She wished they could stay that way for an eternity.

It was Robin who broke the embrace, and for a moment she felt a loss that was overwhelming. He smiled at her, though, in a way that made her heart quicken. One arm still around her, he led her to a fallen log, the remains of a once mighty tree. Together they sat, side by side. He kept his arm around her back and she leaned her head against his shoulder.

"I was so worried for you," he said. "I've never in all my life been that afraid."

"I knew you'd come for me," she said, though she didn't mention the cost. Robin already knew that. She wanted to say something about Will, but she couldn't bring herself to, not yet.

"Chastity gave the book to Friar Tuck," Robin said. "The one Cardinal Francis told you we needed to take to the heart of Sherwood."

"Yes," Marian said, wishing that such unpleasant things could be put off for later. However, she knew they couldn't. Time was running out for all of them. It was still night, though, and the darkness of the forest was near absolute. They were both exhausted from the fight too. As much as she felt an urge to set out immediately, she knew they needed to wait, at least until it was daylight and they'd had a chance to rest. As it was, she knew she needed sleep before she could make such a journey, and she was sure Robin did as well.

"We should rest and set out in the morning," Robin suggested.

"I think you're reading my mind," she said. "I'm just so weary, but we only have six days before the solstice and Cardinal Frances told me we had to complete our task before then."

"It's a big forest. A man could spend months walking in it and never touch every part," Robin said, voice worried.

"We will find a way," she said, just as much to reassure herself as him.

Sitting there with him, out of her tower and away from John

and the Sheriff, she felt free and she realized she was breathing easier. Despite the unknown that lay before them, even her muscles were beginning to relax. A glorious drowsy feeling was creeping over her, and she suspected that with little effort she could fall asleep right where she was sitting. Robin's shoulder made a perfect pillow.

Something soft suddenly nudged her hand. Startled she looked down to see Champion standing on his hind feet, paws braced against the log. She bent down to scoop up the little fox and put him in her lap.

"How on earth did you get here?" she asked.

"Chastity brought him with her to the camp. He must have caught your scent and tracked you out here," Robin said.

She stroked the furry little beast who curled up with his tail over his face. She could tell by his breathing when he fell asleep.

"We'll have to do something about him, so he doesn't get lost trying to follow us tomorrow," she said.

Growing up she'd never had a dog as a pet, and couldn't bear the thought of something happening to the little fox.

Robin reached over and stroked his small head.

"Actually, I think you should bring him with us," he said.

She looked at Robin in surprise.

"What if the journey is perilous? There will be guardians to face, and opponents to defeat." She frowned at him. "I will not place him in danger, not after what we've just escaped."

"I can't explain it," he said, ignoring her ire, "but since I became the keeper of the black arrow things have been... different. I understand the animals even more than I used to, or perhaps they understand me. I don't know. What I *do* know is that he won't be happy unless he's by your side. He might even be a help to us."

Marian bit her lip and looked down at the little creature. All her protective, motherly instincts were kicking in. However, Robin's words had the ring of truth to them, and she couldn't deny it.

"Maybe he is well-named, is Champion," she said.

"It may be that tomorrow we will find out."

They sat together a while longer, saying little. Marian kept breathing the free air with relief that outweighed her terrible sense of loss, and the sense of apprehension about what was to come.

At last Robin led her back to the camp. It was nearer than she would have thought. Things were quiet, most were asleep. Some of the men had erected a crude shelter a little way off, where she found a couple of the female servants from the castle, including her friend the cook, sleeping soundly. They must have decided it was safer to come with the others than stay behind and take their chances with John. Marian felt a twinge of sorrow for each of them and what they might have left behind. Then she curled up with Champion and within moments was sound asleep.

The Sheriff wasn't in the mood to be trifled with, or disappointed. The Hood was dead, but his allies had escaped, taking the Lady Marian with them. They had fled into the forest where they knew he could not go—a barrier his dark practitioners had still not been able to breach. Abruptly, and rather conveniently, the leprous Scotsman had called to him saying they had a solution. When he arrived at the hut, the rest had already assembled.

"What have you found?" he barked as he entered.

The Mad Monk bowed low.

"My lord," he said, indicating the leper with a wave of his hand, "we have found a way for you to penetrate the forest."

"You can cast a spell that enables me to enter Sherwood?" he asked.

"Not you, but a force that you may manipulate," Sera, a gnarled old witch who seemed older than time itself, said. "It's old magic, very old. It took much effort to read the signs, to find it."

"Explain," he demanded.

"There is a force, a creature, who predates much of the magic that protects the forest. In fact, he is kindred to its elemental nature. He can be summoned, and once summoned, he can be given a mission," the Mad Monk said.

"What kind of force?"

"A creature of pure destruction," a painfully thin boy, the disciple of the leprous Scotsman, said, voice eager to please. "Like a storm."

"Yes, but to raise him, it requires the darkest of spells… and a sacrifice. It bodes ill, so say the stars."

The Sheriff turned to look at the pale, waspish man with the nervous eyes and perpetual squint, who spent all his time staring at the sky looking for signs and portents. Desmond was his name. Rumor had it that he didn't so much as relieve his bowels if it wasn't in the stars.

"Does this creature have a name?" he asked, turning back to the others.

"Guy, so named for the grotesque nature of his appearance," the mad monk said.

The Sheriff looked around the room and idly wondered if any creature could be called more grotesque in appearance than those present. Even as his gaze fell upon the Scotsman who had summoned him, a bit of the man's ear fell off onto the ground as if unable to take the weight of his stare. He rolled his eyes.

"And where can I find this… Guy?"

"His resting place is in Gisbourne bog, adjacent to the great forest. Even now he sleeps there," the Scotsman said a bit breathlessly.

"Then what are we waiting for?" the Sheriff responded. "Let us wake him up."

The Mad Monk and the leper lifted the loose-limbed body of Desmond, the astrologer, and tossed it into the thick, murky water. "At least I finally found a use for him," the Sheriff muttered, mostly to himself.

For a long moment the body lay on the surface, suspended by

a brackish scum nearly a hand's breadth thick. Finally the scum cracked under the weight of the corpse and allowed it to sink below the surface.

The Sheriff stared, waiting for something to happen. Dead creatures floated on the bog's surface, bloated and rotting, half-submerged by the weight of their slowly dissolving flesh. The air was so rank, so choked with poison, that the others were having trouble breathing.

Suddenly a man—*no, a creature*—rose out of the bog as though ascending from Hell itself. When at last it stood free of the scum-crusted pond, it was more than a foot taller than the average man.

Ancient demonic designs were inscribed on his arms and his chest, spilling under raw skin across slabs of muscle. Antlers grew from his head, tangled and gnarled like a bramble of wicked bone, and his feet were black cloven hooves. His eyes glowed the crimson of spilled blood. A horsehide cloak and loincloth were his only coverings. He threw back his head and laughed and out of his mouth spilled perversions and filth.

The Sheriff began to smile.

"Welcome back to the land of the living, Guy of Gisbourne."

"What have you called me to do?" the voice that rumbled forth seemed to make the very air and the earth tremble.

"Go into the forest. Destroy the followers of the Hood, particularly whoever is leading them now, and capture the Lady Marian.

"Bring her to me."

CHAPTER TWENTY-EIGHT

It was not quite morning when Marian woke, still exhausted. She lay still for a moment, trying to tell what woke her. A small nose nuzzled her hand, and she lifted it to pet Champion, who was squirming a lot more than he usually did in the morning.

That must have been what awakened her. She would have to tell Chastity that Robin and she were going to take the little fox with them. Then she remembered that Chastity wasn't there. Tears filled her eyes as she thought about her friend. She didn't even know if she was alive, and if so, what horrors were befalling her.

She bit down hard on her fist to keep from screaming in rage and pain. It took a few more minutes for her to regain control. Once she had changed into the men's clothes she used for riding, she finally left the area of the tent and walked slowly to the main campsite. Champion bounded up and down next to her, clearly enjoying the feel of the earth on his paws. She still held trepidations about taking him with them, but she trusted Robin's instincts.

All the men appeared to be asleep except for Little John, who was sitting apart from the rest. When he saw her he looked a little startled at first, and was clearly unsettled to see her in trousers, but quickly dropped into an awkward bow.

"Good morning," she said. "Is anyone else awake?"

"Only… his lordship," he said, voice twisting slightly as though "lordship" wasn't the word he'd initially intended to use.

"He's not a lord anymore," Marian said softly. "Actually, I don't know if you heard, but as of yesterday there isn't a Lord Locksley anymore, either. The Sheriff killed him. Since he had no heirs, John will probably snatch up both Locksley and Longstride lands."

Little John's face twisted. "My wife and children are still living on Longstride land."

Marian could feel the pain radiating off of him.

"If we can defeat John and the Sheriff, then they'll be safe. Everyone will. If not, no one will be safe." She paused, and then added, "I promise you that we will do our best to protect them. Everything that is happening is splitting families apart. I miss my uncle and fear for his safety. You do the same for your wife and children. Robin has lost all his siblings, his father is away and might be dead already, and his mother consorts with the enemy."

Little John's eyes widened at that.

"Lady Longstride?" he asked.

"Yes, she is in league with the Sheriff."

Little John cursed then looked at her sheepishly.

"Beg pardon, milady," he said.

"You said Robin was awake," she said, giving him a little smile. "Where is he?"

"Where is he always?" Little John said, jerking a thumb over his shoulder. "In the forest."

"Thank you."

Marian moved to the edge of the clearing and stood just inside the tree line, letting her eyes adjust to the darkness beyond. Even before they could, she sensed a presence nearby.

"Robin?" she asked.

"Yes. Are you ready?"

"No, but it's time to go."

"Have you eaten?"

She shook her head, then remembered he might not be able to see the gesture in the dark.

"I have some meat and cheese when you are ready."

Apparently he could see in the dark even if she couldn't.

"I need to retrieve the book from Friar Tuck."

"I already got it this morning," he said.

"I didn't realize the friar was awake yet."

"He wasn't, but there are only so many places he could hide something."

Marian's eyes were finally adjusting to the darkness, and she could make out Robin's face.

"Very well," she said. "Let's go then."

He reached out and took her hand in his. Together they began to walk deeper into the woods. She had to trust him to guide her, because she couldn't see the ground. Occasionally Champion bumped against her ankle, so she knew he was staying with them.

"Dawn is coming," Robin said after a while.

"How do you know?" she asked.

"I can feel it."

A few minutes later she saw that the darkness was growing lighter. Soon she could make out Champion, bounding and jumping and running beside them. She could see the ground at her feet, and had no more need of Robin's hand to guide her. She did not let go, though.

As the light penetrated the forest, the sounds around them changed. The nocturnal birds went quiet as others came awake with rapturous song. More creatures began to stir as well.

They came upon a small, ice-lined spring where a family of deer were slaking their morning thirst. With them was a curious-looking creature with fine silver down on its body, and a long flowing mane of hair. It turned as if sensing her stare and she gasped. Its features were far more human than animal. Its eyes quickened with thought, and it dove beneath the surface of the water.

"What was that?" she asked Robin.

"That was one of the fey," he said. "They guard the forest and its secrets. The closer we get to the heart of Sherwood, the more we are likely to encounter them. Some are hostile, others less so."

"When I was little, Uncle Richard would tell me stories about them, but I never truly knew if they existed," she said, wondering now if the king had known all along about these creatures.

"It does not take long for truth to pass into myth," Robin said. "Not that many years ago, everyone knew the fey were real. Now some believe, while others think they are ghosts or devils of some sort. Others choose not to believe at all."

Marian couldn't help but wonder what time would do to the truth of their war against the darkness.

When they had journeyed nearly half a day, they stopped and ate some of the food Robin had brought with them. Champion gobbled down the bit of meat Marian gave him, then settled down on the tops of her feet for a nap.

Robin produced the book from the bag that he was carrying. He handed it to her and she opened it.

"From what I've been able to glean from the instructions here," she said, "it seems that we must overcome challenges by three different guardians, in order to reach the heart of Sherwood.

"According to Cardinal Francis," she continued, "the heart of Sherwood is actually a tree, the Oak of Thynghowe. The book refers to it as an ancient guardian at the center of the forest."

"Well, that's something, at least," he said. "How we're supposed to know it from all the others I guess we'll have to wait and find out."

"The first guardian is of the body," Marian said. "I gather that the challenge is a physical one of some sort."

Robin frowned. "In order to take the black arrow, I had to best the creature that was guarding it. That challenge was a physical one, but there was also a component of strategy. I had to be willing to use the arrow, and it had to pierce my skin, then choose to spare me instead of killing me."

"So, with each of these challenges we must keep our wits about us, and see what is beyond the obvious."

"Yes."

"The second guardian is of the mind and the third is of the soul. Not that I'm sure knowing that helps us at all. How much longer do you think it will take us to find the first guardian?" Marian asked.

"I'm not sure, but this is the farthest I've ever been in this direction. With our next steps the forest will be new to me as well," he warned.

A few minutes later Marian woke Champion from his nap, and the three of them continued on, Robin in the lead and Marian a few steps behind, with the fox keeping mostly between them.

What had to have been a couple more hours passed and worry began to settle into the creases of Marian's mind. It was as though she could physically feel the sands of an hourglass running out as time slipped away from them.

She found herself praying that they would locate the first guardian soon. It was growing even colder as the afternoon was waning, and even though she was moving, the chill was making everything ache—particularly her nose and her fingers.

She could only imagine what they would do when night fell. Robin might be able to see at night in the woods, but she certainly couldn't, and she was already growing weary. She was starting to trip over roots in her path, and feared that they might have to stop for the night without having made any progress.

One more day until all is lost.

Then, suddenly, up ahead of them, directly in their path, Marian noticed two particularly tall, thin trees that grew exceptionally straight. They appeared to be birches, with smooth white bark, and looked like perfect twins. They stood with three feet between them. There was something about them that struck her as peculiar, and she slowed, touching Robin's shoulder and indicating that he should do the same.

Indeed, they were exact twins, mirror images of each other with leafless branches alike in number and placement. She knew that in the world identical people might be born, but she'd never seen trees such as these. They were such an odd sight that they took her mind off the cold and the pain in her fingers and the aching in her joints.

Robin stepped ahead, moving closer to them, then swerved to pass to the left of the trees, instead of walking straight between them.

"Robin!"

He stopped and turned to look at her.

"You've been marching us straight as an arrow all day," she said. "Why are you angling around those trees, rather than passing between them?" she asked.

He blinked at her. "I don't know," he said, frowning. "I just... don't feel like walking between them. For some reason it feels wrong."

"Doesn't that strike you as strange?"

"I suppose so," he replied, still frowning.

"*Can* you walk between them?" she asked.

He looked as if he was about to take a step forward. His weight shifted, his muscles flexed, but he didn't move.

"I don't want to," he admitted.

Marian could feel excitement growing within her. "There must be magic at play, don't you think?"

"I don't know."

She walked forward, catching up to him. As she stepped close to the two trees she felt a sudden aversion to them, a wave of deep dislike. Her eyes slid off them as though she didn't want to even look at them. Something inside her urged her to go around.

She moved toward the side of the one tree then stopped and forced herself to reach out and put a hand on it. It took all of her determination, as though she were actually fighting the muscles in her own arm to make it happen. At last her fingertips touched bark, and she yanked her hand back with a cry.

"What's wrong?"

"It's… hot to the touch. It nearly burnt me. I definitely think magic is at play here," Marian said. "There's nothing else it could be. Something doesn't want us to walk between them."

She felt a glimmer of hope again. Maybe this was the first challenge. From what Robin had said, she had expected to find a fey standing guard. There was nothing that said it had to work that way, though.

"Which leaves us no alternative," Robin said with certainty. "It's exactly what we need to do."

Marian tried to lift her foot, to force it in the direction of the opening between the two trunks, but she couldn't. It was as if her foot had grown roots and was anchored into the ground.

"I can't do it," she gasped at last.

"Nor can I," Robin said, the strain clear in his voice.

"I don't have the strength," she added, and she blinked as she heard the words she'd spoken.

Strength.

"Robin, this is the first test," she said with a gasp.

And we're failing it, she told herself.

CHAPTER TWENTY-NINE

A failure. You are a failure.
   The words had been rattling around in Friar Tuck's mind for hours.

The last man of God, and you are worthless.

When the voice of the evil one came to him, it was sometimes disguised as his own. Other times it had a silken, oily quality to it by which he could tell its true origin. Never before, though, had the voice been that of someone he knew. *You let everyone die. You have disappointed God.*

It was the voice of Cardinal Francis.

Hot tears burned in his eyes. It was hard to denounce a demon when you agreed with it.

A hand touched his shoulder and he jumped, spinning around to see Alan standing there, eyes wide with concern. The elixir had healed his wounds but it didn't have the power to give him back that which had been taken. The bard would never again speak words of wisdom and counsel, never sing and move men to acts of courage.

"I'm so sorry," Tuck whispered before he could stop himself. "It's all my fault. I should never have involved you in all this."

Alan shook his head fiercely. He turned and gestured to the rest of the camp. Then he turned back and touched, first Tuck's heart, then his lips.

"You want me to speak to them?" Tuck asked, gazing out over the survivors. He didn't need to see their faces to feel their fear, their pain. It was evident in their hunched shoulders, their downcast eyes, and the silence with which they were going about their daily rituals.

"I can't speak to them," Tuck said. How could he give them hope, when he held onto none himself?

Alan tapped him again in the chest, harder this time, and nodded, adding an intense glare that seemed to lay bare Tuck's soul.

"He's right," a voice said softly. "It's you they need to hear from."

Tuck turned to find Old Soldier standing beside him, where a moment before there had been no one. It startled him again.

"Would it kill you to make some noise?" he snapped without thinking. He instantly regretted both his tone and his choice of words.

"It might," Old Soldier said, nodding slowly.

"I don't know what to say," Tuck admitted.

"Then you'd better pray for some words," the man told him. "Those people, they don't need a soldier right now. They need someone to minister to them, to remind them that right is on their side and that they're fighting for a higher purpose. I don't think a one of them had ever seen evil quite like that until yesterday. Most are still in shock. If they'd given any thought to demons at all, it was to believe that they might possess men. I guarantee you none of them ever expected to see a devil walking around wearing its own face and skin."

He was right. What Old Soldier was saying was true. Evil had stopped masquerading in England. It had stopped dressing up as men, and had started to wear its own face. Which meant evil didn't think it had anything to fear.

Suddenly he knew just how *wrong* that was. He puffed out his chest, and took a deep breath. Evil was very much mistaken.

He gave Old Soldier and Alan brief nods, and then he strode toward the center of the activity.

"Good Christian folk," he called out.

Everyone stopped and turned to look at him. Taken aback, he calmed himself for a moment. Then he pressed forward.

"Gather 'round, for there is something I must say to you." He threw his arms wide. "We have seen the true face of the enemy, and that is how we know he can be defeated. Christ cast out demons, and he has told his servants to do likewise. We will not let the devil take root here in England. We will eradicate him, yank him out by his roots and burn him until there is no trace left.

"I know you are tired, but God says not to be weary in doing good deeds. And there are no greater deeds than those entrusted to you. I tell you this much, every man and woman of you is carrying out the Lord's work. You're holding this land for all good Christian men, and protecting it in the absence of King Richard, God save him."

"God save him," they said together, quietly.

He had their attention. Turning slowly, he sought to connect with each and every one of them. A few refused, keeping their gaze fixedly on the ground. He knew in a sudden flash of enlightenment that those who wouldn't fight would be slaughtered like animals.

That must not happen.

"We have a plan," he said. "Lord Robin and Lady Marian are even now doing their part to help us win the day. Now is not the time to lose heart. Now is the time to redouble our efforts, because we know the face of the enemy, and we know that greater is the God of the heavens than John the usurper."

Around him heads nodded. He was getting through. He wasn't the most eloquent speaker, but he had truth on his side, and righteousness, and they would speak for themselves.

"When the time comes to strike the final blow, we must be ready," he said. "See to everything that needs to be prepared, weapons first." He paused, then added, "I need two people to spend time with me in prayer."

One man still had his head down, eyes on the ground. He wouldn't fight, Friar Tuck knew that for certain. So he reached out and touched the man on the arm.

"Will you pray with me?" he asked.

The man's shoulders hunched even more, and he shook his head. It was the barest of movements, but his intention was clear.

Tuck dropped his hand.

"I'll pray with you." Tuck turned to see Haylan, the youngest of the stonecutter's boys, standing there, eyes wide.

"Thank you, my son," Tuck said, putting a hand on the child's head.

He turned expectantly, looking for another volunteer. To his surprise Alan stepped forward, his hand raised.

Tuck nodded, keeping a sigh to himself. A mute druid and a small boy. It wasn't exactly what he had been looking for. The Bible did say, though, that wherever two or three gathered together in His name, that God was in the midst of them. Christ also said that truth came from the mouths of babes.

"You two, come with me," Tuck said.

As the encampment began to buzz with activity once again, they moved a short distance away, where they would not be disturbed by the work being done. Placing blankets beneath them to protect them from the frozen earth, they settled themselves on the ground, Tuck on his knees.

Before they could begin a girl ran up to them.

"I'm told to tell you that Jonah ran away," she said. "He won't fight anymore."

Tuck nodded heavily. Without asking, he knew who Jonah was, and he wasn't surprised. He wondered if Old Soldier had sent anyone after him, to bring him back. The location of this place was a secret. Still, the Sheriff and his demons could not enter the forest, so perhaps it wasn't as great a worry as he thought.

"Thank you, child," he said.

"May I pray with you, too?" the girl asked, eyes wide.

"Of course. Sit down here. What's your name?"

"Esther, my mum's a cook in the castle," she said, eyes wide as she sat down and folded her hands.

"That's a good name, Esther. She was a strong woman who saved all her people with her courage," Tuck told the girl who beamed proudly at him.

Alan unfastened his harp. It was a miracle that while the monsters had been cutting out his tongue, they had not destroyed the ancient instrument as well. The bard's fingers touched the strings so gently that the sound was but a whisper, as of an evening breeze. Still, Tuck felt the music wrap around him, emboldening him. He had been wrong. Even without his tongue Alan was still a force to be reckoned with.

Friar Tuck bowed his head and began to pray. He could hear the children joining in from time to time, and underneath it all he heard the golden melody of Alan's harp. There was a lesson in this, too, for him. It mattered not how small or weak the group of faithful who prayed. What mattered was the mightiness of their prayers.

The mighty oaks of Sherwood might as well be made out of straw, for all the notice Guy of Gisbourne gave them. His antlers scraped the lower branches, and occasionally sent one crashing to the snow-covered ground.

Only the thickest, mightiest of trees did he bother to walk around. The rest he walked through. Animals fled before him, but he let them go. They were not the prey he sought.

At last he heard something walking through the forest that did not sound like an animal. It wasn't as swift and sure of foot as the deer and the rabbits. Nor was it as stealthy as the fox or the wolf. This creature walked upright on two feet, instead of four.

He had found a man, one which had become separated from its fellows. One which was not at home in the forest, and knew not its paths nor how to walk them. Guy breathed in deeply. He could smell the creature's fear and desperation. It was a heady aroma, and he breathed deeply.

The man was nearby and coming toward him. Guy concealed himself behind a fallen tree and waited. At last his prey drew nigh. He leaped out from behind the tree, grabbed the man's shirt, and hoisted it high into the air.

"Where are the others?" he roared.

The creature in his hand screamed, and then went limp. Unconscious. Guy dropped it with a snort of disgust. Now he'd have to wait until it regained its senses, before he could torture the location of the others out of it.

"Amen," he said.

Friar Tuck's knees were killing him. He and his small band had been praying for several hours. His stomach rumbled angrily, reminding him that he had missed a couple of meals. They would grab some bread and cheese, he'd see how things were progressing, and discover where his help might be needed.

"Amen," the two children said.

Friar Tuck rose unsteadily to his feet. There was a flash of light so intense it nearly blinded him. It drove him back to the ground.

He gasped as he saw the antlered man-beast from his vision. It was the creature the imps had told him would kill Robin. The thing had a name.

Gisbourne.

His muscles went tight. His eyes were frozen wide as the vision unfolded itself to him. He saw the monster walking through the forest, a mighty scythe in its hand with which it cut down both tree and shrub with equal ease. Then it entered the very clearing in which the camp was located.

Shouts of alarm went up too late. Five men ran forward, led by Old Soldier, and in a moment they were all dead, necks snapped like twigs. The monster roared. It was looking for Robin, but he wasn't there, so it began to kill all who came within its reach. Including the little boy who had been praying with Tuck these many hours.

Hot tears coursed down his cheeks but he couldn't move, couldn't breathe, all he could do was watch as the vision continued to play itself out. Then, suddenly, it was over. All his muscles went slack at once and he fell face forward onto the winter grass.

Then there were hands grabbing at him, trying to lift him. Failing that, they pulled him over so that he was on his back staring up at the sky. Slowly his eyes focused, and he saw worried faces looking down at him.

"Are you alright?" Old Soldier asked.

"None of us will live to see sunset if we do not leave here right now," Friar Tuck said.

All about them was chaos as everyone tried to grab what weapons and provisions they could in preparation to abandon camp.

They decided to move a couple of miles away, to a place where a giant tree had died, but had left children standing in a ring around it. The giant tree had rotted away until it was just a stump but the ground right around it was suitable for making camp.

One that was less exposed.

Much knew the place to which they were heading. As he looked around, he realized that no one at the camp needed him to help carry anything. One look gave him a harsh truth, though. They were far too few, and they possessed far too little—they would need a great deal more, if they were going to defeat John and the Sheriff.

No one was thinking about that battle right now. The immediate concern was survival. A monster had been sent to kill them.

Someone had to think about the days and weeks to come, though.

He waited until he saw his moment and then he slipped unobserved into the trees. Once separated from his fellows he moved as fast as he could, heading for the village. It was good and right that he should do so. He was the only one who could go.

As he made his way through the forest he kept listening. The birds and the beasts who dwelt there might give him a warning if the monster was close by.

He made it to his destination without encountering anyone along the way. Once there he made a beeline for the post in the center of the village, the one that marked the crossroads. This time of day there was a good chance of finding people there exchanging goods, sharing news, or begging for scraps.

He was right, there were at least a couple dozen folks milling around.

He saw the tanner, a young man not that much older than himself who'd been running the family business since the pox took his father. Much walked up to him.

"Hello, good sir," the other man said. "Looking for extra skins for the floor or beds this winter season?"

Much stared at him in surprise. No one had ever called him "sir" before. When last he had spoken with the tanner, only a week ago, there had been none of the deference he was now being shown.

"I hear you're a good man with a knife," Much said softly.

"You heard right," the man acknowledged, giving him a look, "and I've heard that you're friendly with the man who will save us all."

"I am," Much said, glad to hear the words. "He needs help, though. He cannot do it alone."

"I'm not yet ready to live in the woods," the man confessed.

"You don't have to."

"Then what do you suggest?"

"Listen," Much said simply. "Be ready to come to our side, and fight when he calls. Can you do that?"

The tanner thought for a moment, then nodded.

"I can do that."

"Good."

The tanner dropped his voice even lower. "You might want to talk to Georgie. Things have gone hard on him. He might be looking to set them right."

"I will speak with him, thank you."

"Thank you, Much. God bless you." He nodded and walked on, eyes searching the crowd for Georgie. Everyone he encountered gave him a little nod. He wondered if they'd all heard he was friends with the Hood, or if they were merely attempting to acknowledge the murder of his parents.

Bile rose in his mouth at the memory of finding their bodies. He swallowed it down, and pushed the images down with it. He had an important job to do, and he couldn't let anything get in his way.

He spent the next four hours in the village, and by the time he left he had recruited more than he had hoped he could for the battle to come. It was with a great deal of pride and relief that he headed back into the forest, hoping that his friends had all safely made it to the new camp.

CHAPTER THIRTY

Marian was exhausted, and she felt like sobbing in frustration. For far too long she and Robin had tried everything they could think of in order to pass between the twin trees whose magic seemed to be holding them at bay.

They had tried walking backward through the space, but their feet froze just as fiercely to the ground. Robin had attempted to fire an arrow with a rope attached to it, so they might pull themselves through using their arms, but the arrow had stopped before passing between the two trees, clattering lifeless to the ground. They had even tried getting down on hands and knees to crawl through, but with no success.

In a fit of desperation Robin had even tried going behind the trees to see if he could walk through from the other direction. They had discovered, though, that when he went around the trees they disappeared from sight. Wherever the path between them led, it was somewhere that was beyond this area of the forest.

Now twilight was upon them, and it was becoming much harder to see. She was getting desperate. They had spent a whole day and if they didn't manage to make it past the first guardian how could they ever reach the heart of the forest in time to thwart John?

"There has to be another way," Marian groaned as she stood, staring at the obstacle in their path.

"Marian, the book, did it say that more than one person was required to complete this task?" Robin asked.

"It didn't say so directly," she answered, "but it seemed to imply it. Cardinal Francis certainly believed that we both would be needed."

"What if we're going about this all wrong?" he pressed. "What if it's not being strong for ourselves, but being strong for others?"

"What do you mean?"

"I have an idea."

Robin turned his body, angling it away from the opening so he was once again set to pass to the left of both trees. He stepped slowly, purposefully. Then when he had drawn abreast of the tree on the left, he picked up his left foot, but then pivoted on the stationary right one. He slammed his back up against the tree and yelled in anguish.

"It will burn you!" Marian told him.

He stretched his arm out to her.

"Give me your hand, Marian."

She grasped his hand.

"On the count of three, I'm going to yank as hard as I can, and try to propel you through. Do you understand?"

She nodded.

"*Don't let go.*"

"I won't."

"Ready? One, two... Three!"

Robin yanked on her arm so hard that pain shot up the full length. To her shock, though, her feet came free of the ground. She half flew, half fell toward the opening between the trees, and braced herself, wondering if she'd hit the threshold and fall, just as the arrow had.

She kept going, yelped in shock. The forest just past the two trees looked dramatically different than the portion that lay behind her. She started to fall, but kept hold of Robin's hand. As she hit the ground she yanked on it with all the strength left to her, and he came flying through the opening. He landed hard on top of her.

They lay there for a moment, both in pain and with the wind knocked out of them. She looked back between the two trees, but saw only darkness on the other side. They had passed the first gateway on their quest.

Out of that darkness Champion trotted and came up to nuzzle her cheek. *Show-off*, she thought. Clearly the barrier was designed to keep out people, but not the animals of the forest.

Robin rolled off her with a groan.

"Perhaps Champion's the one meant to go after the heart of Sherwood, and not us."

"You were right, though," Marian panted. "About us needing to be strong for each other."

"Of course he was right," a thin, ethereal voice whispered above them.

"Who said that?" she asked, struggling to sit up.

"We did," the voice replied.

"Are you the first guardian?" she asked, still searching for the speaker. Then she blinked in astonishment. The limbs of the two trees rubbed together, and the sound they made formed the words.

"We are," the tree said. "A leader's physical strength must be given to the leadership of the people. You must do for others what they cannot do for themselves."

The voice was like a sighing, similar to when wind would blow through the branches, but so much more distinctive.

"Do you know where we go from here?" Robin asked.

"You must seek the guardian of the mind."

"Where can we find the guardian?" Robin pressed.

"That you must solve for yourselves," came the answer.

"Of course we must." Robin sighed and closed his eyes, the muscles in his jaw twitching.

* * *

Robin rose slowly to his feet and then reached down to help Marian stand. As soon as she was up, though, he had to catch her, as her legs didn't seem to want to support her.

He was exhausted and it stood to reason she would be as well. They had set out early with barely any sleep and the ordeal of passing through the trees had drained what little reserves he had left. Night would soon be upon them and it was time to think about finding shelter from the cold.

He blinked as he realized something. The air around them was cool, but not cold. He looked around at this part of the forest, different from where they had emerged.

Here it was not an early, harsh winter, as it had been on the other side of the gateway trees. Here it was still autumn, as though this part of the forest was untouched by the evil of the prince and the Sheriff. He breathed in deep the heady scents of the life that was growing all around him.

They still needed to rest, but not having to worry about the killing cold was a godsend.

"I think we need to stop for the night."

Marian looked like she was going to protest, but then she reluctantly nodded. "I'm not sure I can go much further right now anyway."

"Exactly. We both need the rest."

He knew she was worried about how little time remained to them. So was he. But pushing themselves to the breaking point was the fastest way to fail, and, quite possibly, to die.

A short distance away from the gateway he could see a giant, felled tree. They could find shelter next to it for the night.

They finished the last of the food that Robin had brought with them and soon after he made a pile of leaves for her to sleep upon.

Shyly Marian lay down, relieved that he would be sleeping

near enough to awake if she had need of him but not so close that she felt unsettled. As it was she felt herself blushing as she drifted off to sleep, realizing that she could hear him breathing.

Robin was up before dawn. He had foraged and found some nuts and berries that he had waiting for Marian when she woke. She glanced at the breakfast in surprise.

"The mighty hunter captured these?" she asked with amusement as she began to eat.

"Somehow, it felt... wrong... to hunt here," he admitted.

"I understand," she said, looking at him intently.

Even in the morning, with leaves stuck to her hair, she was beautiful. In fact, he was certain that she had never looked more beautiful. He forced himself to look away and he cleared his throat.

"Soon as you're ready we can go," he said.

Shortly after they were on their way. Champion had sniffed at the berries before catching a mouse for his breakfast. The little fox trotted along contentedly with them.

Robin looked at everything they passed, not only marveling at how different this part of the forest was, but also marking the path by which they would return. He made sure to turn frequently, looking behind them. The way would look different, after all, when walking in the other direction.

After a while he heard rushing water. It grew louder with each passing stride until finally they stood at the edge of a river. He looked across it and felt both relief and dismay at the same time.

"I think we've reached the second challenge," Robin said.

"What do you mean?" Marian asked.

The other shore was close, alluringly so. Downriver the banks became steep, impassible, and he could hear the sound of rapids. Several large rocks reared their heads above the water.

Upstream, however, the river was even narrower, and appeared more tranquil.

Too much so.

"In finding the elixir I had to cross a stream that seemed peaceful until I stepped foot in it. Then it tried to kill me, and continued to do so until I swam entirely underwater, focused on my goal and not what was happening around me."

"Is that what we're meant to do here, as well?" Marian asked dubiously.

"I'm not sure," he admitted.

"Then perhaps you should ask me," a sing-song voice called out.

Robin turned and saw a girl sitting on a limb of a tree that extended out over the river. She had a narrow face, pointed ears, and very large eyes. She reminded him greatly of the boy who had given him the healing elixir. Only where the boy had possessed green eyes and green coverings, the girl had blue eyes and blue flowers that covered her. The boy had tested him with rhymes.

"Are you the guardian whom we seek?" Robin asked. "The one of the mind, that the book does speak?"

"You don't need to do that with me," the girl said, her eyes growing larger. "You've met Elian, then."

"If he's the boy guarding the elixir then yes, I have."

"He's lazy," the girl said.

"He did seem to enjoy just sitting by the water," Robin said, wondering where she was going with this.

The girl's eyes drifted past him to Marian. "Elian thinks he's clever," she said. "He's not. In order to cross my river, however, *you* will need to be."

"Do you have a riddle for us?" Marian asked.

"Not a riddle so much as a question." The girl smiled, revealing pointed teeth. "How do you cross the river without drowning?"

"Wisdom would suggest that crossing at the calmest, narrowest part would be the safest," Marian said.

"But does not wisdom also tell us that looks can be deceiving?" the girl asked. "What if I were to tell you that somewhere in this river there lived a sea monster, one that devours all who enter? What if I were to tell you that the water here is heavier, it weighs down limbs and clothes and makes swimming nearly impossible? And what if I were to tell you that downriver there are cruel rapids, and a waterfall whose drop has killed many?"

"Then I would tell you that I need to know the safe way across," Marian said.

"My job is not to tell you." The smile grew wider. "My job is to watch you fail and die."

"Elian was not so bloodthirsty as you," Robin said, sarcasm dusting his voice.

The girl creature shrugged. "Like I said, Elian is lazy."

Champion stepped forward, sniffing at the river curiously.

"If the fox gets wet, it will surely die," the girl said.

Marian moved lightning fast to snatch him up into her arms. As she did, Robin stared at Marian's clothes. While the trousers were sensible for the trek and much better than heavy skirts, they were still quite thick and would soak up the water and drag her to the bottom of the river. He couldn't risk having her make the attempt.

"We could build a raft," he said, looking at the trees around.

"The monster will eat you for sure, if you build a raft."

"If he sees us," Marian countered. "We don't even know what part of the river he's in."

"He's either in front of us or upstream, where prey would be most likely to cross," Robin suggested. "Perhaps we can get him to show himself, and I can kill him," he said, hand reaching for the black arrow in his quiver.

"You will only see him when he's eating you," the girl said. It sounded like a taunt.

"Then help us to cross," Marian said. "Please."

"A thousand years, and you're the first to ask for my help," the girl said, sitting up taller.

"Then please help us."

The girl seemed to consider it, but then shook her head. "It is wise of you to ask, though."

"If you will not help us, then at least tell us how we may cross safely," Marian implored.

"It's a wise woman who can ask that. For seeking counsel I will tell you this—take the path you would not take."

"The rapids," Marian muttered. She turned to look at Robin. "We don't have proof of the monster or the heaviness of the water. The paths that it seems most likely we would take are straight across or upstream."

"But we can see the impossibility of scaling the banks further on," he argued, "and hear the rushing of the river."

"The dangers that way are known, at least," Marian said. "If we can find a way to protect Champion, I say we take the known dangers."

As they spoke, Robin studied the blue girl's face to see if there was anything he could read in her eyes.

"She's lying about something," he said.

The girl smiled. "Very good. But which thing?"

Marian pointed. "The rocks downstream look fairly flat on top. They're also dry. Let's use them to cross."

"What if none of them get close enough to the far bank?" Robin said.

"At least we know what lies that direction," she replied, and she shot him a look of confidence. "Sometimes the path that seems most dangerous can be the safest one."

Marian moved down the river embankment a few feet. Just before the bank became impossibly steep, there was a rock two feet away from the slope. Robin was anything but certain, but he decided to trust her instincts.

She perched at the edge of the water, staring intently at the first rock.

"Put Champion here in my pouch," he said opening the top of the bag that held their food and supplies.

Marian deposited the squirming fox inside and Robin closed it over him. "No wet paws for you," he muttered. To Marian he said, "Let me go first."

She nodded and stepped back. He got up to the water's edge, and then was able to step out onto the stone. He paused, waiting for the river to flood over him, or the stone to turn out to be part of the monster's back.

Nothing.

He glanced at Marian, who nodded encouragingly at him.

The second stone was about the same distance away. He made it there, then turned to call out.

"Come on," he said, praying they were making the right decision.

Marian made the first rock, and he breathed a sigh of relief when nothing happened. He then turned and found the next rock.

Slowly they made their way as the path took them downstream. With each step the sound of the water grew louder. They were three-quarters of the way across the river when they rounded a small bend.

Suddenly Robin could see the rapids that they'd been hearing. Jagged rocks were surrounded by violently churning water and foam closer than he had expected. Marian had been right about one thing, though. There were rocks that led them all the way across.

The last rock—the one that lay a mere foot from the far bank—was also at the start of the rapids.

Suddenly he heard a low rumbling sound, something not made by water or stone. The hair on the back of his neck stood on end as he thought about what the girl had said, about their being a monster in the river. Maybe that was one of the things she'd been telling the truth about.

Either way, he had a sudden urge to get to the other side as fast as possible. Still alert for a trap, he kept moving, picking up his pace, but also keeping an eye on Marian. Finally he made it to the next-to-last rock, wide enough for her to join him. The gap between it and the last one was slightly wider, three feet as opposed to two. The final rock was also wet. A slip would send them crashing down into the rapids, where their heads would likely be bashed in.

The sound was deafening.

He took a deep breath. They had come this far. He heard the rumbling again. It was definitely time to get onto solid ground and away from whatever might lurk beneath the water's surface.

We can do this.

He measured the distance to the rock.

Just as he was preparing to jump, Marian shouted. "We need to go back!"

Startled, he lost his footing and almost slipped. He quickly regained it, however, and stood for a moment, staring at the final rock before turning to look back at her.

"What?" he asked. "But, we're so close. Just a few more feet and we'll have it."

"No, there's something wrong here," she insisted. "I don't like it."

"It was your idea to go this way in the first place," he said.

"And I hold to that still, but we need to back up and get around these rapids first." She saw his look, and added, "I feel it, inside, there's something wrong with that rock. I can't explain it, but you just need to trust me."

He stared longingly at the opposite shore. They were so close. He didn't want to give up now.

"Robin, it will take us longer, but we need to go back," Marian said, the urgency growing in her voice. He took a deep breath. Maybe Marian was seeing or sensing something he couldn't. He tried to reach out to the animals here as he did in his part of the forest. None responded to him, though. Whether it was because they couldn't or they wouldn't he didn't quite know.

With a shout of frustration he turned back to Marian. Instead of proceeding back upstream, however, Marian moved on a long series of rocks that brought them close to the shore from which they'd set out.

Maybe that was the answer after all, he thought suddenly. No one had actually told them they needed to cross the river. They'd just assumed it.

When they were within a foot of the original riverbank, he voiced his thoughts.

"I don't think so," she said, "I think the point is to keep going. If we were never supposed to cross in the first place, it would be a great trick, a clever mind trap, but it would also be lazy. Like Elian."

"She most certainly disapproved of that," Robin agreed. Another series of rocks zig-zagged close to the bank, and carried them downstream. The waters rushed and swirled about them and they could see dozens of sharp, jagged rocks all about, but there were still a handful of rocks that sat above the river, their tops flat enough to stand upon. One by one they navigated them until they were past the rapids.

Robin heard a sudden, deep rumbling behind them, much louder than what he'd heard before. He turned and saw movement. It was the stone on which they hadn't stepped—the one he'd thought would take them to the far bank. He stared in fascinated horror as it lifted and fell to the side, revealing the slippery hide of a creature.

That last step would have put them on the back of a monster that was now flipping over on its side, sending spray into the air all around.

Marian followed his gaze and stared, slack-jawed.

"Move faster," he told her.

She clamped her jaw shut, turned, and began negotiating another series of rocks, this path leading them again toward the far shore.

Every time Robin landed on a new rock he tensed all of his muscles, hoping fervently that it didn't shift beneath his feet. They began to ache with the effort. At last they saw a final rock that led to a gentle slope in the bank.

"Marian," he called, and he pointed to the rock.

She stared at it for a moment, and then shook her head and

pointed to another one that was slightly larger, but farther from their destination. She leaped onto it, foot slipping.

He shouted and tried to lunge forward, even though he knew he couldn't catch her if she went into the water.

Miraculously Marian regained her balance, and then leaped to the other side, grabbing hold of a tree root to help pull herself up. He followed, and when his feet were on dry ground Marian picked up a pebble and threw it at the rock she had rejected.

It sunk under the weight of the pebble.

"How did you know?" he asked.

She shook her head. "I didn't. It just seemed off, though. The first one that turned out to be the creature was slightly wet looking, and none of the others on the path were. That one seemed... too easy, I guess."

"You passed the test," a familiar voice said.

Robin turned to see the girl standing on the shore beside them. Her chin didn't even come up to his chest.

"A ruler must be willing to hear advice, weigh the evidence they have, listen to their instincts, and be flexible enough to change course quickly," she said in a matter-of-fact sing-song. She wore a smug expression.

Robin nodded. "Your instincts were correct," he said to Marian.

"Thanks," she breathed. "There's something about this place—I feel more attuned to it. It's almost as if it is an extension of my body, or vice versa."

His pouch squirmed. He opened it and pulled out Champion, whom he set on the ground. The fox stood stiffly, then shook himself, taking quick gulps of air. Then he stared at them as if to say, *never again*.

"Where do we go from here?" Marian asked the second guardian.

"To the Oak."

"Show us the way."

"You already have that which you need to find it," the girl creature said.

"I don't understand," Marian said.

"I knew you were coming. I knew of your need long before you did. In preparation I gave you a gift, and I see that you have cared for it as I knew you would."

Marian glanced down at the little fox.

"What do you mean?" she asked, her heart beating a bit faster. "How could he be a gift?"

"He is a woodland creature, born in the shade of the Oak itself, with the instincts to return if brought far enough by one who had raised him." The blue girl smiled at the look on Marian's face. "I took the kit from its mother, left it for you to find. If you were worthy, if you were the one, it would be your child, you its mother, and it would one day lead you home."

Marian stared in astonishment as she remembered when they had found Champion. Even then Robin had been surprised that the kit was so close to the road. It hadn't been an accident then; they were meant to find him, to care for him. And Robin had been right. They needed to bring him along on this quest.

"Lead him one hundred steps that way." The guardian pointed with a long, bony arm. "Then let him lead you."

Marian nodded. "Come on, Champion," she said, her voice quavering slightly.

She began to walk in the direction the guardian had pointed and the fox went with her, bouncing along. Robin followed.

She counted her steps and as she approached one hundred she slowed, and then stopped. She looked down at the tiny bundle of red fur.

"Take us home, Champion," she whispered.

The little fox looked up at her, tongue lolling out of the side of his mouth. Then he suddenly cocked his head and turned, his nose twitching. He smelled something that had caught his interest. He took a step, then another. Trotted a few feet away and then turned, as though anxious to make sure she was following.

She did so, and when she had reached his side he took off again, forcing her to hurry to keep up.

Little John returned alone to the old camp. Friar Tuck had begged him not to go, but there were weapons they'd left behind, and he wasn't going to abandon them if it could be helped.

Plus moving was the only thing that kept him from feeling like the cold was freezing his very marrow. He had never been fond of ice and snow, and this winter, coming so hard, so early, it just seemed to chill him in a way he had never known. It was unnatural, but he didn't like to think about such things if he could help it.

He didn't like breaking camp, but at least it gave him the ability to move, and chase away some of that freeze deep inside.

He didn't know if he believed in the friar's visions. He wasn't sure what he believed in anymore, but he knew that a good steel blade would protect you from a lot of evils.

Everything seemed quiet as he entered the small clearing. He made a beeline for the things they'd missed, sitting behind a log. He would grab what he could and be gone within a minute. Not enough time for some great monstrosity to descend upon him.

He stooped down and began slinging the extra bows over his shoulder. The quivers would be next and then he'd carry the swords in his arms.

A sudden, foul stench assaulted his nostrils, like an animal dead and rotting. It was so terrible he thought he was going to retch. He stood, turning to see where the smell could be coming from.

Not five feet from him stood a monster who loomed taller than him—something he had never imagined. It had a head crowned with blood-stained antlers.

CHAPTER THIRTY-ONE

Champion bounded ahead, leaping through the undergrowth and knocking snow from the shrubbery. At times he pulled out of sight, over some ridge or down some hollow. Even so, they were able to follow his trail.

Finally they climbed a ridge, Robin pulling Marian up behind him. They turned and gasped in awe.

Down the other side, in the center of a long canyon, stood the mightiest oak they had ever seen. It loomed far above the canyon floor, a vision of symmetry, its boughs still green as spring and thick with foliage.

"That's…" Robin struggled for the word.

"Astounding," Marian finished.

Tears formed in Robin's eyes. "I could stare at it forever."

Marian took his hand.

"It calls to me," he said. "It wants me to draw near."

"I feel it, too." And she did, like a knot of homesickness behind her breast.

"Then let us heed the summons."

They made their way down the slope and across the flat ground of the canyon bottom. It was chilly in the shade of the primordial oak, but not bitter like the winter air had been on the other side of the gateway.

In front of the tree they found a very tall man.

He sat, impossibly long legs crossed beneath him, eyes closed as though in prayer or meditation. His grayish skin was covered with markings, ancient symbols, only a few of which Robin had seen before. Before him on the ground lay two swords, both of silver that shone brightly.

They came to a stop in front of him.

Marian cleared her throat, and the man opened eyes that were slitted like a cat's. He regarded her calmly.

"Are you the third guardian?" she asked. "The one of the soul?"

"I am."

"We are here to place a book at the heart of Sherwood," she said.

"You would be queen," the man said, and he turned to Robin. "Are you king?"

"I have no desire to be king," Robin replied quietly. "I do, however, need to stop John from destroying all of England." As he spoke, he was unable to take his eyes off the symbols.

"In order to do that you need a king," the man said. "So, if not you, then who?"

Robin was about to respond when Marian spoke up.

"We are here to receive the right to rule as king and queen," she said. "What must we do?"

Robin shot her a puzzled look, but remained silent.

"To be a ruler, a true ruler, you have to be willing to sacrifice for the people, for the land."

"We have already sacrificed much," Marian said.

"But not all," he informed them. "You've bled for it, yes, and you are willing to die for it, but can you sacrifice the thing you love for it?" the tall man asked. "And along with it, your hopes for your own future?"

Marian looked at Robin.

"One person may claim the prize," the tall man said. "Only the one."

Robin stepped back. "Then I forfeit to her." This time she wore the look of surprise.

"That is not good enough," the tall man said. "Not good enough by half."

"You should have come alone," Marian said to Robin.

"He would have never found here without you." The tall man leaned back, pushing the swords forward with his foot. "No victory without sacrifice, children."

Robin stared at the swords. There had to be another way. None of these tests were ever quite what they seemed.

I will not fight Marian. That, at least, was a certainty, and he was sure she would feel the same. "What shall we do?" he asked her.

She stared hard at the tall man. "There is no way for one person alone to pass the first guardian, the trees, is there?"

"No," he answered.

"Two must pass, two must cross…"

"In order that two may battle. There is no winner without blood being spilled, no sovereign, no saving your world."

"I suppose we duel." Marian picked up the swords, holding one out to Robin. They were heavier than they looked, the weight of them in the tip of the blade. He didn't take it.

"I have a sword," he said.

The tall man smiled. "The blade of iron and steel, stained by the hand of the invader in the blood of your people." He shook his head "You cannot use that to gain the sovereignty. Defend it? Yes, but not to win it."

Reluctantly Robin took the sword from Marian. The moment his hand gripped it, something changed, it was though the sword was speaking to him, much like the black arrow. His flesh tingled where it touched the weapon and inside him all the rage, all the aggression, he had ever felt and more swelled up like a wave.

Across from him Marian's teeth were gritted and there was a wild, savage kind of gleam in her eye.

"King through combat," Robin breathed. "The stronger, the faster."

"The old ways," Marian hissed.

"You are quick, children," the tall man said wryly.

Marian raised her sword and slid back into the on-guard position. Terror rose up in Robin, the equal to his anger. Try as he might, though, he couldn't stop himself from raising the tip of his sword. It was as though his arm and the sword were in perfect agreement with each other, possessing each other, and were ready to slash Marian to ribbons while the part of him that loved her, that would never harm her, could only watch helpless and horrified.

"Do you know how to use that?" she asked. "You are a bowman, after all." And what terrified him most was he couldn't tell if she was expressing concern, or mocking him.

"I've a passing knowledge."

"I learned from the Lionheart himself," she said, "so you will have to do your best."

"She is correct." The tall man stood, and he looked at Robin with eyes that seemed to see inside of him. "You can not make mockery of the Thynghowe by not striving to win. The sword will not allow it. You are committed now. Only one will stand. Her or you."

"I won't harm her," Robin protested, even though he knew there was no way he could stop himself.

"Enough talking." Spinning, Marian lunged at Robin.

The sound of steel upon steel rang across the canyon, rolling up the walls and skipping over the ground. Marian's heart was breaking and she wanted to scream in her anguish, but there was nothing she could do to stop it. The sword pulled out of her all her skill, all her speed, all her agility.

Robin and Marian parried back and forth, striking at each other. Marian had been taught a controlled form, keeping her blade close to her body to block attacks, and then using the strength of her shoulder to push her own blade in short chops and thrusts.

Robin swung his sword with reckless abandon, sending it in wide arcs and sweeping cuts. He used the entirety of his body, twisting at the hips to hack and slash as if he were a woodsman clearing a path. He committed his full body to each strike. Against a less skilled opponent he would have destroyed their defense, crashing over it like a flood over a hut, and cutting them down. However Marian was too skilled, too quick, too clever in her own mechanics. She was the mongoose to his serpent, avoiding the bite of Robin's blade while still striking with her own. Despite the difference in their styles, they were evenly matched.

Neither was winning.

Desperation began to slowly outweigh her pain and her fear. If one of them did not win, if they both fell dead of exhaustion, then John would win and he would destroy everything they had worked to protect.

She could do nothing to stop herself. Indeed, part of her felt rage and violence and was glorying in the combat. That was the work of the sword, too. If she could not use her mind to overpower the sword, to lose on purpose, then she needed to stop fighting the sword. She needed to embrace it and the strength it gave her and use all her wits to find a way to defeat Robin.

Marian shoved her agony into a corner of her mind. She couldn't think of him as the man she had grown to love. He was only the obstacle between her and the salvation of England, and any obstacle could be removed if one was clever enough and committed enough.

She counted Robin's blows until she found his pattern, the rhythm into which his body naturally fell.

Just like dancing, King Richard had told her in their early lessons. *If you watch your opponent long enough, you can find his steps. Learn the pulse of their flow and you can cut in.*

Richard... she thought wistfully. Then she pushed that

emotion, too, to the side. It was a weakness she could not afford. She focused in on Robin. And in a flash, she knew how she could let the sword taste blood.

Robin cut three times, changed direction to slash, then stepped back. Without letting him know what she was doing, she led him into his pattern.

Cut, cut, cut...

Slash...

Back.

Then she struck.

Spinning on her heel as he was mid step, she pirouetted, sword arm fully extended. The flat of the blade whipped around. Robin stumbled as he twisted to get his sword up in time to parry.

As she felt the impact of his blade on hers, she lunged and bent her elbow, using the force of her body to push his sword out and away from her. Rolling into his reach she trapped his sword arm with her free hand, drove her foot into the hollow of his thigh for leverage, and clubbed his wrist with the pommel of her sword.

His fingers flew open and his sword flew away.

He stood there stunned as she slashed her sword across his chest, deep enough to cut, shallow enough to save. Blood seeped through his tunic and as he stared down at it she snatched up his fallen sword. She stood there, quivering in rage. She had won, she knew it, but the urge to finish him was overwhelming.

The tall man had said bloodshed, but he had never said anything about death. Why then did the swords not acknowledge her victory?

A sudden flash of insight crossed Robin's face.

"The swords were crossed. Cross them, Marian."

Her right arm quivered, ready to thrust forward, but she quickly swung her left hand and clanked the swords together so that the blood on her sword was also touching his sword.

Just like that, the swords released her.

With a sob of relief she dropped them. She stepped over them, grabbed Robin by the front of his tunic, pulled him close, and kissed him on the mouth as hard as she could.

When they were done, she turned to the tall man.

"There, defeated."

He nodded his head gravely. "A leader must be willing to sacrifice all that they love for their people. A wise leader also knows the difference between sacrifice and slaughter, understands that leadership is not clear, not black nor white, but understanding and embracing all the shades of right and wrong. Do not rejoice too long in your victory for I know of what is happening out there, and it is most probable that one of you will yet have to lose the other... or lose all."

Then, with that somber warning, he disappeared. Before they could even react, the mighty Oak of Thynghowe split open. With the sound of groaning wood, the trunk yawned apart as if cleft by a giant's axe. Golden light spilled out from the inside, bathing them in its warm glow. A fragrance lilted out of the opening, the scent of some intoxicating flower.

Inside the tree hung two torcs.

She grasped his hand, and they moved closer.

The torcs nestled on a pair of pegs, their circles entwined. The one on the left was slender, made of a bright gold and woven of dozens of thin strands that twisted around one another, mimicking the pattern of ancient knotwork, and ending in the form of birds.

The one on the right was thicker and crafted from a dull grey iron. It also wove from strands but these were thick, nearly the size of Marian's last finger. Its ends were capped with the heads of boars, cunningly carved from the iron and with sharp tusks jutting from growling mouths.

Marian reached into the opening.

Robin touched her arm. "It cannot be this easy."

"This wasn't easy."

"You know what I mean. Why did we bring the book, the one the cardinal gave his life to put in your hands, if we could just reach inside and take these?"

Marian frowned. "You are right." She pulled the book from her pouch. Opening it, her eyes went wide, and she found that the pages had gone blank. Frantically she flipped through them, each one bare of the words and symbols she'd seen before.

At the end she found a phrase.

"What language is that?" Robin asked, looking over her shoulder.

"English."

"No, it's not."

"Of course it is."

"Marian, that is not English. It's a scribble of shapes and symbols."

She turned her head, looking at the book from the corner of her eye. In the blur of strained vision the words morphed and she caught a glimpse of what Robin was talking about. The line written in the book was in an indistinct scrawl, unreadable to her.

When she looked at it full on, the words became clear. This must be what the cardinal was talking about in regards to her ancestry. Perhaps only someone with her blood could see the words and understand them.

She took a deep breath.

"I'm going to read them."

"If you are able."

"I am able. 'Worthy of honor. Worthy of glory. Worthy of worship. Too humble to seek them. Strong enough to hold. Brave enough to fight.'" With each sentence her voice rose. "'Wise enough to rule. I stretch forth my hand and lay claim to the heritage of Thynghowe. I lay claim to the very sovereignty of this land.'"

Marian cried out the last words, and then held her breath.

Silence.

"I expected something to happen," Robin said with a frown.

"So did I," she admitted, and she reached in and took hold of the iron torc. It chimed as it slid free of the gold one. She turned toward Robin with it in her hands. "I need you to open this."

"Why?"

"So it can go around your throat."

"I am not the king."

"You heard the guardian," she insisted, "and Cardinal Francis sent us here to claim the sovereignty. We must do as he instructed, or he will have died for nothing."

"I am not worthy."

"You *are*," she said, becoming impatient.

"No," he said, sounding like a child. "I don't want it."

"And this is why you are worthy, Robin of Longstride." Tired of their disagreement, she thrust the torc toward him. He took it, gripped the carved boars' heads, and pulled. The metal was stout, but with a struggle he opened it up. Then he handed it back to Marian.

"Lean down," she said.

He did. She slipped the torc around his neck. Like the glow, it was warm.

Nothing happened.

"Well," he said. "I expected something."

"What did you expect?" she asked.

"I have no idea."

"How does it feel?"

"Heavy," he replied. "Heavier than iron should."

"Well, that's something."

Pushing on the ends he closed the torc so it wouldn't slip off his throat. He nodded toward the tree. "Your turn."

Marian lifted the gold torc, and was able to pry the soft metal open. She slipped the torc around her throat, and pulled the ends closed.

"Well?" he asked.

"It…"

Light exploded from her.

It blasted out from her chest, so bright that Robin could see the outline of her bones. He cried out and covered his eyes as the wave of magic swept over him. He blinked it all back, and when his vision cleared he found Marian suspended in front of him, floating a few feet off the ground.

"Marian!" he cried, and he took a step toward her. Then he stopped.

She didn't seem to be in pain. Golden sparks swirled around her, and a wind he did not feel whipped her hair around her face. Her mouth opened, and she sang, her voice transformed into something beautiful, angelic.

The notes fell out into the air, and he wept at her feet.

They were almost back at the camp and Marian wanted nothing more than some warm food and to curl up and go to sleep.

It had taken an hour for her to come back to herself, back at the tree. Retracing their steps, they found that the tests had vanished, and the distance was surprisingly shorter. Champion danced around their feet, carefully avoiding the risk of being kicked.

Several times Robin asked her if she felt any ill effects.

"No," she said. "I don't even recall what happened. One moment I put on the torc, and the next you were standing there, looking at me as if I had grown an extra nose. You looked quite silly, really."

"At least I kept my feet firmly on the ground," he said, and he laughed. There was a worried edge to it, however. She felt strange, unsure what was to come next. All she knew was that they were going to make it back well before the solstice.

In fact, the cardinal had told her she just needed to accomplish the task before solstice. So, they had done it. Still, something wouldn't let her quite breathe. She didn't know how this was going to help them to defeat John. A terrible suspicion kept rising in her mind that it hadn't been about defeating him, but about stopping him from gaining even more power than he already had.

Robin stopped suddenly, every part of him going still.

"What is it?" Marian asked, and she glanced around for any new threat.

"Something terrible has been here," Robin muttered.

CHAPTER THIRTY-TWO

"Stay here," Robin said softly.

Marian shook her head fiercely. "Whatever it is, we face it together," she said.

It wasn't the time to argue, so he nodded, moving forward quietly as they continued for the clearing.

The camp had been abandoned, and hastily. They had taken the essentials, leaving only the debris of their passing.

"What happened here?" Marian whispered.

He didn't reply, and reached for the black arrow. As they moved to the center of the clearing, his eyes fell on a still, bloody figure.

"Little John!" he cried as he rushed forward.

The giant of a man had been beaten half to death. His face was swollen almost beyond recognition. Robin's mind reeled as he wondered what manner of man was strong enough to best John Little. There were no cuts, was no evidence of a sword or a club. Whoever had done this had used only their fists.

"Is he dead?" Marian asked from behind.

"No, he's still breathing," Robin said, knowing he should be grateful for that.

Then the hair on the back of his neck raised suddenly, and he felt a bird's wing brush the crown of his head.

He spun around and saw a nightmare striding across the clearing toward them. His heart flew into his throat. His first thought was that the hideous form was one of the guardians of Sherwood. With the next breath he realized that couldn't be, because nothing so evil called the wood its home.

He heard Marian gasp as she followed his gaze.

"Run," he said.

Her mouth opened and he whirled on her.

"I said to run!" he shouted.

Marian hesitated only a moment more, then turned and slipped into the woods.

Swinging his bow into his hand, he pulled arrows, one by one, and sent them at the creature as quickly as he could. They struck the antlered giant and each one burst into splinters. The creature charged forward.

Robin's hand moved, and he felt his fingertips brush against the black arrow. Surely it could fell the giant beast. He yanked, but the arrow didn't move, remaining instead firmly lodged in his quiver as though it refused to be drawn against this enemy.

Cursing, he dropped the bow and drew the sword at his side. He cast his eyes around, looking for some advantage.

"That pigsticker will be no use against me," the thing growled, its voice that of a feral creature.

Robin didn't answer, moving to the left and up a small rise. The creature still towered over him but he was on more even footing.

The thing turned, black eyes gleaming as it closed in.

Robin swung the sword over his head.

The creature lifted a massive arm to block the strike. The limb was covered in ancient symbols, painted in woad.

Cannily Robin changed the direction of his strike, whipping the long blade down and lunging forward, low and fast. The edge of the sword sliced against the thing's knee, biting deeply. Robin felt the impact up the blade, up his arm, and into his teeth.

The skin parted, but did not bleed.

Had this thing been mortal, then the razored steel would have sheared through not only skin, but also muscle, tendon, and bone.

The creature reached for him and he spun away, big, blunt fingers dragging unsuccessfully across the back of his cloak as he rolled down the rise, using the natural shape to aid him. He came up on his feet to the side of the creature and thrust, using his body weight to drive the blade into the spot where a man would be soft, the hands-breath of skin between hipbone and ribcage.

The point dug in, puncturing skin only a finger-width deep, then slipped away as if he'd driven it into an iron pot.

This time the hands snagged his cloak.

The creature jerked him back as if he were a toddler, lifting him off his feet and swinging him around to slam into the ground. All the air rushed out of his lungs and tried to take them with it. His vision went black as he was lifted again, dragged by his cloak as if it were a leash.

Or a noose.

His eyes were blurry but clearing. He was held aloft as if he were a baby rabbit, and nothing more.

"That is a good sword," the monster observed. "It cut me. It was crafted by an artisan, not simply a smith."

Robin couldn't respond. He was doing all he could to keep conscious.

The creature reached toward his throat, pushing the knotted cloak away to reveal the iron torc.

"I'll take that."

The creature grabbed the circlet of iron, fingers digging into Robin's throat, cutting off his air, and pushing him further toward the darkness.

The hand twisted and yanked it off Robin's neck, then dropped him to the ground. Looking up, he saw the thing turn and grab something from the air, no… some*one*.

Marian had launched herself at the thing, knife in her hand, as it stood over him. The thing caught her as if she were a child and held her aloft as she thrashed and twisted, trying to put her blade into its eyes.

Robin struggled to his feet, moving to help her.

The creature casually swung the iron torc against Marian's head. The metal connected and she went limp in his arm.

Robin lunged forward.

The torc sang against his skull, and the world went dark.

Friar Tuck sagged in relief as Robin's eyelids flickered, and then opened.

"Where?" Robin asked.

"We are in the backup camp location."

"Marian?"

Friar Tuck shook his head. "We were hoping you could tell us. All I found at the old campsite were you, Little John, and Marian's fox. You must have been attacked by the monster we abandoned the camp to avoid. Alan believes it could be an ancient elemental entity called Guy of Gisbourne."

"He took Marian and the torc," Robin said, struggling to sit up. "We need to get them."

"You're not going anywhere in the shape you're in," Tuck said, putting a hand on Robin's chest and managing to push him down with hardly any effort.

"I have to," Robin protested weakly. "You don't understand. The torc bestows kingship. John can't be allowed to possess it." He peered up, desperation in his eyes. "Tuck, there's no telling what he'll do to Marian."

Still the friar did not move his hand.

Robin closed his eyes and for a moment Tuck thought he had lost consciousness again, until he spoke.

"What of John Little, does he live?"

"I do, and I look a fair sight better than you," John said shuffling up behind them.

Tuck looked at Little John. The man was a mess, limping, beaten, but still standing. He was looking down at Robin with a strange expression on his face. Tuck couldn't read it, but he did know it was the first time in a long while that the giant hadn't looked at Robin with hate in his eyes.

"I'm guessing you ran into the same thing I did, with no better luck killing it."

Robin opened his eyes and slowly shook his head. "I won't fail again."

"If this Gisbourne took Marian to John," Tuck said gently, "then what do you think you're going to do? You couldn't defeat him when you were whole. How will you do it as you are now?"

"I don't care," Robin said. "I can't leave her to torture and death. I love her." He pushed away Tuck's hand and struggled to sit back up. "If the monster kills me this time, so be it, but I can't abandon her."

Friar Tuck dropped his eyes. He had suspected as much. It was a good thing, the feelings Robin had for her. Right now, though, they would only get in his way.

"What you can't do is abandon your people," he said. "Too many are counting on you."

"That's why I have to go. If we lose her, if John claims the torc, we're all dead anyway, not just those here, but their families, and their neighbors, and all the good men and women of England," he said, pushing Tuck's hand off his chest. "I might not be able to swing a sword right now, but I can still fire an arrow, and I've got one just for this occasion. As long as it doesn't fight me," he said, locking his jaw.

"Friar Tuck!"

Tuck turned and saw Much running toward them.

"What is it?" he asked the young man.

"I've had word from a friend who was delivering food to the castle. She saw the Lady Marian being brought there unconscious. However, she thinks—but she's not positive—that John and the Sheriff might have slipped out of the castle a little later, taking Lady Marian with them. She didn't know where or even for sure if they had gone. None of the stable boys knew either. I've sent for those that will fight with us, telling them to come now."

Robin blinked at Much.

"Our young friend has been busy," Friar Tuck explained. "Even if we have more men, though, that won't help us if we don't know where to send them."

"I know someone who can find her, wherever she is," Robin said.

"Who?" Tuck asked.

"You said you found her fox."

Marian was bound in the middle of a circle of stones. She had never seen the place before, but it felt sick. The ground beneath her feet was dying. The grass had withered to nothing.

She didn't know if Robin was alive or dead. He had been awfully still when the beast had knocked her out and taken her from the camp. She'd drifted in and out of consciousness, only to wake in this vile place.

John, the Sheriff, Glynna Longstride, and several others stood nearby. The others wore cloaks, and had the hoods up so she could not tell if they were strangers, or persons she knew. She looked in vain for the monster that had brought her there but didn't see him.

Thank God for small favors, she thought, and immediately regretted the blasphemy.

"Ah, the little princess is awake," John said, turning to look at her. "You know, I've always thought it was going to be a great moment when you fell beneath my knife. Now thanks to you I have the torc, and with your sacrifice, I will become the rightful king of all of England. Neither Heaven nor Earth will dare to dispute it."

"Do what you will, but you will never be the true king," she said. "They will come for me."

"Of course they will, but they'll be looking in the wrong place. You see, we made a grand spectacle of parading your unconscious body around the castle before we left. Your friends will look for you there first—and what they'll find instead is their doom."

The monster, she realized. That's where he was—at the castle, waiting to destroy whoever came for her.

Robin struggled not to let his men see his pain. *His men*. He wasn't sure when he'd come to think of them that way, but there it was. At any rate he needed them now more than ever.

Much had gone to fetch the men he'd recruited, and escort them to the camp. The boy had grown up a lot, seemingly in the span of a few short weeks.

"This is the moment we've been waiting for," he said. "Our chance to put an end to Prince John's reign of evil. If we fail, the chance will never come again. You're hurting, and you've lost much, but this is your opportunity to take back at least some of what you've lost." He glanced over at Alan. "Or, at the very least, take your vengeance for it."

"No bloody way are we following you to another slaughter," one man shouted angrily.

Before Robin could say anything, however, Old Soldier turned and hit the man so hard that he fell down unconscious.

"Enough of that talk," the old man growled. He turned back. "We're with you, Lord Robin." Others nodded and voiced their agreement.

"So are we!"

Robin turned to see Much entering the clearing, with more than two dozen men following him. He nodded, and Much beamed at him. He'd done well. When this was over he'd need to make certain the young man received the credit he was due.

If they were both still standing.

"Marian is the key," Robin said. "If nothing else happens,

we have to get her out. The trials she survived granted her sovereignty over this land. Rescuing her is our mission."

"You focus on doing that, getting in and getting her back, if she's the key to ending all of this. The rest of us will do what we can about the others," Little John said. "Whatever may come."

Glynna stared at Marian, a mixture of feelings running through her. Mostly she felt glee that the princess would soon taste the knife.

It didn't sit well with her, however, that it would be to further the fortunes of Prince John, and increase his power. Her man should be king, not the whining brat.

For the moment, it was her job to guard the prisoner while the others finished their preparations.

"Lady Longstride, please, you have to help me," Marian said.

"That title means nothing any longer," Glynna said, and she gave the girl a withering look. "Regardless, I don't *have* to help you, and I won't."

"Think of all that's happened because of John," Marian implored. "We've all lost so much to him. You've lost three of your children."

"Three? Then Robin's dead is he?" Delight coursed through her at the thought.

Marian blinked and then frowned.

"No... I don't know," she said, seemingly startled by the reply. "I was talking about Robert."

"Robert?" Glynna said. "Robert's off with his father."

Marian's eyes widened. "You don't know, do you?"

"Know what?" Glynna asked, her pleasure turning to irritation. "What are you talking about?"

"Robert is dead," Marian said. "I'm so sorry. The king sent him back to make certain his kingdom was safe. The Sheriff... the Sheriff killed him."

Glynna blinked at that, struck through by the thought. As much as she'd always hated Robin, she had liked her girls, in an abstract kind of way. Robert, though, had been her pride and joy. So strong, so handsome, the envy of all.

She glanced over uncertainly at her lover. If this was true, why would he not have told her?

"How do I know you're not making that up?" she asked.

"I know where he's buried," Marian said. "You can see for yourself."

Glynna took a deep breath. "'Tis no matter. If the Sheriff killed Robert, he must have had reason to do so."

Marian stared at her in revulsion. "How can you be so callous over the death of your own children?"

Glynna settled a hand on her belly. "Herein lies my true child, the one that shall rise to a greatness never imagined by the others. He will have his father's strength and my cunning. He will feast upon the weak and the foolish. He shall make the lesser man his footstool." She narrowed her eyes. "He's hungry now."

Marian recoiled.

"My pet," the Sheriff called.

Glynna turned, her momentary annoyance with him forgotten as her blood sang.

"Remember, my love—the princess isn't for eating," he said.

His men were concealed down by the road, ready to go wherever Robin would lead them. He alone had taken the small creature as close to the castle as he dared. He just hoped that the bond between Marian and her pet would allow him to pick up her scent.

He was just about to set Champion down when he turned and saw something that caused him to gasp in shock. He fought the urge to vomit.

There, mounted on a pike in front of the castle gate, was the head of his cousin, Will Scarlet. Despite the distance, there could be no doubt. One of his eyes was rolled halfway back into his skull, while the other was gone, no doubt to some scavenger. The skin was white, the lips dark as a bruise.

Robin stared for a moment, blood thundering in his ears.

Will was dead.

He had known it, but a part of him had hoped that somehow it wasn't true. He just kept staring. In his arms Champion began thrashing back and forth. He should put the fox down, he knew, then find Marian before John could do the same to her.

He didn't hear the whisper of sound behind him until it was almost too late.

He ducked as a sword cut through the air right above his head, whistling as it passed him. He turned to see the creature that had beaten him and taken Marian. It held the blade that had been Robin's.

"Guy of Gisbourne," he ground out as Champion leaped to the ground.

The thing stopped for just a moment before letting out a deep, rumbling laugh.

"I thought I killed you," it said as if relishing another try.

"I'm harder to kill than most," Robin said, mind working furiously as he stepped backward, trying to put distance between himself and the monster. He needed just a few feet and then he could use the arrow, so long as it would let him this time. But he couldn't risk bringing it out in close quarters, allowing the creature to snatch it away. Maybe the arrow had been protecting itself in a similar way during the last encounter. By the time he'd gone to use it, the monster had been nearly on him.

Then he realized something else.

The beast hesitated when I called it by name. The creature was ancient, and a similarly ancient magic would have been used to raise it. In that kind of magic, names had meaning, and granted power. To know the name of a thing was to have influence over it.

There had to be a way to use that to his advantage.

"This time I am going to take this fancy sword and stick it in your guts." Guy of Gisbourne swung again, and Robin dove away, toward the castle wall.

He scrambled to his feet and slung his bow into his hand. Moving back he pulled a regular arrow and let it fly.

It struck the creature in the throat and ricocheted off, tangling in the thick twisted hair hanging off his head. Guy of Gisbourne growled, and stalked forward. Robin moved quickly, angling them away from the castle to avoid attracting attention, launching arrow after arrow, only to watch them bounce off one after the other. The monster threw back his head and laughed. "Your arrows are not as well made as your sword."

Robin's hand closed on the black arrow.

"Try this one on for size."

The arrow came free. Swift as thought he notched it. It sung to him as he let it fly.

It struck Guy of Gisbourne in the chest, sinking to the feathers. The creature looked down, mouth gaping. He staggered back a step, hand moving toward the notched end that now jutted from his breast. His fingers brushed it once, then twice, then fell limp by his side.

He swayed as there was a crack and the antlers broke loose from his skull, one skewing sideways, loose and forlorn, the other tumbling to the ground. Black fluid poured from his open mouth as he dropped to his knees. His eyes fluttered, rolling back, and he fell sideways to the earth.

The arrow would not pull free.

The skin into which it sank had gone hard, until it felt like winter earth under his hand.

He cursed and pulled again, fingers cutting on the stiff edge of the black fletching.

People stood around him. He heard their voices.

He defeated that?

What is he doing?

Why does he care so much about an arrow?

Do you see that thing? It is a monstrosity.

Giving up, Robin stood.

He was surprised to see Little John standing next to him. He was looking in the direction of the gate, toward where Will's head was. They needed to take that down. They didn't have time, though.

"It's not right, what they did to Will," the big man muttered, anger seething in his voice.

"They've killed every noble who dared to speak up," Friar Tuck said as he handed Robin a jug.

"Every free man, too," Robin said.

He took the jug, expecting the burn of whisky, and found only cold water.

"You did well."

Robin shook his head. "It isn't done yet."

"Look around you," Tuck said, gesturing. "These men will follow you into Hell itself."

Robin pulled his newly retrieved sword. "Then let's get them to it, before they lose their nerve."

A small yip caught his ear from inside the castle gate. A wave of emotion swept through him, and he started jogging down the road.

"What is it?" Friar Tuck called.

"The fox! He's picked up Marian's trail."

CHAPTER THIRTY-THREE

"Carry on."

The Sheriff's voice was harsh.

Standing over Marian, his hands raised, John didn't take time to look. He'd just finished cutting symbols into his own arms and the blood ran thin and quick, dripping off his elbows and onto her as she lay bound on a flat stone altar.

They were in one of Richard's hidden gardens, recently remodeled for his own purposes.

The distant sound of fighting, outside of the wall, caused John to pause and turn.

"They sound close," he said.

"My men will stop them," the Sheriff grunted. "Carry on."

Marian struggled against her bonds. "Stop this, John. They're coming. They will save me. You can preserve yourself by stopping this now."

"Stupid girl," Glynna hissed. "In just a few moments he will have ultimate power. There is no use in begging for your life."

"I would never beg for my life," Marian answered. "I simply offered mercy—far more than he would give." She rolled her head to look at Glynna. "And I wasn't talking to you, whore."

Hands on her stomach, Glynna turned to the Sheriff. "If he won't finish, then let me kill her."

"I'll finish," John said.

"Then do so."

John turned back to the book in his hand. Before he could begin reading the door to the garden burst open with a crash.

The intruders spilled into the garden, clashing swords with a cadre of dog soldiers, Friar Tuck and Little John just steps behind Robin himself. Once inside the open space they moved apart.

The Sheriff turned to Glynna. "Make him complete the ritual. I will deal with these mongrels."

"Your will be done."

He turned and stalked toward the fighting, drawing his greatsword from its scabbard. She watched him, feeling things tight and low inside her. The baby kicked, breaking her lust for the Sheriff and putting her mind to the task at hand.

John was staring at her when she turned back.

"Get to work," she growled "or I will pull your eyes from your skull."

He peered down at the book, and began the incantation.

The dog soldier in front of him fell, his neck turned completely around from the blow he'd delivered with his quarterstaff. He spun and found that another one had just run a sword through Timothy, who he'd known since they were infants.

As the young man slid off the dog soldier's blade Little John dealt a blow to the back of his knees, cutting him to the ground. He dropped onto the thing's back, hooked his staff under its chin, and pulled back with all his might. He felt the bones of the dog soldier pull apart, separating until it quit fighting underneath him.

He let the corpse loose and stood.

Looking around he found most of the enemy had been overwhelmed, and the ones left fighting were hemmed in by his fellow fighters.

He also saw too many people he knew lying still on the ground. It only added to the roil of emotions he had been trying to keep in check since the beast had attacked him at the camp.

He was weak, vulnerable. They all were. There was nothing he could have done to kill that creature. Robin had found a way, though—even broken and hurting worse than Little John imagined he was.

Somewhere in all there he had been reminded of the boy he had once known and cared for, the fearless child who was not afraid to fight and who loved freedom more than anything. Freedom was what Robin was fighting for. Little John just wished he could have looked past his own anger and pain to see that faster. Not for his own freedom did Robin fight, but for everyone's.

Another dog soldier rushed him and he bludgeoned it to death. His arms were knots of pain, bruised purple up and down so that no normal skin color showed, and with every blow he dealt he thanked God for Old Soldier, who had pushed him so hard. Taught him that pain in battle was meaningless, that it was just something to push down into the fire in your belly, adding fuel to it so that you never stopped fighting.

The old man was a dozen feet away, piling up bodies faster than could be imagined. Old Soldier had never given up faith in Robin. He had been right. Robin and the Lady Marian were all that stood between the people of England and death at the hands of the prince and his demons.

His eyes found Robin, who had just cut down an opponent, his face spattered with gore. As Longstride stepped over the body, the Sheriff appeared behind him, raising a sword that ran with blood.

He bellowed out a warning and began to move.

Robin heard a roar that sounded like a bear. He jerked his head and found the Sheriff trying to cut it off.

He barely raised his sword in time. Even so, the blow tore it from his hand. Off-balance, he stumbled, dropping to one knee.

"No more!" the Sheriff roared and his jaw distended, opening into a maw. His voice changed, becoming inhuman. "No more shall you plague me, human."

The sword raised again.

Robin pulled the knife from his belt, but it wouldn't be enough. There was nothing he could do but watch the sword fall and end his life.

Marian... he thought.

He turned to see her one last time.

Suddenly Little John was there, plowing into the Sheriff and carrying him to the ground.

Robin scrambled to his feet. The giant lay on top of the Sheriff, bruised arms clamped around the man. The Sheriff screamed something not meant for a human throat and struggled to get free. Little John held tight.

He looked up at Robin, blood trickling from his mouth.

"Go save her," he slurred. "I'll hold him while I can."

Little John squeezed the Sheriff tighter and tighter. He remembered what the miller's boy had said—that at the monastery arrows hadn't even phased the devil. He didn't know if a sword would be capable of decapitating the monster. He would have loved to have tried, but he had no blade, and his quarterstaff lay on the ground, just out of reach.

Beneath him the Sheriff thrashed like a wild thing. Curses spewing from his lips seemed to actually darken the air around them. Little John didn't know much about magic or demons, so he did his best to ignore them and focus instead on what he did know.

He knew that he was the strongest man in England, and even bloodied and battered nothing could change that. He might not have been able to take on the Gisbourne creature, but the Sheriff was much smaller.

He flexed his arms, squeezing tight.

Harder! Squeeze harder!

In his mind he heard Old Soldier barking orders at him, orders he'd never actually said, but what John imagined he would be saying if he was standing there now.

Squeeze as if the lives of everyone you've ever known depended on it, because they do!

So Little John, strongest man in England, flexed the muscles on his mighty arms and squeezed the Sheriff as tight around the chest as he could. He squeezed until the Sheriff actually stopped cursing because he could no longer draw air into his lungs.

He kicked at John's legs, but his legs were like mighty tree stumps, immovable, unshakeable. He could kick all day and it would matter not.

Suddenly John heard a sharp cracking sound and realized with a rush of glee that the Sheriff's armor had cracked in two. He redoubled his efforts, shouting in defiance of the man, the prince, and all their monsters from Hell.

King John spoke the final word. The spell hung in the air around him. It made the cuts in his own flesh sting as if vinegar had been poured into them. The dark energies pulsed around him.

All he had to do was spill Marian's blood.

He looked down at her, the knife in his hand.

She stared back at him, defiance writ on her face.

She had his brother's eyes. They were honey brown and fierce.

Glynna Longstride leaned toward him.

"The time is here. Do the deed."

The potential in the air pulled at him, making him sway on his feet.

The blade seemed to move of its own accord.

He closed his eyes.

Something lifted him off his feet.

For a second he thought he had completed the ritual, and was floating.

Then the pain set in.

John tilted, spinning in the air.

He'd been tossed, like so much garbage. As he struck the ground he rolled, the knife flying away.

The man in the hood was at the altar. He put his hands on Glynna and pushed, knocking her down. There was a blade in his hand and he slashed apart the ropes holding Marian as she leaped off the stone.

He looked at John as if to move on him, then thought better of it and turned. Pulling on her arm, he took her away.

The magic in the spell remained, but now it was agony.

Little John was winning, he could feel it. The Sheriff was struggling less. *Hold him*, that's what he'd told Robin he'd do. He was beginning to think, though, that he had a chance to kill him. He was doing his best to crush him to death, but the man was withstanding pressure no human could.

Because he's not human, he told himself.

Suddenly he thought of all the times his mother had sat with him at bedtime when he was a child. He began reciting the Lord's Prayer out loud as he kept trying to squeeze the life out of the creature below him.

"Our Father which art in heaven, hallowed be thy name."

The Sheriff opened his mouth in what looked like a scream of agony, but no sound could emerge still. He was weakening. Little John could feel it, sense it, and he began to shout the words louder.

"Give us this day our daily bread. And forgive…"

He did not know how much time had passed. He did not know if Robin had saved Marian and ended the prince. All he knew was that he wouldn't let go, not ever.

He heard a whisper of sound above him and sudden searing pain as a sword was shoved into his back. He cursed in his mind. The Sheriff's soldiers, he'd forgotten all about them.

* * *

The little prince was screaming in anguish and Glynna didn't know what to do. She looked everywhere for her love, and finally she saw him, striding toward her, armor cracked and hanging off, blood covering him. Somehow it made him look that much fiercer.

"What do we do now?" Glynna asked. Her hands went red, coated in the blood that slicked over his chest.

"We finish it."

"Can we?"

John threw the knife and the book onto the altar. "We need her," he shouted, his face twisted in fury. "The sacrifice has to be of royal blood. Don't you understand?"

The Sheriff pinned him with his gaze. "I understand that fact perfectly, little prince."

"What does that mean?" John asked, spittle flying from his mouth.

"Just this."

A white-hot blade, smoke rising off it, appeared in the Sheriff's hand and he struck upwards, shoving it up into John's sternum and piercing his heart.

John's eyes went wide.

"Did you really think that *you* had summoned *me*?" the Sheriff asked. "I whispered in your mind for so many nights until you finally knew how to conjure me, but it was not so that I could be your servant. It was so you could be my sacrifice." He smiled. "You have served me better than most."

Robin stopped, jerking Marian with him. They stood over Friar Tuck, who knelt beside the body of Little John. The big man had been stabbed a dozen times.

"He died for me." Robin's voice sounded strange.

"He sacrificed himself so you could save me."

Friar Tuck stood. "We must go."

* * *

The Sheriff hung the iron torc around his neck, pulling it closed.

Glynna looked at him.

"You have a question, my dear?" he asked.

"I thought something would happen," she said "Are you now king?"

The Sheriff laughed. "No, I can only wear this for a short time. Only a human with a soul may wield true sovereignty."

"Then what shall we do?"

"Deliver unto me the victory."

"Tell me how."

His hand fell on her stomach and he spoke a word of power that caused a contraction to rip through her from mid-thigh to breastbone.

As they approached the gate and freedom, a high-pitched keening sound yanked Robin's head around. He looked for the source and then saw his mother, grabbing her distended belly and staring down at the ground.

Thick, black fluid was flowing out of her, forming a pool on the ground beneath her. As he stared in horror she threw back her head...

...and *laughed*.

"My love! Our child is coming!"

Fighting revulsion, he pushed Marian ahead of him beside the fat friar, and yelled to the survivors of his band of men.

"Go, go, *go!*"

The Sheriff caught up to them by the main gates.

Robin grabbed Much's tunic as the boy ran past.

"Get Marian and the men back to camp!" he shouted. "I will attend to the Sheriff."

Much nodded and changed direction, running off to do as he was told.

All Robin could do now was distract their pursuer, lead him on a chase away from the others. Fortunately, the devil's attention was already on him. He turned and staggered toward the forest, moving slower than the rest so that the Sheriff would follow him. Given the extent of his injuries, it wasn't a difficult ruse.

A horse galloped by, riderless. Robin grabbed the animal's reins and yanked it to a halt. He managed to drag himself into the saddle and kicked the beast forward. The effort caused his injured limbs to sing out with pain.

He turned his head to make sure that the Sheriff was following. He saw the man grab a horse and mount it. Two dark shadows slithered down the Sheriff's legs and dropped to the ground. His pets.

The creatures leaped forward, and Robin kicked his already terrified horse as hard as he could.

They streaked toward the nearest section of the forest. A shadow flitted past, visible out of the corner of his eye. The horse screamed in terror and reared, slowing their progress. Robin maintained his seat and kept urging the animal forward.

Something snapped at his leg and Robin kicked out to the side. Hot breath tickled the back of his neck and he swung his arm backward, knocking the other creature to the ground, where it fell beneath the clamoring hooves.

He could hear the Sheriff's horse bellowing right behind him.

Just another fifty strides.

His horse bucked suddenly, then moved to the side, nearly unseating Robin and sending new bolts of pain through him. He ducked as the Sheriff's sword came at him. The animal reared up, then crashed back to all fours. Robin screamed and kicked the animal again and it shot forward. Forty strides. Thirty. *Almost there...*

Twenty. The horse tripped and fell heavily to the ground, screaming in terror. Robin went sailing through the air. He tucked his body and rolled when he landed, doing his best to ignore the pain. As he got up he saw the Sheriff's horse collide with his own and they both went down. Spinning, he ran for the woods.

Moments later he fell, just inside the boundary.

The Sheriff's pets howled in rage as they reached the edge of the trees—the mystic wall that would not give way. Robin scrabbled backward, trying to blend into the dark, in case the Sheriff had a bow with which to shoot an arrow into the forest.

The sound that reached his ears wasn't anything born of a human throat. The man bellowed his frustration, to the point Robin thought he could feel it vibrating up from the ground. *No, not a man*, he thought. *A demon.* As Robin dragged himself further into the forest, he vowed never to forget that.

EPILOGUE

Darkness gave way to light, and Robin realized he had been unconscious. He had crawled farther into Sherwood than he had thought. Every fiber in his being throbbed in agony, and the cold did little to numb it.

Around him he could hear voices whispering.

They were talking about him. As his eyes managed to focus, he realized that he was surrounded on all sides by fey. They were staring intently at him.

"He is a good man, worth saving," Elian said. He was the sprite who'd given Robin the elixir. His was the only face Robin recognized, and most of the forms were shadowy and vague.

"He is no such thing," another voice growled. This one he didn't recognize. "Because of him, Sherwood has been desecrated by the Gisbourne. We should kill him for that alone, regardless of his other crimes."

What crimes? he wanted to ask. He wanted to speak, to defend himself, but he was too weak. He couldn't even force his lips to open.

"We should vote," a third voice said. "Kill, or save."

"There will be no vote!" A new voice rang out, cutting through the rest. Murmurs of surprise filled the air.

A moment later Marian stepped into his sight. At least it

looked like Marian, but she was somehow transformed. Light seemed to be shining from her, or through her. Champion walked by her side, but the fox seemed changed as well.

"We shall save him," she said, "but we will let the world think he is dead, so that none will look for him while he heals." One by one the fey bowed their heads, deferring to her edict.

"Marian," he managed to whisper at last.

She bent over him, her hair free and loose.

"Don't worry, Robin of the Longstride, I won't let you die too."

In the harbor, under the thin light of a half-moon, a battered ship coasted to a stop against the charred remains of the dock.

ACKNOWLEDGEMENTS

Thank you to James for being such a great collaborator and fellow bringer of mayhem. Thank you to Steve Saffel, a terrific editor, for all his support. To the entire team at Titan, you are the best band of Merry Men we could hope to work with. Thank you to Howard Morhaim for being a terrific agent. Thank you to Scott, my love. Thank you also to my family, friends, and fans for all your love and support without which none of this would be possible.

—DV

Thank you to Debbie, my co-conspirator. Thanks to D.E.O. Steve Saffel who did drive this book further down the road than we were originally going to go. Thank you to Howard Morhaim and his staff. The behind the scenes Titan posse. Thank you to every Merry Man out there no matter your gender, you are welcome one and all to our Sherwood.

I couldn't do any of this without my own fated love, Danielle Tuck.

—JRT

ABOUT THE AUTHORS

Debbie Viguié is the *New York Times* bestselling author of more than four dozen novels including the *Wicked* series co-authored with Nancy Holder. In addition to her epic dark fantasy work Debbie also writes thrillers including *The Psalm 23 Mysteries,* the *Kiss* trilogy, and the *Witch Hunt* trilogy. Debbie plays a recurring character on the audio drama, Doctor Geek's Laboratory. When she isn't busy writing or acting Debbie enjoys spending time with her husband, Scott, visiting theme parks. They live in Florida with their cat, Schrödinger.

James R. Tuck is the author of the *Deacon Chalk* series and a modern Lovcraftian adventure series, coming soon. He is also a professional tattoo artist, an accomplished photographer, and podcaster. He lives in the Atlanta area with his lovely wife Danielle.

ROBIN HOOD: DEMON'S BANE

MARK OF THE BLACK ARROW

A vast darkness is spreading. If left unchecked, it will engulf the world, and so Richard the Lionheart must depart England on a holy mission. In his absence, the safety of the realm is entrusted to his brother, Prince John.

When the king departs, black sorcery begins to grip the land. Horrific creatures stalk the forests, yet the violence they commit pales when compared to the atrocities of men. A handful of rebels fight back, but are doomed to fail unless they can find a hero to lead them.

"A thrilling page-turner brimming with mystery and intrigue!" Nancy Holder, *New York Times* bestselling author

"This bleak and bloody telling of the Robin Hood story makes engaging reading." *Starburst*

"Thrilling fantasy entertainment!" *Rising Shadow*

CHAOS QUEEN: DUSKFALL

Stuck with arrows and close to death, a man is pulled from the icy waters of the Gulf of Nahl. Winter, a seemingly quiet young fisherman's daughter, harbours a secret addiction that threatens to destroy her. A young priestess, Cinzia, must face a long journey home to protect her church from rebellion. A rebellion sparked by her sister.

Three characters on different paths will be brought together by fate on one thrilling and perilous adventure.

"*Duskfall* is a delicious mix of Jason Bourne, dark fantasy, and horror. Husberg has written the kind of debut that has me thrilled for the future of Fantasy." Steve Diamond from Elitist Book Reviews, and author of *Residue*

"A fascinating mystery that slowly unfolds, cultures and religions in conflict. Enjoy." Melinda Snodgrass, author of *The Edge of Ruin*

THE DRAGON'S LEGACY

The last Aturan King is dying, and as his strength fades so does his hold on *sa* and *ka*. Control of this power is a deadly lure; the Emperor stirs in his Forbidden City to the East, while deep in the Seared Lands, the whispering voices of *Eth* bring secret death. Eight men and women take their first steps along the paths to war, barely realizing that their world will soon face a much greater threat; at the heart of the world, the Dragon stirs in her sleep. A warrior would become Queen, a Queen would become a monster, and a young boy plays his bird-skull flute to keep the shadows of death at bay.

AVAILABLE IN 2017

For more fantastic fiction, author events, exclusive
excerpts, competitions, limited editions and more

VISIT OUR WEBSITE
titanbooks.com

LIKE US ON FACEBOOK
facebook.com/titanbooks

FOLLOW US ON TWITTER
@TitanBooks

EMAIL US
readerfeedback@titanemail.com